THE BEACH STREET
KNITTING SOCIETY AND YARN CLUB

THE BEACH STREET KNITTING SOCIETY AND YARN CLUB

Gil McNeil

hachette
BOOKS

NEW YORK   BOSTON

Hachette Books
Hachette Book Group
1290 Avenue of the Americas
New York, NY 10104
www.HachetteBookGroup.com

Printed in the United States of America

RRD-C

Published in hardcover by Hyperion: March 2009
This Hachette Books special price trade edition: November 2015

10 9 8 7 6 5 4 3 2 1

Hachette Books is a division of Hachette Book Group, Inc.
The Hachette Books name and logo are trademarks of Hachette Book Group, Inc.

The publisher is not responsible for websites (or their content) that are not owned by the publisher.

The Library of Congress has catalogued the hardcover edition of this book as follows:

McNeil, Gil
    The Beach Street Knitting Society and Yarn Club / Gil McNeil.
        p. cm.
    ISBN 10: 1-4013-4080-6
    ISBN 13: 978-1-4013-4080-3
    1. Widows—Fiction. 2. Family—Fiction. 3. Knitting—Fiction.
4. England—Fiction. I. Title.
    PR6113.C58B43 2009
    823'.92—dc22

                                                        2008054591

ISBN 978-0-316-35382-3 (special price pbk.)

Book design by Jennifer Ann Daddio
Title page photograph © Vladimir Grekov / Dreamstime.com

For Joe

CONTENTS

THE BEACH STREET
KNITTING SOCIETY AND YARN CLUB

SHOW ME THE WAY
TO GO HOME

It's seven o'clock on Monday morning and the movers have been here since six. They're busy packing up crates in the living room and tutting because I've lost the kettle, which must be in one of the boxes they've already put in the van; only I've lost my list so I'm not sure which one. I'm sitting in the kitchen finishing the border on Jack's new blanket and trying to calm down, but even the familiar rhythm of knitting isn't doing the trick. If death, divorce, and moving really are the top three most stressful things you ever have to get through with your clothes on, it's a complete bloody miracle that I'm still standing; although I've got some kind of weird spasm in my back, so it's more of a stoop and shuffle, a bit like the Hunchback of Notre Dame, as Archie helpfully pointed out yesterday, only without the bells. Somehow I think this is going to be a very long day.

"Llamas don't go like that, stupid. They do this."

Archie's making a spitting noise. Llamas? How did they get onto llamas? Damn, I've been zoning out while they ate breakfast and it sounds like a mega-bicker might be brewing.

"Yes, they do. We did them in our animals project, but you don't know, because you're only in the first class, which is the Babies."

Jack smirks; since he's six and three quarters and Archie's only just five and a quarter, one of his favorite things is reminding Archie that he's the Baby, and Always Will Be. And Archie's already furious because Jack got the last of the Weetabix and he was forced into adopting advanced I-am-not-eating-Shreddies maneuvers while he was still half asleep, so he narrows his eyes and glares at Jack. "It's not the Babies, you stupid, and it was on telly and they can spit right on your head, even if they're standing a long way away they can. It's great."

Oh dear, I think I know what might be coming next.

He spits at Jack in a llamalike fashion, and Jack shrieks and spits back. Any second now they'll be punching each other, and Jack's already got a massive bruise on his forehead from last week in Tesco when he ended up on the wrong end of a large bottle of fabric softener.

"Stop it, both of you. Now."

They ignore me and start shoving each other. I think this may be a good time for something from Mummy's Little List of Useful Threats.

"There won't be television for anyone who pushes their brother. None at all. But there can be cartoons for anybody who isn't being Silly."

There's a freeze-frame moment while they consider this. If I nip in quick with a competitive moment, I might be in with a chance. "I wonder who'll be first to get dressed today. I bet it'll be me."

As I walk toward the kitchen door, I'm pushed sideways by a blur of small boys racing for the stairs: pretty much everything's about who can be First in our house, which seems particularly hard given how many hours I spent studying books about sibling rivalry and doing all the things you're meant to do; the usurper baby bought the one Formerly Known as Prince a special present when he was born, and praise was heaped on anyone who spent more than ten seconds with the weeny one without poking him with something pointy. Although actually it was me doing most of the book stuff, because Nick said I should stop fussing and it was all bollocks and he once broke his brother's arm in two places by pushing him out of a tree, but that's just how boys are, and they laugh about it now; which isn't strictly true, since James got quite thin-lipped when I mentioned it last Christmas. Sometimes it feels like I'm stuck on permanent peacekeeper patrol, playing piggy in the middle and championing the virtues of peace and love like some mad old hippie, apart from brief moments of tenderness, when you catch a glimpse of what they might be like when they're in their twenties and have stopped punching each other. Dear God. I'm definitely not cut out for this level of stress first thing in the morning.

Ted, our chief moving man, comes into the kitchen and looks at my cup of tea suspiciously. Damn.

"Have you found the kettle then, love?"

"No. I've tracked down a saucepan, but I still can't find any more cups. I could wash this one and we can take turns, if you like?"

I'm having visions of a relay team of moving men lining up for their turn with the Cup. Christ. It looks like I'm going to be as useless at moving as I have been at packing; it's been complete chaos here for weeks, endlessly searching for things that have disappeared into plastic crates and trying to keep chirpy so the boys don't get too rattled. Maybe I should nip out and get some teas from the café down the road, because Ted has been giving me very wounded looks, and the boys have taken advantage of the fact that I'm having a beverage crisis to start shoving each other again. This just gets better and better.

"I'll go up and get the boys ready, and then I'll sort something out, shall I?"

Ted nods. "Good idea, love. Only we need our tea, it keeps us going."

I'm walking toward the stairs when the doorbell rings, and if this is one of those we-were-in-your-area-and-wondered-how-many-new-windows-you-would-like-fitted-absolutely-free-of-charge salesmen, I think we can safely say he's definitely picked the wrong bloody doorbell.

It's Ellen. The cavalry have arrived. Hurrah.

"Hello, darling. Happy moving day. Everything all organized?" She gives me a hug.

"Sort of. This is Ted. Ted, this is my best friend, Ellen Malone."

Christ. This is my best friend; I sound like a ten-year-old. We'll be wearing matching hair bands next.

Ted stands with his mouth slightly open; not only is Ellen looking particularly stunning this morning, in tight black jeans and a tiny pink T-shirt, and gold sandals, which are bound to be Prada or something equally exorbitant, but she's also the senior news anchor with Britain's Favorite News Channel, so she's in your living room at peak times on pretty much a daily basis.

She gives Ted one of her Big Smiles. "Hi, Ted, lovely to meet you."

He mumbles something and seems rooted to the spot, which happens so often Ellen hardly notices it anymore, as she doesn't notice when people follow her round Waitrose and peer into her basket, or lurk behind her in the street smiling and waving in case there's a camera crew hiding somewhere.

"Put the kettle on, darling. I'm dying for a coffee."

"Sorry, it's vanished."

"Like magician abracadabra vanished? How clever."

"No, you twit, vanished as in packed in a box only I don't know which one and I've lost my list. And there's only one cup."

Ellen gives me one of her Are-You-a-Total-Idiot-or-Just-Pretending? looks, which she usually reserves for politicians who make speeches instead of answering the question she's asked them. Ted is still standing slack-jawed, and appears to be reeling from my telling one of Britain's Favorite Broadcasters to stop being a twit.

"Well, let's sort something out, shall we? I know, you couldn't be a complete angel could you, Ted, and pop down the road to the café and get us all a coffee? Only I'm desperate."

She gives him another Big Smile and hands him a twenty-pound note, and he makes a faint choking noise. Christ, he'll be asking her to autograph it in a minute.

"Do you . . . I mean, would you like . . . ?" He's gone very red now and is clenching his fists in order to speak. "Do you take sugar, or I could nip down to Starbucks if you like, I know a back way so it wouldn't take long, it would be no trouble, no trouble at all. And you get a wider selection there, my wife likes those frapping things; I could get you one of those, if you like."

He's starting to babble; and if you don't rescue people once they go into the land of babbling, it can take ages before they come back out; we once got stuck for nearly half an hour with a woman in a noodle bar who told us in very graphic detail all about her dad's knee operation when Ellen was doing a state-of-the-nation's-health week, and in the end I had to use our emergency get-this-nutter-off-me technique and surreptitiously text Ellen so she could pretend an alert had come through and she needed to get back to the studio.

There's a deafening crash upstairs, and my maternal radar, which can see through walls and up staircases, detects that my gorgeous boys are jumping on my bed and one has just overshot the runway.

"I think I'd better go up before they break something."

"I'll come up with you, shall I, darling? And Ted, whatever you think, if you're sure it's no trouble, but if you do go to Starbucks I'd love a skinny cappuccino with an extra shot, and a banana muffin, and Jo, a caramel macchiato, darling?"

"Yes, please."

"And, actually, why don't you get a few muffins while you're there, Ted, whatever they've got. Thanks so much, you're a total star."

If she kisses him now, and Ellen's very fond of kissing people, sometimes total strangers, I think Ted may well have a cardiac moment. But fortunately she goes for another megasmile instead, and he goes an even darker shade of red; I really hope he's not going to pass out or anything, because, to be frank, I could do without my chief moving man swooning himself into a heap. The rest of the team—which consists of a very thin work-experience teenager called Kevin, who looks about twelve and manages to do most of the heavy lifting without disturbing his hair gel, and an older man called Eric, who doesn't say much but grins quite a lot—have been standing in the living room doorway watching Ted, but they spring into action as he finally surfaces from his reverie.

"Right, let's be off, then. Kevin, go and get the back of the van shut, and get a move on, will you, we haven't got all day. The lady wants a coffee."

Ted is walking toward the front door muttering "Skinny extra shot banana" when Eric steps forward.

"I don't like them muffins, guv, they're all bits."

"Is that right, Eric? Well, thanks for letting me know. But I wasn't planning on getting you one as it happens, so get in the van and stop moaning."

Ellen starts walking up the stairs, and I follow her, marveling that someone with such a small bottom can have such a major effect on people, because I know from bitter experience that if I'd tried to send Ted off to Starbucks with a twenty-pound note he'd probably have told me to sod off, or disappeared for hours and charged me overtime, instead of desperately speeding round the back of the high street chanting his skinny-extra-shot-banana mantra. And even though I know Ellen spends ages in the gym with her personal trainer, Errol, and a small fortune on massages and facials and highlights and low-lights, I still can't help feeling it's bloody unfair that she looks like it's all completely natural and effortless and she's about ten years younger than me, even though she's two years older. It's bloody annoying, actually, and she's definitely the kind of woman you'd want to kick in the shins if she wasn't your best friend.

Ellen's the person I call first when I'm having a crisis, and she texts me rude jokes or choice bits of gossip when she's in the studio, sometimes even when she's on air and they're doing the sports or the weather. It was Ellen I called the night Nick came home from another six-week stint in Jerusalem to say he'd got the foreign correspondent job; he was supposed to have been back for Valentine's Day, but he was two days late, and he'd only had time to give me the highlights before he went up with the boys for bedtime stories, so I texted her while I was clearing up the supper things. They were always the ones to watch, Ellen and Nick, right from when we all first met on the BBC training course. They both had that slight shimmer on camera which natural television presenters always have. Rather than the slightly glazed look that was all the rest of us could manage when we were doing our studio training; I even managed to develop a mystery stutter, and fell right off my chair during one particularly tricky session. But I was much better on the production side, and by the end of the course, I could edit a piece better than both of them put together, and we ended up getting the top three marks. Although that all seems like a very long time ago now; like another life entirely.

I was still pottering in the kitchen tidying up and thinking about us having to move abroad for the new job, and whether it would be Johannesburg or Jerusalem, which both felt quite scary, or Moscow, which would just feel freezing, when Nick came back down from story time. And I was about to ask him where he thought we'd be going, when I realized he had some more news to share, something he was less sure about, and I remember thinking, *I bet it's bloody Moscow,* as he started making some fresh coffee and patting his hair down like he was preparing for a big piece to camera, some crucial bit of breaking news that would change everything. Which as it turned out it did, because the really big news was that he'd been having an affair, for just over a year, with a French UN worker called Mimi. A whole year when he'd been coming home with all his dirty laundry, demanding shepherd's pie at midnight and saying he was exhausted, and then disappearing into the garden with his mobile phone. A whole fucking year.

He'd worked up a big speech about how he hoped we could be civilized about the divorce, because it was just one of those things, and he was very sorry, and he hadn't meant for it to happen, but he was sure we could work something out, and Mimi loved kids and she was really looking forward to meeting the boys. And that was when it got through to me, because I'd been weirdly numb until that point, like I'd been catapulted into a parallel universe where, if he'd only stop speaking and

finish making the coffee, everything would be back to normal.
But suddenly I could see my boys being shuffled around airports, and I realized he was serious, and that's when the shouting started.

I'm not usually very good at shouting, but this time I really
gave it a go, and he was so bloody calm, like he was repeating
lines he'd been rehearsing in the bathroom mirror, which,
knowing him, he probably had; he kept doing his sympathetic-
but-professional face, like he was interviewing someone who'd
just had their house blown up with most of their family in it,
which in a way, of course, I had. And he was so controlled
and professional, right up until I threw the milk jug at him.
The look on his face was priceless, a mixture of fury and
panic and a glimmer of admiration; I don't think either of us
thought I'd ever be the kind of person who'd hurl china about.
But God, it was worth it, even though it was me who had to
crawl around afterward sweeping up all the broken pieces.
And then he got furious and said I was being hysterical, and I
said if he thought this was hysteria he was in for a big surprise,
and if he thought he was going to be shuttling my lovely boys
halfway round the world he could think again, and he stormed
off in a huff saying I was being totally unreasonable, slamming
the front door so hard one of the pictures in the hall fell down.
I was still picking up bits of glass when Ellen turned up, in full
studio makeup and clutching a bottle of champagne ready to
celebrate the new job.

We were sitting at the kitchen table when the policeman
arrived, looking very nervous and fiddling with the hem of his
fluorescent jacket, and he didn't really look at me but kept

talking to Ellen while his radio crackled and he told her there'd been an accident and Nick had been in a car crash and the car had hit a big tree, and I remember thinking, *I'm always telling him to slow down and maybe now he'll bloody listen and stop driving everywhere on two wheels,* and then the policeman's radio started crackling again and he went very pale, and Ellen started to cry.

And then she just took over, especially in the first few days, when everything went foggy. She came with me to the hospital, to the side room with the curtains drawn and the young nurse who kept asking us if we wanted a cup of tea, and she dealt with everyone who turned up with flowers and cards, the press and all the people from work, and she was the one who sat with Nick's parents, who'd been so proud of him and couldn't seem to grasp that their golden boy was gone and wanted someone to blame. She was completely stellar.

Mum and Dad came over from Italy and tried to be helpful but pretty much just got in the way, like they usually do, with Mum wanting special attention all the time and Dad looking for jobs to do round the house and drilling holes in things, and my brother, Vin, came home and took care of the boys and helped me cope with Mum and Dad. Without him and Ellen, I really don't know how I would have managed. Not that I did much coping. You always hope that you'll be one of those stalwart people in a crisis, kind and generous and capable, but now I know that in fact I'm crap in a crisis, silent and incapable. The only thing I really seemed to be able to do was sleep. For hours. It was like I was half unconscious, deep heavy numb sleep that left me more tired when I woke up. Ellen and Vin were busy sorting out the funeral and negotiating with Nick's mum, who wanted something very formal, with everyone in black veils and the boys in suits and a Jacqueline Kennedy moment with them stepping forward to salute, with trumpets if we could manage it, and an eternal flame in the middle of a Sussex churchyard. But they kept on going, and avoided the trumpets but arranged for music instead, Mahler and Elgar, and Vin lit candles, hundreds of them, and Archie wanted to know if it was someone's birthday. Ellen had got a huge bunch of silver balloons for them to release at the graveside, which I wasn't sure about because I thought there was a strong chance Archie would want to take them home, but it turned out to be very beautiful, and that was when I really lost it and behaved like a proper grieving widow, sobbing and holding the boys too tight, until Gran helped me back to the car, patting my back like she used to when I was little, stroking my hair and telling me it was all going to be all right, while Ellen and Vin took Archie and Jack for a walk.

The boys are showing Ellen how high they can bounce on my bed when I get upstairs.

"Stop jumping, now, or you'll break the bed."

Archie's bright red and breathless, and still bouncing. "You can't break beds, Mummy. You're just being stupid."

Ellen laughs. "Don't be cheeky, Archie, or I can't give you your present."

He sits down immediately, and crosses his arms and legs like he does at school when they sit on the mat for story time.

Ellen's usually got something highly unsuitable in one of her trendy bags, and today is no exception; she delves into a huge Tod's leather tote and hands them each a potato gun and a large potato. How perfect. Now we can all dodge potato pellets for the rest of the day.

Jack flings his arms round her waist. "Oh, thank you, Aunty Ellen, thank you ever so much, I've always wanted a potato gun, forever actually, but Mummy wouldn't let me have one."

He gives me one of his My-Life-Is-Hopeless-Because-of-My-Dreadful-Mother looks (patent pending) and starts poking at his potato with the end of the gun. If I don't stop him, there'll be bits of potato all over the upstairs landing carpet, and I'm trying to leave the house as tidy as possible for the new people, because Mrs. Tewson in particular strikes me as someone who will be deeply unamused at finding bits of potato all over her new landing; she's already asked me which cleaner I use on the kitchen tiles, which I'm pretty sure was her idea of a subtle hint.

"Hang on a minute, Jack. Let's get you dressed, and then you can take your guns out into the garden. I wonder if the squirrel will be out?"

This does the trick, because they're both desperate to vanquish the naughty squirrel who eats the bird food we have to put out on a daily basis since Jack overdosed on sodding nature programs. I keep meaning to write and ask them how they manage to avoid getting tangled up with marauding squirrels every time they try to hang their nuts up, but I've got a feeling my letter might end up in the loony pile.

"The squirrel will be very surprised if we get him with our guns, won't he, Mummy?"

"Yes, Archie."

Ellen snorts. "He might just collect the bits of potato and go home and make chips."

Archie giggles, but Jack gives her a rather worried look. "Squirrels don't eat chips, Aunty Ellen, they haven't got cookers."

"Oh. Right."

"Yes, they eat nuts and berries. Mostly."

He looks at me for a spot of maternal approval. He likes confirmation when he's got something right.

"That's right, Jack. Now let's finish getting dressed, and Archie, please stop doing that, sweetheart."

He's jabbing his gun into a black plastic bag full of clothes; I've run out of suitcases, and these are mostly I'll-never-wear-this-again-but-it-was-bloody-expensive things. Suits I used to wear to work, and small summer dresses I can't get into any-more, which I like to think I'll be wearing again one day, when I wake up miraculously three stone smaller with a proper job, which doesn't involve squirrel hunting with potato guns. And that's another thing: I thought sudden bereavement was meant to make you go all pale and wan and lose vast amounts of weight, but I seem to have done rather the opposite. Possi-bly because I've spent too many consoling hours with the biscuit tin; but it was either that or vodka, and at least you can still do the school run when you've been mainlining Jaffa Cakes all day.

"I want to wear my Spider-Man outfit."

"Not today, Archie."

I'd quite like to avoid moving in fancy dress if we possibly can, but after a fairly concentrated round of stamping and shouting, we agree on a compromise; he'll wear the top and trousers but not the face mask that he can't actually breathe in and that makes him sound like a mini–Darth Vader. And he'll wear his wellies to go out in the garden, even though officially Spider-Man wouldn't be seen dead in a pair of wellies. He's still huffing and tutting as they go downstairs with Ellen for Squirrel Wars: The Final Revenge, while I try to work out what I need in the bags I'm taking with us in the car.

Our first night in the new house seems like a fairly crucial moment, and I want to get it right, and we'll need Archie's night-light for definite, or he'll never get to sleep. And Jack's favorite dinosaur pillowcase with his name on it, and warm pajamas in case the boiler's as useless as the survey predicted. God, I'm feeling really nervous about this; they've both been quite keen on the idea of moving so far, but I think that's because we'll be so near Gran, whom they adore, and not just because she tends to slip them bags of fluorescent sweets when she thinks I'm not looking. I think they know I'm more relaxed when we're there, which means they can relax, too. Gran's house has always been my place of safety, with summer picnics, and flannelette sheets in winter with a faint hint of lavender and a hot-water bottle, because Gran thinks electric blankets have a tendency to go berserk in the night and boil you while you're asleep. But given how much more clingy and prone to tears they've both been over the past few months, especially Jack, they might change their minds when we get there. Jack hates change of any kind, and even a new cereal bowl can set him off, so I'm thinking a whole new house might be a bit of a challenge.

I've already put his old baby blanket in the car, because I'm pretty sure he'll want it tonight; Archie's never really gone in for special blankets, although he did get very attached to a yellow plastic hammer for a while, mainly because he liked hitting Jack with it. He even used to take it to bed with him, until the magic fairies came and cheekily swapped it for a Captain Incredible outfit while he was asleep. But Jack used to carry his blanket everywhere, and it's resurfaced over the past few months. I'm knitting him a new one, which was meant to be done in time for the move, but I'm still finishing the border, so that's another thing I've failed to organize properly. But at least knitting it has kept me sane over the past few weeks, when everything else has felt so out of control. He chose a seaside theme in honor of his new bedroom, so I've done pale blue cotton squares, with a darker sky blue border, and all the squares have fish motifs knitted into them, some more fishlike than others, but he loves it already, so I'm hoping it'll help him sleep, because he's been waking up with bad dreams again recently.

I've just finished putting the bags into the car when Ted arrives with what appears to be Starbucks's entire stock of muffins for the day, carrying in the gray cardboard trays and brown paper bags while the boys hop up and down with excitement at the prospect of a Muffin Mountain.

"It's a feast, Mummy, look. A proper feast. And I can have two, or even more if I like, Aunty Ellen said I could."

"Well, let's have a drink first, and see how you go, shall we, Archie?"

I'm trying to divert his attention long enough to get some juice down him before he starts on the muffins, but I don't know why I'm bothering, because he can eat incredibly quickly when he wants to. He's like a hamster; he simply bulges out his cheeks so he can fit more in.

Jack's drinking his juice, looking very chirpy.

"The squirrel's hiding up his tree and he won't come down, so we're shooting him up the tree, and it's great."

"Well, finish your drink and you can show me, love. Ellen, do you want a muffin? Only I'd get in quick, if I were you."

"No, thanks, darling. I might just have a small piece of Archie's, though." She looks at Archie, who crams the remainder of his muffin into his mouth as quickly as he can and tries to smile at the same time. "Or maybe not."

We wander back outside with our coffees and watch the boys racing around firing at invisible squirrels.

Ellen sighs. "This is the closest I've been to a bloody potato for months."

"Ellen, we had chips last week, on the beach, when we went down to look at the shop."

"Well, I didn't have many, and I had to do an extra session with Errol to make up. You know, I worked it out once, and I've spent weeks of my life on that fucking treadmill. Christ, when did we all decide we had to be so bloody perfect?"

"When we decided to become a Media Star?"

"Star, my arse. They've taken on another new girl, did I tell you? Alicia something, looks about twelve, legs up to her armpits, and she's shagging management, I just know she is, only I haven't worked out who yet. Probably Tim Jensen, but the makeup girls are on the case, so we'll know soon enough."

The women who do the makeup are a top source of gossip;

they tease out everyone's secrets while they're slapping on the foundation, and if you don't spill the beans, they make you look like a drag queen. Whenever you see someone reading the news with a particularly orange face, or pantomime eye shadow, you can be sure they've been holding back top nuggets.

"So that'll be another bloody nymphet after my job. Christ."

There's been a rash of nymphets recently, parachuted in by management without any proper training, and they usually crash through a couple of bulletins before they get sent off to the regions to try to pull themselves together.

"What happened to that other one? The dark-haired one Brian Winters brought in, who kept going on about what people were wearing on serious stories? The one who said 'Well, I can tell they're very upset, Ellen' when you were on a live link to Scotland Yard and you asked her how they were reacting to yet another inquiry saying they'd totally screwed up."

We both laugh.

"I rather liked the sound of her."

"So did Brian Winters, until his wife found out. They didn't renew her contract, so she wrote 'Wanker' on his car, with bright red nail varnish, Dior Rouge, I think. It was fabulous. Security must have seen her, but they pretended they hadn't."

"How brilliant."

"I know. She went right up in my estimation, I can tell you. But no wonder everyone keeps moaning on about young women today drinking themselves into stupors and taking their tops off in pubs. What the fuck's the point of being all ladylike and refined when you're up against lying bastards like that? Or saddled with some bloody New Man, pretending he doesn't mind if you earn more than him while secretly he's fuming? New Man, my arse. You know Zara's husband, Adam, who works in the City, thinks he's God's gift?"

"The one with the hair?"

"Yes. Well, she just got promoted to the top job in the last shuffle at LTV, and do you know what? She told him she's been downgraded to executive assistant and she says he's loving it. She's earning a bloody fortune, but instead of smuggling in shopping bags because she's spent too much of his money, she's smuggling them in because she's spent too much of her own. Can you believe it? She says he'd have a breakdown if he knew. Honestly, I'd bloody take my top off in pubs if it wouldn't end up in the fucking papers."

"Yes, but at least we're allowed to earn more than the boys now, even if they do hate it."

"Yes, technically, but not if you still want them to speak to you. God, I hate New Men. It was better when they were honest; you could be a typist or nurse or a waitress, and if you made it through in anything else you were a nutter and they left you alone. But now you get all this ball-breaker crap, while they sponge off you and moan about their masculinity being threatened."

"Bring back the good old days? When all you had to do was find a nice boy, marry him, and stay at home and polish things?"

"Exactly. Until you finally snapped and woke him up one night by stabbing him in the neck with your nail file."

"I don't think that happened very much, did it?"

"It happened to my aunty Dorothy; she got Uncle Brian right under his ear. He was always telling her she was stupid at family lunches, stuff like that. But the worm eventually turned."

"Was he all right?"

"Yes, just a couple of stitches, but I don't think he slept very well after that."

We're both cackling as the doorbell rings.

"Sod it, I bet that's Mrs. Parrish. You know how she kept coming round with food parcels before the funeral. Well, she's at it again, only now it's sorry-you're-moving snacks. She likes to chat, and it all takes ages."

"Do you want me to go?"

"Oh, yes, please, that'd be great."

Ellen comes back clutching a tinfoil tray of brownies.

"She just wanted to say she hopes you're very happy in your new home and you're to ring her, if you want that telephone number. What's that all about, then? Fixing you up with a hot date?"

"Hardly. Her husband died a few years ago and she joined some widows' group, and she keeps trying to recruit me. She's brought me all the leaflets and everything, and apparently you're meant to go through stages: acceptance, denial, and anger. Or it might be the other way round."

"Well, a group might be good, you know, meeting new people and all that."

"Yes. New tragic people."

"True. Actually, a shag would be much better."

"Please, that's the last thing I need, and anyway, I wouldn't know what to talk about; unless they were into *Spider-Man*, I'd be in serious trouble."

"I wouldn't worry, darling, they prefer it if you just listen. And nod admiringly—that always goes down well. It's when you start talking that it tends to get complicated."

"It would feel like I was cheating on Nick."

She gives me a Look.

"I know, but it would. I can't explain it. If there was a group for Widows Who Were Just About to Get Divorced, I'd bloody join it, I definitely would. It's absolutely crap; I can't be a poor widow, mourning the loss of the love of my life, and I can't be a Just Divorced and Still Fuming, either, so it's hopeless. You really know you're in trouble when there isn't even a support group you can join."

"Well, never mind, they're all full of moaners, in England anyway. I bet there'd be one in New York."

"Yes, but it's quite a long way to go on a Tuesday night, isn't it?"

"I know, I've just had one of my brilliant ideas. I'll be your group. It'll be great. I'll call you up once a week and do my special therapy voice, and you can tell me how you're feeling and I'll tell you that you need to get laid and it's all your mother's fault. Which is the truth, and it'll save you a fucking fortune. It'll be perfect. God, these brownies are great."

"She's such a nice woman, but I do get fed up with talking to people who use that special tone of voice, like you're some victim of a disaster who might start screaming at any moment."

"Well, you are."

"Thanks very much, that's very supportive. I think I may be getting a glimmer of how your new therapist role might work, and I wouldn't give up the day job yet if I was you."

"Well, it is a bit tragic, you've got to admit; your husband drives his car into a tree just when he's got a big new job and you'll finally start having some proper money to play with, and then you find out the bastard's taken out a second mortgage without telling you, and you've got to sell up and go and live in the middle of nowhere and work in your gran's bloody wool shop. How much more fucking tragic can you get?"

She's smiling, but I know she's half serious.

"Yes, but I keep telling you, it's my shop now—we've signed the papers and everything—and it's not the middle of nowhere, it's only half an hour from Whitstable, and you can hardly move there for Londoners in stripy sweaters. It's always heaving with them being all nautical and trotting round the fish market every weekend. And anyway, you know how trendy knitting's getting; it'll be a new start, which is what we need, and I can make enough money to feed us all at the same time. At least, I hope I can."

"Yes, in Notting Hill maybe, but not Nowhere-by-the-Sea."

"Yes, but I can't afford Notting Hill. I can't afford anywhere Hill, not in London, and there'll be no rent on the shop, so with the money from selling this place and Nick's work policy, I can pay off the mortgage here and get the new house and still have a bit left over to get the shop sorted. I've told you, it's the only thing that makes sense."

"Yes, but it's not a bloody career, darling, twiddling bits of wool about all day. You were a great news producer, and you should come back to work. I could get you back in with us, you know I could."

"Yes, I know. Tom Partridge called me a few days ago. Was that down to you by any chance?"

"No."

"Ellen."

"Well, I might have mentioned something, possibly. So what did he say?"

"Oh, the usual: how sorry he was about Nick, and how he always needed good freelance producers, and how family-friendly they were now, so if I was interested we should meet for a drink."

"Family-friendly, my arse. He sent Kay Mallow off to do that earthquake story when she was only just back from maternity leave, deliberately, just to make a point. She was stuck there for nearly two weeks, frantically texting lists to her husband, who's still guilt-tripping her about it. Anyway, Tom's a serial shagger, everybody knows that. His wife's on Prozac. I saw her at a drinks thing last week and she's got the thinnest legs you've ever seen, she looks like a really pissed-off whippet. And she never took her eyes off him, all night."

"Exactly. So I'd get a few night shifts to start me off, working for a charmer like him, and then if it worked out I'd be back on peak times, full-time, late home every night, and working flat out to pay for the nanny. It doesn't make sense; it's got to be better to try and make the shop work."

"Maybe."

"I don't want the boys to lose Nick and then lose me, too, out working all hours, racing round the shops in a panic about supper, and answering to idiot management, who are all ten years younger than me and wouldn't recognize a good piece of editing if you stapled it to their heads. No, thank you very much. I'd rather work in M and S. At least you get discount on the food. And the people are nicer."

"True. But you know how to handle the boys in suits, you know you do."

"Maybe, but I'm not sure I want to, not anymore. I know the plan was always that I'd go back as soon as Archie was at school, but I'd been thinking about trying something different for ages, retraining or something, and now there's no money for that."

"Well, don't blame me if you go mad down there and start knitting loo-roll dolls."

When I took Ellen down to show her the new house and the shop, she managed to find a knitting pattern for loo-roll covers involving crinolines and lots of pink wool, and she still hasn't recovered; Gran's a terrible hoarder, and there are boxes and boxes of old patterns, balaclavas and appalling sweaters with birds on them, and pram sets and bed jackets—although I quite fancy the idea of bed jackets.

"Damn. That's your surprise birthday present ruined."

"I just don't want you so far away, that's all."

"Ellen, it's only a couple of hours' drive, and the house has got a phone, you know; the shop has, too, come to that."

"Yes, but I won't be able to nip round after work."

"Ellen."

"Yes?"

"Stop it right now, or we'll both end up in tears. And I've promised myself today is a no-crying day."

"All right. Sorry. I suppose you might land a hunky fisherman, and you can knit him a new net and stand on the quayside wearing a black shawl when the weather's bad; it'll be like *The French Lieutenant's Woman* meets *The Perfect Storm.*"

"Yes, and knowing my luck, I'd get swept out to sea, and that would be the end of that. Anyway, we haven't really got a quayside, only the old pier and a couple of boats with huts on the beach where they sell fish. But you have to get up really early."

"Well, bloody get up early then. It could be a whole new business opportunity. You could be the Rick Stein of Kent, only without the yappy dog."

"I think I'll stick with the wool shop for now, thanks. Less clinging onto trawlers in bad weather."

"Mummy, Mummy, tell Jack he's got to stop shooting me. He nearly got me right in my eye, and I could have been seriously ninjured."

"It's *injured*, Archie, and Jack, stop it, right now."

"He started it."

"I did not. Liar, liar, pants on fire. Pants on double fire."

Jack is doing what I think the police would describe as loitering with intent, lurking behind a tree and loading his gun with the last bits of his potato; time to go back inside, before we have to make a detour to the hospital for potato pellet removal.

By the time the solicitor calls to confirm that all the money has landed in the right bank accounts, it's nearly three and we're on the point of complete hysteria trying to keep the boys from killing each other in an empty house with no telly. They're still bickering as we drive off, so it's only me blinking back the tears as Ellen stands waving: she was here on the day we moved in, when we ate fish and chips in the garden and Nick managed to collapse an old deck chair we found in the shed while he was still sitting in it, and we all laughed so much I thought I was going to be sick, or go into labor.

I was eight months pregnant with Archie, and it was a really hot Easter that year, and we were so excited about the house, even though we couldn't really afford it, but Nick was adamant we could do it up and make a fortune, which turned out to mean I spent hours balanced up a stepladder and the fortune would disappear into a secret second mortgage. Bastard. I scraped off wallpaper and spent hours sanding all the floorboards and buying endless Smorgflapp door handles from IKEA, while his main contribution was the occasional glance at a paint chart before he was off on another story; I had to paint the kitchen three different shades of pale yellow before I got it right. And now here we are, the three of us, off to make a new life by the sea without him.

The bickering from the backseat is reaching a whole new level as I join the queue for the traffic lights.

"Stop it now, both of you. I know, let's sing a song, shall we?"

I'd put some music on to lessen the tension, but Archie squirted the radio with his water pistol last week. I start singing "Ten Green Bottles," but there's a marked silence from the back.

"Are we nearly there yet?"

"No, love, we've got to do the motorway first."

"Yes, Archie, stop being such a baby. It's ages yet, ages and ages. When will we stop for our picnic, Mummy?"

Picnic? I don't remember saying anything about a picnic. "It's much too cold for a picnic, Jack."

It may be July, but it's gray and cold, and the forecast is for torrential rain; probably just when Ted and the boys are unloading all our furniture.

"Eskimos have picnics, and they're on ice, so it must be cold. They probably have them in their igloos. If there was snow, we could make an igloo and it would be great. And anyway, you promised."

"When did I promise?"

"You said we could have picnics. You did. By the sea. At our new house. And I've been looking forward to it. All day, I have."

"Yes, Jack, and we will. We can have a picnic tomorrow, if you like, and play on the beach. But not on the day we move in."

He tuts. "Yes, but you said, you did, and that's a lie and that's not very nice, you know, Mummy, telling lies."

Here we go; he will now recite from his ever-expanding list of Lies My Mother Has Recently Told Me. I think he's keeping it for when he's older, probably for some kind of legal action, and even though he can't remember to bring his packed-lunch bag home from school, he has crystal-clear recall of the day I went to the hairdresser and promised to be back in an hour, only to come back three hours later with unscheduled highlights to find Nick had forgotten to give them lunch, and they were both running on empty and entering the twilight zone, lying on the living room floor kicking lumps off each other while Nick watched football. I think I'd better try a spot of what I believe they call positive behavior modification in all those help-me-my-child's-a-total-sod books. In other words, bribery.

"What about if instead of a picnic we stop at a Little Chef and have pancakes? How does that sound?"

Bingo. They start concentrating on scanning the horizon for red-and-white signs.

God, I wish the bloody radio worked.

2

ELSIE AND THE AMAZING TECHNICOLOR CARDIGAN

I'm sitting in a Little Chef surrounded by enormous lorry drivers, all texting their friends and moaning about the weather because it's pouring, and one of them is complaining that he's supposed to be in Doncaster by ten, which, given that we're only twenty miles from Dover and it's nearly six, is going to be a bit of a challenge, unless Ferrari have started making lorries.

"I love pancakes." Archie's got maple syrup in his hair.

"Do you? Well, that's good, sweetheart, but try to be a bit more careful. You're getting very sticky, you know."

"I like being sticky. It's one of my best things."

I've only ordered a coffee, since I ate too many brownies earlier on with Ellen, who's just texted me: *Good luck on first night, will call later. Love you. PS. Look out for hunky fishermen.*

"Did Daddy like pancakes? I can't remember."

Jack's giving me one of his anxious looks. He's been doing his Did-Daddy-Like-This routine quite a lot lately; I think he's worried he's starting to forget him.

"Yes, he loved them."

He nods, satisfied.

Archie pauses between mouthfuls. "Yes, and he liked lots of sauce."

"It's not sauce, you stupid, it's syrup. Mable syrup, that's what it's called."

Archie looks momentarily crestfallen but rallies by jabbing Jack with his fork. Jack screeches, and the lorry drivers start giving us Looks.

"Archie, that was very horrible, and if you do it again you'll have to have a baby spoon. And Jack, please stop teasing him, and it's *maple* syrup, not mable. Let's just finish eating, shall we? Gran will be waiting for us."

"Yes, and the lorry might be there, and I can help, can't I, Mum? I can help carry things. Ted said I was a very strong boy."

"Yes, Jack."

"I can help, too. I'm strong, too. Look." Archie holds his plate above his head.

Great. More mable syrup in his hair.

They both get free lollipops at the till to keep sugar levels at an absolute maximum, and there's a brief but very bitter exchange about whose turn it is to sit in the front, which I solve by putting them both in the back, so they sit united in hatred, jiggling about and singing silly songs with the occasional rude word thrown in, which I'm pretending I can't hear, until we get our first glimpse of the sea.

Broadgate Bay is definitely one of those seaside towns where the tide went out a long time ago and looks like it's staying out. But among all the bungalows and bucket-and-spade shops, there are signs that things might be on the turn: heritage colors have started to appear on a few front doors of the Victorian terraces, and there are geraniums in the occasional window box. People who can't afford Whitstable have begun moving in, and the library in the high street still looks very grand with its gray stone columns and steps, and we've got a new art gallery, even if it does mainly sell posh birthday cards and pretty watercolors by the kind of artists you'd be very surprised to find on the short list for the Turner Prize, unless Stormy Sunsets become a special new category. And Gran says the local council's getting very excited about the competition for Best Seaside Town (Small), and we're in with a good chance this year because the judges are fed up with the same places always winning so they've changed all the rules.

As we drive down Beach Street past the shop, I can see Gran's done a new window display in honor of the competition, with what looks like a pyramid of red, white, and blue wool, a few sweater patterns pinned to the green felt on the back wall, and a vase of dusty plastic flowers; so I think a new window display might be moving up to the top of my list.

The shop looks quite faded, and the gold "Butterworth's Wools" lettering has gone patchy from all the sun and salt, which is something else that needs sorting, but I think I'll wait for a while, because I'm thinking of changing the name. McKnits is the favorite so far; officially I'm still a Mackenzie-Jones, since Nick and I combined our names when we got married, just after Jack was born. Nick liked the idea of being double-barreled because he thought it looked better on-screen, although I was never that attached to Jones. I don't hate it as much as Vin does, though, especially when Gran calls him Vinnie. Officially, he's Vincent, which is down to Mum being Artistic, so I'm lucky I only got stuck with Josephine. I did try going for Jo-Jo in my teens, but it didn't stick. I think you probably need silk tassels to pull off being a Jo-Jo.

I'll ask Gran what she thinks about McKnits, because I think a change of name would be good; it would signal a new start. But I don't want to offend her; the shop's been in the family for years, and she started working the week after she married Grandad, just after the war started and he was sent off on a naval destroyer from Dover. He only got home for one leave before he was blown up somewhere in the Baltic; she showed me all his medals once, with her wedding album full of black-and-white photographs, and a bundle of letters with tiny, neat writing and rows of kisses at the end of each one, and a silk Valentine's card, with red ribbon faded to pink. He was only twenty when he died, and Gran moved in with old Mrs. Butterworth, and had Mum, and then gradually took over and ran things herself. So she might mind if I change things too quickly.

She's standing by the front gate as we arrive, waving a duster.

"How was the journey? Terrible I bet, I've been listening

to the radio, and they said there was one of them hatchbacks on the motorway."

Archie's yelling, "We're at the seaside, we're at the seaside!" and trying to find his fishing net.

"A tailback?"

"Yes. You poor things, you must be exhausted. Come on in and I'll put the kettle on. I brought the spare one from the shop so we could have a nice cup of tea before the van gets here. Mind you, it takes an age to boil—I think the element's furred up. I keep telling Elsie we need to get one of those metal things you put in and they collect up all the bits. Mrs. Lilly's got one and she says it's marvelous. Have you got one, love?"

"What? Sorry, Gran, no, I haven't. Archie, please stop that, and Jack, leave things in the car and we'll bring them in later."

"But I need my blanket for tonight."

"Yes, I know, but don't start unpacking things now. We haven't even got the beds in yet."

He sighs, and Gran gives him a hug.

"I've done the front room and given the bedrooms a quick wipe-over. Dust as thick as anything there was, you know, but I don't think Gladys can have bothered. She always was a bit flighty, if you ask me. She used to stay out all hours, you know."

Somehow I can't quite see Gladys Tilling staying out all hours. She's got to be at least as old as Gran, and Gran's eighty next year.

"Did she? When was that?"

"In the war, dear, she was very partial to the Americans

at the base. Her and May Prentice, they'd come back all hours, with their stockings in their handbags, if you get my meaning."

"Sounds like fun."

"Yes, but not with her Ted off in the desert getting shrapnel in his head. Mind you, he wasn't exactly the full shilling before he went, but he managed very well; you'd think a head full of bits of metal and that'd be it, but he went on for years, and he could always tell you if there was bad weather on the way. Well, I just hope she's happy in Australia, because it's a long way to go at her age, you know, even if your daughter has got a pool and does barbecues every night. You wouldn't catch me going all that way for a sausage. Do you want a hand with that, dear?"

"No thanks, Gran, it's fine. The moving men should be here soon."

"Yes, and you've got to watch them, you know, make sure they don't pinch your valuables—they're all at it."

"They'll have a hard job, Gran, unless they're into Lego."

"Well I'll be keeping an eye on them; it's always in the *Gazette*. They start off all charming, and then as soon as your back's turned they're in your bag before you can say 'mugger.'"

Archie giggles. "Granny said 'bugger.'"

"Granny said 'mugger,' Archie, and don't start being rude."

"They're probably tired from the journey, aren't you, my lambs? Come on, let's see if Granny's got anything nice for you in her bag."

Great. More sweets.

I ferry bags in from the car and get panicky about how much there is to do while the boys run around the front garden having a sword fight with a rather overgrown gorse bush, and then the sun comes out and I start to feel that maybe things might be all right after all, even if the house does look much more dilapidated now that all Gladys's things have gone. We've got a big front garden facing the park, and we're only a five-minute walk up the hill from the shop and the seafront, and there's a gate round to the back garden, which is full of overgrown flower beds and brambles. There's a garage, which I'm particularly excited about, even if it is full of old planks at the moment; it'll be great not having to scrape ice off the car in the winter. Although we probably won't need the car so much here because the school's only a ten-minute walk across the park, so I'm hoping for far less refereeing in moving vehicles in the mornings, and the bracing sea air will help wake us all up. In theory.

The house is an Edwardian seaside villa according to the estate agent, but it's nowhere near that grand, and every room needs redecorating. All the walls are covered in the kind of wallpaper that hasn't come back into fashion and never will, or horrible old paint that's chipped and faded. But it's got a lovely, solid feel to it, and you can see the sea if you stand on tiptoe in the bathroom, and there are fireplaces in most of the rooms so we won't freeze if the boiler conks out. And there's a big, solid front door, with an old-fashioned door knocker, which will make a nice change from that bloody doorbell at the old house, which made me jump every time someone rang it. I think I always half expected it to be the police again with more bad news.

Gran's making a start on the kitchen cupboards as we go back in. She's brought a bucket full of cloths and brushes and bottles of bleach, and is in her element, tutting and scrubbing away, humming hymns to herself; she's always humming, and today it's "For Those in Peril on the Sea," but she moves on to big band tunes if she's tackling anything tricky, and she's doing a pretty nifty medley of Glenn Miller's greatest hits when Ted and the boys turn up and start filling the kitchen with crates.

The cupboards look pristine to me, but Gran's not convinced and is still busy bleaching things, and there's no point arguing with her since she just pats you on the arm and says, "Yes, dear," and then completely ignores you and carries on. She may be quite small, and she's definitely got smaller over the years, but apart from a slightly collapsed look when she's tired, she still looks the same as she did when we used to come down for our summer holidays. Neat and tidy, with her hair done every week in the salon next to the chemist's, a perm that looks like a helmet for the first couple of days, and then goes soft and wispy, busy with her pinny on, smiling and humming away to herself; blue eyes, and soft hands.

I put the kettle on to make tea, and notice that the old fridge Gladys left for us is making weird chuntering noises. But I can always put stuff in the larder if it conks out; it's freezing in there, with thick stone shelves, which remind me of Mrs. Bridges and *Upstairs, Downstairs.* Maybe I'll learn how to cook mutton and make game pie, and get into making jam and pickles and have all the jars lined up with pretty labels: only to be honest, the last time I tried making jam it wouldn't set, for hours, and then it suddenly set solid like peanut brittle and I had to get it out of the pan by bashing it with the garlic press, so perhaps I'll just stick to lining up all my packets and jars in there if I ever work out which crate they're in; so far, all I can find are stacks of plates and a collection of old dusters, with the dustpan but no brush, and a small piece of milk jug.

Our sofas are looking dwarfed in the living room, so it'll be a case of spacious rather than gracious living, but my bedroom's going to be great, with no more gaps in the wardrobe where Nick's things used to be. Actually, with no wardrobe at all, since the old one collapsed when they tried to take it apart to get it down the stairs. There's a built-in cupboard, though, and I'm going to paint everything violet, or pale pink, and have a white cotton duvet cover without having to worry about Nick spilling coffee all over it while he's reading the papers. And I'll get dangly glass lampshades and a bedside table. Nick thought bedside tables were suburban; he liked piles of books and papers with his radio balanced on top, and then he'd lose his alarm clock under the bed, so if he had an early call I'd wake up to the sound of him swearing and rootling about under the bed trying to grab it before it woke the boys up.

God, I wish he was still out there somewhere, spilling coffee all over someone else's duvet; sometimes I forget, and then it catches me all over again, like pressing on a bruise; duller and less sharp, but much bigger. And because I'm so used to him not being around for weeks at a time, I forget and think I'll tell him something next time he calls, usually something about the boys, and then I remember.

That's the thing I hate most of all, really, because he might not have been the world's most devoted father, but he was their dad, and they loved him. I've spent so long preserving the lovely Daddy image, buying presents from him and covering up for his lack of even basic knowledge of their latest likes and dislikes, and now he's not around the myth is even bigger, and I'm stuck with it. Forever. Just like when he used to plan to take them out and then his phone would go and he'd be off to Heathrow and I'd have to step in like some crap courier service trying to deliver on his promises of paternal largesse but always failing to deliver the goods on time. And it's never going to change now; he'll always be their lovely Daddy, whom they lost. And it's not bloody fair.

Maybe if I hadn't given up working, things would have been different: it wouldn't have felt like he was always off somewhere while I stayed at home folding washing and losing touch with him. I'd have been out there, too. I did try working part-time when Jack was little, but the shifts were a nightmare, and I could never count on Nick being around, so it was all too complicated. And I hated the way I wasn't taken seriously anymore, like I'd been invisibly demoted just because I'd had a baby, whereas for Nick it wasn't an issue. That's the thing about having children; it's all the invisible stuff that really gets you. And now I'm doing it on my own, which wasn't how we planned it. Although in lots of ways I was always on my own; Nick would never have considered moving sideways for a while to accommodate the boys. He never remembered who liked their juice in the blue cup or their bedside light left on all night. He'd have been totally screwed if this was the other way round, if it was me that was gone, and him left with the boys.

But still, I wish he was out there somewhere, not bloody remembering.

It's nearly ten by the time Ted and the boys finally leave, and even though Gran tries to insist she's fine walking home, it's a long walk up the hill to her bungalow, and it's pitch-black outside, so after a short tussle she relents and lets me drive her back. We have to make a complete circuit of the bloody seafront thanks to the new one-way system, but Jack and Archie are thrilled to be out in the dark, and Gran gives us a running commentary on practically everything we pass.

"Look, that's Mr. Pallfrey, he lives in your road, and he shouldn't have a big dog like that if he can't control it—it chased the milkman right down the road last week, you know, and he was ever so upset. He says he's going to report him if it happens again, and I don't blame him."

Mr. Pallfrey's being pulled along at quite a pace by a very large dog. Jack closes his window. "Does he bite people, Gran?"

"Don't you worry, petal, he's as soft as anything; he'll lick you silly if you let him. And that's the house Lady Denby's bought, look, that one there."

We pass a posh-looking house with wrought-iron gates, right at the end of the seafront. Lady Prudence Denby's our local aristocrat, who dominates all the local committees and is usually accompanied by a couple of Labradors and her husband, George, who can never remember anyone's name and calls everybody Moira. They sold their country estate last year, for a small fortune, to Grace Harrison, the twice-Oscar-nominated, BAFTA-winning all-round mega–film star, who wanted to return to her Kentish roots, according to the papers, only not in the backstreets of Gravesend, where she grew up, but in a more picturesque version, involving a hundred and twenty acres and a Georgian manor house with a lake. The whole town's been agog ever since.

"She's having five new bathrooms, you know, that Grace Harrison, all in marble, and a new sunken bath that's big enough for six people, although why you'd want a bath that big is a mystery to me—just think of the cost of heating all that water. And Mrs. Palmer at the post office says she'll be moving in when she comes back from America, although how she knows I don't know, she's always carrying on like she knows more than everybody else, which is ridiculous because she didn't know about the pub being sold, did she? I found that out myself, from Betty. Anyway, it seems daft to me, spending all that money on a house and then never living there. More money than sense, some people."

"It's probably a good investment."

"Oh, probably, but it's very selfish, getting everyone all excited and then not even bothering to turn up."

"That's probably not her fault, you know, Gran. It's the same with Ellen, people just make things up she's supposed to have said and everyone believes it. And most of it's complete rubbish."

"Yes, but Ellen's a lovely girl, well, apart from the language. Oh, I meant to say, the new people at the Anchor moved in last week, and she looks foreign to me, lovely dark hair, and he's a young chef, from London. Looks a bit like that one who swears all the time, that Jamie Gordon."

"Gordon Ramsay?"

"Yes, and who'd want that kind of language in their kitchen, I ask you. I bet his wife's mortified."

I bet she isn't. She's probably far too busy buying designer outfits and amusing pieces of jewelry.

"Although I'm sure he could cook you a lovely dinner if you asked him."

Somehow I can't see Mr. Ramsay popping round to make me supper and battling with the ancient Belling. But I'm pretty sure we'd all learn some new swearwords if he did.

"And they've got a little boy who looks the same age as our Jack, and a little girl, Betty told me. The wife was in, getting milk, and you'll never guess what the girl's called: Nelly. I thought that one went out of fashion years ago."

I'm never really sure about people who go in for Special Names for their children, while the rest of us just try to avoid anything that rhymes with *willy*. I think they're probably all suffering from some kind of attention-seeking-by-proxy disorder, and I'd bet serious money there isn't a mother of a Beowulf out there who wouldn't benefit from a sharp slap on closer acquaintance.

I pull up at Gran's, and she leans over to give me a kiss.

"Now don't you get out, the boys will get chilly. Are you sure you don't want me to stay over? It'd be no trouble, you know."

"No, Gran, we're fine, honestly."

"Well, you can always ring me, you know, if you get worried or anything. It's your first night, so you're bound to be feeling nervy, and I can be right over."

"Thanks, Gran."

Honestly, what kind of wimp does she think I am?

"I'll pop round first thing and we can make a start on the rest of those crates. Shall I bring some breakfast? I've got a nice bit of bacon from the butcher's."

"Lovely."

She turns to the boys. "Be good boys for your mum then, and no larking about. Straight into bed, promise?"

They both nod.

The drive back is much quicker, since we don't have to do the seafront tour, and we see Mr. Pallfrey still battling with his dog as we turn in to our street.

"I need a dog, you know, Mummy, I really do, we should get one, tomorrow. Can we, please? It'd be ever so handy."

"How would it be handy, Archie?"

"I could tell it to bite people if they're horrible."

I know without looking that he's giving his brother a menacing look. Jack's never been that keen on dogs, let alone ones who've been trained by his brother to bite on command.

"Dogs aren't allowed to bite people, Archie. Ever."

He sighs.

As I'm tussling with the front door, it starts to drizzle; it's really dark and I can't see the key properly. Christ. Just when I'm thinking it can't get any worse, a huge dog races up the path and starts leaping about barking, hotly pursued by Mr. Pallfrey, who comes puffing along full of apologies and tries to grab the end of the lead, while Jack cowers behind my legs and Archie screams with delight. Bloody hell. He's running round and round in circles now, wagging and barking and licking everyone, and having a fabulous time. I think he must be a wolfhound or something, because he's the size of a sodding donkey.

"I'm so sorry. Trevor, *sit!*"

Trevor ignores him.

"You're Mary Butterworth's granddaughter, aren't you?"

"Yes. We've just moved in, and I can't get the key to work. Archie, get up. You'll get mud all over your coat."

Jack's obviously feeling braver now he's realized Trevor hasn't actually mauled anybody, and he risks a stroke and the bloody thing goes into another round of leaping and barking. I'm still frantically turning the key round and round, and finally the door opens and I switch the light on and everything gets slightly better; more Benny Hill, and less Hound of the bloody Baskervilles.

"Sit, Trevor. Sit."

Trevor gives Mr. Pallfrey a supercilious look and runs back down the path, hotly pursued by Jack and Archie.

Dear God. So much for a nice quiet bedtime.

Mr. Pallfrey looks mortified. "I'm ever so sorry."

"Don't worry about it. We love dogs, honestly—Archie was just on at me to get him one."

"Well, think long and hard about it, that's my advice, and don't get a lurcher, whatever you do, because he's still growing. He's my daughter's, really, she got him as a puppy, lovely little thing he was, but she doesn't have the room now."

We look toward the gate, where Trevor's standing silhouetted in the moonlight, appearing every inch the obedient canine, while Jack and Archie pat him.

"Lord knows how big he'll be when he's finished." He finally manages to grab him and they head for home, waving and barking.

"There you go, Archie. That's why we're not getting a dog."

Archie looks at me like I'm mad, his face still flushed with excitement. Even Jack's been converted to the newly launched Canine Campaign. "Oh, Mum, please, we could have one just like Trevor, and then they could be friends, and it'd be great, he could come to school with us and be in the playground. And if we didn't like our packed lunch, he could eat it."

Archie gives his brother an admiring glance. A dog that eats your sandwiches: what a brilliant idea.

After a protracted round of teeth brushing and arguing about dogs, they're in bed at last, sparked out and asleep, and I'm downstairs trying to unpack the crates in the kitchen. Everywhere I look there's another crate full of things that should be in another room, or in the bin. And I'll have to sort out the telly tomorrow, because they both practically went into shock when they discovered there was no Sky, and I think I'm going to need as much backup as I can get over the next few weeks.

I'm unpacking china when Ellen calls. "How's it going, darling?"

"Great. The rooms are much bigger than I remembered. The boys have unpacked all their trains and the track upstairs, and there's still a load of space."

"God, I loved that film."

"What film? Not *Thomas the Tragic Tank Engine?*"

"No, *The Railway Children.* I loved it—still do, in fact, although I always end up sobbing at the end. That bit where Jenny Agutter runs up the platform shouting 'Daddy! My daddy!' Christ, it gets me every time."

There's an awkward silence, and I'm pretty sure we're both

thinking it doesn't matter how many platforms Jack and Archie run along shouting "Daddy!"—he won't be appearing out of the mists. Actually, I'm starting to feel tired and cold.

"And the mother was great, too."

"Ellen, nobody loves the mother in *The Railway Children*. It's all about the kind old gentleman and the dad, or Perks at the station."

"Well, I loved her, and when you sell your first ball of wool, I'm going to come down and we'll have iced buns for tea. Deal?"

"You're on."

"You were right this afternoon. This is just what you all need, a new start by the sea. The boys will love it, and I can come down for detox weekends. It'll be great."

"Promise?"

"Yes. Now, enough about you, let's talk about special me. I've had another fight with Jimmy."

Ellen likes to keep a few men on the go at the same time, and it can get pretty confusing, but I think Jimmy's the one who's a freelance sound engineer, and a bit of a sulker.

"He's on about me helping him get a contract again, but I'm not keen; I mean, what if we've had a fight and he's on one of my shifts? I'll end up sounding like I'm standing in a bucket. Christ, you'd think I'd learn."

"Are we talking about Dirty Harry, by any chance?"

"Yes. Who I saw the other day, by the way, at a drinks thing, looking gorgeous."

"Ellen."

"I didn't talk to him."

"Ellen."

"Well, I might have texted him."

"So you're seeing him when?"

"Next Friday, for a quick drink after work. But only a drink. And then I'm coming down to you for the weekend."

Harry's been a bit of a blind spot for Ellen for ages; he's a brilliant cameraman but pretty wild, and he tends to disappear off on jaunts and come back with all sorts of unexplained bruises and fabulous stories. She just can't resist him. A bit like me and Walnut Whips, only much better for your thighs.

"So we'll expect you on Sunday afternoon, then, around teatime?"

"Don't be like that. I'm going to be firm this time."

"Right."

"I am. Cool and calm and in control."

"Okeydokey."

"But if the cool thing doesn't work, will Saturday afternoon be all right?"

"Of course. Vin might be around, too."

"Oh, good. Has he stopped doing his Jacques Cousteau thing then?"

Vin's a marine biologist, and tends to be off counting plankton when he's not surfing and lounging about with the kind of blond girlfriends who look good in wet suits.

"No, but he's back while they de-barnacle the boat or something, so he's coming down to stay and help me sort the house out. I was thinking we might start this weekend by painting everything white."

"Less of the 'we,' darling, if you don't mind. You can do the DIY and I'll do cocktails."

"Yes, but not those pink zombie things like you did last time. I can't move after one of those, let alone paint ceilings."

"That's because they're mostly vodka, darling. I'll do you a PG version. More pink, less zombie."

"Perfect."

By the time I'm in bed, it's nearly one, and I've gone right past the totally knackered stage and straight into staring into the darkness. I can't find my sodding duvet, or any sheets, and I'm too exhausted to look in any more bloody crates, so I'm shivering under a motley selection of Archie's old cot blankets and Jack's old duvet cover with the purple stains from a sugar-free Ribena incident, lying listening to the sea and trying to convince myself that it's lovely and soothing, and a far superior background noise to the London traffic I'm used to, but it's not bloody working. The sound of the waves crashing on the rocks down by the pier seems to be getting louder, and I'm getting colder by the minute. Christ. If it's going to be like this every night, I'll have to buy earplugs. I think I'm having a slow-motion panic attack, wondering if I've done the right thing moving us here, and whether the house will fall down before I've had a chance to get rid of that horrible wallpaper in the hall, when I'm suddenly inspired to make a List. Making Lists always makes you feel like you're in control, so it's a Top Plan.

Right. Number one, buy gallons of matte emulsion, and rent a sander. Two, get a new hammer because the old one's got a dodgy handle; and three, find my bloody duvet. And finish Jack's blanket and sort out a new window display for the shop. Something that doesn't look like someone's just chucked a few balls of wool in and then gone home, maybe with a seaside theme, with buckets and spades and shells. I could hang some net up and knit some fish shapes. I'd probably need twenty or thirty, in cotton, maybe, oranges and blues, and maybe some silver ones, too, and I could knit some seaweed in dark green, in chenille or something velvety. Actually, I think I may need to be Getting a Grip now, because I'm lying here obsessing about knitting seaweed and it isn't really helping.

"Mum, I had a horrible dream and the sea came right in the house and we were all drownded. I hate this house. I want to go back to London."

Jack's standing in the doorway, looking pitiful.

"It was just a dream, darling. Come and snuggle in, and you'll be fine. Go and get your duvet, but be very quiet so you don't wake Archie."

"I'm already waked up."

Excellent. Archie's dragging his duvet along the floor behind him; no need to vacuum the upstairs landing for a while then.

"Snuggle up now, it's very late."

"Can we have a story?"

"No."

Two small wriggling boys, and a corner of a child-size duvet. I'll be asleep in no time.

Gran appears at half past seven the next morning, with a packet of bacon and a new loaf, looking full of energy. God, I really hope she's not planning on doing this every morning. I'd forgotten about her early starts: the only drawback to spending the summer holidays at Gran's was being hoiked out of bed at the crack of dawn every day. Vin used to refuse to get up, but I never had the nerve, and this morning's no exception. I'm downstairs putting the kettle on before I'm even half awake while she starts cooking the bacon and humming "Onward, Christian Soldiers."

"You sit yourself down and let me do that. You looked completely done in last night, you know. Did you sleep well?"

"Yes, fine, thanks."

Actually, this is surprisingly true, despite dreaming about being shipwrecked and getting tangled up in seaweed and having to cut myself free with the bread knife before I could swim to shore. At least it was better than the one where I'm driving the car on the motorway with the boys in the back and the steering wheel comes off in my hand.

"One egg or two?"

"Just bacon for me, thanks, Gran."

"You can't have just bacon, that's not a proper breakfast if you've got a busy day in front of you. I'll do you one. Go to work on an egg, isn't that what they say?"

Not for the last thirty years they haven't, but never mind. "I'm fine with a bacon sandwich, honestly."

She sniffs, which means she doesn't approve but doesn't want to make a scene. "Shall I do the boys scrambled eggs, then?"

"Lovely."

Her chances of getting either of them to eat scrambled eggs

are almost zero, but it's the thought that counts, and at least it'll stop her obsessing about what I'm eating.

They come downstairs and start running round the table, clapping their hands and shouting "Bacon, bacon," and seem thrilled to find someone is finally providing them with a proper cooked breakfast.

Gran starts to crack the eggs into a bowl.

"What's the plan for today? Only I said I'd pop in to see Betty later, and I've got the Bowls Club this afternoon, and bingo tonight, for the Lifeboats."

"I thought I'd do some more crates, and then I want to go into the shop and see if the new stock's in yet."

"Right you are then, lovey."

I'm really looking forward to seeing the new stock: I've met most of the reps over the past few months, and they've shown me their new autumn ranges and told me about discounts and bulk orders, and in-store promotion kits, most of which were either too big to fit in the shop or required ordering vast quantities of the new ranges that I didn't particularly like, but the Rowan rep turned up with all sorts of gorgeous samples in beautiful colors and I got carried away, to the tune of a small fortune in anybody's money. Particularly mine. Which I'm trying not to think about.

"They've asked me to be ladies' captain, you know."

"Who have, Gran?"

"The Bowls Club. It's a lot of work, mind, arranging all the matches and everything, but I think I'll do it, now I've got the time. Only you're to say, you know, if you need me to help out in the shop or anything. I don't want you getting exhausted—these two are enough to keep anyone busy."

She gives me a sideways look as she stirs the eggs.

"Yes, but they'll be back at school soon, and then I'll have every day until three, and Elsie says she'll do the afternoons and extra in the holidays, so it's only Saturday mornings really, if that's still okay with you?"

"Of course it is, pet."

Archie's stopped running round the table and is giving me one of his Determined looks, which usually means trouble.

"I'm not going to school. I'm staying here, to play with the dog."

Great. I can go to prison for failing to get my five-year-old to be a regular attender, and the RSPCA can take the dog into care.

"Don't be silly, Archie. They've got lovely things in your classroom, paints and a sand tray, don't you remember? And we're not getting a dog."

"Yes, but you have to sit on the mat at school. You always have to sit on the stupid mat."

"But only for stories, and you love stories."

"I can have my stories at home with you."

"I'll be working in the shop, so you'll have to come with me and sit and be very quiet. But if you're sure you want to be at home like a baby when Jack goes off to school, I suppose we could do that. I'm surprised, though, now you're such a big boy."

"Well, I might go, just to see what it's like, only I haven't decided yet."

I pour myself a cup of tea, and there's a marked silence when Gran presents the boys with their bacon and scrambled eggs.

"I don't like jumbled-up eggs."

"Yes, you do, Jack. Your mum used to love them scrambled when she was your age. Just you eat up like a good boy, and then we can go down to the beach."

Jack stares at his plate, while Archie starts eating with extra lip-smacking sound effects.

"Can we take our fishing nets? Because we might catch a big fish, there might be a whale, and we could keep it in the bath."

Jack rolls his eyes. "You couldn't get it in your net, silly, a great big whale, the pole would snap."

"It might want to be friends, and it could swim up by itself. You don't know."

"Tell him, Mum."

"You can both take your nets if we can find them, and your buckets, and we can go fishing for crabs off the pier later, if you like, but you'll have to eat your breakfast first, Jack. Try some of your egg, properly, and then if you don't like it, you can leave it. But it was my favorite when I was little, so try some."

He takes a tentative forkful. I'm really hoping Gran isn't going to launch into her waste-not-want-not routine, because it's not going to work with Jack, who could be a major food fusser if he was given half a chance, so I pretty much go for the one mouthful and then if you don't like it don't eat it but don't whine approach, which has worked pretty well so far, apart from cauliflower and avocado.

"Actually, it's quite nice."

Gran smiles. "There's a good boy."

He grins at me as Gran gets up to pour herself more tea.

I unpack more crates upstairs while the boys finish breakfast, and get thoroughly absorbed in arranging sheets and pillowcases in neat little piles in the big linen cupboard on the landing, which has slatted wooden shelves and smells faintly of mothballs. The house may be in chaos, and I still don't know where half my clothes are, but at least I've got an impeccable arrangement of sheets and towels. By the time we're dressed, Gran's managed to unpack a vast collection of half-used tins of paint downstairs, so I stack them in the garage while Gran tries to get the boys to stop dueling with their fishing nets before someone gets poked in the eye. I'm beginning to feel rather nervous about going into the shop now we're actually down here and moved in; it all feels a bit like the first day of school after the holidays, only I haven't had a holiday. And my back's starting to hurt again, so I'm doing a rather stiff-legged trudge as we head off down the hill, while Gran tells the boys how Vin and I used to sledge down it in the snow, and Vin once shot right across the road and nearly onto the beach.

I'm having visions of a Cresta Run of solid ice outside the shop and Archie disappearing under a bus balanced on my best tea tray as we continue our royal progress down Beach Street, with Gran stopping to talk to practically everybody she meets, while the boys run ahead and then run back again, waving their fishing nets and trying to get her to hurry up. The shops haven't changed much over the years; the butcher has the same plastic parsley among all the white china trays, and the pink china pig, and Parsons's has still got metal buckets and mops hanging outside and smells of glue and wood shavings, like it always did. We go in to say good morning to Mr. Parsons and Archie knocks a coal scuttle over, and then we're outside the florist's next door to our shop, and Mrs. Davis comes out to say hello carrying a plastic tub full of yellow roses.

Elsie's waiting for us, standing behind the old-fashioned counter with the glass top when I push open the door, which sticks so you have to give it a bit of a shove; that's another thing I must get sorted, because people are always half falling into the shop after shoving too hard. The bell jingles, and keeps on jingling as the boys each have a turn at opening and closing the door.

"Aren't you going to come and say hello to Aunty Elsie?"

They shuffle over, suddenly shy, while Gran casts an expert eye across the shelves and spots some of the new stock, a mohair-and-silk mix in bright acid colors, which will knit up into lovely, delicate wraps and shawls. "They look expensive."

I can tell she's not sure, and I don't really blame her, because Elsie's bundled them all together in a complete clash of colors. She's put the new cottons next to them, too, all shoved in together, right next to some acrylic baby wool in a revolting shade of sickly green. Next to salmon pink. Maybe she was just trying to be helpful, or maybe not, but I'm itching to move them.

Gran puts her bag on the counter. "I see you finished your cardi, Elsie."

Elsie nods and gives us a twirl. Dear God, it's got zigzag stripes, in every color imaginable, and it makes her look like one of those Peruvian poncho people who play the panpipes outside Tube stations wearing hats with earflaps, mixed with a hint of Missoni, if they'd suddenly gone color-blind and went in for double knitting. If you look at it for too long, you start to feel dizzy.

"I could knit you one, too, if you like, Jo, and we could wear them in the shop."

Bloody hell.

"That's kind of you, Elsie, but we need so many things knitted up, for samples and the window and everything, I was sort of counting on you for that."

I'm very pleased with myself with this diplomatic answer, and I can tell Gran's impressed, too, because she gives me a surreptitious wink.

"Well, you just let me know, because I like to have a few things on the go, and I can do pretty much any pattern, if I say so myself. I could always do you one in between anything else that needs doing."

Bugger. I'll have to think of something, and quick, because I'm getting visions of myself stuck behind the counter looking like a loony. Desperate times call for desperate measures.

"I've been thinking about doing a new display for the window, for the Best Seaside competition, and I'd like to knit some fish shapes, in cotton, in some of the new colors, so maybe you could help me with that?"

Elsie purses her lips and looks annoyed. "I'm not sure that's a good idea, it all sounds very modern to me."

Bang goes my cardigan, I hope. Elsie hates change, and anything Modern is to be avoided at all costs as far as she's concerned, since it tends to involve Bad Manners, or Sex. Or both. Often at the same time.

Gran's trying to hide a smile. "Well, I think it sounds lovely, and Jo's always been clever with things like that, you know. She used to do me lovely shell pictures when she was little."

Elsie gives me a rather sneering look. "Yes, but a window's a bit bigger than a picture, you know, and our ladies like a nice tidy window."

I think I should probably step in now, before they go into one of their bickers. They've been bickering for years, and Gran usually loses, which, come to think of it, is probably why she didn't give up the shop ages ago: she couldn't face telling Elsie.

"I'll do the window, Elsie, if you're not sure, but maybe you could do a shawl for me. There's a nice pattern in one of the Rowan books, which looks quite fiddly, but I'm sure it won't be a problem for an advanced knitter like you. And I'd like to have a few things in the new colors to encourage people."

I've already knitted one in silvery gray, with tiny silver beads knitted in round the edges, which took me ages but was worth it. Ellen's tried to "borrow" it twice, which is always a good sign.

Archie opens the shop door, keen to be off to the beach.

"I'll take these two off, then, and see you later back at the house?"

"Thanks, Gran."

She's humming as she goes out, but Elsie's still looking pretty ruffled.

"Shall I make us a cup of tea, Elsie?"

"No, I'll do it, it's no trouble."

Elsie loves making tea; it's one of her favorite things.

"Did you bring the kettle in with you? Only your gran borrowed it yesterday."

Damn. I knew there was something I meant to bring. "Sorry, I forgot, but I can go back and get it."

"There's no need for that, I brought mine in from home. I thought you might forget, what with moving in and everything. I won't be a minute."

She's looking slightly happier as she goes upstairs, having scored points on the kettle front, which is good, because I'd really like to avoid upsetting her if I possibly can. She's worked here for years, and having her walk out in my first week would be a disaster, because, apart from anything else, she's the only one who knows how to open the till; you have to wiggle the number 8 and press the Total key at the same time, and I still haven't got the hang of it. And she's completely reliable, and happy to come in at short notice, because she likes to be out of the house and away from her husband, Jeffrey, who's recently retired, and who's been a source of constant disappointment to her. They live two streets up from the shop; she'd like one of the new bungalows up by Gran, but Jeffrey's not keen; actually he's not that keen on anything except his allotment, where he grows giant onions, which have to be taken to the local shows in his wheelbarrow. They've got one of those silent marriages, where people seethe away for years never saying anything, like living inside a pressure cooker on a very low heat, where everything goes soft and pulpy, simmering away for ages, forgotten, until the lid finally blows off and you end up with bits of turnip all over your kitchen ceiling.

I've always had a soft spot for Jeffrey, because he made a sledge for me and Vin when we were little, and he used to play cricket with us on the beach with their son, Martin, who was a couple of years older than us, and once chased Vin right along the seafront, wearing his cowboy hat and firing at him with his cap gun. Martin moved to Cheltenham after he got married, but he's back at home now, and going through a very messy divorce, according to Gran; he works in computers, and his wife, Patricia, left him for the U.K. sales manager and now insists on being called Patsy and drives a Mercedes sports car. Gran says Elsie's thrilled because she never liked the wife, who once bought her a satin nightdress with a matching dressing gown for Christmas, which wasn't from M & S so she couldn't take it back, and now she's got Martin back home she's cooking all his old favorites for him, which must be rather mortifying for him, since he's over forty. But I bet he daren't tell her to lay off the eggy soldiers, because she's not the kind of woman you'd want to cross, especially if she happens to be your mother.

I'm standing looking at the shelves while Elsie's upstairs, and planning how I'm going to move everything around, with all the nasty pastels in the back room, along with all the white baby wool and the multicolored acrylic double knitting. Although I think I might wait until Vin gets here, and maybe do it on a Sunday, when Elsie's safely at home boiling sprouts and battling with her Yorkshires. The back room has got the same dark wooden shelving as the front, divided into squares, and the same dark wood floor, but there are quite a few spaces with not very much stock, and a table with a couple of chairs, and all the patterns in an assortment of old cracked plastic folders next to the door to the stairs. The kitchen and loo are upstairs, and the storeroom, packed with old display units that used to twirl round but don't anymore, and boxes full of oddments of material and tinsel, along with all the clutter Gran's collected over the years. I'd like to try to open it up as a workroom and more shop space, if I can ever work out how to get rid of all the rubbish.

I'm wondering how much it would cost to hire a skip, and where on earth I'd put one if I did, since it would pretty much block the road, when Mrs. Davis comes in from next door, with a big bunch of sunflowers. "I just wanted to say a proper welcome, love."

"Oh, how lovely. Thank you."

Elsie barrels down the stairs to see what's going on.

"Look, Elsie, aren't they lovely?"

"Very nice." She gives Mrs. Davis a hostile look.

"I can't stop, but pop in any time if you need change or anything. It's amazing how you run out if you get busy. See you later."

Elsie's standing back behind the counter with her arms crossed, still looking hostile; there was a mini-drama last year when they fell out over change, I think, something to do with pound coins.

"Wasn't that kind of her?"

"Oh, yes, very generous, but you've got to watch her, you know, or she'll be in and out all day wanting change for ten-pound notes, although why she can't go to the bank like the rest of us is beyond me. And anyway, we haven't got any vases so I don't know where she thinks you're going to put them."

"Yes, we have. There's one in the window, isn't there?"

I open the door in the partition and reach through to pick up the glass vase with the faded plastic tulips.

Elsie tuts. "I spent quite a long time arranging them, actually, but never mind. I'll go and get the tea, shall I? Only there aren't any biscuits, I'm afraid. We used to have biscuits a while back, but your gran stopped buying them."

She's looking seriously put out now. Bugger. I think this might be the perfect time for an olive branch. "I could get some, if you like."

"I don't like bourbons."

"Okay."

"Or gingersnaps—your gran's very partial to those, but they repeat on me. I quite like digestives, though. Or custard creams."

The way she says "custard creams" makes it fairly clear they're the top choice.

"Right, well, I won't be a minute."

Bloody hell. From television news producer to biscuit girl; I think I'd better get a few packets, because it looks like I may be needing them.

Elsie's got a mouth full of custard cream when our first customer of the morning, Mrs. Stebbing, comes in. She buys three balls of lemon four-ply and a pattern for a matinee coat for her goddaughter's new baby, who looks like a fairly chunky boy when she shows us the photographs, and not an obvious choice for a delicate lemon jacket with a lace design on the front. Then old Mrs. Marwell comes in, or tries to, but she can't get her wheelie basket through the door. By the time we've got her in, there's a slightly awkward moment when she can't remember what she wanted, but then it comes back to her, with a bit of prompting from Elsie. She's knitting another sweater for the church, for the orphans in Africa, and she wants to look in the bargain basket, where we put any odd balls left over from different dye lots; usually the cheaper things with a high percentage of man-made fiber, which wash well if you don't mind a sweater that builds up static. Quite a few of our old ladies knit things for the church, and they're quite happy using up odd balls of wool, so the sweaters often have one yellow sleeve, and one red, with a bright blue middle, like weird versions of Mondrian paintings, only warmer. I think this might be a good time to launch another one of my Top New Ideas, now I've got the custard creams as backup.

"Mrs. Marwell, do you think it would be useful if I started a charity basket? I was thinking we could ask people to bring in any leftover wool from home, and we'd put in our spare stock, like we do now, and it would all be free, for people to use for charity things like blankets or sweaters."

"Oh, I think that would be wonderful, dear, really wonderful, because it does add up, you know, and my pension doesn't go as far as it used to."

"Right, well, let's start now then, so that'll be no charge, since it's for charity, so put your purse away, and if you've got any spare wool left, bring it in next time, and put it in the basket. Someone's bound to be able to use it for something."

She's thrilled, and goes off promising to tell all the ladies at the church about my marvelous new idea.

Elsie's looking thin-lipped again. Oh dear.

"I meant to talk to you about that first, Elsie, but it doesn't seem right charging them, does it, not when it's for charity. And we've got so much stuff just sitting upstairs."

"Well, that's as may be, but I hope you know what you're doing, because they'll all be bringing in all sorts now, stuff they've had in their cupboards for years."

"We can always throw it out if it's too manky."

She sniffs; I think she's trying to decide if *manky* is a rude word.

"Have you got any more ideas, any more things you want to change? Only I'd quite like to know beforehand, and that way I can help you avoid making too many mistakes. Because it's not as simple as it seems sometimes, you know. When you've been doing it for as long as I have."

"Nothing major, moving things around a little bit, and putting the newer stock in the front, and new window displays. I'd like to start a group, invite people in for a glass of wine—people are starting them all over the place, and they're really popular. Not just in wool shops, people meet in pubs and cafés, too. They call them Stitch and Bitch groups."

"I'm not sure that sounds very nice; I don't think our ladies would like anything like that. Couldn't you call it something nicer?"

"Yes, but that's the whole point, Elsie. We need to attract new ladies—I mean women—into the shop."

"I know, what about Knit and Natter? That's much nicer."

"It doesn't sound so much fun, though, does it?"

"Would you want me to work on any of these evenings, because I do have to get Jeffrey's supper, and what with my

Martin being home, too, and in at all hours with his work, I sometimes end up cooking twice of an evening. And he can be quite a fussy eater, you know. It's all salads and sandwiches, and he won't touch fish fingers anymore, and he used to love them when he was little."

I think maybe Martin's been Making a Stand after all, which is rather impressive of him.

"No, I'll do them. Gran says she'll have the boys, and it'll only be one night a week, but we need to try new things, we really do, otherwise the shop will never make any money and we'll have to close, like so many of the other small shops have. Anyway, I think it'll be fun. Now then, shall we have another cup of tea and get started on the stock check? Only Gran will be back with the boys soon and I still need to look through these orders."

"I'll go up and make a fresh pot. Would you like another biscuit?"

"Please."

Christ, I'll end up completely spherical if she carries on at this rate.

I know Elsie's nervous of change, and I'm feeling pretty nervous about it myself, but the shop only made two thousand pounds' profit last year, which according to the books I got from the business section in the library is the retail equivalent of being in the kind of coma where they either start playing your favorite music and sticking pins in your legs or else turn the machines off. And the books say the vital thing you need in a shop is a detailed profile of your core customers, like the supermarkets do when they send you money-off vouchers for couscous with your club-card statement, even though you bought it only once, by mistake, and your children refused to eat it because they said it looked like sick. At the moment my core customer is called Doris, and she's a hundred and eight, and she may not be able to remember where she's put her front-door key, but she knows the price of four-ply down to the last penny within a hundred-mile radius. What I really need is a few more in their mid-thirties, called Tara, or something ending in *ee*, who like beautiful glossy pattern books, and won't faint if you ask them to pay eight pounds fifty for them. If they're buying pastels for a baby, they want raspberry or nougat, or duck-egg blue, never peach. Nectarine possibly, and sage greens and caramels and creams, in pure wool or cotton mixes. Or silks and mohair. Tara wouldn't know how to knit a matinee coat if her life depended on it, but she'll have a go at a poncho, and I know she's out there somewhere, because all the reps are saying wool sales have gone through the roof recently, especially for the more expensive ranges. So I just have to find out where she lives round here, and keep Doris and her friends happy at the same time. Bloody hell. Still, it could be worse; I could be wearing a multicolored zigzag cardigan made entirely of man-made fiber and getting small jolts of static electricity every time I touch anything vaguely metallic. Although I've got a horrible feeling it may be only a matter of time.

3

SAND AND WATER

I t's Friday morning and I'm wedged in the shop window trying to be Artistic with cramp in my arm. I finished knitting
the fish last night, with Gran's help, and now they're all
bobbing around on lengths of nylon thread looking very nautical, especially the stripy ones, which look rather like angelfish,
only woollier. I'm stapling some dark blue net to the Peg-Board
partition on top of the silver net I put up earlier; I'm aiming for
an impressionistic, wavelike shimmer, but so far it's all going a
bit *Blue Peter*. People keep stopping to wave at me through the
glass, which is embarrassing, and I've got sand up both my
sleeves.

"I don't know how on earth we're going to get all that sand
out, you know. It'll be a devil to clean up."

I think we can safely say that Elsie's still Not Keen.

"We can use the Hoover."

"You'll have a job. That old thing can barely suck up a bit of fluff, let alone a load of dirty old sand. What are these things meant to be, then?"

She hands me one of the papier-mâché starfish I made with the boys at the weekend, which probably wasn't one of my best ideas, especially since there are now bits of newspaper glued to the kitchen floor, the side of the fridge, and the soles of my flip-flops. I must try to remember that Art with Small Boys is best left to professionals, or people with ready access to tranquilizers.

"They're starfish."

She sniffs. "I'm not sure I've ever seen a purple starfish, but never mind. I'll make a start on tidying up in the back, shall I? Those pattern books are in a terrible muddle again."

"Good idea."

Christ. Beam me up, somebody; she's driving me mad this morning, and if she carries on like this, I may have to staple her to something to keep her out of my way. I wonder what she'd look like covered in dark blue net.

Apart from Elsie and her comments, and being stuck in this bloody window, everything has been going rather well; we've been in the new house for nearly a fortnight, and we've got a fully functioning telly now, thanks to Billie turning up in her Sky van, with a special belt for holding all her tools and a relaxed attitude to being trailed round the house by boys watching her every move. Although I think she'd underestimated just how much they'd been missing *SpongeBob SquarePants*, because she went very red when they both kissed her good-bye.

The really good news is that Vin's arrived, with his new

girlfriend, Lulu, who's been a huge success, not least because the boys think her name is completely hilarious. And instead of spending all day lounging about and looking glamorous, like her predecessor did, sipping water and refusing to eat anything with more than three calories in it, she helped me paint the big wall in the hall yesterday, which was good of her, particularly since she got the dodgy roller with the wobbly handle.

The boys are in seventh heaven in the new house, and if they're not out in the garden making camps with most of my sheets, they're on the beach, or campaigning to go fishing in the harbor, where they like to spend hours trying to catch teeny crabs while I lose the will to live. And there's definitely less bickering since they've gone all Famous Five. I think all the fresh air is knackering them; and if they do start niggling, Vin holds them upside down by their feet until they stop, which isn't a technique I've seen in any of the books, but it works pretty well, and I'd give it a go if I didn't think I'd drop them on their heads.

I'm trying to drape a piece of orange nylon fishing net over some driftwood when there's a loud banging on the window, which nearly gives me a heart attack. I've been having visions of crashing through the glass and ending up in a heap on the pavement for most of the morning, and it looks like this might be my moment. But it's the boys, with Gran, and she's very impressed with the window.

"It looks so pretty. You're very artistic, you know. I'd never have thought of anything like this. What are those purple things?"

"They're the starfish the boys made."

"Well, aren't you clever, boys?"

They nod.

"Morning, Elsie. Doesn't it all look lovely?"

Elsie sniffs again. "I liked it the way it was, but this is nice, too, I suppose."

Gran turns to me. "I better be off, then, love. The match is due to start soon."

She's wearing her special blazer and her white pleated skirt; they like to look smart at the Bowls Club, especially when they've got a match on, and if you turn up in a velour tracksuit like Mrs. Chambers from the baker's did, they make you go straight home again and get changed.

"Thanks, Gran, and I hope you win."

"We left Vinnie in bed, bless him, but we took them in a cup of tea, before we left."

We wave her off down the road.

Archie starts giggling. "When we took Uncle Vin his tea, guess what, Mum? They were doing kissing, him and Aunty Lulu, they were."

He makes a series of very realistic retching noises.

Jack puts his hand up, like they do at school.

"Yes, and Uncle Vin said a swearword. And it was a really bad one. Shall I tell you?"

"No, thank you, darling."

"It was the F word."

I'm pretty sure I can hear Elsie smirking.

"I'm sure it wasn't, Jack, and anyway, grown-ups are allowed to do different things than children, I've told you before. They can make their own minds up."

"Yes, and it's not fair. I want to make my own mind up. I might want to do swearing." He's giving me his most determined look.

"When you're a big boy, you can decide."

"Yes, but when will I be a big boy? How long?"

"When you're as old as Uncle Vin."

He gives me a stricken look. "I can't wait that long. I can't. It's just ridiculous."

"It's just ridiculous" is one of his new catchphrases.

"Give me a few more minutes to finish the window and we can go to the beach, how about that? You could both go and stand outside and tell me where things need to go, if you like. That would be really helpful."

They have a lovely time standing outside gesticulating increasingly frantically while I tip shells into little piles and do another quick spot of net adjusting, until I hear them starting to recite their favorite rude words, presumably as a practice run for when they're older and can unleash them on an unsuspecting public. Apart from the ubiquitous *willy* and *bum*, *bugger* features pretty heavily in their list, which is probably down to me while I was painting the hall. Mrs. Davis comes out from next door with a bucket of chrysanthemums and gives me a little wave. *Christ, she'll be thinking we're having a family Tourette's moment*; but she doesn't seem to notice, and then I remember she's got four grown-up sons and a staggering number of grandchildren, so she's probably fairly familiar with the word *bugger*.

"I'll be off, then, Elsie. I'll see you tomorrow around one."

She's standing behind the counter, pretending to sort

through the patterns. "It's no trouble to come in earlier, you know."

"No, it's fine, you have a nice lie-in for a change."

"I don't hold with staying in bed, I don't think it's healthy. I like to be up, getting on with my jobs, and what with Martin being home now, there's always plenty to do; I don't know what he does with his shirts, I really don't. They take a lot of starching to get them right; people don't seem to bother nowadays, but I like to do them properly. But Saturdays can get very busy, though, so you just call me if you need any help."

I'm not quite sure why she thinks I might need backup. I've even been practicing opening the till when she's not looking, and I'm really counting on a nice session in the shop without her breathing down my neck and tutting, so I can finish moving things around. Which is probably why she's so keen to come in.

"I'm sure I'll be fine, but thanks."

The beach is very hot and crowded when we arrive, and we have the usual sunscreen tussle, with Archie having a mini-meltdown when some goes in his mouth, before they're off with their buckets and I'm left trying to find the plastic top to the sunscreen tube, which has somehow managed to vanish again; it's vital I find it so I don't end up filling my handbag with another layer of sun cream, like I did last week. I've just found the bloody thing when Jack comes back with a bucketful of shells.

"Look, Mum, my bucket's nearly full and I've got some really good ones. Do you want to see?"

He tips them, along with half a bucketful of wet sand, all

over my legs, which I suppose will save me exfoliating if I try the fake tan thing again; although the last time I tried, Nick said I looked like I had a vitamin deficiency or was recovering from terrible burns.

"Well done, sweetheart, they're lovely."

"Are we going home for lunch?"

"I thought we could get some rolls from the baker's and have a picnic."

I'm hoping to give Vin and Lulu a few hours' peace, especially after their rude awakening earlier.

"Can we have chips, then?"

"Maybe later, when it's lunchtime, we'll see."

He runs off bellowing "Archie, Archie quick, she says we can have chips," and mothers with far more nutritious lunches in mind turn and give me disapproving looks. Damn. I'm starting to recognize a few of them, and was hoping I might get to talk to some of them before we're all standing in the playground at school doing the vague smiling thing you do when you don't know anybody's name but want to look friendly. They'll all know me as Chip Mum now, and I was hoping for something slightly more upbeat.

I never really managed to crack the school-gates routine in London. It was all very cliquey, and I never got beyond the cheerful nodding stage; probably because I'm crap at making new friends, unlike Ellen, who'd be our best chance of a gold if it ever becomes an Olympic sport, which it definitely should be because it's a lot more useful than bloody pole vaulting or cycling round in circles wearing weird helmets. I didn't fit in with any of the groups in our old playground; the working mums were the nicest, but they were always racing to get to work, so we never got beyond the occasional birthday party tea. And the nannies and au pairs who used to meet in the café in the park and do impressions of their employers didn't like mums joining them. So that left the posh mums, who were frighteningly glossy but brittle-looking, chatting into tiny mobile phones and driving massive Jeeps with lots of tinted glass, really badly, causing mini–traffic jams wherever they went, and I simply didn't have the right sort of clothes for them.

There was a brief flurry of interest when one of them spotted me with Nick in Sainsbury's and promptly invited us round to supper; I think she quite fancied having a real live Television Reporter sitting at her dining table, which would have been fine if he hadn't been on a flight to Jerusalem while we were starting on the rack of lamb in an herb crust. But she was persistent, and asked us again a few weeks later, when Nick was just back from another trip and completely knackered, so he only managed a brief bicker with a banker called Roger, with a wife who appeared to be called Pod, before he practically fell asleep at the table. And after that my temporary membership in the yummy mummies was rescinded.

The most scary ones were the Alpha Mums: the I-used-to-have-a-Proper-career-but-I-gave-it-all-up-for-the-children-and-now-I'm-quite-bored ones. God, they were relentless. Organizing birthday parties four months in advance, with the same skills they'd employed in mergers and acquisitions, busy networking on the PTA and lobbying to become school governors and racing their kids through after-school programs that were so complicated they required advanced time management skills just to get to Wednesday. They made me feel like a complete amateur, wildly underprepared and chaotic, only just managing to get to school on time while they'd been up at six making brioche and fermenting things. And if you had one of their kids to tea, they always arrived with special instructions: wheat allergies or a penchant for eating only white food or taking all their clothes off at unusual moments. Or they couldn't come until five because they had a viola class, or Japanese, or advanced maths, and they'd either behave so perfectly they were like Stepford children and made yours look like lumpen yobs, or they were so appalling you longed for someone to come and pick them up. Never anything in between.

I think most of them were secretly desperate for a good nanny and a job that didn't involve making your own Play-Doh, but of course they'd never admit that, so I'm really hoping things will be a bit more relaxed down here; at least there won't be anyone who used to be earning a six-figure salary before she sprogged, or many takers for Mandarin Chinese for Toddlers. And I'm going to make much more of an effort, so I hope I won't end up doing quite so much nodding at the school gates like one of those dogs in the backs of cars. But I think I'll start tomorrow, when the chip thing has died down a bit.

Jack comes running back with Archie. "Here you are, Mummy, I got some fabless ones."

He's got a tiny bit of sand on his shorts but is otherwise totally pristine, whereas Archie looks like he's had a tricky half hour in quicksand and only just managed to get away.

"Let's get you dry, sweetheart."

"We're having chippers for lunch, aren't we, Mummy? Jack said, and I love chippers. Best of all, I do."

He's doing a celebratory dance while I try to de-sand him.

"Yes, but not yet. It's not lunchtime yet."

"Chips, chips, chips. We're having chips."

Oh, good. More disapproving glances.

I retreat inside our beach hut, which I'm loving more and more; we used to make camps in it when we were little, and I'd spend ages sweeping up sand with a pink plastic dustpan and brush and arranging plastic cups, and making Gran drink luke-warm water with daisies in it, while Vin stood guard with his plastic ax in case of Viking invaders, which was embarrassingly stereotypical when I look back on it, but what we didn't realize was quite how brilliant beach huts are for grown-ups. There's no staggering up and down the beach carrying half a ton of as-sorted kit, or sitting shivering behind a windbreak being sand-blasted and praying for rain so you can go home. And best of all, there's no more wriggling out of wet swimming costumes under sandy towels or showing your naked bottom to half the beach. It's just completely brilliant, and the council have painted them all different colors, and ours is a lovely pale blue. I'm having a little therapeutic sand-sweeping moment when the boys come back with a new friend.

"Can he come and have chips with us, Mum, because he loves chips, don't you?"

Archie's doing his best pleading look, and the new boy's nodding enthusiastically. He's got lovely big brown eyes and a very serious expression.

"I do. I really love them."

While we're doing the obligatory let's-go-and-ask-your-mummy chat, I discover he's called Marco, and he's the same age as Jack, but with far nicer manners. In fact, he's a total charmer, and before I know it all three of them are off to see his mum, who comes over with them to introduce herself, and presumably check I'm not a nutter. She says she's called Constanza, and holds out her hand as if to shake hands, which seems rather formal, and then she says everybody calls her Connie, especially in England, where nobody can pronounce Constanza, and she's just moved into the pub with Gran's Gordon Ramsay, who's actually called Mark. They met when he was in Tuscany, cooking in her uncle's restaurant.

"And he was called Marco, too, which is coincidental, isn't it, and he's my favorite uncle, although he drives Silvia into madness, but she can be a difficult woman, very sharp, but she makes really good gnocchi, very light, and with sage, but not too much sage, or it can be too much. Too powering. And so, hello, and lovely to meet you."

She's still holding my hand, with Marco jiggling up and down, trying to start another round of chip pleading, and then there's a huge amount of arm waving and the occasional Italian word, *basta* mainly, which I think means stop it right now or I will have hysterics, or it might be *pasta*, in which case it's her alternative plan for lunch, and then she smiles, and I can see where Marco gets his beautiful eyes from.

"So, we have panini, and perhaps we have lunch together, yes?"

"That would be lovely."

She's got a great tan, and bright pink fingernails with her

hair up in silver clips, and she's wearing a long white embroidered shirt and pretty sandals, so I'm particularly glad I'm wearing one of my new flowery shirts today, although I wish I wasn't wearing such battered old flip-flops.

"Marco, where is Nelly?"

They both look toward the sea.

"Go and get her, please."

He runs down to the sea and retrieves a small girl, who despite the fact that she's wearing a sundress, appears to be swimming away from him as fast as she can.

"She loves to swim. It's her favorite thing. I was the same, I think. But the sea is warmer at home."

Nelly is brought back, dripping wet.

"Antonella. You promised. Only to your knees."

She's a paler version of her mother, with lovely dark hair, which has gone into little wet ringlets.

"I want to swim."

Nelly's certainly determined for someone so tiny, and there's lots of arm waving going on as we make a tactful withdrawal with Marco to the chip shop.

Calm has been restored by the time we get back, and we sit eating chips and delicious ham rolls, which are somehow even more delicious when they're called panini. Connie tells me about buying the pub, and how they've had to borrow money from everyone they know, including Mark's old boss, and most of her family, and I tell her if the shop hadn't been Gran's, I'd have needed to borrow money from everybody I know, too.

Archie and Nelly seem very taken with each other and are planning a major castle-building extravaganza after lunch when it starts to rain, so we huddle inside the beach hut clutching our chips, and Archie spills his juice all over my feet while Connie tells us this never happens in Italy, and really it's very beautiful how the English weather can do many different things in one day, and aren't these little houses lovely, and maybe we can all live in one if we run out of money. The sun comes out again after a few minutes, and then Vin and Lulu arrive and we make a pot of tea on Gran's old Primus stove while the kids make a start on their sand castles.

Vin's getting anxious because Archie and Nelly are enjoying flattening their castles almost as much as they're enjoying building them, and he's worried they aren't keeping up with Jack and Marco. "Do you think I should help them?" He quite likes helping where sand castles are involved but gets rather tense if things are bashed flat while he's still in construction mode.

Lulu shakes her head. "You're hopeless. Stop being so competitive, Vin. They're fine."

"Well, I'm off for a swim, then. Anyone fancy joining me?"

Vin's a very strong swimmer, especially if he's not accompanied by anyone wearing armbands. But his idea of a nice long swim tends to be other people's idea of a coast guard incident, so I'm hoping Connie doesn't join him, unless she was a former member of the Italian Olympic team, because it would be such a shame to end our first afternoon together with Vin giving her mouth-to-mouth. And I'm still not convinced he knows how to do it properly; he worked as a lifeguard when he was doing his A levels, and spent the whole summer showing off and practicing the kiss of life on my friend Laura, but I'm sure he missed some vital bits, because it just looked like snogging to me.

"If Nelly sees you are swimming, she will come, too. She loves to swim."

Vin's putting luminous sunscreen on his nose. "That's fine."

I'm pretty sure he thinks he'll soon tire her out and then he can dump her back on the sand while he has a proper swim, but Nelly doesn't give up that easily. In fact, it looks like he might have finally met his match; she's like a little seal, and she just keeps on going. He's very impressed, when he finally manages to get her back out.

"She's got so much energy, it's extraordinary."

"I know. My mother says we should feed her less meat."

Lulu hands Vin a towel. "She sounds like my grandmother. She always used to bang on about children not having too much rich food, and then they'd all sit down to crumpets and cake for tea, and we'd get palmed off with bread and butter. Horrible old bag."

She obviously still minds about the lack of cake, and I don't really blame her; if I tried something similar with the boys, they'd probably call the police.

"I love your English teas. I keep telling Mark we should do afternoon teas, in the restaurant, with muffets. I loves muffets. And scones."

Lulu smiles. "I think you might mean muffins."

"Oh yes, I love them, too. And honey. And English jam. Damson is the best I think, or raspberry. But Mark says he wants to run a restaurant, not a tea shop, and he can be very stubborn. He wants a vegetable garden, and we've already got chickens, and now he wants pigs. Honestly he does. And piglings. But if he thinks I will be looking after piglings, he will be having a very big surprise. My family stopped being peasants years ago, and if I want to live in dirt, I can go back to Calabria."

"I think chickens are sweet."

Connie gives Lulu a puzzled look. "Do you? Well, you must come and see them, take some home with you, please. Because they are everywhere. There was one in Nelly's bedroom last night. Horrible things. Eating my flowers."

We head home at about five, after promising to go to the pub for supper later; Connie says the kids can watch DVDs upstairs if they get bored, and it'll save me cooking, which is great, especially as Ellen's due to arrive soon, with Dirty Harry. They're back on again, and she's completely blissed out about it, and I can't wait to see her and show the house. Not that it's looking much different from the last time she saw it, but still.

I'm washing shells in the kitchen when they arrive. Harry looks even more handsome than I remembered, with his non-designer stubble and his battered old leather jacket. He gives me a long hug and whispers "I'm so sorry" in my ear, which confuses me, so I stand holding the washing-up brush having a panic attack about him being on the verge of confessing something tricky until I realize it's the first time I've seen him since Nick died. He gives me another hug as he goes out into the garden with Vin.

Ellen's standing watching me. "So, what do you think?"

"About what?"

"About the state of the dollar against the euro. Come in, Number Twenty-six, your time is up. Harry, of course."

"Lovely. You make a perfect couple."

"I know, we do, don't we, and it's so great, because he's being much less annoying this time; no long silences, or going out for croissants and not coming back for three weeks."

"He only did that once, and to be fair, he did text you, didn't he? And it was work, wasn't it?"

"Yes, but he still should have called."

"Yes, but then you'd have gone berserk with him, wouldn't you?"

"Yes."

"Well, they don't tend to call if they know they're going to get an earful."

"Funnily enough, that's exactly what he says. But a girl likes to be able to have a bit of a rant when she's been waiting three fucking weeks for a croissant."

"Less of the F word please, Aunty Ellen, when your godsons are awake."

"They're at the bottom of the garden."

"Yes, but Jack's on a new Swearing for Children mission, and he's got hearing like a bat; he can hear a packet of crisps being opened anywhere in the house. Honestly. Try it if you don't believe me."

She laughs. "Fair enough. The house is looking fabulous, darling, or it will be when you've finished."

"In ten years, possibly. I just don't think I'll have the time, not with the shop."

"It's very Vintage, you know, mixing old wallpaper with chintz, very eclectic. Christ, what on earth are they doing out there?"

There are hammering noises coming from the garden.

"Making a camp, with bits of wood from the shed. Vin tried a few little improvements and it fell down, so he's pretending he did it on purpose."

"Well, I don't want to worry you, but there's a bloody huge dog running round out there now."

"That'll be Trevor. He pops round most days."

Actually, I'm getting rather worried about Trevor. He keeps turning up, and sitting outside the back door looking hopeful and waiting for the boys to come out to play, which they do at every opportunity. And we've got a growing collection of semi-deflated footballs to prove it.

"Christ, if something that size turned up in your garden in London, you'd call in Armed Response."

"He's very friendly."

"He'd bloody have to be, he's the size of a horse. He's just knocked Archie over, flat on his back."

"No he hasn't, that'll be Archie taking a dive. He loves rolling round on the grass being licked, it's one of his new Best Things."

"Some bloke's turned up now."

"Does he look embarrassed?"

"Very."

"That'll be Mr. Pallfrey, come to fetch Trevor."

"So have you made any other new friends, apart from old men and giant dogs? How's Elsie?"

"Driving me mad. She told me off yesterday for putting the pound coins in the wrong bit of the till."

"Sack her. I've told you. Just say, 'Elsie, you are the weakest link. Good-bye.' She'll like that. They all love Anne Robinson, old bags like her."

"I can't. All the other old bags would boycott the shop. And anyway, she doesn't mean it."

"She bloody does. Miserable cow."

Vin comes back in. "Are we talking about Elsie, by any chance? I've told you, tell her to cheer up or chuff off. I don't know what's happened to my bossy big sister, I really don't."

"She had kids, that's what happened. You can't be bossy with babies, not unless you're a complete cow, so you get used to compromising and cajoling and eating the leftover bits at supper, which isn't exactly ideal training for being ruthless. It would be a perfect way to reprogram people, anyone a bit too fond of bossing and shouting. Make them look after a two-year-old for a whole week, with no buying in staff and no locking anybody in cupboards. Heads of multinationals, chief executives, former presidents, it'd be great television, Ellen: I'm an important person, get this toddler off me."

"I'll tell the boys upstairs, but somehow I don't think they'll buy it. Bit too close to home for most of them, I'd say."

"Anyway, I don't want to be ruthless. I just want everyone to be happy."

"And world peace. Don't forget that."

"Piss off, Vin. Or should I say Vinnie?"

"Don't you start. It's bad enough with Gran. Lulu's started calling me it now. Just don't go all hippie on me, that's all I ask. You can keep everybody happy and still tell Elsie to bog off, you know. It would make me happy, for a start. Is there any juice? Only I could do with a drink. Oh, and Mr. Pallfrey says he's very sorry, again, and he's getting some trellis for the top of his fence. Not that Trevor's going to have any problems with a bit of trellis, but at least he's showing he's willing."

Ellen snorts. "Juice? Are you joking? We can do better than juice, can't we, darling?"

Oh dear. I think she might be talking pink zombies.

By the time we get to the pub, I'm feeling no pain, and my face has gone numb. Ellen brought some champagne with her, and I always go a bit numb when I drink champagne, not that I get much practice. And she made us pink zombies, too, so it's a wonder I can still walk at all. Connie greets us with a flurry of kisses like we're long-lost friends, looking very glamorous in a black beaded top and black trousers. We're all in jeans, and I'm worried we look a bit scruffy, apart from Ellen, who's wearing a chiffon top that manages to be see-through and yet rather demure and Miss Marple at the same time, which is clever.

"There's a table in the garden, if that's all right, or you can be inside if you prefer." Connie puts her arm round me, like we're old friends, which is nice.

"Oh, no, outside would be perfect."

There are candles in glass lanterns and comfortable wooden seats with cushions, and the food's fabulous. Even Ellen's impressed, and she's a hard girl to please when it comes to restaurants. She tends to order things that aren't officially on the menu, or in different combinations with different sauces, or no sauce at all, and she usually takes so long to order you can tell the waiters want to stab her with their pencils, but Connie's very patient with her, and only winks at me once. The home-made burgers go down very well with the boys, and the chips are perfect, and there are great salads, and pasta with clams, or a creamy sauce that's so delicious Harry almost licks his plate. Connie comes to sit with us while we're having coffee, which arrives with a plate of dark chocolates and little cubes of quince jelly.

"That was so brilliant. Can we go into the kitchen and con-gratulate the chef?" Lulu's obviously been very well brought up.

"Oh, good, I'm so pleased. He wasn't happy with the sauce for the orecchiette, but I told him it was fine."

"What do you mean, fine? It was bloody brilliant."

Connie smiles at Harry. "I'll bring him out later and you can tell him, please. We've been quite busy tonight, and it's our first week being properly open, so it's good, I think. I'll get you some more coffee, and amaretto, yes?"

We sit sipping and chatting. Connie takes the boys up to watch *Charlie and the Chocolate Factory*, and Archie's so tired he'll fall asleep as soon as the film starts, which will be a bonus for Jack and Marco. Nelly's supposed to be asleep, too, but keeps appearing in the garden in a long white cot-ton nightie, like a little fairy, flitting about under the trees in the twilight and talking to the chickens until Connie chases her back upstairs. It's still warm, and everything feels rather magical.

Ellen's asking Vin about Mum and Dad.

"Venice was great, but Mum's still as mad as ever, and she's got a special plan to get us all over there for Christmas, which my clever sister was meant to get us out of, but she blew it."

"I did not."

"Yes, you did."

"But she'd already got Dad to get the tickets, and she knows Gran used to close the shop until after New Year, so I couldn't use my best excuse. And then she started going on about getting sodding capons, and I was outmaneuvered, as usual."

"I still think you could have thought of something."

"I'm quite looking forward to it, actually."

We both look at Lulu like she's mad.

"Well, I am, and if you'd had as many boring Christmases in Chipping bloody Malden as I have, with your grandmother trying to stop you eating brandy butter while your mother force-feeds you mince pies behind her back, you'd be looking forward to it, too. I think she's a laugh, your mum. At least she's not all twinsets and boring like mine."

"That's one way of putting it, I suppose."

Vin shakes his head. I think Lulu's trying to be diplomatic, which is sweet of her, because Mum can be a bit full-on when you first meet her: actually, she can be a bit full-on when you've known her for years. Her latest nonsense is insisting on being called Mariella, instead of Mary, which will infuriate Gran when she finds out. They're living in a collapsing palazzo because Mum's met some count, who sounds as mad as a bucket but far less useful; she's restoring his frescoes while Dad runs around trying to catch bits of marble before they fall into the canal, and Vin says he's invented some new kind of mix of lime mortar and superglue, only you have to be careful not to get stuck to pillars or you have to chisel yourself off.

Mum's always been a bit of a challenge: not content with

turning up at school in tie-dyed clothing and throwing off the yoke of domesticity by making embarrassing phallic-looking pottery, she started Doing Courses, and now she's a proper picture restorer and she's been dragging Dad round Europe ever since he retired from teaching. He was the deputy head at Vin's school, which was pretty terrible for Vin, especially on parents' evenings, when Mum used to go round with all the other parents, making sarcastic comments and pretending she didn't know Dad.

"If she starts calling me bloody Vincenzo again, I'm pushing her in a canal. And she wants us to get Gran over, too? Fat chance of that."

Gran's one of the few people who can ever stand up to Mum. The only person, really. Which is another reason why we all love her so much.

Ellen puts her coffee cup down. "You're both being big babies, Venice is fabulous, and the shops are amazing. You'll have a brilliant time."

"Yes, but not with Mum, Ellen, honestly. She bargains for everything, even in the supermarkets, it's awful. Anyway, it's all right for you, you only do a couple of days with yours before you escape to somewhere glamorous: Barbados again this year, is it?"

"I'm working. But after that I'll be off somewhere hot on the first plane I can find. With Harry, if he's still around. Or his replacement, if he's fucked off looking for croissants again."

"Charming, darling. Nice to know I'm irreplaceable in your life."

"Oh, but you are; it would take me ages. Hours, at least."

Connie comes out with Mark, who's finally managed to get out of the kitchen and is looking knackered. He's very tall, and rather shy, until he starts talking about food.

"I want to keep it simple, and not have to keep reinventing things. I'm not interested in pomegranate salsa and all that bollocks. Slow Food is more my thing. Simple food in season, and time with my kids; otherwise there's no point."

While he's talking to us, Nelly appears and climbs up his leg, like he's one of those practice climbing mountains, with different-colored handholds for increasing degrees of difficulty, and he moves her around his back rather absentmindedly, finally draping her across his shoulder and stroking the back of her neck with his thumb as she settles in for a cuddle. She's half asleep by the time he carries her back inside, and we've all gone into a sort of trance watching him.

Ellen looks at Connie. "God, he's gorgeous. Does he stroke the back of your neck like that?"

"Sometimes."

"Then you're a very lucky woman. Christ, he can cook supper for me any time he likes."

Connie stiffens slightly; I don't think she's entirely warmed to Ellen, who can be a bit overpowering when you first meet her, especially if she's had a couple of pink zombies and is flirting with your husband.

"You might have to book a table, because we're getting very busy."

Harry laughs. "Well, he's right about the Slow Food thing, anyway. Eating local stuff and not flying kiwi fruit three thousand miles has got to be right when you think about it. Jo, you could start the same thing with your shop. Slow Food, Slow Clothes."

"It doesn't have quite the same ring to it, though, does it?"

"Oh, I don't know, I think it sounds rather good."

Ellen nods. "Sounds very chilled out, as long as we don't have to wear Slow Shoes, too; I'd definitely draw the line at hippie sandals."

"I love mine." Lulu holds her leg up so we can all admire her Birkenstocks.

I think she must have done ballet at some point, because she can get her leg up very high. It's quite impressive, until she loses her balance and falls off her seat. Actually, I think we may all have had slightly too much to drink.

Ellen helps her up. "Yes, but the surfer girl thing works for you, darling, mainly because you do actually surf. Right?"

"Yes."

"Well, there you are then. The rest of us just look like we're shuffling along in our slippers, like little dumpy, shuffling people, which is not a good look. I need my heels, preferably with 'Prada' written on them somewhere, or 'Jimmy Choo,' or 'Gucci,' with little snakeskin straps."

"Christ, she's starting on about bloody shoes again. Stop her, someone."

"Shut up, Harry."

"Three bloody hours, that's all I'm saying. I bet you've never spent three bloody hours buying a pair of boots, have you, Jo?"

"Not recently, no, but that's mainly because Archie starts rearranging the displays after about five minutes."

"What a brilliant idea."

"Harry darling, if you try rearranging the stock in Gucci, they'll call security and have you thrown out."

"This plan's getting better by the minute."

"Talking of security, I'd better go and make sure the boys aren't trashing Connie's living room."

Connie gives me a mini-tour on the way up. She's particularly proud of the kitchen, which has been refitted with huge stainless-steel ovens and a walk-in cold room, so I know where to come when our fridge finally gives up. She says she'd like to redecorate and put a new bathroom in, but they've blown all their money on the ovens.

"Mark doesn't notice, he'd live in a tent if the kitchen was good, but I've told him, for one year, yes. Then we have to make changes, or I will go back home."

"He was so sweet with Nelly. Is he always that relaxed with them?"

"Oh yes, they can do anything with him. It's only the difficult things, the things they don't like, that I have to do."

"I know what you mean. I asked Nick to get them new school shoes once, and all three of them came back with new trainers, with flashing lights on the back. They were thrilled."

She smiles. "And where is he now, your Nick?"

There's an awkward pause while I try to work out what to say.

"Oh, you are divorced, yes?"

Bugger. She's really going to mind this next bit.

"No, although we were going to, I think. I mean, he'd just

told me he wanted a divorce, but then there was an accident, a car crash. And he died. In February. Just after Valentine's Day actually."

She's gone rather pale, and I give her a weak sort of smile. She's the first person I've managed to say this to all in one go, and I'm quite pleased with myself; usually I only get the car-crash bit done and they go all sympathetic and I feel like I've somehow given them the impression that we were the perfect happy couple, tragically torn apart by fate.

For someone who talks so much, she seems very comfortable with long silences, which is rather nice.

She takes my hand.

"And now you cannot be angry with him, because he is died. Yes?"

"Yes."

"How very terrible."

"Yes."

She squeezes my hand again.

God. At last. Someone who gets it, without me having to explain.

We check on Nelly as we pass her room, and she's fast asleep, clutching a fairy wand with a silver star on top, looking angelic, and then we walk along the corridor to the living room and Archie's asleep, too, but he surfaces as soon as Connie turns the telly off.

"I was watching that, I was. We've been doing Oompah-Loompah dancing, and stupid Jack said I'd got a wonky willy, so I hitted him with a cushion."

Marco starts giggling.

"Well, never mind, it's home time now."

They all start trying to prove how Not Tired they are, and Jack treads on Archie's hand while he's trying to find his shoes, so Archie shoves him and he falls over. Connie's trying to get Marco into bed, and failing, as I shepherd my two back downstairs.

I'm dreading the walk home because Archie gets pretty explosive when he's tired, but it's surprisingly painless, mainly because they get piggybacks from Harry and Vin; Archie's sitting on Harry's shoulders patting him on the head and yelling "Faster!" as we get to the house, and it's all going rather well until we spot Trevor on the horizon, pulling poor Mr. Pallfrey along at quite a pace, and before we know it the dog is joining in the fun and they're starting an impromptu game of nocturnal football. Mr. Pallfrey looks mortified, but Trevor's having a lovely time.

"Does anyone want a drink? Tea, Mr. Pallfrey?"

"Oh, well, if you're sure, that would be lovely."

Bloody hell.

Mr. Pallfrey ends up in goal, with Lulu in the other goal by the tree and Ellen doing her cheerleader routine.

"I need pom-poms."

"Sorry, I've just run out."

"Well, can't you knit some quick, because I need something to shake."

"Ellen."

"Yes?"

"Five minutes, all right, and then it's bedtime."

"Fair enough, darling. I'll be the ref. Have you got a whistle?"

"Not on me, no."

It's nearly an hour later when I'm finally tucking the boys into bed. Archie's on the blow-up mattress in his room so I can sleep in his bed, and let Ellen and Harry have mine. He's exhausted and falls asleep almost immediately, but Jack's still got things to Share.

"I scored three goals, Mum."

"I know, darling. Lie down now."

"And Trevor nearly scored as well, Mum. If he'd stopped running he would have. Dogs don't really know how to play football, do they?"

"Not really. Now lie down properly."

"But we could teach him, though, couldn't we?"

Great. We can have football training for dogs in the back garden every day; we'll probably end up with a pack of them popping round for a bit of penalty practice.

"No more talking now, Jack, it's sleep time."

"I had a piggyback all the way home, didn't I?"

"I'm turning the light off now, love."

"But Dad used to give me the best piggybacks, didn't he?"

"Yes, darling."

"And he used to play football with me sometimes, didn't he?"

"Yes, lots of times."

Actually, he didn't; he wasn't a playing-games-in-the-mud kind of dad. He'd shout encouraging things from the sidelines in the back garden while he was reading the papers—but only if he was in the bloody country, of course.

"And he used to take me swimming."

"Yes."

Once. And he lost one of Archie's armbands.

"He was the best dad in the whole world, wasn't he, Mum?"

"Yes, darling."

"And when I go to heaven he'll have seen me getting my goals, won't he?"

"Yes, sweetheart, I'm sure he will."

I'm standing outside his bedroom door now doing silent crying again. Fuck it. Double fuck it. I'm so angry, and if there is a heaven, I hope he's stuck up there watching, and feeling guilty, except I suppose that would be hell really, watching your children struggle to make sense of it all, building up their memories as they turn you into the best dad in the world. And I don't even believe in heaven or hell, I just thought it might help them if they could think of him as being in heaven. Archie seems to mix it up with all the other things that he half knows are make-believe, like Father Christmas and the tooth fairy, and he doesn't seem worried that he'll forget Nick, or that his dying had something to do with him. But Jack's more complicated; he went through a heartbreaking phase in the first few weeks, asking me if Nick was angry with him for all sorts of half-forgotten things like breaking the towel rack in the bathroom, or putting plasticine in the dishwasher—like Nick even knew, or would have remembered. He seems more settled about it now, though, like he did when he first went to school; he's resigned himself to it, but it has left him that little bit more anxious, and more fragile. And I can't fix it for him, so I end up feeling guilty. Nick dies, and I feel guilty. It's absolutely bloody typical.

"What are you doing up there, darling?" Ellen's whispering from the bottom of the stairs.

"Nothing. Just checking they're asleep."

"Well, hurry up. Vin's opening another bottle of wine and we're going to play strip Scrabble. And Harry's practically dyslexic. He can't spell to save his life."

"I'll be right down."

I'm opening up on Saturday morning at ten past nine, with the help of two aspirin and my sunglasses. God, I never realized the seaside was such a terrible place for hangovers, but there's just too much light and I've got a crick in my neck; Archie climbed back into his bed at about three, so I ended up on the blow-up mattress and spent the rest of the night feeling slightly seasick and having my shipwreck dream again. The boys are at home with Vin, who heroically staggered downstairs as I was leaving, so they'll be watching telly for most of the morning, while Vin drapes himself somewhere dark and tries to recover from not knowing how to spell *rivet*.

By the time I've had my first cup of coffee, I'm feeling slightly more human: opening up the shop is definitely one of my favorite times of the day now. Mrs. Davis is putting her buckets of flowers out while I wind out the awning, and our postman, Sam, stops to tell us about his six-week-old baby, Jackson, who sleeps all day but is awake all night. We commiserate and say they grow out of it, which isn't strictly true but we're trying to be encouraging because he's got dark circles under his eyes and looks exhausted, and then I make a start on moving the last of the horrible pastels in between serving a dribble of customers. I'm just thinking about another cup of coffee when Ellen and Lulu arrive, both wearing dark glasses and bearing croissants. Hurrah.

Lulu puts the paper bags on the table in the back room. "We thought we'd bring you breakfast; the boys are watching cartoons at full blast and Vin and Harry are playing trains and we couldn't stand the racket."

Ellen nods, very slowly. "She's not kidding. They've got train track all over your living room floor and they're bickering about where to put the tunnel. There's boxes of the stuff everywhere."

"That's down to Nick. He just kept buying more bits for it and then he'd spend hours laying out some complicated pattern, and yell at them if they touched it. I was seriously thinking of buying him a stationmaster hat for his birthday."

They both smile, and the memory of him lying on the floor laying out train track makes me feel slightly wobbly, which I think Lulu notices.

"Anyway, we've come to help, so is there anything you want doing?"

Ellen gives her a pleading look. "Anything that doesn't involve moving your head too much, and can we have coffee first, please, or I think I might pass out. All this sea air really does you in, doesn't it?"

Lulu takes her sunglasses off. "That's better, I feel more awake now. Shall I put the kettle on? It's upstairs, isn't it?"

"Yes, and the milk's in the fridge, and don't worry about the door, it's broken, so if it falls off, just slot it back on the hinge thing."

"Okeydokey." She goes upstairs, humming.

"Christ, she's a bit chirpy, isn't she?"

"She's just young, Ellen. We were like that once."

"Thanks very much, that's very encouraging. And why have you got a fridge with a detachable door?"

"Because it still works and it's only for milk for the shop so it's not worth getting a new one."

"You're not going to turn into one of those mad women who collect bits of string, are you?"

"Definitely."

"God, that's a fabulous color." She picks up a ball of one of the new winter yarns in sage green with flecks of black.

"Yes, madam, and it knits up beautifully. You could have a scarf, or a shrug, in next to no time."

"Not if I was doing the knitting I couldn't, darling, and anyway I'm not that convinced by shrugs, not unless you're sixteen and some old bastard asks you what you're planning to do with your life."

"What about a scarf then?"

"Actually, I was thinking about a sweater, for Harry. The symbolism appeals to me. Me sitting knitting for my man. Very postfeminist, don't you think? Although the chances of us still being together by the time I've finished it are pretty slim."

"You seemed great last night."

"Oh yes, it's all hunky-dory at the moment; he's off on a job next weekend, ten days in Moscow, some drunken Russian oil mafia special, but he's already booked dinner with me for the night he gets back. If he doesn't end up with a one-way ticket on the Trans-Siberian Express, that is."

"Well, that sounds like progress: advance bookings."

She nods. "Christ, every time I move my head I feel like I'm going to fall over. Do you think I could manage a sweater then?"

"Maybe a scarf might be better to start with, and you could knit him a pair of gloves too, or maybe mittens—the fingers on gloves can be tricky, but mittens are easy, and they'd help keep the cold out in Moscow."

"Brilliant. Will you help me get started?"

"Sure."

"And we can put them on one of those strings you put gloves on. I used to have them when I was at school, inside my school coat."

"So did I, but Vin always used to pull one end, so I ended up with a glove under my armpit."

"Bastard."

"I know. He did it most mornings, while we were waiting for the bus."

"Another bonus of being an only child, darling: nobody pulling the string on your gloves."

Lulu comes down with the coffee and we start looking through the folders of patterns, but Ellen won't consider anything where the models look spacey, or have funny hair, which discounts pretty much all of them until we finally find an Aran pattern with a family who appear to be standing halfway up a mountain, and by the looks of things they've just had a big fight. Probably about the kids being forced to wear sweaters with bobbles up the front.

"Is that plait thing tricky?"

"The cable? Yes, it can be—you need an extra needle—but we can miss that bit out and do a plain version, with some rib. The mittens look easy, though."

"Actually, I'm rethinking the mitten thing. I think a scarf might be enough of a challenge to start with."

"Well, if you're just doing a scarf, we don't need a pattern. I'll start you off and you can keep going until you get bored."

"It'll be a bloody short scarf then."

Lulu's looking through the Rowan books. "Some of these are beautiful. I think I'll do this tank top."

"Have you done Fair Isle knitting before?"

"I don't think so. My mum taught me to knit, but I haven't done any for years."

Ellen sighs. "I wish my mother had taught me stuff like that, instead of concentrating on advanced sulking. What's Fair Isle knitting, anyway? It sounds rather sweet."

"It's when you knit with lots of different colors and carry the wool along the back. It's fairly easy if you don't get the wool tangled, but you have to make sure you keep it loose enough or it pulls everything out of shape."

We look at the pattern Lulu's chosen, which is a fairly simple shape, in lots of fabulous colors.

"This will be fine, or you could do a plainer version, with fewer colors. That way, instead of six balls of the main color and four of the contrast colors you'd be okay with eight."

"Are you sure? Isn't that a lot less wool?"

"Yes, but that's why they design patterns with so many different colors: so you have to buy a ball of each, even if it's only for a couple of rows."

"Well, if you're sure, that'd be great, and it'll save me a fair bit, too, won't it?"

"About nine quid, yes. If you were paying for it, which you're not."

"Oh, but we want to pay. Don't we, Ellen?"

She nods. "Christ, I've done it again. Has anyone got any more aspirin? I think I need a booster dose."

I show Ellen the Aran-weight wool, and she chooses a flecked gray and black, and Lulu goes for a pretty felted tweed in a lovely plum color, with a ball of slate gray and one of violet for her contrast colors. I check the labels on the plum to make sure they're from the same dye lot, and tell her she should be fine with five because she's knitting the smallest size, but I'll keep a ball aside for her, just in case.

"Do you do that, for normal people?"

Ellen laughs. "Speak for yourself, darling."

"No, I mean do you keep wool for all your customers?"

"Yes. All the shops used to do it years ago, when people couldn't afford to get all their wool in one go; most of them make you buy the whole lot now, and then let you return any balls you haven't used. But Gran carried on with the putting-it-by thing, and I think it's nicer. And you don't get loads of wool being returned all squashed. Elsie tends to weigh it, though. She's convinced people sometimes use a bit and then pretend they haven't, but I'm trying to get her to stop, so I've hidden the scales."

"Do people really do that?"

"I don't think so, but that doesn't stop Elsie doing her *Crimewatch* routine. They had some woman a few years ago who went through a phase of knitting up a ball and then deciding she didn't like it and unpicking it, and then bringing it back for a refund. Gran said you could see it had gone all coggly, but they both knew her, and she was starting on HRT, so they just gave her a refund and put it in the bargain bin."

Ellen puts her cup down. "They all sound like nutters to me."

"Some of them are, but most of them are lovely. Although what I really need are much younger ones who buy all the expensive stuff."

"How much do you make on one ball of wool, if you don't mind me asking? Don't say, if you'd rather not." Lulu's gone a bit pink.

"Of course I don't mind, and it varies, but it's about half, usually, including VAT. The pattern books don't have VAT, but the loose patterns do."

"I haven't the faintest idea what you're talking about, darling, even if Lulu has. Tell me in money."

"On a seven-quid ball of wool, I make about three quid."

"And what about the VAT? Who does all that?"

"Mr. Prewitt. He's been doing the books for years, so we just note down the sales in the cashbook and he does the rest. He's very deaf, so you have to shout, but he's really sweet."

"Well, it all sounds very complicated. Have you decided about the group idea yet?"

"The Stitch and Bitch thing? Yes, I'm definitely going to give it a go."

Lulu's busy casting on. "What's Stitch and Bitch?"

"Like a reading group, only with knitting. I'm thinking of starting one in the shop."

"That sounds good."

"Yes, and I've been thinking, darling, you could do special cocktails. I'll teach you how to make pink zombies so you can really liven things up; it'll be like one of those Ann Summers parties, only without the batteries."

"I was thinking more like a book group to be honest, Ellen."

"Well, be careful, because mine's gone weird ever since Miranda joined. She's doing a Ph.D. or something pointy like that, and she keeps lecturing us about symbolism, and then they all start showing off and I'm left sitting there hoping nobody talks about the middle bit because I skipped it. Do you know, she even asked me to leave a few weeks ago, because she said I was too disruptive."

"What did you do?"

"I outflanked her, of course."

Lulu looks impressed. "How did you do that then?"

"I got them invited to an awards lunch full of celebs, as my special guests. They all loved it, except Miranda, who couldn't make it that day. Shame."

I almost feel sorry for Miranda, because it's a very bad idea to tangle with Ellen. She's one of the most generous people in the world when she's on your side, but she also holds a grudge longer than anyone I've ever known, and settles scores, big time, sometimes years later. People think they've got away with it, and she suddenly creeps up behind them and gets them in the back of the neck. Metaphorically speaking, of course. Usually.

"And that fucker Steve Simpson was there, looking like he'd been on the sunbed again, which is quite brave, given how much plastic surgery he's had. They'll probably go in one day and find most of him has melted."

Steve used to co-anchor with Ellen, and when they were on a shift together they were known as the Anchor and the Wanker.

"He seems quite nice when you see him on the telly."

Lulu's really terribly sweet.

"Well, he bloody isn't. He used to elbow me out of the way and spread his stuff everywhere, and he never knew what was going on, which really pissed me off. People think we just turn up and read what's put in front of us, but we don't, we do at least an hour or two before each shift, catching up on what's going on, reading background notes, sometimes more if it's a big day. But I saw him off eventually. I managed to talk for nearly nine minutes when that siege in Russia broke, with just a crap map and a couple of photos, and trust me, nine minutes is a fucking long time live, with everyone running around trying to get the satellite link back up and find out where the fuck the town is, and he just sat there, being totally useless. It was brilliant. They moved him after that; he's our business correspondent now. And he's fucking useless at that, too."

I cast on Ellen's scarf for her, and we sit chatting while we knit, which is exactly how I want the group to be, only maybe with slightly less swearing: relaxed and friendly, and just the kind of thing you'd fancy after a long day at work, or at home with the kids.

"Wasn't Mr. Pallfrey sweet last night, when we were playing football? Although that goal was definitely a foul."

I think Lulu's still rather aggrieved about scoring an own goal, with a little help from Trevor.

Ellen laughs. "It's nice to know you've got such mad neighbors to keep you busy down here, darling."

"He's not mad, it's just Trevor's a bit too lively for him. Anyone fancy another coffee?"

"Yes, please. And a brandy if you've got any; I'm still feeling a bit fragile."

"Sorry, I'm a bit low on brandy at the moment."

"How low?"

"Very. We don't get much call for it, funnily enough, not with this being a wool shop."

"There you are, then, that's a perfect job for Trevor the Wonder Dog; he's the size of a fucking St. Bernard. He can trot around doling out restorative shots. You'd make a fortune, and it would knacker him out."

"I'll mention it to Mr. Pallfrey."

While I'm upstairs waiting for the kettle to boil, I realize Ellen's right; I've had more neighborly moments down here in a few weeks than I had in all the years we lived in London. I think I only spoke to the people next door once, when the water main burst in the high street and our water was turned off. They weren't very friendly, and both drove matching silver Audis and got very annoyed when I parked my car in what they liked to think of as their second space, even though it was right outside our house. Apart from them and Mrs. Parrish, I never got past the occasional wave with any of the other people in the street. In fact, I think I was rather lonely, which isn't something I'm going to have to worry about down here, since I couldn't be lonely if I tried, what with Trevor popping round, and Gran, and Elsie keeping me on my toes in the shop.

Ellen's managed to drop a couple of stitches by the time I get back downstairs, so I sort them out for her, and then we sit trying to work out what to put on the Stitch and Bitch card for the window. I've got some pale pink postcards from the art gallery, and lots of shiny silver stars, and I'll do one for the newsagent's and the library notice board as well.

"What day are you going for?"

I hand Ellen the card, since she's doing the writing with her posh fountain pen.

"Thursday. Gran doesn't have anything that night, so she can look after the boys."

We try out different lines, and discard most of Ellen's because they sound slightly rude, before we finally settle on

Absolute Beginners
Want to learn to knit?
Join our Stitch and Bitch group
Here every Thursday, 7-9 P.M.

I've just finished sticking the card in the window when Elsie arrives, with a tall man with very short hair, who looks like he's just got out of the army; he's pale and looks a bit shell-shocked, but that may be because Elsie's gone into pursed-lips mode again.

"I see you're going ahead with your group then; I still don't like the name—our ladies are very polite, you know, and I don't think that sort of thing will appeal to them. I hope you won't be too disappointed when nobody turns up. Anyway, I've brought my Martin along to look at upstairs for you. He's ever so good at carpentry, always has been, and it's turning into quite a nice little sideline for him, as well as his computers job. Isn't it, Martin?"

She gives him a slight nudge. "You remember Jo? You used to play together in the summer when she came down to stay with her gran, with her brother, Vincent."

"Yes, of course I do, Mum. You look completely different from the last time I saw you, Jo, much bigger—I mean taller, more grown-up."

He's gone red.

"I suppose it must have been at least twenty years ago?"

"Yes, that sounds about right."

There's an awkward silence while he looks at his feet.

"So you're after some shelves?"

"Yes. I want to turn upstairs into a workroom, with more shop space. I got a quote from the man who did Gran's roof, but it was way more than I can afford. I thought I might just go to IKEA and get something cheap."

He flinches at the mention of IKEA. "I'm sure we can do better than that. What sort of wood were you thinking of?"

"Sorry?"

"For the shelves."

"Something cheap that I can paint white I suppose. Chip-board?"

He flinches again. "I've got some lovely oak in the shed—it's been drying for years, so it's ready now. Or there's pine if you prefer. I could stain it, or wax it. I prefer wax, myself. It respects the wood more."

I'd forgotten he and Jeffrey collect wood in the big shed in their garden. It used to be Jeffrey's workshop, but I suppose it's Martin's workshop, too, now.

"That sounds lovely, but won't it be really expensive?"

"No. Dad got it for free when the builders were gutting somewhere. He always keeps an eye out for good timber, and I do the same, so we're running out of space. I saw some lovely floorboards in a skip the other week, but we haven't got the room. It's a terrible shame what people throw out; with just a bit of work they'd have been beautiful."

"Well, if you're sure, that sounds great. I'd pay you for your time, of course."

Elsie looks pleased. "I'm sure you'll find his rates are very reasonable."

He gives her a pained look.

"It's more of a hobby, really. I wouldn't want to charge you—if you could just cover the cost of anything I need to buy, that'll be fine."

Elsie tuts. "Don't be silly, Martin. I've told you, there's no point in selling yourself short all the time, letting people walk all over you, like someone we won't mention. I'll take you up and show you the room while I put the kettle on, I'm gasping for a cup of tea. Would anyone else like one? Miss Malone?"

Ellen's doing her Britain's Favorite Broadcaster smile.

"No, thank you, Elsie, we've just had one. What a fabulous cardigan."

"It was quite a lot of work, but I've had lots of comments."

"I'm sure you have."

I think I notice a flicker of a smile on Martin's face, but he covers it up very well as they go upstairs.

"Quick, let's run away before she comes back."

Lulu laughs. "She seemed quite keen on you."

"Yes, but that soon wears off. Trust me, she'll be banging on about too much sex on the telly any minute, like I've got anything to do with what they get up to on Planet Drama. So that was Martin, the man with the tragic haircut. And who is the someone we won't mention? The wife, I suppose."

"Probably. Elsie always hated her. And what was the matter with his haircut?"

"It looks like his mother does it for him. Gorgeous eyes, though, and great jeans. I love a man in old Levi's, and if he's into carpentry, he'll be good with his hands, which is always useful for helping you get through those long winter evenings."

"I've known him for years, Ellen, he's like a cousin or something. It would be too weird, and anyway he's in the middle of a divorce."

"Well, you could help take his mind off it then. Let me give him the third degree and I'll let you know."

"Don't you dare; he'd probably go into shock, and anyway, a

dalliance with Elsie's nearest and dearest is the last thing I need: she's bad enough already."

"True. Oh God, here she comes."

Elsie brings her tea down with her and starts telling Ellen about a play she watched which was full of Bad Language, and then Martin comes back and starts talking to me about wood and obsessing about shelf widths and drawing me pictures of dovetail joints. I'm practically in a coma by the time he's finished, and Ellen's pulling faces behind his back while Elsie serves Mrs. Davis, who's ostensibly come in for some navy double knitting for a school sweater for one of her grandsons who's got very long arms, but actually so she can tell Ellen she's seen her on the telly and she thinks she's very clever, and to tell us that she's seen the postcard in the window about the Stitch and Bitch group.

"My daughter-in-law Tina's in the shop with me today, Graham's wife, nice girl even if she can't cook to save her life, and we were just talking about her wanting to learn to knit, so she might come to your group, dear. I can look after Travis for her, although I'll have to put my bits and bobs away, because last time he was round he broke two of my glass donkeys."

Elsie's standing with her arms folded.

"Well, I better be off, then, but lovely to meet you all." Mrs. Davis nods at Elsie and goes out.

Elsie tuts again. "I'm sorry about that; I might have known she'd be in. Never misses out on anything, that one."

"I thought she was lovely."

Elsie gives Ellen a disbelieving look.

Lulu starts putting her knitting away. "Can we have some lunch soon? I'm starving."

"Good idea. Let's go back and see if the boys are hungry. Have you got everything you need, Martin, all the measurements?"

"Yes, thanks. I'll get home and do some preliminary sketches, so you can see the sort of thing I mean, shall I?"

Oh, God. Preliminary sketches? I just want some simple shelves, not something that requires technical drawings.

"That would be great. I'll see you on Monday, Elsie. I'll drop the boys at school and be in around ten. Mrs. Brook might be in later for that blue cotton, it's all ready in a bag, behind the counter."

Elsie's looking happier as we're leaving, and Ellen does her Grand Exit routine and kisses her, and Martin, who looks as if he might pass out.

"Lovely to have met you."

He mumbles something and starts backing toward the stairs.

"Bye, Elsie."

We walk along the high street giggling like nutters.

"You shouldn't have done that, Ellen. The poor man, it'll probably take him all day to get over it."

"What, kissed Dovetail, do you mean? It was very useful research, if you ask me, and he smells very nice, sort of pine with a hint of lemon. You should definitely reconsider, darling."

"Stop it. He's doing preliminary sketches of shelves. You heard him."

"He was a bit Rain Man I suppose. Shame. Nice eyes. I like green eyes on a man. But what with the tragic hair thing, maybe you're right. Bugger. I thought I'd found you someone to play with. Let's go to the pub for lunch and see if we can't dredge someone else up. There must be someone under sixty around here who goes fishing."

"Well, if there is, I don't want him dredged up, thank you very much. I've got quite enough on my plate without any mad fishermen. God, you're like some demented matchmaker trying to pair everyone off."

Lulu laughs. "I wonder what the boys will be doing when we get home."

"Lying on the sofa surrounded by chaos and trains, probably. Although you never know, maybe they'll have prepared a light but nutritious lunch and the magic fairies will have tidied up all the train track."

Ellen puts her arm round my shoulders. "How long have you been having these delusions, darling?"

"Well, they might. I'm looking on the bright side. The Stitch and Bitch group might be a huge success, and Elsie might stop tutting, and Martin might make the shelves without giving me any more Top Wood lectures. And there might be so many customers in the shop we have to get a second till."

"Yes. But in the meantime, I think the pub's a top plan. I'm craving a vodka and tonic with lime and lots of ice."

"Okay, let's go home and see the extent of the damage, and then adjourn to the pub."

"Finally, a plan I can really get behind."

4

STITCH AND BITCH

"Where's your book bag, Archie?"

He gives me a puzzled look, like I've asked him to find the lost city of Atlantis.

"You had it last night, love, when we did your reading. Where did you put it after that?"

Another blank look. Brilliant; we'll have to play Hunt the Book Bag while I covertly try to finish making two packed lunches without anyone realizing it's cheese again.

"Go and look by the coats, and hurry up with your Weet-abix, Jack, for heaven's sake."

"I hate cheese. I really do."

Bugger. Archie's crept up behind me again.

"Just find your bag, will you please."

He wanders down the hall, muttering, looking for all the world like he's got hours to spare, whereas in fact we're on the verge of being late. They've only been at the school for a month and we've already been late twice, three times if you include the morning it was foggy, but everyone was late that day so I don't think it counts. But they're much more relaxed about red-faced parents running in as the bell's ringing than our old school was, thank God, although it still makes me feel like a crap mother, especially when the head, Mr. O'Brien, is in the playground, looking young and perky in his corduroy trousers and baggy sweaters, being trailed by a gaggle of children. He's always surrounded by children; he's like the Pied Piper, only without the rats.

So far the new school's been a big success. The teachers are lovely, especially Archie's Mrs. Berry, who goes in for dangly earrings and lots of bangles, and clinks when she walks. Her classroom's pretty chaotic, but all the kids seems happy, and Archie's reading is definitely improving, so she gets top marks as far as I'm concerned. Jack's Mrs. Chambers is less clinky, but she seems just as popular, and she does art for the whole school, so her room's full of paintings and tinfoil sculptures, and she's got clay, which Jack adores. So all in all they've both settled in remarkably quickly, which is a big relief.

Archie's finally tracked down his book bag and is sitting on the stairs, waiting for me to do his shoes up, even though they've got Velcro straps, which he can do himself. There's a mini-scuffle as Jack starts up the stairs to brush his teeth, and then the yelling starts.

"He did that on purpose, he did, Mum, tell him, he treaded on me on purpose."

"I did not, he won't let me get past, stupid fat baby. Move."

"Jack, stop it. And Archie, do your shoes up."

Jack glares at me. "It's ridiculous, that's all. Just ridiculous."

He stomps off upstairs and then comes back down with toothpaste all over the front of his sweatshirt, so I do a quick spot of dabbing with a damp cloth while we're putting our coats on.

"Mum, Ben Taylor says my anorak makes me look like a minger."

Archie's busy having a hopping competition with himself but pauses, balanced on one leg, ready to defend his brother against enemy forces disparaging his anorak.

"Well, Ben Taylor's a minger. I'll tell him for you, if you like. I'll go right up to him and say, 'You're a minger,' and then run away. I can run really fast, you know. I can run like the wind."

Jack grins. "Yes, I know, you're quite a good runner for your age."

Archie hesitates, not sure whether "for your age" is a put-down, until Jack smiles at him.

"Yes, I am."

I'm still trying to work out if *minger* is as rude as it sounds, and needs to join our banned-and-never-to-be-heard-again list.

"I think Ben sounds very silly, and you should ignore him."

They both look at me and roll their eyes.

"You can't ignore him, Mum, or he'll just keep doing it, it's like Archie and Harry."

"Come on, let's go. We need to walk quickly today, so no looking for conkers or we'll be really late. And what's like Archie and Harry?"

There's a silence as I close the front door.

"Jack, what's like Archie and Harry?"

"Harry just kept being horrible to Nelly all the time, that's all. He kept calling her Nelly Belly. But now he's stopped."

I've got a funny feeling I'm not going to like this.

"What did you do, Archie?"

"Nothing."

"Archie."

"I just pushed him a little bit, and he fell right over, on purpose. And Nelly gave me some of her biscuit, and it was chocolate."

"Archie."

"And then he cried, but he's a big baby and it was only pretending crying. And we had to sit on the mat and Mrs. Berry said it was horrible to call people names and he mustn't do it again. And you mustn't push people or they can get hurt, and I had to say sorry."

"Right, well, that's right, because you could really hurt someone, pushing them. And did you say sorry nicely? Hold my hand now, while we cross the road."

"No, I didn't. I said I was sorry he fell over but I wasn't sorry I pushed him because calling people Nelly Belly was much more horribler than a little old push, and he's a big baby for fussing. And if he doesn't want to get pushed he should shut up calling people names. And Mrs. Berry smiled, I saw her, and I got a sticker in painting, for Good Trying, but I got a hole in my paper and everything, so I think it was for pushing Harry really."

"I'm sure it wasn't."

Actually, I'm pretty sure it was.

"The best thing to do when someone calls you names is just ignore them. They'll soon stop when they see you don't care."

"Yes, but Nelly did care."

I don't want to encourage him in his role as self-appointed playground enforcer; he's already got quite enough of the Vin side of the Jones family gene pool to be going on with, even if it is sweet of him to defend Nelly like that.

"Try to be extra friendly today, to show you've forgotten all about it."

"But I haven't."

"Archie."

"Oh, all right."

A very small girl is ringing the bell so enthusiastically she's almost falling over as we walk through the gates; they don't go in for the rather brutal lining-up-in-the-playground-in-total-silence thing our old school used to favor, so stragglers can merge in with everyone else instead of doing the walk of shame across a silent playground. There's a great deal of cheerful milling about, and you're allowed to go inside with them and help hang up their coats, which seems to lead to much less stress and far fewer tears, so I don't know why all schools don't do it; it's so much friendlier. But I suppose not all of them are interested in being friendly as long as their test scores are high enough.

Connie's waiting for me in our usual spot by the bench under the big conker tree, as Jack and Archie go straight into their classrooms. Having Marco as a ready-made friend has really helped Jack a lot; he was so nervous on the first morning he couldn't eat any breakfast, even though I'd made his favorite toasted bacon sandwiches. Archie had three, and seemed completely relaxed; he plays with Nelly every lunchtime, especially Narnia, their new favorite game—Nelly's either the Witch or the Lion, and Archie's usually the Wardrobe.

There's a last-minute flurry of people arriving, including two small girls who refuse to get off their bikes and a girl from Archie's class who he calls Nettle, which can't be right. She's having a last-minute ponytail adjustment when one of the big boys arrives with his leg in plaster, with his two younger brothers trailing behind him and doing impressions of his limp; he stops every few steps and turns round and they freeze, like they're playing a new version of Grandmother's Footsteps, and he gets more and more annoyed with them until Mr. O'Brien comes over and the two shadow limpers start walking normally again.

Connie laughs. "Look at the little one, he's doing it again."

One of the toddlers has just been retrieved from Reception, which he tries to infiltrate most mornings. He tends to get very narky with his mum when she brings him back out, and he's sitting down in the playground and taking one of his wellies off this morning, to stress quite how irritated he is.

His mum sighs. "Ben, please don't do that. Let's put it back on."

He takes his other boot off, and chucks it as hard as he can. It's easy to forget just what total nightmares toddlers can be; you remember all the chubby kisses but forget the constant battles and earsplitting shrieks, it's like post-traumatic stress disorder, but in reverse. Connie retrieves the wellie and takes it back to him, and says something in Italian, which I'm guessing is along the lines of "Aren't you a little bugger?" but it sounds so lovely she gets rewarded with a cheeky smile. Maybe we could start a new trend: swearing at your child in a foreign language. Nobody would know, and you'd get to unburden yourself without feeling like someone was going to call Social Services. I think it could be a real winner, and I'm definitely going to get her to teach me a few handy phrases.

We're walking toward the gate when I notice a woman heading our way holding a pile of pamphlets, wearing a sensible navy skirt and loafers, and a padded jacket with a silk scarf knotted over pearls. Christ, I hope she's not another über-Tory out recruiting. I've already had one in the shop, asking me to join the local Conservatives Mean Business, or Mean Conservatives in Business or whatever they call it, and the only way I could get rid of her was to out myself as a lifelong Labour voter, so now she keeps popping in with annoying and vaguely racist leaflets and trying to convert me; I think they probably get a special merit badge if they convert people to the Right Path. Or possibly a rosette.

She smiles at us, but it's a rather scary smile.

"I'm Annabel Morgan, and I'm president of our PTA."

Oh, thank God for that.

She hands us each a leaflet. "I'll be more than happy to answer any questions. This is my fourth year as president, so I know about most things, if I do say so myself. The committee were so insistent I felt I had to stand again, although I would have been more than happy to let someone else take the reins for a while, more than happy. It's a great deal of work, as I'm sure you can imagine, but we all have to do our bit, don't we?"

There's something about the way she talks that makes you think she's moved heaven and earth to keep hold of her presidency, and what's more she'd knock you flat with a bulldozer if you tried to stand against her. I think she's probably one of the I'm-a-very-important-person PTA types, who are always telling you how busy they are, and tend to have unpleasant children, who you start out feeling sorry for, for having such appalling mothers, and end up wanting to hit with a beanbag. There are nice PTA people, of course, who make cakes and spend ages sorting through lost property and covering all the books in the library in sticky-backed plastic. They're usually the ones who end up volunteering to drive leftover kids home after parties; who, funnily enough, often turn out to be the children of the Very Important Types, who are just too busy being Special to remember to pick them up.

"It's not obligatory, of course, but we do like to welcome new parents and ask them to join us. We're raising money for more IT equipment at the moment, which is so important, I'm sure you'll agree."

"Oh, yes, definitely. I've been meaning to find out about the PTA. How much is it?"

"Ten pounds a year."

"I'll bring the money in tomorrow, then. I can't promise much in the way of help during school time, because I'll be busy in the shop, but I'll certainly do what I can."

"Oh yes, you're Mary Butterworth's granddaughter, aren't you, from the wool shop, with the wonderful new window display?"

"Yes."

"So clever. Although I do tend to pop up to town when I'm knitting for Harry. I only like to use pure wool—he has such very sensitive skin."

"Well, come in next time you're passing, because we've got lots of new stock in."

She smiles, but in a way that makes me feel like I've just knocked on her front door and tried to sell her a packet of dusters.

"Actually, I did want a little word, on another subject, if you've got a moment."

She looks rather pointedly at Connie.

"This is Connie Maxwell. She and her husband have just taken over the Anchor."

She nods at Connie. "I hear the food's rather good now. We must book a table soon."

There's an awkward silence, and Annabel looks at Connie as if she were a waitress who's lingering too long at her table.

"I hope you won't mind my mentioning this in public, so to speak, but there was something else I wanted to discuss. Your son Archie is in my son Harry's class, I think."

Oh. Bugger.

"Yes, I think he is."

"There was an unpleasant incident yesterday, not the sort of thing we want to encourage at all. But I don't suppose he mentioned it, did he?"

"Oh, yes, we were just talking about it, actually, and I'm sure it won't happen again."

"Well, I was rather hoping he might apologize, perhaps after school, with both of us present? Harry said he didn't do it properly yesterday, and I do think it's important for our children to realize that we will not tolerate violence, don't you?"

She's speaking quite slowly, and very loudly, as if she's dealing with people who aren't as clever as she is. Christ, they're always terrible bullies, the Very Important Types.

"I think it was just a little bit of pushing, wasn't it? And Mrs. Berry seems to have dealt with it."

"Yes, Mrs. Berry, who we all adore, of course, but she is sometimes, well, she doesn't always focus on things quite like she might, and Harry was terribly upset last night."

Connie makes a fuffing noise. "So was Antonella."

"I'm sorry?"

"My daughter, Antonella, she was very upset also, and if Archie is saying sorry, then Harry will say sorry to Nelly, yes?"

"I'm afraid I don't quite understand you. You're from Italy, aren't you? We love Italy. We were in Florence for Easter last year—so civilized."

So not only is she the leading light of the PTA but she's also a cosmopolitan jet-setter. At least I think that's the impression we're meant to be getting.

Connie glares at her. "Archie was only, how do you say, sticking out for Nelly."

Connie's looking quite angry now, so I think I'd better step in and try to sort this out or there might be a bit more pushing in the playground.

"Apparently Harry's been teasing Nelly, for a few days, calling her silly names, which is very upsetting when you're only little—quite upsetting when you're big, too." I try a small smile, but Annabel's having none of it, and some of the other parents are definitely listening. How perfect; at this rate we'll be banned from the PTA before we've even joined.

"I've talked to Archie, as I said, and he does know that pushing people is wrong, and I'm sure Harry knows he mustn't tease people. And Mrs. Berry will keep an eye on things. But if you think it would help, why don't I have them all round to tea? They can all make biscuits, they always love that, or if you'd rather ask them to apologize again, then I imagine you meant Harry would apologize to Nelly, too, didn't you? Otherwise, we'd be sending out a very mixed message, wouldn't we?"

Annabel gives me a terrifying look, like she'd set the hounds on me if only she had some handy. Actually, I can just see her sitting on a horse like a total snooter, blowing a bugle.

"Yes, well, I'm so glad we had this little chat. It's so important to be vigilant, of course, but perhaps if we keep an eye on things for now . . . I must just pop into the office—official business, you know, it never stops, there's always so much to do. So sweet of you to ask Harry round to tea. I'll look at the diary and get back to you, shall I? Super."

She nods at the other parents as she storms across the playground.

Bloody hell.

Connie mutters in Italian, including something that sounds like "porking Madonnas."

"You must teach me a few phrases. They'll be so handy for Venice with my mum."

She laughs. "In Venice they have different ones."

"Yes, but she won't know that."

"Are you really having Harry to make biscuits?"

"I bloody hope not, but it was the only way I could think of to shut her up."

We seem to be receiving lots of extra smiles and nods as we walk to the gates, so I get the feeling our president isn't quite as popular as she likes to think she is; but I'd also be willing to bet a fair bit of money that our chances of winning anything in a PTA raffle in the next year or two are now extremely slim. Not even the ubiquitous third-prize box of squashed chocolates from the local shop. And guess who'll be holding the sick bucket on any coach trips if she's got anything to do with it. Double bugger.

I spend the rest of the morning in the shop, trying to recover from my moment with Mrs. Morgan, thinking of brilliant things I should have said, and having rather gratifying mock conversations with myself, until I realize that Elsie's giving me funny looks, so I move on to panicking about teatime with Horrible Harry, because last time we made biscuits, Archie got icing all over the floor and I practically had to chisel it off: maybe flapjacks would be better, although how I'm going to persuade him to make flapjacks with his newly sworn enemy is anybody's guess.

I'm finishing sorting out the room upstairs, ready for the Stitch and Bitch group tonight, with Elsie popping up to tut every now and again. She doesn't like the floorboards and thinks we need a proper carpet, even though I've crawled around for hours washing and waxing them. But even she's got to admit it's a vast improvement on how it was. Vin and Lulu helped me clear the bulk of the junk before they left, and three trips to the tip and twenty quid to the bin men later, I've finally got rid of the last of the rubbish. I've really missed them both since they left; Lulu keeps sending me funny text messages describing how ridiculous Vin's being; he always gets terrible jet lag, and makes a huge fuss about it, and since they're on a three-week squid-counting project somewhere off Australia, they had a really long flight. But texts aren't the same as having them here.

All sorts of forgotten treasures have emerged from the piles of tat upstairs, including a lovely old wooden tailor's dummy, which I've put downstairs in the shop wearing a pretty cardigan I knitted up in Scottish tweed in storm grey and draped with a mohair shawl in marmalade: Gran and I have come up with a new, simple shawl pattern, which knits up really easily and looks great, and I've written down the pattern and printed copies at home and we've already sold two, which is encouraging. And I've unearthed a collection of old vases and some lovely raffia baskets, which I've filled with odd buttons and ends of ribbon, and some cardboard show cards from the 1950s, advertising new brands of wool, which I've stuck up on the walls and on the staircase. But the top things by far are the red knitted Advent calendar, with a little pocket for each day, and the knitted Nativity scene, which Gran and Elsie made years ago: Mary looks rather pissed off, and the baby Jesus is very pink, with bright yellow hair, and the camels have got massive humps and tiny legs, but it's fabulous. The donkey looks just like Eeyore from *Winnie-the-Pooh*, and there are two very grumpy-looking sheep. Gran used to put them in the window every year, but then she moved on to fairy lights and a tinsel tree and somehow it all got lost in a box, but I'll definitely be using it again this year. Only I think I'll knit some cloaks for the figures, to tone them down a bit, and possibly a new baby Jesus that looks a bit more newborn and a bit less Miss Piggy.

Elsie's been in her element dusting things as they came out of the boxes, and Martin's been in and shown me his drawings for the shelves, which looked very detailed, but I'm sure they'll be great. He's made a start on the back wall, and fixed the door to the kitchen so it closes properly, with Elsie following him around wittering on about how clever he is, which must be rather mortifying for him; but he handles her very well, mainly by ignoring her most of the time, and whistling. In fact, the boys have been so impressed with his whistling-when-your-mother's-being-annoying technique that they've been trying to whistle ever since, so a great deal of puffing and blowing goes on every time I ask them to do anything they don't fancy, which is rather annoying, especially when we're walking to school.

Elsie's still not happy with all the new space, though, because apart from the lack of carpet, she wants to turn the room into a staff room, particularly now it's looking so cozy. I've put up some old chintz curtains from Gran, and Lulu helped me clean up the fireplace, which was hidden behind a pile of boxes. It's got lovely old hearth tiles, which I spent ages scrubbing and polishing before I tracked down a chimney sweep, who covered the whole thing with soot when he pressed the wrong button on his vacuum cleaner. But it's looking very pretty now, and

Mr. Pallfrey's given me a stack of logs from an old apple tree that fell down last winter, and they smell wonderful, and Gran's given me her old coal scuttle, and when the fire's going, the whole shop seems warmer.

I'm sitting by the fire in the armchair I've brought in from home and trying to work out if I've got enough chairs round the table when Elsie comes up to make tea. She's put the shop door on the latch again, even though I've asked her not to when both of us are in, but I think I'll pretend I haven't noticed.

"It's looking good now, don't you think?"

"I still think we need a carpet."

"The table looks good, too, doesn't it? And it gives us so much more room in the back of the shop."

"Yes, but people liked it downstairs, you know; they need somewhere to look through the patterns."

"There are still chairs down there, Elsie, and it makes so much more sense having it up here, in the workroom, don't you think?"

I've decided to keep calling it the workroom to remind her that she can't annex it as her personal domain.

She purses her lips. "I'll put the kettle on."

The shop bell rings, and I go downstairs to find Lady Denby rattling the door. Elsie races past me and practically curtsies as she opens the door, and Lady Denby sweeps in, followed by two large black Labradors.

"Just wanted to say jolly well done. Excellent. I've just come from the meeting. Algie, sit. Clarkson, if you can't behave yourself you'll have to stay in the car. Now, where was I? Oh yes, the silver medal, Best Seaside thing, first time we've won in decades, marvelous. Your window was given a special mention by one of the judges, highly artistic, something along those lines, so jolly well done, and keep up the good work, because we want a gold next time."

"How wonderful."

"Yes, isn't it? I see you've changed the shop name. McKnits, very clever. I like it. I don't approve of changing the names of things as a rule, can't see the point of it, but I must say I think this is an improvement. Makes you think of Scotland and all the glorious heather—used to do a lot of shooting up there when I was younger."

"I'm so glad you like it. Mr. Taylor only finished the painting yesterday."

"Taylor? Do I know him?"

"He does most of the shops here, I think. Gran's known him for ages."

"Little man, unfortunate hair?"

Elsie giggles, and is rewarded with a sharp look.

"I've got him now. Good. I like to encourage people to use local tradesmen where possible. Used them myself when we moved. Cost the earth, of course, and that stupid boy broke two vases, and chipped a rather important plate. But still, at least you know who you're dealing with. Clarkson, what on earth are you doing?"

He is licking Elsie's shoe, much to her embarrassment.

"Stop that right now. Always been a nightmare for shoes, this one. Eats them, given half a chance."

"It's no trouble, Lady Denby, none at all."

Elsie's stuck in a sort of a half curtsy now; if a common or garden Labrador came bounding into the shop and started licking her shoes, she'd throw a complete fit, but she's obviously prepared to make an exception for an aristocratic one.

"Yes, well, keep up the good work. Excellent. And there'll be a presentation at some point, I imagine, local press, that kind of thing."

Elsie makes a squeaking noise, and Lady Denby fixes her with another beady look, then turns to me.

"I'll ask someone to let you know, when the arrangements have been made. Used to knit myself, years ago, you know, but my eyes aren't up to it now. I used to do socks, nice thick ones, and they lasted a damn sight longer than the rubbish they sell now, I can tell you. Yes, well, I can't stand here all day. Must get on. Good morning."

She sweeps out again, followed by Algie and Clarkson, who gives Elsie's shoe a longing look as he's yanked sideways through the doorway.

Elsie's thrilled. "Well I never! Imagine her coming in here. And our window being specially mentioned. Imagine."

I think she's gone into some sort of trance.

"Tea?"

"Yes, please, dear."

I think we may need to be opening an emergency packet of custard creams.

The boys are both uncharacteristically lively when I collect them from school, which makes a nice change from their usual monosyllabic routine of all right, fine, and what's for tea? Archie's been doing PE and he's lost one of his socks, and has got his sweatshirt on back to front, and Jack's been helping Mr. O'Brien put pictures up in the hall.

"And I got a Good Helping sticker, look, and I'm going on the Golden Board, Mum."

"That's lovely. Well done, sweetheart."

"And in assembly I have to stand up and get a clap. If your name's on the Golden Board you get a clap. From everybody." He looks at Archie, triumphant.

"And I did jumping in PE, and Mrs. Berry said I was very good. Look, I'll show you."

Archie leaps along the pavement in a series of very energetic jumps. "And we played Narnia at playtime, and we let Harry play. That was good, too, wasn't it, Mum?"

"Yes, Archie, that was very good."

And let's hope he tells his bloody mother.

"And he was Aslan, and he had to chase us, but he got fed up because he couldn't catch us, so he didn't want to play anymore, but then Max was Aslan, and he was great."

"Did Nelly play?"

"Yes, she was the Witch, she's always the Witch, she likes it best. And I caught two wolves in my Wardrobe. Like this." He grabs Jack round the shoulders.

"Get him off me, Mum!"

Archie lets go.

"I was only showing her, stupid. But they were only in the first class, the ones I caught, so I let them go because they're only babies. Not like me, because I'm in the big boys' class now. That was kind of me, wasn't it? I expect I'll be on the Golden Board next, for being kind, if I tell Mrs. Berry."

Jack rolls his eyes. "What's for tea, Mum? Not shepherd's pie. I hate shepherd's pie."

"I love shepherd's pie, it's my favorite." Archie grins at me.

I've got half a pound of mince in the fridge and was rather counting on shepherd's pie. Bugger.

"Spaghetti?"

"With cheese on top?"

"Yes."

They both do their celebratory dance routine, which involves a great deal of bottom wiggling. Spaghetti Bolognese it is, then.

Gran arrives just after six, while I'm still clearing up. Archie loves Bolognese, but he does like to give his pasta a thorough twirl before he eats it, so Jack and I have to sit at the other side of the table if we don't want to be wearing sauce for the rest of the day.

"Shall I put the kettle on, Gran?"

"I'll do it, dear."

"I'll finish the washing up then."

"Did you have pasta tonight?"

"Yes."

"I thought so. I'll put his shirt in to soak, shall I?"

"Please."

Gran loves battling with stains. She boils all her flannels, and bleaches her dishcloths every week. It's a whole different world.

"Will you be wanting me to have them next Friday by any chance?"

"No, why?"

She goes rather pink.

"Nothing, really, it's just a friend of mine, Reg Coles, from the Bowls Club, he's asked me round for a bit of supper. He keeps asking me, and I usually put him off, but this time he says he won't take no for an answer, and he's such a nice man, a real gentleman, always has a clean shirt on, not like some of them, with stains all down their sweaters. His wife died a few years back, but he keeps everything spotless. Only I'm not sure."

"About what?"

"Well, I don't want people talking."

"People are always talking, Gran, I wouldn't worry about that. What does Betty say?"

"Oh, she thinks I should go, but then she would, wouldn't she? Just look at the pickle she got herself into with that insurance man."

Betty had a whirlwind romance a few years ago, after her husband died, with the man from the Pru. They had a weekend in Brighton before he confessed that his wife wasn't actually terminally ill in hospital but was visiting her mother in Leeds, and due back home any day.

"Did she ever see him again, after that weekend?"

"No, but she says she's got no regrets. She's terrible, you know, she said it made a nice change."

We both smile.

"Well, I think you should go, Gran."

"There's no harm in a bit of supper, I suppose. And he's very kind, he says he'll come to collect me later, to save Connie driving me home. I was telling him that she always drops me off every week and he says it would be no bother. So I said half past nine. Is that all right, dear?"

"Perfect."

She smiles.

Crikey, first it's supper and now he's driving her home. She's never been that keen on what she calls gentlemen friends, because she thinks they're Common. Stan from the greengrocer's seemed quite fond of her a few years ago, and I remember him bringing round brown paper bags full of fruit, but she never showed the slightest bit of interest, so I think he gave up after a while. God, I hope Reg doesn't turn out to be some kind of geriatric Romeo, with "friends" all over the south coast, or I'll have to go round there and sort him out. Although Betty would probably beat me to it.

"Shall I take the boys up for their bath, pet?"

"Yes, please, Gran, and don't let Archie put the bubbles in, or they'll be up to the ceiling again."

She smiles. "I still don't know how he managed to get the whole bottle in."

"No, neither do I. I was only getting a towel out of the cupboard."

"You need eyes in the back of your head with that one, not like our Jack. He's as good as gold, bless him."

"I've put a chair next to the bath so you can sit down. Don't go kneeling or anything."

"Right you are, dear. And I think you're right, I will go to supper with Reg. People are always talking, and most of it's rubbish, so why should I care?"

"Exactly."

Connie arrives at the shop as I'm putting more logs on the fire. She's got her knitting in her bag and is carrying a large greaseproof paper parcel, which means Mark has made us another treat; last week it was a polenta cake, which was so delicious we had to cut the last slice into slivers to avoid unseemly tussling.

"It's pear and almond. I've already had some, and it's very good."

"I bet it is. Tell him thanks from me, will you, Connie? I think word's getting round and people are starting to come just for the cake. Maybe we should forget about the knitting and open a tea shop."

She shakes her head. "No thank you. One restaurant is quite enough."

Everyone's arrived by half past seven, and we're sitting round the table upstairs with the curtains drawn while Tina tells us about the latest exploits of her son, Travis, whom we all adore, mainly because he's not ours; he's very bright, and a total charmer until he gets bored, when he's hell on wheels.

"He was out on our roof on Sunday. Honestly, I nearly died. I'd put him in his room, for a time-out, you know, like they do on the telly, but he climbed out the window, and they never do that on the programs. It took us ever so long to get him back again. Graham had to hold a plate of biscuits out the window in the end."

Tina runs the local hairdresser's, where Gran gets her shampoo and set every week.

"You wonder what he'll come up with next, don't you?"

"Not really, Linda, not if I can help it. I'm just thankful we got him back in before he fell off. Graham was as white as a sheet."

Linda laughs; she works in the salon with Tina, and they've been friends for years. "Why didn't he just climb up a ladder, your Graham? I mean, firemen are supposed to be good up ladders, aren't they?"

"Yes, but he likes a full crew and the blue lights going before he climbs up things nowadays, and anyway, we haven't got a ladder anymore, not since your Pat borrowed it. I don't suppose you could get it back off him could you, next time you're talking?"

"I could ask my solicitor, I suppose."

Linda's in the middle of divorcing Pat, who's moved in with a nineteen-year-old called Kimberly, who used to work at the salon as an apprentice before she got sacked because she was incredibly lazy and terminally stupid.

"I suppose I could tell him I want to do a swap—I'll go for custody of the ladder and he can have the kids. That'd wipe the smile off his face."

"Give Kimberly a bit of a turn, too, I shouldn't wonder."

Linda smiles at Tina. "Wouldn't it just."

Cath puts her knitting down. "Livvy climbed up onto the roof of our garage once, when she was little."

Olivia goes pink and gives her mother a furious look; she's sixteen, going on twenty-six, and thinks her mother is a complete idiot, like you do when you're sixteen. And sometimes quite a bit older than that, actually.

"Mum, you're being really embarrassing. Again. And I've told you, my name is Olivia, not Livvy. Livvy makes me sound like a baby."

Cath hesitates, and Linda gives her a sympathetic look. "I don't want to worry you, Olivia, sweetheart, but that's what mums are for, being embarrassing. Didn't you know? It's all part of the job—they give you a book on it in the maternity ward. And from what we've seen so far, your mum's very low-key. You should hear my mum if you want embarrassing. She marched right into the bus shelter near our house once, when I was 'saying good night' to Kevin Lucas when I was about your age, and she slapped him so hard he fell right over."

"I've always wanted to kiss someone in a bus shelter."

We all turn to look at Maggie.

"Well, I have."

"Take it from me, it's not all it's cracked up to be—bloody freezing, from what I remember, and pretty embarrassing when the bus comes and you don't get on."

"Yes, but still, I'm definitely going to add it to my list of things to do before I die. Oh, damn it, I think I've gone wrong again. I've got a hole in the middle now. Is that from dropping a stitch?" Maggie holds up her knitting for me to see.

"Probably. Let's have a look."

I show her how to pick up the stitch that's formed a mini-ladder; she's making a cushion cover, in different shades of purple and gray, which is quite brave for a beginner. But you can tell she's going to be a serious knitter, because she loves all the different textures. She works at the local library, but she's also an artist in her spare time. She's quite shy when you first meet her, but her paintings are enormous, apparently, and rather rude, according to Gran, so I'm dying to see them.

"My mother used to make me play the piano when people came to tea, and I absolutely hated the piano. I still have nightmares about it. I'm sitting on the stool and I can smell the beeswax polish and hear the clock on the mantelpiece, and I've got absolutely no idea what I'm meant to be playing. And then I wake up. God, I'd have had so much more fun with someone called Kevin."

"Is everyone ready for some cake?"

There's a chorus of appreciative murmuring, so I go into the kitchen and start putting glasses on the tray, and Olivia comes in and offers to help.

"You can take the tray in for me, that would be great."

"I was wondering . . . I hope you won't mind, but Mum said you wouldn't, only, well, if you ever needed a Saturday girl, or anything like that, I'd love it. I really would. If you ever needed anybody. Only I'm trying to save up, for clothes and stuff, and Mum makes me do jobs if I want extra money, like doing the cleaning. In the house." She pauses, for the full horror of this to sink in. "Which is so not fair. I hope you don't mind me asking."

"Of course not."

"I do babysitting, too. Only not babies, because Mum says I'm too young. But little ones, you know, toddlers and stuff. I take Jack Palmer to the park sometimes—his mum's just had a baby—and he's so sweet, I really like it, actually, only don't tell Mum, will you?"

I smile at her. "I promise. Let me think about it, would you? I don't need anyone in the shop right now, but I might need someone to babysit."

"Great. I'll take this tray in, shall I?"

"Please."

I carry in another tray with the coffee and a bottle of wine, and we sit eating cake and trying to think of new words for *delicious*, because Linda says it's much better than that, and she's right. We finally agree on *delectable*, and Connie promises to tell Mark. I'm really enjoying myself tonight; I was too nervous for the first couple of weeks, trying to make sure everyone was having a good time and getting the complete beginners started off, but it's much easier now I know people.

Linda's moved round the table and is sitting next to Angela Prentice, who's so timid and quiet she's like the Invisible Woman; she practically quivers when she speaks, and she's married to Peter Prentice, the local estate agent who sold me the house, who's got to be the most pompous man in Broadgate. He's on all the local committees, and takes himself very seriously, and when you see them together, Angela's usually trotting along at least ten paces behind him, dressed like a Mormon in long, shapeless skirts and head scarves. But Connie and I reckon there's something going on underneath all the quivering, because Peter sits outside in the car every week looking stony-faced when he collects her, and she's making a fancy white baby blanket for her daughter Penny, in a complicated feather stitch with a picot border, on tiny needles. And she's asked me if she can leave it at the shop while she's working on it, so we're thinking Peter probably doesn't approve. We're determined to solve the mystery, only we're building up slowly because we don't want to frighten her. So far all we've managed to find out is that Peter doesn't like courgettes.

Linda's trying to persuade Angela to try some cake.

"No thank you, although it does look very nice."

"What about a glass of wine then?"

"I don't really drink, apart from at Christmas."

"It's nearly Christmas. Go on, give yourself a treat."

"Well, maybe just a small glass."

Linda pours her half a glass. "Is the blanket for your daughter?"

"Yes."

"When's the baby due?"

Connie and I lean forward slightly.

"January."

"Is it your first grandchild?"

"Yes."

"I bet you can't wait."

"No, it's all very exciting."

"Where does she live, then, your daughter? Penny, did you say her name was?"

"Yes. She's in Manchester."

"Her work's up there, is it?"

"Yes."

Angela takes a tiny sip of her wine and I notice her hands are shaking, and I'm pretty sure everyone else has noticed, too.

She puts the glass down on the table and picks up her knitting.

"Oh dear, I think I've made a mistake." She gives me a desperate look; she's usually a very precise knitter, although her tension is so tight you can almost hear the stitches squeak, so I think she probably just wants rescuing from Linda.

"Let's see, oh yes, here. That's easily fixed. Just go back a row, and pick it up there. How are you doing, Linda?"

Linda grins and shows me her knitting. "Fine, I think."

She and Tina are making squares for a blanket for the latest Davis baby.

"I'm really enjoying it. It's so nice in the evenings when I'm watching telly, it makes me feel like a proper mum, sitting there knitting. And it stops me eating crisps, too."

Tina nods. "I like it, too. It's nice having something to do when Travis is asleep and I'm waiting for Graham to get home."

"I like it because it helps you pass the time while you're waiting for something exciting to happen."

Tina smiles at Olivia. "You'll end up with a very long scarf if you're waiting for something to happen round here, love."

I move round the table and sit next to Connie, who's doing a complicated flower pattern on a cotton cardigan for Nelly in pale lavender, with bright pink centers for the flowers; she's quite an experienced knitter, but we're changing the pattern slightly to make the sleeves shorter, and she wants to use different colors and knit beads in as well, so I'm showing her how to thread the beads onto the wool when Maggie asks me how to add in a new color.

"You just need to remember to wrap the wool round each time you change colors or you'll get holes. Put it round like this, yes?"

"That's so clever. I thought you had to carry the wool along the back or something complicated like that."

"You do, in Fair Isle, but this is intarsia, which is better when you're doing solid blocks of color."

"It's much easier than I thought it would be."

"Most things in knitting are, really."

"Especially if you've got someone who knows what they're doing explaining it to you. Did you decide what you're doing for your window? Are you still thinking about an autumn theme?"

"Yes, I thought I'd do autumn leaves and scarves, and conkers, and maybe a branch propped up, to hang the leaves on."

"Knitted leaves, do you mean?"

"Yes, and pom-poms, in oranges and reds."

"That's a good idea. God, this wine's lovely. Where did you get it?"

"From Connie."

"It's Passito di Pantelleria. We get it from my uncle, and it's one of my favorites. We buy all our wine from him—it's much cheaper for us, and much better."

"You couldn't get me some, too, could you, next time? I'll pay you, of course. Only it's so delicious."

Connie smiles. "Sure."

Linda puts her knitting down. "There, that's another square finished. You never know, we might actually get this done before the baby's born. What else are you planning for the window, Jo? You'll have to do something special for Christmas, you know. You've got to keep up your standards now we've won the silver medal; I hear Her Ladyship came in to tell you."

"Yes, she did, and Elsie nearly fainted."

She laughs. "I know. We heard all about it from Betty. It's good, though, us winning. It's about time the local council did something useful instead of just buggering up the roads. There was another crash along on the front, on Monday. A lorry was trying to overtake a bus, silly sod. He wasn't badly hurt or anything, but someone's going to get killed along there one of these days. Oh, God, sorry. Me and my big mouth. I'm sorry, Jo."

For a minute I'm not sure what she means.

"I was so sorry—about your husband, I mean. It was so awful."

There's a silence. Damn. I sort of assumed they all knew, but we've never actually talked about it.

"Yes, it was."

"And the poor boys."

"Yes, that was the worst part really, having to tell them."

"Of course."

"I'm still not sure I got it right."

Waking them up in the morning, and trying to find the right way to explain, with Jack asking me why if Nick was at the hospital the doctors couldn't fix him.

Maggie coughs, as if she's about to say something, but Connie beats her to it. "Yes, but no sad things here. We all just relax, yes? And leave the sad things for other times."

Cath smiles at her. "Exactly."

Everyone's still looking at me.

"Right, well, I'm definitely having the last piece of cake now."

Linda looks relieved. "Go on, love, you have it."

Everyone relaxes, but they're all much more affectionate when they're leaving, and Olivia hugs me, which she's never done before. Connie drops me off on the corner of our road, and I kiss her good night, in a non–bus shelter kind of way. She's been teaching me some Italian phrases, and I want to try them out.

"Porqui misèria, it's cold tonight."

"No, *porca*, not *porky*. Porca misèria."

I try again.

"Perfect."

"Oh, look, here come Mr. Pallfrey and Trevor. Porca misèria, I hope the boys are asleep."

She laughs.

I walk up the road, thinking about kissing boys in bus shelters. It might be a bit late to start now, but you never know. Maybe I should make a list like Maggie's, of things I want to do in the next few years. Not in the house, or for the shop, just for me; I've always wanted to learn Italian, so maybe I could find a local class. It would really annoy Mum, which would be a hidden bonus, but I'm not sure there's enough room in my brain for too much new information; something else would get wiped out to make room for it. I'd come out of my class chock-full of fabulous new vocabulary and discover that I couldn't remember where I'd parked the car. God knows what useful things I've jettisoned already, just learning a few phrases, but I can't find my front-door key, so I have to knock on the door, which gives

Gran a bit of a turn. We're in the kitchen when Reg arrives to
drive her home, which wakes Archie up, so I wave them off
and then go up to settle him back into bed. But he's having
none of it and wants a story. And a drink. Porca misèria.

I'm in the shop the next morning, standing behind the counter
rummaging through a drawer full of buttons, when a woman
comes in, wearing sunglasses and talking on a tiny black mobile
phone.

"Where the fuck are you, Bruno? I'm in a wool shop—you
can't miss it, the window's full of fish. No, I'm not joking. Why
would I be fucking joking? So if you could just stop driving round
in bloody circles and get over here, I'd be seriously grateful."

She turns to me and smiles, and suddenly I know who she
is. Jesus Christ, Grace Harrison is standing in my shop giving me a megawatt smile. The same smile she gives George
Clooney just before she jumps off the bridge holding his hand
in *Falling into Love Again*. The smile that greets Ralph Fiennes
when he gets back from a vital mission as a Second World War
pilot in *Wings and a Prayer*. Bloody hell.

"I'm sorry about this. I'm trying to avoid a photographer."

When she says "photographer," she gets the kind of expression on her face that you'd get if someone had just walked up to
you and been sick all over your shoes. At least I think she does;
it's quite hard to tell with the dark glasses.

I can't think of a thing to say. I'm standing here like a total
lemon, completely mute with awe. Christ.

"My car will be here soon."

"It's probably stuck in the new one-way system, it's really awful, the traffic gets stuck by the bus stop, along the seafront, and nobody can get past."

Great. Now I'm babbling like a loon.

Her phone beeps.

"Yes, I've just been hearing about the bus stop. I thought you'd had special training in counterhostage maneuvers. Didn't they do bus stops? Just get here as soon as you can."

She clicks her phone shut and gives me another dazzling smile. "I'm sorry about this. Would it be all right if I wait in here?"

"Of course."

Like I'm going to say no, please wait outside on the pavement. I'm guessing she's trying to decide if I'm going to ask her for an autograph or go into another blurt about the traffic; God, it must be awful, launching people into idiotic babbling everywhere you go, just like Ellen, but much worse. So it's probably quite important that I act like a normal person, preferably before she leaves.

"Would you like a cup of tea while you're waiting?"

"No, thanks."

"Or coffee? Or juice? I've got some apple upstairs, I think."

So not quite so normal after all then.

"No, thanks."

"I'm even starting to scare myself now."

She smiles again. Actually, I wish she'd stop doing that, because it's really not helping in the Pull-Yourself-Together department.

"I'm not your greatest fan or anything—I mean, I haven't got a room full of your posters or anything weird like that. It's just, well, I think you're great. Sorry, I'm doing it again, I'll shut up now, but let me know if you need anything. Anything at all."

Oh, God.

"Great."

She walks toward the back of the shop and stops by the shawl I've draped over the dummy. "This is gorgeous."

"It's in that mohair on the shelves behind you."

She turns to look. "Great colors."

"I know, they're lovely, aren't they? There are lots more, only I haven't got them all in stock. But it only takes a day or two if I put an order in. The shawl takes three balls, so it comes to just over twenty pounds. And you'll have some left over, for a flower, like these ones, so it's worth it."

Oh, my God, I can't stop. I clench my toes in an effort to stop talking as I pass her one of the knitted flower brooches I've made, with the sparkly silver beads in the middle. It took me ages to do the first one, but now I've got the hang of them they're easy, and they're selling really well.

"Gorgeous."

"I've got the shade card here somewhere."

I scrabble through a drawer and pass her the cream card with all the swatches on it.

She takes her glasses off. "I love the names. I think I'll have the Marmalade, and Candy Girl, Dewberry, and Jelly—oh, and the dark brown, and three of the flower brooches, in whatever colors you've got."

Bloody hell.

"I've run out of Candy Girl, but I've got all the rest, I think, and you'll need the pattern. It's just a sheet of paper because it's one of our own patterns, but it's very easy to follow. Have you got needles?"

"Sorry? Oh, I see. No, I meant ready to wear."

"Oh, right."

"Can you do that?"

"Yes, of course."

Actually, nobody's asked for anything knitted up yet, but other shops do it, so I'm sure we can.

"So how much is that? Around a hundred quid?"

She's probably used to getting massive discounts, but five shawls are going to take a lot of knitting. Still, it will be brilliant publicity, if I can tell people. I wonder if she'd mind.

"That'll be fine, but can I—"

"So that's five hundred quid in total, yes?"

Christ.

"No, that's far too much."

Somehow I don't think anyone's going to be nominating me for a Businesswoman of the Year award just yet.

She smiles. "Trust me, it's a bargain. Add on the flowers, too, and actually I'll want four, including this one."

She's wearing jeans and a pretty chiffon top, a bit like one Ellen's got, only in blues and greens, under a long black coat. She picks up one of the larger flowers in different shades of green, with tiny purple beads in the center, and pins it onto her shirt.

"You take credit cards, right?"

"Yes. I only got the machine last week actually."

She opens her handbag, which I think I've seen in one of those what-the-A-listers-are-queuing-up-for-now features, except I don't think A-listers do queuing, and she hands me a very smart black wallet with dozens of different credit cards in it, which all look slightly different from the usual ones, and are either black or gold.

"Is one of these MasterCard?"

She hands me a black card, which looks nothing like mine; I wonder if it's still got a PIN number. Christ, I don't know how to work the machine if she hasn't got a PIN number. Please let me not balls this up. Please let it work and not start beeping or eat the paper like it did last week, when I pressed the wrong button and the paper disappeared inside the bloody machine.

"Do you know your number?"

"No. But I know someone who does. Hang on a minute."

She makes a call and enters the number, and the receipt prints out. Hallelujah.

As I'm handing the receipt to her, the shop door opens and a man walks in, with a camera.

"Fuck." She turns instantly and walks through to the back of the shop as he raises the camera. I can feel her panicking; it's just like when I was out with Ellen and there was a rumor that she was having an affair with one of the other anchors, who was married with kids, and the snappers were all camped outside her flat. And she wasn't having any affair with anyone. But he was, with the new girl doing weather.

Actually, I'm not bloody having this.

I step in front of him and block his way, and there are definite advantages to not being waiflike when you're trying to block someone's shot; there's a blur of clicking and flashing, which Ellen says they do to intimidate you, even when they're not getting any kind of picture. And it's bloody working.

"Can I help you?"

"Out of the way, love. I just want Gracie."

"I'm afraid that won't be possible, not right now, and since my shop is private property, I'm afraid I'm going to have to ask you to leave."

I take a step toward him, and my knees are shaking so much I feel like I'm walking on stilts, but he starts to back through the doorway, while I try to remember what Ellen said about keeping calm and being friendly but most important Keep Moving.

I close the door, slide the top bolt across, and go through to the back.

Grace is standing behind the door to the stairs. "Where did you learn to handle snappers like that?"

"My friend Ellen sometimes has them after her. Not like you, of course, but still, sometimes."

"Oh, right. Well, that was great."

"Not really. He's still waiting outside on the pavement, and we haven't got a back door."

"Of course he is. Don't worry about it. He'll be joined by his mates any minute—they never go away until they get something. But at least this way I get to do my face. Have you got a hairbrush?" Her phone beeps and she answers. "Yes, I know. Wait there."

She turns to me. "The car's outside. Hairbrush, and a mirror?"

"Upstairs."

"What's upstairs?"

"Our workroom, and the kitchen."

Thank God it's not still full of crap.

"Is the light better up there?"

"Yes."

"Then lead the way."

It's completely fascinating. We go upstairs and she sits at the table and I hand her the mirror from the hook over the sink in the kitchen, and she gets a black nylon makeup bag out of her bag and there's a flash of little brushes and tubes and she's transformed: her eyes seem huge, and a much darker brown, and her face is more defined, somehow. And her lips look fabulous. I'm tempted to ask her what kind of lip gloss she's wearing, but thankfully I manage to restrain myself.

"If you don't give them something, they just make you look like shit. Christ, my hair's gone really weird since I've been pregnant."

I can't believe she's just told me she's pregnant. All the papers have been full of is-she-or-isn't-she? pieces for weeks.

"That's why they're after me, we've just released it. It's been all rumor up to now—fed by my agent, no doubt; he's such a bastard—but I wanted to wait until I'd had all the scans, just in case."

She suddenly looks vulnerable as she puts her hand across her tummy, which seems pretty flat to me, with only the slightest hint of a bump.

"It worked out better not to confirm anything officially, for obvious reasons."

I'm guessing she means her on-off relationship with Jimmy Madden, the bad-boy rock star who most women under thirty would like to shag senseless, according to a recent poll for Channel Five. And who most men would like to actually be—or at least know, so they could go to his parties. But it's all definitely over now, if the papers have got it right, and after a series of Graceless and Shameless headlines, they're all running pieces on Our Gracie, putting her back up on the pedestal they spent so long knocking her off, while simultaneously monstering Jimmy.

"Do you have kids?"

"Yes, two boys."

"I keep having the weirdest dreams. Did you do that?"

"Yes, especially with Archie."

"Really horrible dreams?"

"Yes, flippers, Siamese twins, aliens, everything."

She smiles. "And they're fine?"

"Yes. Noisy, and incredibly messy, but absolutely perfect."

She smiles again. "And is their dad around?"

"No."

"Sorry. It's just I've been wondering what the single-parent thing might be like. For obvious reasons."

"I think it's pretty much the same as the two-parent thing, if you're not desperate for money, and if you've got family to help you."

We both smile this time, because if she started counting all her money right now, I doubt she'd be finished until the middle of next month.

"It's bloody hard work, and they can be incredibly annoying sometimes, but I wouldn't change it for the world."

"Did he bugger off?"

"No. He was about to, but there was an accident. A car crash, actually."

"Serves the bastard right, then. Oh fuck, I can't believe I said that. I'm so sorry. Fuck." She looks completely mortified.

"You're pregnant: blame it on your hormones. I was always blurting things out when I was pregnant. I still do, especially when I've got a major film star in my shop. You might have noticed?"

She laughs and unties her hair and brushes it with my manky old hairbrush, which I keep by the sink. "How do I look?"

"Absolutely beautiful. Stunning."

"I'm liking you more and more. Right, well, let's get this over with. Oh, and give me a bag, will you? Actually, a couple would be great, then they can do Amazing Grace, out shopping for her baby."

"Right. Bags. With wool in?"

She looks at me like I'm slipping back into loon territory again.

"Yes. I'll pay for it later, or get someone to bring it back. Only no pink or blue."

"Okay."

Somehow I don't think this is an elaborate ruse for shoplifting. Blimey. Grace Harrison is going to be photographed coming out of my shop, carrying two of my new shopping bags with "McKnits" on them in pink lettering. Thank God I got the paper ones instead of the nasty cheap plastic, although I wish now I'd gone for the thicker paper.

We go downstairs, and I put a selection of pretty cottons into two bags while she waits out of sight at the foot of the stairs.

"Pale yellows and peppermint and lots of white?"

"Great. And don't stay by the door when I go out, go straight back in. They'll come in as soon as I've gone, and ask you what I bought. Say baby wool, and I knit like the clappers, have done for years. Actually, do people knit like the clappers?"

"Not unless they've got a machine, which rather defeats the point."

"Well, I've been knitting for years and I haven't just started since it got trendy, and you've known me for ages, and I'm very happy, and excited about the baby. But nothing else, okay?" She gives me a rather fierce look.

"Sure. Got it. Long-term advanced knitter, old friends, no idea about anything else."

"And when the shawls are done, you can come to the house—I'll get someone to call you. Thanks, you've been great."

She kisses me, without actually touching my cheek, and she smells lovely, and then she's gone, into a blur of flashing lights. I think I can see Mrs. Davis out there, but there's quite a crowd, and a massive black Jeep with tinted windows. Elsie's going to be furious when she finds out what she's missed; I'll never hear the end of it. A young woman and an older man come in and ask me exactly the questions Grace said they'd ask, as soon as the car drives off. Bloody hell.

As soon as they've gone, I ring Ellen. "You'll never guess who's just been in the shop."

"Dovetail Martin with a special plank to show you?"

"No. Grace Harrison."

"Fucking hell!"

"I know."

"What was she like?"

"Lovely."

"Bugger. I hate it when they're lovely. It's so much better when they're complete arses and then you can hate them. Is she stunning?"

"Breathtaking."

"Damn. They've just confirmed she's five months pregnant, like we didn't know already. Is she huge?"

"No."

"This is just getting worse. No word on Daddy, I suppose? Still off availing himself of all the Class A drugs he can get his hands on, by all accounts."

"I know. She said."

"What did she say?"

"That she's pregnant."

"Everybody knows that, darling. What did she say about Jimmy?"

"Nothing."

"Well, if she pops in again, bloody ask her, would you?"

"No."

"Charming. She didn't happen to tell you if it's a boy or a girl, did she?"

"No."

"God, this could be fabulous for you, darling. A VIP customer, just what you need. And then you can pass me top snippets."

"I'll have to knit the shawls first, and then I've got to take them to her house. Her people are going to call me, apparently. It's so exciting. And I'm not in the snippet game anymore, remember?"

"Oh yes you bloody are, if they're for me. Look, I've got to go, darling, I'm late for a meeting—some bollocks about maintaining standards in the modern news environment. Or why we shouldn't run live links to lying-bastard junior reporters on destroyers in the middle of war zones before we've checked that they're not actually still in dry dock. But get cracking on the knitting and call me the minute you're done, so I can prep you for your next meeting. And when her people call you, ask them if you can release it, the shawl thing, I mean. It'll be great; you'll get features on it, for sure."

"I think I'd better wait until I've knitted them before I ask anyone about releasing anything. She might change her mind or something, and then I'd look like a complete idiot."

"That's my girl, always look on the bright side. Bye, darling."

As I'm putting the phone down, Gran comes in, shaking with excitement.

"Betty rang me. Is it true? Grace Harrison? What did she buy? Betty said she'd got bags. Was she nice? Oh, those pepperonis are awful."

"I think you mean paparazzi, Gran."

"Yes, horrible people, making people look silly. What a terrible way to make a living. And look what they did to Princess Diana. Mind you, if she'd stayed at home it would never have happened—everybody knows they drive like maniacs in France. Mrs. Marwell was over there last year with her son, you know, and it took them four hours to get out of Calais and she said she'd never been so frightened in all her life. She got some lovely biscuits, though, like little pancakes, in blue packets."

By the time I've sorted Gran out, Elsie arrives, furious at having missed out but desperate for every last detail, so I have to go through it all again, and then the three of us sit knitting shawls while Gran and Elsie hold court in the shop, entertaining a stream of customers who pop in for a mini-purchase and a mega-debrief; Elsie even temporarily suspends hostilities with Mrs. Davis, because she stood right by the car and can provide fascinating details like how long it took before she stopped having black spots in front of her eyes after all the camera flashes.

I escape for a quiet moment upstairs by the fire. I'm meant to be doing a supermarket shop, but I can't quite face it, not after my Hollywood moment. It feels like someone else should be doing mundane things like buying sausages for tea, so I sit knitting and try to calm down. That's one of the best things about knitting: once you get past the mystery dropping-stitches stage, it's brilliant at helping you relax. Even your breathing starts to slow down, and I bet if you were hooked up to one of those inflatable armband things, you'd find out your blood pressure was going down, too. Whenever I feel out of control, I find myself wanting to knit, and the rhythm of the rows and the feel of the wool through my fingers usually sorts me out; even when I'm knitting a shawl for a major movie star, and I've got to finish it as quickly as I can, so I can pop round to her country mansion and collect useful snippets for Ellen. Actually, maybe I should just try to forget about that for a while. But still. Bloody hell. Grace Harrison, in my little shop. Bloody hell.

5

DIVAS DON'T KNIT

I've spent the past few days frantically knitting shawls, and being glared at by Annabel Morgan in the playground while assorted parents come over to ask me what Grace Harrison was really like, and did I get her autograph, and is it true that she's got eight bathrooms inside her house, like I'm her new best friend and have all sorts of secret information to share; although if I was, the last thing I'd be doing would be blabbing about it to all and sundry, unless I wanted to set a new world record for becoming a former new best friend. It's amazing what one mini-moment with someone famous can do for you; the shop gets a mention in most of the papers, with pictures of Grace holding her shopping bags, and Elsie and Gran are both keeping copies in their handbags, ready to show people. But since there isn't anyone within a five-mile radius who hasn't already seen them, they're having to make do with knitting leaves and making pom-poms for the new autumn window display, because Gran says we've got to keep our standards up now we're famous.

Connie's been enjoying herself, too, and we've developed a sort of double act in the playground whereby she fills in any details I forget, like how pregnant Grace looked and what color her top was. We've sold so much of the mohair I've had to reorder twice, even though Gran and Elsie promised me they'd keep quiet about the shawls until I've delivered them and made sure she's not going to change her mind. So it's all been a bit twilight zone, and I'm due round at Graceland tomorrow, so I'm finishing the last shawl before I pick the boys up from school. And I'm really hoping that Trevor the bloody Wonder Dog doesn't come round to play while I'm trying to wrap things up in tissue paper, because I'm not very good at tasteful yet elegant gift wrapping at the best of times, and whenever he's around, the boys end up covered in mud, which I don't think is really going to help.

I'm sitting by the counter knitting while Elsie's upstairs having a break when Ellen calls. "All set then, darling, shawls at the ready?"

"Pretty much. I got the tissue paper and ribbon like you said, but mine and Gran's are slightly bigger than Elsie's—she knits really tight."

"Why am I not surprised? How's Dovetail doing?"

"Fine. He's got two shelves up and they look great, but he's obsessing about knobs now."

"Do shelves have knobs on Planet Martin then?"

"No, but he doesn't like the wicker baskets I was going to

put the oddments in. He says glass-fronted drawers would be better."

"Right; quite pushy, isn't he?"

"Very, when it's about wood. Not at all on anything else; he's almost completely silent most of the time. He gave me a hell of a shock the other day. I was in the kitchen humming a happy tune and doing a little dance routine, like you do, especially when you've just been out and got a doughnut for your lunch."

"What sort of routine? Tango, or fox-trot?"

"More of a jive, really."

"Right. So you're jiving in the kitchen with a doughnut—"

"Yes. And I turned round and he was standing in the doorway, just watching me and smiling. I nearly dropped my cup."

"Bless. What did he say?"

"Nothing, thank God. And then Elsie came up. She bosses him about terribly, she never stops. And she's made him a bobble hat."

"Does he wear it?"

"When she's around, yes, but he takes it off pretty sharpish when the coast's clear. Are you all right? You sound a bit tired."

"I'm fine, but I need a break. Can I come down to you for a few days?"

"Of course you can. That would be lovely."

"Tomorrow?"

"Sure."

Something's happened, I know it has. Her mini-breaks usually involve facials and massages in sacred yurts, not small boys and shabby spare bedrooms.

"Have you had any more e-mails?"

Ellen gets lots of fan mail, most of which is perfectly harmless—notes and homemade calendars with kittens on them—but occasionally something more sinister turns up. Last year there was a series of weird cards with cryptic messages about how she'd be hearing the good news soon, and we were worried a religious cult was planning to kidnap her, but it turned out to be a poor woman who'd stopped taking her medication and thought Ellen was her secret twin sister. Last week she got one saying she wouldn't have to wait much longer, from some anonymous address with no name, and then another one saying "I'm watching you" and "He's not good enough for you," which pressed quite a few alarm bells, particularly with me. But Ellen has just joked about them, so far.

"Yes, there was one yesterday."

"What did it say?"

"I like your new boots."

"What?"

"I was wearing them the night before, when I left work."

"Christ."

"Now don't go into one. Brian Winters has already called in Special Branch."

"Good. What did they say?"

"Take extra precautions while they make inquiries, which means they've got no fucking idea. But Brian's sorted me out a security guard. He's called Gary, and he bloody follows me everywhere. I can't even go to the canteen without him trotting along behind me. And he's got weird eyes, like he's looking at you, but not."

"They've given you a security man with a squint?"

"No, he's ex–Flying Squad or something, so he does that scanning thing, looking behind you all the time like he's about to shoot someone. Not that he's actually got a gun, but you know what I mean."

"How's Harry handling it?"

"I haven't told him. He'll only go all *Die Hard* on me, and I hate bloody Bruce Willis—he always looks so pleased with himself. Anyway, it's bound to be some sad nutter in a bedsit who just wants a bit of attention."

"Well, he'll certainly get some when Special Branch smash his door down."

She laughs. "Look, I'm sure it'll be fine, so don't go on about it, all right? But tomorrow's okay with you?"

"Yes, of course, I'd love it. But I still think you should tell Harry."

"Yes, but I'm not going to, so shut up. He's off to Germany for some environment thing. Christ, he's never does anything useful like specials on luxury spas. Who'd want to watch a documentary on a load of recyclers anyway?"

"Friends of the Earth?"

"Oh, please, enough already with the green guilt-tripping. He's been banging on about global dimming for bloody weeks."

"What's that, then? How we're all getting stupider and stupider?"

"It's the new Armageddon scenario; something about all the pollution getting trapped so it blocks out the sun. It's so depressing it just makes you want to jump off a cliff."

"Well, I'd get a move on, because it'll probably only be a two-foot drop from Beachy Head soon, what with the seas rising."

"You could always learn to knit underwater."

"I think that might be least of my worries actually; I'll have to bulk-buy snorkels."

"I still don't get how global warming means we're all going to wake up surrounded by bloody permafrost like in *The Day After Tomorrow*. Although Dennis Quaid's fucking gorgeous, and I love skiing, so it might not be all bad."

"I don't think there'll be lots of après-ski in the Second Ice Age, Ellen."

"I bet there will, there'll be fuck-all else to do. And knitting will be a vital survival skill, so you'll be able to do everyone a sweater. It'll be great, so stop worrying. What time are you due round at Gracie Mansions tomorrow?"

"Eleven."

"Well, make sure you remember to say the local paper wants to do a piece."

"But they don't."

"No, but they will once we've made a few calls. And not just *Tragic Seaside Weekly*, either. And I want every detail, especially anything about Mad Jimmy."

"So I should read any letters that I find lying around? 'Dear Grace, let's keep our marriage secret until the triplets are born.' That kind of thing?"

She laughs. "That would do very nicely, thank you. What are you wearing?"

"I haven't decided, but don't start with the fashion tips—you know they only confuse me."

"Jeans and your black cashmere sweater."

"Which isn't actually cashmere."

"Yes, and one of your chunky scarves, the gray one with the bobbles, and your black boots."

"Not very glamorous, is it?"

"No, but you can't outglam a Diva. You're going for hand-made and authentic, relaxed and discreet; someone she can confide in about her recent relationship issues."

"So I can get straight on the phone and blurt to you?"

"Precisely. So I'll see you around four?"

"Great. Shall I make fish pie for supper?"

Fish pie is one of Ellen's favorites, and I've got one in the freezer. I'll get some carrots on my way home from school with the boys, because they're her favorites, too.

"And carrots?"

"Of course."

"Perfect, and then I'll come Bitching and Stitching with you on Thursday. Harry's still loving his scarf—he wears it all the time—so I was thinking I might have a go at a sweater for him. I've really been missing the boys. I can't wait to see them."

"You fibber."

"I have. I've already got them a present."

"I hope it's not more of those bloody microrobots, because they nearly drove me mad shooting out from under the fridge. I can't tell you how much food I dropped on the floor until I worked out how to get the batteries out."

"No, it's a bow and arrow, a proper one, with feathers and everything, and a big target thing you can put up. It's great. I got it for Jack's birthday, but I'll get him something else now, and they can share."

"Share? You'll be lucky."

She laughs. "They'll be fine."

"Well, don't blame me if you end up with an arrow stuck in the back of your head."

"Bye, darling. See you tomorrow."

God, I hope she's right and the e-mails turn out to be nothing. I suppose if Special Branch are on the case, and Gary's watching her, then it'll be fine. Although I'd still like to ring Harry so he can be on the lookout for nutters, and I bloody would if it didn't mean breaking one of the cardinal rules of sisterhood. But if it's not sorted out soon, I'm going to call him, and she knows it, which is probably why she's told me.

I drive up to the gates of Graceland at five to eleven the next morning and get out of the car to press the silver entry-phone button on the brick pillar, congratulating myself on being on time. But as I reach forward, there's a buzzing noise and the gates slowly start to open, so I have to leap back into the car, banging my shoulder in the process, which isn't very elegant, and then I stall the car. Christ, I hope nobody's watching; there's a camera mounted on top of the wall, so I surreptitiously rub my shoulder and try to calm down before I get my first proper glimpse of the house. Bloody hell. It's like something from Jane Austen, not quite Pemberley, but pretty close, with landscaped lawns as far as you can see, and a tree-lined avenue up to the house. Someone must spend hours on one of those drive-along lawn mowers keeping the grass looking this good, and I'm guessing it's not Grace.

There's a lake in the distance, and a vast circular drive in front of the house. I'm half expecting to see Darcy emerging from the lake and people drifting about in muslin dresses. It's the kind of place that usually has car parks and green National Trust signs, and I wouldn't be surprised to find a hut selling lavender drawer sachets and guidebooks as I'm parking next to a selection of posh-looking cars to one side of the house. I wish I'd remembered to wash the car, which looks even more sordid than usual next to all this gleaming splendor. I think expensive cars must have some special kind of dirt-repelling paint, although I bet I get lots more miles to the gallon than any of these gorgeous objects do. I probably get more miles to the gallon than the bloody lawn mower.

As I'm walking round to the front of the house, I'm bracing myself for a butler, but the door's opened by Grace, in bare feet.

"Hi. Fuck, this stone's freezing. Come in." She turns and shouts over her shoulder, *"Maxine!"*

I recognize the skinny woman in jeans and a gray cardigan who darts out of a doorway; she brought the shopping bags back the day after Grace had been in the shop, and told me to put any media calls straight through to her, in a rather firm manner. She's looking harried.

"Get me some shoes, would you, Max?"

I follow Grace into a huge room off the hall, with old leather armchairs and two enormous emerald green velvet sofas, and a fabulous Persian carpet in shades of blue and green. The wallpaper is a deep blue-turquoise peacock-feather pattern, and it's absolutely beautiful; I wonder how much it costs for a roll. Probably more than my budget for the whole living room.

"Have you been here before?"

"No. It's beautiful."

"Thank God for that. We had someone round yesterday, the woman who used to own it, and she kept going on about how much better everything was in the good old days. She nearly drove Maxine demented. Do you know her?"

"Lady Denby?"

"Yes. Is she a nutter?"

"Slightly eccentric possibly."

She laughs. "We couldn't get rid of her, and she'd got two mad dogs with her who kept licking everyone's feet. Amazing. Oh, great."

Maxine has appeared, clutching a selection of shoes, and Grace takes a pair of green suede ballet shoes that match the green of her wrap dress. She's looking very beautiful, even though she doesn't appear to be wearing any makeup at all, unless it's that tricky no-makeup look that takes hours to get right.

"Would you like a drink, coffee or tea or a juice?"

"Tea would be lovely."

"Pomegranate for me, Max, and tea."

Maxine turns to me, with a rather superior look on her face. "We have Earl Grey, jasmine, broken orange pekoe, mint, herbal, or fruit."

I hesitate. Oh, God, now I don't know what kind of tea I want.

"Or we have English breakfast, if you prefer?"

"That would be lovely."

She smiles, and I can't help thinking I've just failed some special kind of tea test.

Grace is sitting on one of the velvet sofas by the fire, which is very grand, with huge logs burning in the hearth and making the whole room feel warm, in a non-inglenook kind of way, and without the faintest hint of a coal scuttle.

"So show me, I'm dying to see."

"Oh yes, of course."

I pass her the bags with the shawls in.

"Pretty paper." She rips open the first one and holds up the chocolate shawl to the light. "Perfect."

She's still ripping paper and holding up shawls when the door opens and a man walks in, carrying a tray.

"Room service, madam. And I want a tip."

"I'll give you a tip, Ed. Bugger off. I'm busy."

"Charming. I only need a quick word."

"Why are you here, anyway? I didn't think you were coming down until tomorrow."

"And miss watching Mr. Fitzgerald doing his meet and greet later on? Not on your life."

He gives me a cursory look.

"This is Jo. She runs the local wool shop."

There's a hint of a smirk as he turns to me, but he hides it very quickly. "Lovely to meet you, Jo. Sorry to interrupt, but I need a quick word with Grace about our plans for tomorrow."

"I've already told Maxine."

"Oh, have you?"

"Yes. And I think I'm going to be knitting."

She smiles at me, one of her mega-smiles, and Ed looks at me and then back at Grace.

"I'm sorry? I don't think Divas knit, darling."

"Oh yes they bloody do, they're all at it. Julia Roberts, Uma Thurman, Kate Moss, Sarah Jessica Parker. Ring any bells?"

"Never heard of them."

She smiles.

"I can be knitting things for the baby, in my lovely new home."

"Oh, right. Yes. I can see how that might work actually."

"I'm so glad you agree."

Ed laughs.

Grace takes a sip of her juice, and then turns to me and smiles again.

"We've got Daniel Fitzgerald coming to do some photographs tomorrow, and everyone's rather jumpy about it. Except me, of course, because I love him."

Christ. Even *I've* heard of Daniel Fitzgerald. He does fashion photographs, but he also does brilliant portraits, and there was a piece in one of the papers about him a few weeks ago, where they called him Fitzcarraldo, because he's so relentless when he's working. I think I may have worked out why Grace is looking so fabulous this morning.

Ed snorts. "If you love him so much, why did you say he was a total nightmare last time?"

Grace gives him a rather cool look. "I was joking."

"And can you do the knitting thing, then?"

"Of course I can. Jo can help me."

Ed's shaking his head when Maxine comes back in, looking agitated. "He's here."

"Who?"

"Daniel Fitzgerald. He just buzzed at the gate and said he got here quicker than expected and could he come in to say hello."

"I hope you told him to bugger off."

There's a silence.

"Bloody hell."

Ed looks quite pleased. "See, this is exactly what happens if you don't let me organize things."

Maxine glares at him. "It's hardly my fault if he turns up early. He's not due until two, I only spoke to his stupid assistant yesterday, and we confirmed times and everything."

Ed smiles at her. "Well, maybe you should have told Fitzcarraldo."

The doorbell rings, in a very aristocratic servants'-bells-ringing kind of way; no novelty door chimes here, which is a shame because I was rather hoping for "Hooray for Hollywood."

"Well, go and let him in, unless you're planning on leaving him standing outside."

Maxine and Ed go out.

"Damn. I was going to change."

Grace looks down at her dress, as if she's forgotten what she's wearing, then picks up the marmalade shawl, drapes it round her shoulders and knots it slightly to one side, and pins on one of the matching flower brooches.

"I'm serious, about the knitting, if you'll help me?"

"I'd love to."

"You'll have to be on call, for emergencies."

"There aren't really emergencies in knitting."

"There will be with me, trust me."

"Right, well, yes, I'm sure I could do that."

"And I need it to look right, if I'm knitting in photographs. I don't want some old bag writing saying I'm doing it upside down or something. Are you free tomorrow for a couple of hours? Because it would be great if you could be around."

"What sort of time?"

"Maxine will give you all the details. Actually, can you knit upside down?"

"Not really."

"Thank God for that. My mum always used to say I had two left thumbs. She made all my clothes when I was little, but I was useless at sewing."

I smile, and manage to resist the temptation to say I already knew about her mum making her clothes, because it was in an interview she did. I know about her dad disappearing when she was little, too, and then resurfacing when she got famous, and how they had some sort of reconciliation before he died. Her mum died a few years after that, and the press were at the funeral when she got so upset she had to be practically carried back to the car. They ran it on the news. God, it must be awful: people you've never even met thinking they know all about you; and not being able to bury your mother without the press camping at the graveside. It must be so hard to feel safe, anywhere.

The door opens, and Maxine ushers in a tall man with dark hair, in jeans and a leather jacket.

"Daniel, darling, why are you so fucking early? I haven't even had time to get dressed."

"You look dressed to me, angel."

They hug, like long-lost friends.

"I had a meeting in town but I couldn't be arsed, so I thought I'd just come straight down to see my favorite girl."

"Well, I'm thrilled to see you, darling, you know I am. Have you brought your people with you?"

"I don't have people, angel, just Tony, and he's gone on to the hotel to check in all the gear."

"Drink first? Or would you like the grand tour?"

"Tour, please. Nice little place from the outside. Bit small for you, though, isn't it?"

"Yes, it's a fucking struggle, but we're coping. This is Jo, by the way, she's my knitting coach. Come on then, let's start upstairs. I'm getting quite good at this now."

Knitting coach. Bloody hell. I'm having visions of whistles and stopwatches as we go upstairs, and somehow I don't think I'd be getting the tour if it weren't for Mr. Fitzgerald, but it's all completely fascinating. We troop round with Grace acting as our guide and Maxine supplying background details on paneling and provenance, and even though we go into only about half of the rooms, you just know the whole place has been done up to the same ultrahigh standards and there's no spare room with a clothes dryer up in the corner and hideous wallpaper. Everything matches, in a nonmatching kind of way, with lots of florals, sort of William Morris meets minimalism, with wonderful stark colors in among all the faded pastels.

The views from the windows upstairs are stunning; I'm

thinking one lawn mower wouldn't be nearly enough as we go up and down landings and staircases, and into a warren of guest rooms with en suite bathrooms bigger than my bedroom. There's a kind of faded gray and pale blue color scheme going on, with lots of old floorboards and rugs, and fabulous silk quilts on the beds. God, imagine living somewhere this beautiful.

I'm so dazzled by the time we're trotting round outside that I nearly fall into the swimming pool, which is lined with slate and has glass walls that slide back so it becomes open-air at the touch of a button, with a view over the fields and steam gently rising from the water. The boys would love it here. If there is a knitting emergency, and I have to race round here, maybe I could bring them with me, although, on second thought, I'd probably never get them to leave, so perhaps not.

"Does anyone fancy some lunch?"

"Great. I'm starving."

"You don't count, Ed, you're always starving. What about you, Jo?"

"I'd love some."

I get a frosty look from Maxine.

"So what should I be knitting tomorrow, Jo?"

"What about a baby blanket?"

She smiles. "That sounds perfect."

I get another cold look from Maxine as we walk back to the house and into the kitchen. Maybe she hasn't made enough sandwiches or something.

Christ, if I ever win the lottery I'm going to have a kitchen just like this one, except maybe on a smaller scale. There's lots of granite and brushed steel, but without it feeling too clinical, and the biggest refectory table I've ever seen, and comfortable wooden chairs with cushions instead of those trendy plastic ones that make your bottom go numb. The leather sofa in the bay window looks like six people could sit on it and still have room to move their arms, and there's a sort of fireplace halfway up the wall, which might be one of those special pizza ovens, only with a massive Aga and an industrial-size stainless-steel hob, I can't see why you'd need to stick your pizzas in the wall. A young man called Sam is making salads and fruit smoothies, and humming to himself, looking like Jamie Oliver only not quite so pleased with himself. I'm half expecting to see a camera crew lurking somewhere, filming him slicing up pears. He's talking to a man called Bruno, who's probably the Bruno from the shop. He must be Security because he's got rippling muscles and is eating a giant sandwich.

Maxine starts putting out plates and glasses.

"Can I help?"

She gives me a surprised look, and a small smile. "No, it's fine. But thanks for asking."

The food's delicious, with great bread warm from the oven, and a choice of salads that all taste different, unlike the mishmash of lettuce and tomatoes that I manage to produce. Maxine and Sam disappear, and Ed keeps darting off to take phone calls, while Daniel and Grace talk about the plans for tomorrow. Apparently, the magazine people will arrive early in the morning with a stylist called Gwen, and a makeup woman called Tess, who Grace likes, and a hairdresser called Sven, who she doesn't, and he's been told he can't bring his yappy dog with him, which has really upset him. Daniel's talking about photographing Grace by the lake. I hope it doesn't rain, because there's often sea mist mixed in with a light drizzle here in the mornings, and somehow I can't see either of them being very good with drizzle.

"I could be knitting by the lake. What do you think?"

Daniel looks rather surprised. "Sure, that works for me, if that's what you want. We could try you in a boat if you're up for it—the water would be great if the light's right. Have you got a boat, preferably something old and wooden, nothing too flash?"

"*Maxine!*"

Actually, I can see how that could get quite annoying after a while.

Maxine appears in the doorway, with a glass of water in her hand.

"Have we got a boat?"

"Yes, but it's pretty shabby. Shall I get it painted?"

God knows how she thinks she'll manage to get a boat painted overnight round here: even buying a loaf of bread can take you twenty minutes if Mrs. Baintree's behind the counter at the baker's.

"No, it sounds perfect, as long as it still floats."

Grace smiles. "If I end up falling into my lake, you'll never hear the end of it, you know, will you, Daniel?"

"I'll dive in to rescue you, angel, I promise."

Bloody hell. I'm really hoping I won't have to do the knitting coach thing in a boat, because I'm not very good in small boats—or big ones, come to that.

They move on to gossiping about people I think I've heard of, but since they use only first names, I'm not sure. But it's still quite exciting hearing about who is back in rehab and who has completely lost the plot. Then Sam reappears to make coffee, and an herbal tea for Grace that smells revolting, so I'm very pleased I went for English Breakfast earlier. I tell Grace I need to pick up the boys soon, but I'll bring the wool and a selection of patterns over tomorrow morning.

"Perfect. But nothing too complicated."

"Of course."

Daniel looks surprised. "Are you a local then?"

"Yes."

He smiles, and Maxine comes back in and pours herself a cup of coffee as Grace starts peeling an orange. "Give Jo the times for tomorrow, will you, Max? She's got to go and get her boys from school."

"Sure."

I walk back to the car half thrilled and half terrified. I'm sure I'm not the right person to be teaching film stars to knit, but still, I'd better sort some wool out for her; if I'm quick, I can nip into the shop before I collect the boys, and then we can go straight home ready for Ellen. I'll have to ask her if she can collect them tomorrow, just in case I can't get away in time, and then there's the Stitch and Bitch group tomorrow night, so it's going to be a busy day. I'm at the top of the hill when Ellen rings to say she's already at the house, because she got away early, so I end up going straight back to tell her all my snippets.

She's very impressed. "This could be the start of a whole

new life for you, knitting guru to the stars—you'll be off to L.A. before you know it. You'll have to get into organic wool, and knit mufflers."

"Aren't they car exhausts?"

"Jo in *Little Women* was always knitting mufflers. Or was that Mary, the wet one who dies?"

"That was Beth. Mary was the one who went blind in *Little House on the Prairie*."

"Oh yes. God, I adored that when it was on telly; perfect for Sunday-morning hangovers."

"I read all the books, over and over. I really loved them, especially the mother, who was like the perfect antidote to mine, always making buttermilk pancakes and doing things with molasses, instead of making sculptures like willies and telling you off for being Suburban."

Ellen laughs. "I haven't had pancakes for ages. Let's make some."

"Can we do it later? Only we've got to get the boys soon, and if I'm going to be filling the kitchen with smoke, I think I'd rather wait until they're home. They love making pancakes."

"Sure. Do you do the setting-fire-to-the-brandy thing?"

"No. But I set fire to the tea towel last time. Will that do?"

My celebrity status in the playground gets another massive hike when practically everyone recognizes Ellen as we arrive and walk over to Connie. We're attracting lots of covert glances, and Annabel Morgan stomps past looking positively furious, writing things on her clipboard as the kids start coming out. Archie shows Ellen his painting of a boat, while Marco and Jack tell us they've both been moved up to the top table for maths; technically none of them are supposed to know which groups they're in, but they all do and the bottom group does lots of coloring in, which is always a bit of a giveaway. We start walking home, and Nelly shows us how high she can jump, unfortunately sparking off a jumping contest, which culminates in Archie trying to leap over a litter bin and rather spectacularly winding himself. He lies on the pavement panting for maximum attention, but miraculously rallies when I suggest buying a drink.

"Can it be Ribena?"

"Yes, if you're careful with it."

He grins.

"Come on, she says we can have Ribena."

They race to the sweetshop, where Nelly starts a campaign for sweets as well as juice, which ends up with her kicking Marco, so Connie marches her home in disgrace, with Marco adopting a tragic limp.

Archie's outraged.

"Poor Nelly. She only wanted a little sweet."

"No, she didn't, she wanted a whole big packet." Jack's clearly on the side of big brothers who get kicked in the shins.

"Come on, I need to go to the shop before we go home. Jack, try to walk a bit more quickly, love, or we'll never get there."

"Do we have to?"

"It'll only be for a minute. I just need to get something, and then we'll go straight home."

He sighs.

"Aunty Ellen might have a present for you when we get home, if you're both sensible."

They perk up instantly and start speed-walking to the shop.

Elsie takes them both upstairs with her when we arrive, so they can have their drinks and talk to Martin, who's sanding things because he's got the afternoon off work. They're whispering about biscuits as they go up the stairs, while I start sorting out a basket of wool for tomorrow, and Ellen looks at patterns for sweaters and makes disparaging comments about the models.

"Look at this one, he looks like a total psycho—I bet he's called Malcolm. And look at this one, he looks like a mugger."

"Everyone looks like a mugger when they're wearing a balaclava, Ellen."

I'm sorting through my spare knitting needles when the door opens and a man comes in. "I thought this must be your shop. Great window."

Bloody hell, it's Daniel Fitzgerald.

He smiles.

"Did you knit those fish in the window?"

"Yes, she did."

Ellen's looking interested.

"Ellen, this is Daniel Fitzgerald. Daniel, this is Ellen Malone."

He does a slight double take.

"From the news, right?"

Ellen gives him one of her best smiles. "Yes, and it's lovely to meet you. I'm a great fan of your work."

She's flirting with him. Oh, God, this could take hours and hours, and the boys will be wanting their tea soon.

"So what brings you to sunny Broadgate, Daniel?"

"I'm escaping from the hotel. I've got a four-poster bed with bloody curtains, and everything's got a different pattern on it. I'm not kidding. It was so bad I had to close my eyes and feel my way to the door."

"Oh dear."

"It's a great deal worse than 'Oh dear,' trust me."

"It sounds a bit like Eastgate Manor."

"That's it."

"It's very popular for weddings, I think. I've never been there, but some people seem to like it."

"Well, some people should be fired out of cannons, then."

Ellen laughs. "Have they got cannons?"

"Oh yes, in the baronial dining hall; with suits of armor, and great big metal things up on the walls with spikes. Actually, it's the perfect place for an S and M weekend, never mind a wedding."

Ellen smiles. "It sounds like most of the weddings I go to, there's always a hint of S and M about them, don't you think? All that promising to honor and obey."

He laughs. "I'd never thought of it like that."

I'm putting the needles in the basket for tomorrow, and since he's here, I think I'll ask him if he likes the colors I've chosen. I've gone for coffees and creams, and caramel and buttermilk, with a lovely pistachio green, as well as some navy in case she wants something stronger.

"This is the wool for tomorrow. Are the colors all right, do you think?"

"They look great to me. Apart from this." He picks up the navy.

"What's the matter with it?"

"It'll look dead."

"Oh, right."

Dead wool; who knew?

He looks around the shop. "This place is amazing."

Ellen smiles. "That's because Jo's got impeccable taste. You should have seen what it was like when she first got here. It was pretty tragic, I can tell you."

The boys come clattering back down the stairs, followed by Martin and Elsie, who's heard Ellen's "tragic" comment and gone all thin-lipped.

"I wanted to show you this, Jo."

Martin's holding a small glass drawer knob.

"Or I could get the larger ones, if you prefer?"

"No, they look perfect, Martin, thanks. Really nice."

"I wanted something simple, and these were the least fussy."

Archie's hopping up and down by the door, with a large Ribena stain on the front of his school sweatshirt.

"Can we go now, Mum? You said Aunty Ellen's got us a present, so we need to go home."

"In a minute, Archie."

"You always say that."

Daniel looks sympathetic. "My mum always used to say it, too, and it was always more than a minute. Anyway, lovely to see you again. Is there anywhere decent to eat around here, by the way? Only I don't think I can face that hotel."

"The pub's very good, the Anchor, just up the hill."

"Great. Thanks."

Ellen smiles at him. "We'd come with you—the food's fabulous—but Jo's made a fish pie. Actually, why don't you come and join us? She makes a great fish pie, and you'd be more than welcome. You, too, Martin."

"I've got a hot pot in the oven, on low." Elsie's standing with her arms folded, looking thunderous.

I could kill Ellen sometimes. She's always doing things like this, and the house is in a complete mess, so it's not the ideal time to be inviting round famous photographers, or infuriating Elsie by diverting Martin from his hot pot.

"Well, maybe another time?"

Martin nods, looking uncomfortable.

Daniel turns to me. "I'd love to, if you're sure that's okay with you?"

"Of course. It would be lovely."

Ellen looks very pleased. "We're just about finished here, so come round with us now, if you like, unless you've come in to buy some wool? There's a whole Zen thing going on with knitting, you know."

"I'm sure, but I think I'll pass, if it's all the same to you. I'm not very good with Zen stuff, unless it's motorbikes. Actually, I'm not very good with them, either."

Ellen gives him one of her Big Smiles.

Bugger.

As we walk home, Archie tells Daniel how he plays Narnia at school, while I frantically try to work out how to expand our supper so there's enough for all five of us. I've got some extra potatoes, and I can do some peas as well as the carrots, and make a plum crumble—Mr. Pallfrey gave me some plums at the weekend—but still. Damn. Archie and Jack are having a who-can-make-the-best-lion-noises competition as we're walking up our road, so that'll be Trevor on full alert, while Ellen and Daniel are talking about some new restaurant in London where they take themselves so seriously they throw people into the street if they don't make enough fuss about the food. Maybe I should try that later on, when the boys refuse to eat anything with plum in it.

I'm peeling potatoes while Ellen and Daniel drink coffee and the boys watch cartoons, and it's all going much better than I thought it would: Daniel seems oblivious to the state of the kitchen surfaces, and I'm almost starting to relax when there's the unmistakable sound of Trevor at the back door and the boys race outside. Five minutes later, Ellen's making Mr. Pallfrey a cup of tea and Daniel's in goal.

Mr. Pallfrey's brought me some more plums, wrapped in newspaper. "I've just been up at the hospital, and they've given me a date for my operation. So I'll be getting my new hip after Christmas."

He gives me a nervous look; I'd noticed he'd been limping more lately, but I thought it was just down to being dragged along behind Trevor twice a day.

"I'll be glad when it's done, of course, but I wish they'd get on with it. And my Christine says she'll come down for the week, after I'm out of hospital."

He smiles faintly, but I think he's rather frightened.

"Let me know if you need anything, won't you?"

"Oh, I'm sure I'll be fine, but, well, there was one thing, and I wouldn't ask, but since he's so fond of you and your lads, well,

I was wondering, would you take him out for his walks for me? Christine can only get a week off work, and I think it might take a bit longer than that before I'm properly back up to scratch."

Bugger.

"Of course we can, the boys will love it."

He looks very relieved. "It'll be the end of January—they're sending me a letter—so I thought maybe we could go out for a few practice runs, beforehand like."

"That would be good."

"Only he gets a bit overexcited sometimes."

"I'm sure we'll be fine."

Ellen's biting the side of her mouth and trying not to laugh.

"Well, I'd better take him home for his tea. But thank you, that's really set my mind at rest, I was starting to fret about it."

"The boys will really look forward to it."

Unless it's raining, of course. Or snowing. Or he pulls us into the bloody sea.

Mr. Pallfrey puts his cup in the sink and turns to Ellen. "Well, it was lovely to have met you again, and you just keep up the good work. I always look out for you now on the news, and you do a proper job, not like some of them, balanced on sofas with their shirts half undone. Right then, I'll see myself out."

Trevor takes a bit of persuading but finally succumbs, and Mr. Pallfrey's whistling as they go off down the road. The boys come in covered in mud, and Daniel's dabbing at his jeans at the kitchen sink.

"It's a long time since I've had this much mud on my trousers."

"Welcome to my world."

He laughs, and I take the boys upstairs for a quick bath while the pie's in the oven.

When I get back downstairs, Ellen's pouring wine.

"Cheers, darling, I put the potatoes on, like you said. Here, have a drink. It's not every day you become an official dog walker as well as knitting guru to the stars."

"Just don't, all right? He's hopeless when he's on his lead. I'll have arms like an orangutan by the time we've finished."

Ellen smiles. "Yes, but just think, you won't need to go to the gym for weeks."

"I don't even belong to a gym, Ellen, let alone go to one."

"I know, but I'm looking on the bright side."

"Well, bloody stop it, will you?"

I tell the boys the good news about Trevor while we're eating supper, and they're thrilled.

"But we'll have to be very sensible. Archie, are you listening? No running or shouting, because we'll be helping Mr. Pallfrey after his operation, and it won't be very nice if we lose Trevor for him, will it?"

"We won't lose him, Mum. He always comes right back if you let him go on the beach, Mr. Pallfrey says he does. But sometimes he goes in the sea."

Daniel laughs.

"And I can hold his lead, can't I, because I'm the biggest?" Jack smirks at Archie, who bristles.

"Yes, but I'm the strongest. I've got big muscles, haven't I, Mum? Look." Archie holds up his arm, which looks particularly puny in his pajama top, probably because the pajamas used to be Jack's and have gone rather baggy.

"They'll be even bigger if you eat up all your carrots."

Daniel puts his glass down. "You sound just like my mum. She was always telling me to eat up things—she still does, in fact."

"Mine used to make me eat fried liver and onions. To build me up."

Jack and Archie give Ellen a horrified look.

"So thank your lucky stars it's only carrots your mum's forcing on you." She winks at them, and Jack puts his fork down. Great. He's never been that fond of carrots.

"Less of the forcing, if you don't mind, Aunty Ellen. We love our vegetables in this house. They're very good for you, aren't they, Jack?"

He sighs. "Yes."

Daniel winks at him. "What other terrible things does she make you do, apart from eating vegetables?"

"She makes us have apples for packed lunch, and not biscuits. And everybody else has biscuits."

"Anything else?"

Archie puts his hand up, which makes Daniel smile.

"We can only have Coke at the weekends."

Daniel chokes slightly, and Ellen laughs.

"Actually, Archie, I bet Daniel knows quite a few people who only have Coke at the weekends."

Archie gives him a sympathetic look.

Time to change the subject, I think.

"Did Trevor like your new bow and arrows, Jack? And eat up please, love, or there won't be any time for telly."

"Yes, although he bit one of my arrows right in half. But he didn't mean to."

Daniel nods. "He scored a couple of pretty good goals, too. You could make real money with that dog, you know."

Archie looks at him like he might be slightly mad. "Dogs can't play proper football. They're not allowed."

"Oh, right, of course."

Ellen sniggers. "Fancy you not knowing that, Daniel."

"Have we got pudding, Mum?"

"Yes. Plum crumble and vanilla ice cream. Or just ice cream for people who don't like plums but ate up all their carrots."

Everybody claps.

I make coffee, and then we do ten minutes of reading books on the sofa before they turn the telly on, while Ellen and Daniel stay in the kitchen. They're still sitting talking at the table, surrounded by dirty plates, when I go back in.

"Archie's reading's coming on really well now. Did you hear him?"

"Yes, and I love the way he does his special reading voice, and all that Annie Apple stuff, it's so sweet. Here, have another drink." She passes me my glass.

"I'll just get these sorted out first. There's another bottle in the pantry, if you want it."

I start putting the plates in the sink.

Daniel stands up. "We'll help. In fact, sit down and we'll do it." He turns to Ellen, who looks rather unconvinced. "I'll wash and you can dry, yes?"

"Do we have to do it now?"

"Actually, there's no hot water, I used it all for the bath. I was only going to put them in to soak."

"Thank God for that." Ellen celebrates by opening the second bottle of wine and giving us all refills. "Here's to leaving things to soak."

Her phone beeps, and she looks at the screen and sighs.

"It's my mother. She's starting her annual Christmas maneuvers early this year, and she's driving me demented. She's had my dad out shopping every day this week."

"Don't mention Christmas, please. I'm trying not to think about it."

"Is this the first since it happened?" Daniel's looking uncomfortable.

"Sorry?"

"Since the accident?"

"Yes, sorry, I didn't realize what you meant. I thought you were talking about my mother—she's summoned us to Venice and I'm trying not to think about it. But yes, this will be our first Christmas in this house and everything."

Actually, the only advantage of going to Venice is we won't have to spend our first Christmas here on our own. Nick really loved Christmas; he said it was the triumph of hope over experience, and anyone who didn't like Christmas was a miserable bastard.

But then it wasn't him who had to do all the shopping.

"Venice is fabulous at Christmas."

"I'm half looking forward to it, really, but my mother can be a bit of a handful sometimes."

"Mine, too, but I go home every year, even though I always say I won't. All of us go home, and there are always fights. I've got three brothers, and they all bring their kids. But it's great."

Ellen smiles. "Are you the youngest?"

"Yes, and my mum spoils me rotten, washes all my clothes and irons things no normal person would iron. I've tried hiding my stuff, but she always finds it."

Ellen laughs.

"You can mock, but let me tell you, never trust a man who doesn't love his mum. It's a dead giveaway."

"But not if he's propping her up in a rocking chair in the attic when she's been dead for years, right?"

"No, that's not a terribly good sign, and if he's got 'Mother' tattooed somewhere, that's not always good, either."

We're all giggling when Jack comes in, with Archie in his wake, to complain that Archie won't stop singing.

"And he's doing it really loud. Tell him, Mum, because I can't hear the telly."

"I can sing if I want. Mrs. Berry says I'm a lovely singer, only I have to stand at the back, because I can go much louder than some of the others. I'll show you, if you like."

He starts belting out "I Can Sing a Rainbow," complete with arm movements, while Jack puts his hands over his ears, and we're on the third chorus of red and yellow and pink and blue as I'm taking them up to bed, with Jack starting to whine.

"Why can't Aunty Ellen come up and read us a story?"

Last time Ellen read bedtime stories she fell asleep on Jack's bed, and when I went up to investigate, the boys were both up, building a Lego castle in stealth mode, silently passing each other bricks in the darkness, like they were on a submarine and trying to avoid being picked up by enemy radar.

"Not tonight, love. It's too late."

"Well, will you read one, just a little one, please?"

"All right, but only five minutes, if you both do your teeth properly, with no pushing."

They race for the bathroom, and Archie spits on Jack's hand by mistake, which prompts a stewards' inquiry, and then Jack pulls the cord on the bathroom light so hard the little plastic toggle comes off. Again.

By the time I'm back downstairs, after two encores of "We're Going on a Bear Hunt," Daniel's talking on his phone and Ellen's rather drunk.

"He's calling Tony, to come and pick him up. Who's Tony?"

"His assistant, I think."

"Oh, right. Is he good-looking?"

"I've never met him."

"Shame."

"Shall I make some more coffee?"

"No. Let's play strip poker."

Oh, God.

"Sorry, the boys were playing Snap at the weekend, and half the cards have gone missing."

"Well, I'll make some more."

"Right. And how are you going to do that then?"

"With my special pen."

Daniel finishes his call.

"Tony's on his way, but he drives like a total old git, so fuck knows how long it'll take him. But I missed a treat at dinner, apparently; he says it was like the living dead. With baby sweet corn."

"Get me some paper and I'll make the cards."

"Ellen wants to play strip poker."

"Excellent news."

We both look at Ellen, who's humming to herself.

Daniel grins. "Won't it be rather tricky playing poker with half the cards made out of bits of paper?"

"No, it'll be great, because I'll be the only one that knows what they are, and then I'll win."

"Top plan."

By the time Tony arrives, Ellen's still busy making her cards.

"Do you have to go? I've nearly finished."

"Sorry, but I try to make it a rule not to do any stripping if I've got to work in the morning. Call me old-fashioned; it's just the way I am."

We walk into the hall, and I hand him his jacket. Ellen's still humming.

"Perhaps I should change my mind. I'm rather good at poker."

"She's a terrible cheat."

He laughs. "I kind of guessed she might be. Well, thanks, both of you, for an enchanting evening. And that was a great meal, Jo, you're a lifesaver."

"My pleasure."

"I'll see you tomorrow at Graceland, then?"

"Yes."

"Night."

We wave him off and then go back into the kitchen.

"Coffee?"

"No, more wine, I think, and some water, so we can rehydrate. What a nice man."

I put the kettle on.

"Actually, I think he fancied you."

"Don't be daft, Ellen."

"Or maybe it was me. I kept getting mixed signals."

"I didn't get any signals at all."

"Yes, but your aerial's been down for years, darling, so that's not surprising. But I definitely think he was up for something, and so is Dovetail, if he can ever get shot of his terrible mother. Didn't you see his face when she said she'd got her pot hot in the oven?"

"It's hot pot. It's a kind of casserole."

"Whatever. There was definitely something, only I'm not sure what. Actually, I think I might have drunk slightly too much."

"You don't say."

"That's why I thought the strip poker was such a good idea."

"Yes, brilliant—one of your best, I'd say. Let's play strip poker with an international photographer who spends most of his time watching supermodels getting their kit off. I suppose you thought it would be a nice change for him to see a pair of M and S pants."

She laughs.

"We wouldn't have gone that far, you fool, I would have

caused a diversion or something. And anyway, I'd marked all the cards—well, most of them. And it would have been very valuable research."

"On Planet Loon maybe."

"Have you got any chocolate?"

"Not really, only my emergency Kit Kats."

"Well, this counts as an emergency."

"What does?"

"Me wanting some chocolate."

Ellen's got such a terrible hangover in the morning that she stays in bed while I take the boys to school; and I'm not feeling exactly pristine myself. She's planning a day on the sofa watching daytime telly with her sunglasses on, and I promise to call her if I need her to pick up the boys. Archie manages to smuggle the new bow and arrow into the back of the car while I'm searching for a spare set of keys for Ellen, so we have a frank exchange of views when we get out at school, which culminates in me wrestling the bloody thing off him just as Annabel Morgan walks past; still, at least it's nice to know that I've brought a smile to someone's face this morning. After a thirty-eight-point turn, which blocks all the traffic outside school, I'm halfway to Graceland when I realize I've forgotten to put any earrings on, and I've got a mayonnaise stain on the knee of my jeans due to rather overhasty packed-lunch maneuvers, which is great, obviously, since I'm going to be surrounded by media professionals for the entire day.

Maybe if I put some lipstick on I might feel slightly more ready for a magazine shoot, and less like I should be going straight back to bed. I rootle around in my bag, but the lid's come off the tube and the lipstick is covered in fluff. If I was a proper grown-up, I'd have an emergency makeup bag in the glove compartment, full of pristine Clinique and Clarins and an atomizer filled with my favorite perfume. But since I'm not, I have to do my best with an old ChapStick and a tissue, which only manages to make the stain on my jeans look marginally worse. Christ.

The collection of smart cars by the house has grown significantly by the time I arrive, so I'm assuming the magazine people are already here. There's no sign of Daniel, but Maxine's much more friendly than yesterday as she's taking me up to see Grace.

"It's been bedlam all morning."

I know just how she feels. "Oh dear."

"We're having a bit of a crisis because Grace hates all the clothes."

"Well, I don't want to get in the way. I can always come back later."

Possibly minus the mayonnaise stain.

"She said to bring you straight up."

"Oh. Right."

God, I hope she's not going to be throwing any Diva-like tantrums, because I'm not really in the mood. I wonder if Maxine's got any aspirin.

Grace is in one of the blue-and-white bedrooms we saw on our tour yesterday, sitting in front of a huge mirror, with massive foam curlers in her hair, and a woman dabbing powder on her cheeks.

"Great, you're here. I'm nearly done, and then we can grab ten minutes."

She's wearing a bronze silk strapless evening dress, and a rather major diamond necklace, and the room is full of people unzipping black nylon bags and hanging up clothes. She turns to a woman who's wearing a purple floral smocked dress over black leggings and gold stilettos—so I'm guessing she's either the stylist or someone else Creative.

"I'm just going downstairs, Gwen."

"Okay, darling."

"And I'm not wearing that blue thing, okay?"

"Sure. I knew you'd hate it. I told them, but they always think they know best."

"And you can tell Sven if he tries to backcomb my hair I'll have Bruno escort him off the premises. And trust me, Bruno's not the kind of escort Sven's used to."

"I'll tell him."

"I'm not joking."

"I know you're not. That's the best bit."

They both laugh.

Blimey. It sounds like Sven might be in for quite a trying morning.

We go downstairs to the room with the green velvet sofas, and Maxine brings in some tea and we sit looking at baby-blanket patterns, and it all gets rather bizarre; sitting talking about knitting with someone wearing a ball gown, with curlers in her hair and a fortune in diamonds hanging round her neck.

She decides on a very simple pattern of knitted squares with a garter-stitch border and starts looking at colors.

"These two are pretty together."

She holds up the coffee and the caramel.

"Let's start with the coffee."

I show her how to cast on, and she concentrates, watching me closely, and then puts her hands in exactly the same position as mine.

"Like this?"

"Perfect. You're a really quick learner."

She smiles. "What do I do next?"

"I'll show you how to do a knit stitch—it's the basic stitch that everything else is built on. It's really easy."

She's done nearly four rows when Daniel comes in, looking very chirpy.

"We're ready whenever you are, angel."

"I just need to finish this row."

"What are you making?"

"A blanket for the baby."

"Great colors." He winks at me.

"There, I'm done." She hands her knitting back to me and turns to Daniel. "Five minutes?"

"Great."

"Is Sven up there?"

"Yup, ready and trembling."

"Good. Come up with me, Jo, and I can do some more while he takes these rollers out."

Half an hour later we're outside by the lake and she's sitting knitting on the stone steps, in a kind of cloud of bronze silk, which is reflected in the water, with her feet bare, looking absolutely stunning. She must be freezing, but you'd never know it: she looks completely relaxed, without even the faintest hint of the fixed serial-killer grin most of us end up with in photographs. And even though you know it's her job, it's still incredibly impressive, especially with so many people watching her and darting forward to tweak her hair or makeup.

"That's gorgeous, angel. Just look down a bit."

She looks down.

"I'll be out of the top of this dress any minute. Being pregnant certainly does wonders for your cleavage."

Daniel laughs. "So I can see. Move the knitting to the left, just a bit . . . bit more. Perfect."

She carries on knitting but glances up occasionally. She's got something on her cheeks that catches the light.

"Beautiful."

She smiles.

The magazine people are all in a huddle, nodding and looking very chic in various shades of black and gray; I think you must have to be anorexic to work on fashion in magazines, so I'm trying not to stand too close to them. They're not particularly friendly, especially Stella, who I think is the boss because Ed keeps getting her glasses of water and generally fussing round her, and she keeps summoning Daniel for little chats. She gave me a quick but very thorough once-over when I arrived, but I don't think she was terribly impressed with my Look. I thought my Aran cardigan would be perfect for standing around outside in the cold, even if it has gone rather baggy, but now I just feel like I'm a one-woman tribute to Starsky and Hutch.

"Let's try the rowing boat. We've set it up on the lawn, round by the trees."

There's an ancient bleached gray boat propped up on the lawn, with the house behind it, surrounded by silver reflectors, and a rather anxious-looking Bruno standing to one side, but Grace doesn't seem the least bit thrown by being asked to get into a boat in the middle of her lawn and climbs in without a murmur. The boat wobbles and tilts, and Tony and Bruno rush forward, but it settles and Grace sits down.

"Great. I love it. Just let me check the light."

"Jo, can you come here a minute?"

Daniel and Tony are moving umbrellas, adjusting the tripod, and peering at light meters.

Grace hands me her knitting. "It's gone wrong."

"You've just dropped a stitch here, that's all." I pick it back up for her.

"Thanks. Christ, I'm fucking freezing."

"Shall I get you a shawl or something?"

"No, just give me your cardigan for a minute."

I take it off and wrap it round her shoulders.

"It came out bigger than I wanted it to."

"Did you make it? God, how long did that take you?"

"Not long—it was on big needles. But Archie adopted it, he liked wrapping himself up in it while he watched telly and putting his legs down the sleeves, which hasn't helped."

She laughs, and the boat rocks slightly. "You must bring your kids round sometime. I'd like to meet them."

Daniel comes over. "Ready when you are, angel. Will you be wearing that, then?"

"Sadly, no."

He grins.

The sun keeps coming out and then going back in again, which makes Daniel swear and swap cameras, but finally he's finished and we all go inside for coffee and mini-croissants, which Sam's just made, along with almond pastries and plates of fruit. The magazine people look at the pastries with varying degrees of longing, but nobody actually eats anything, apart from me and Tony, who wolf them down. Grace is upstairs getting into her next outfit, and Daniel's on the phone, arguing with someone in Paris.

"If you wanted to crop my stuff, you should have fucking asked."

Tony rolls his eyes. "They never learn."

Grace comes in, wearing layers of white beaded silk and beautiful soft white trousers.

"I can't do these bloody trousers up; Gwen's had to cut a chunk out of the waistband." She puts a hand across her tummy. "And it's only going to get worse."

Actually, she does look slightly more pregnant today.

"Sam, can I have one of my teas please, darling?"

"Coming right up." He passes her a tiny almond pastry.

"Great. My favorite."

Ed comes over to us. He's been standing with Stella, but she's gathered her troops around her and they're all busy writing things down in smart leather notebooks.

"It's going brilliantly, isn't it? And you looked amazing, darling, bloody amazing. And very calm, which makes a nice change."

She flicks a flake of pastry at him. "I think it's the knitting—it's really helping me to zone out."

"Let's put it in all our contracts, then, and Jo can be on standby. She can be like our horse whisperer."

"So what does that make me then? Fucking Red Rum?"

"Fabulous legs, highly strung, loves winning things. Sounds spot-on to me."

She puts her hand on his shoulder. "You're like the opposite of a horse whisperer, did you know that, Ed? Every time you open your mouth I want to kick you."

He turns and kisses her hand as Maxine comes over.

"They're ready whenever you are."

"Right. Tell them five minutes." She sips her tea. "So remind me, it's Emily Pankhurst, right?"

Ed nods.

"And Simone de Beauvoir."

"Yes."

"Right. Christ, I hate fucking interviews."

She turns and smiles. It's really strange; she seems perfectly normal, and then she'll move or smile in a certain way and you suddenly remember who she is, which is a shock, every single time.

"Thanks very much, Jo. Let's fix up another session soon—talk to Max. Right, Ed, let's get this over with, shall we? And no pulling faces like you did last time."

"I'm sorry, but she was so stupid I couldn't help it. 'When did you first realize you were beautiful?' Please."

Grace laughs.

Maxine starts to gather up the cups, so I collect the ones on the windowsill along with some plates of half-eaten fruit and put them in the kitchen.

"Thanks. Have you got your diary with you?"

"Yes, it's in my bag. Actually, where is my bag?"

"In my office—you left it in the living room. I'll just finish up in here and then we can go and get it."

"Are you off, then?" Daniel hands his phone to Tony.

"Yes, in a minute."

He takes a step forward, but Tony mutters something about bandits at twelve o'clock and nods toward Stella, who looks like she might be wanting another little word. Daniel sighs, and smiles, and there's a faint hint of something, a sort of mini-frisson as I start gathering up more cups, but I've got no idea what it means; he's probably just being friendly, or he's going to ask me for Ellen's number or something. I'm totally out of practice at this coded conversation stuff. I lost my decoder a long time ago, and it was never that reliable in the first place. Someone can ask Ellen out for a drink and she'll instantly translate this into either "I'd like to rearrange all your clothing in a non–Trinny & Susannah kind of way," or "I'd like to talk about work." And she's nearly always right, whereas I was always getting it wrong before I met Nick, particularly at university, where I crashed and burned so many times I practically gave up. But with Nick it was different. He asked me out for a drink, and pretty much never went back to his flat again, except to collect his clothes.

"I hope you have a great time in Venice."

"Thanks."

He smiles, but Stella's hovering now, looking very irritated.

"Daniel, could I have a word?"

"Sure."

He winks at me, and Tony hands him a coffee as I follow Maxine to her office, which is at the side of the house. It all seems very organized, with a year planner up on the wall covered in neat black writing.

"It must be quite a job keeping track of everything."

"Yes, sometimes."

"What was that about Emily Pankhurst and Simone de Beauvoir, with Ed? If you're allowed to say, of course. I don't want to know anything that's confidential or anything."

She smiles. "Ed sits in on most of her interviews; we always have copy approval, but it's useful to have someone with her, and she was checking what she's going to cover; what's already out there, what we're giving them that's new, that kind of thing. They're both scripts she's talking about at the moment."

"Oh, right. Well, I'll definitely go and see them, if she does them."

"They're pitching the French one as the Bogart and Bacall of existentialism."

"I bet Jean-Paul Sartre would be thrilled."

She laughs. "Probably not, he sounds like a right bastard in the script. Did you know he left his whole estate to some other woman when he died?"

"Did he? How bloody typical."

She smiles. "So, what about next Friday? We're away until Wednesday, but Friday would work, around ten."

"That would be lovely. Should I bring anything, apart from more wool?"

"Whatever you think. She tends to really go for things

when she gets into them, so bring extra, and we'll pay you, of course, for your time and everything. I'll send you a letter. We ask everybody to sign a confidentiality agreement. I hope that's not a problem?"

She's gone all steely again.

"Of course not."

"Good. Do you have a day rate?"

"Not exactly. It won't be the whole day, anyway, will it?"

"Probably not, but I'll check with Ed and we'll come up with something for you."

"That would be great. And I meant to ask you, can I say something, in the shop I mean, about the shawls? That wouldn't breach confidentiality, would it?"

"No, that's fine, you can say she bought them. But if the press ask you about anything else, we need you to put them onto me."

"Of course."

"Great. We'll see you on Friday, then."

⎯⎯⎯

Ellen's watching telly when I get home, and looking much perkier than when I last saw her.

"I've got a bottle of champagne in the fridge. I thought we could celebrate."

"Celebrate what?"

"Your glorious new career. How was it?"

"Extraordinary. She's so beautiful it's almost as if she's not real, and then suddenly she's normal again."

"Top moment?"

"Watching her knitting in a rowing boat in the middle of the lawn."

"Sounds very Special. How was Daniel?"

"Very busy, I didn't talk to him much."

"You idiot."

"Ellen, seriously, I'm sure he was just being friendly last night."

"Maybe. We'll see."

"They've asked me to go back next week for another knitting session, and she's started on a baby blanket and she really seems to like it."

"Well, I'll drink to that, and there's something else we can be celebrating, too, because they've found my weirdo stalker. And guess what? It was bloody Gary."

"Security Gary? Christ."

"I know. He was asking why I wasn't in, Jess rang and told me all about it. He wanted to know where I was apparently, and Brian got suspicious and asked why he was so interested, and Gary punched him. God, I wish I'd been there. His nose was bleeding and everything, Jess said it was brilliant. And then he ran off."

"Have they found him yet?"

I think I might go and double-lock the front door.

"Yes, the silly sod just went home—hardly master-criminal behavior, is it? And then he hit two policemen, so he's in custody, and they reckon he won't get bail. They take it really seriously when it's police officers you're popping. So it's all sorted."

"Thank God."

"That's got to be worth a glass of champagne, don't you think?"

"Definitely."

"So, about the Bitching thing tonight, is there some kind of initiation ceremony? Do you have to unravel a ball of wool and sing a special song while you stab yourself in the leg with a knitting needle, or anything like that?"

"No, but we'll make an exception for you, if you like. And no swearing if Olivia's there, because she's only sixteen."

"Then she probably knows more swearwords than I do."

"Yes, but I don't think her mother would appreciate you running through them with her."

"Who's the quiet one again?"

"Angela Prentice."

"I'll concentrate on her then."

"She's very shy; she hardly speaks at all really."

"Don't you worry about that, I'll soon get her out of her shell. I'm very good with shy people."

Oh dear. I think Angela might be needing more than a piece of cake and a sip of wine tonight. Actually, I think we all will.

6

TRICK OR TREAT

The weather's gone absolutely freezing, with thick frost every morning, and the radiator in my bedroom doesn't really work, so I'm sleeping with two duvets and a woolly hat. But when I woke up this morning, I was boiling hot and breathless, like I'd hurtled straight into menopausal hot flushing, which wasn't exactly encouraging, until I realized I'd left my electric blanket on all bloody night. And feeling like you've been parboiled isn't the ideal way to start the school run, and I forget Jack's PE bag, so we have to walk back to get it, which makes us late. All in all, it's been a sod of a morning, and it's only five to ten.

I'm standing behind the counter in the shop surrounded by pom-poms and knitted leaves for the window, trying to write a list of Things to Do Today without hyperventilating. Elsie's gone right over the top on the pom-pom front, and now she's moved on to knitting a Christmas tree, like one made from lots of little sleeves she saw in a magazine, in different shades of green, and she keeps muttering about fairy lights, because she says it'll be Christmas before we know it and she wants to get a head start. Christ, I wish I could get a head start on something—anything really—instead of feeling on the brink of total chaos all the time. The past few weeks have been manic. Grace has finished her baby blanket, and I've knitted the border for her and done all the sewing up, and now she's making a baby cardigan while she's in Paris having meetings about the Simone de Beauvoir film. And Ellen's texting me daily because Harry's sweater keeps going wrong, and she snapped one of her bamboo knitting needles, and had an altercation with the assistant in John Lewis because they'd run out of the size she needed, so I had to post some to her at work, which meant queuing up in the post office on Pension Day, which took ages because everybody chats.

The local paper have done a piece on the shop, with a picture of the shawl Grace bought, unfortunately modeled by Elsie over the top of her mad cardigan: she was so desperate to be in the picture I just couldn't stop her. But despite the mortifying photographs, we've still had lots of new people coming into the shop, some from as far away as Maidstone, which is all very gratifying, and we've been pretty busy, although there are days when we only have three customers and one of them is Mrs. Marwell, who comes in for a biscuit and a quick sift through the charity basket. Ellen's badgering me to contact more papers and magazines, but I'm putting it off until after Jack's birthday party, when I can either work out a way to persuade Elsie not to wear her bloody cardigan again or work out how to keep her out of the shop for a day or two; maybe Martin can help me with that. He's nearly finished the shelves, which look great, although he still wants to give them another coat of wax, according to Elsie, but he's away on a training course in Coventry, so he'll do it when he's back.

I'm about to make a start on the new window display, after threading pom-poms onto transparent nylon thread, and stabbing myself in the finger repeatedly in the process, when Gran arrives. She's wearing her Big Coat, which makes her look about three feet wider than she actually is.

"Morning, dear. You look peaky, are you feeling all right? There's all sorts of bugs going round, you know. Mrs. Denning was only just telling me, that winter-vomiting one is back, and they've closed two wards at the hospital, so she's got her mother back home, which doesn't seem right, does it, not at ninety-six? She's got no idea where she is, poor thing, she calls everyone Nurse, even Mr. Denning, and he's a big man, nothing like a nurse. Promise me you'll put something in my milk if I ever get like that. Are you feeling sick at all?"

"No, I'm fine, Gran, and you don't drink milk."

"Yes, but if I was going doolally I wouldn't know that, would I? Or you could put a pillow over my face. One of those ones off my spare bed would be good, they're quite firm."

"Gran!"

"Promise?"

"No."

"It'll set my mind at rest. I wouldn't want to be making a spectacle of myself. Just promise me, there's a good girl."

"All right. I promise. Now, can we change the subject, please?"

I wonder if you can be arrested for promising to euthanize your gran with the pillows off her spare bed. I bet you can, especially round here.

She smiles and pats my arm. "You do look pale. Are you sure you're not coming down with something?"

I don't think I'll tell her about the electric blanket—I'd only get a lecture.

"I'm fine, honestly."

She shakes her head, then looks at the pile of pom-poms. "Are you doing the window now? I'll stop and help if you like. I'm not due at the Lifeboats until later, and I don't like the look of you at all: you'll probably end up facedown in the window if you're not careful; it's a tricky job to do on your own. Where's Her Majesty this morning, then?"

"She's in after lunch."

"I still think you should have told her, she's got no call pushing herself into photographs like that; she's always doing it, you know. When they opened the new café along the front, she was there, bold as brass, sitting at one of the tables by the door. And she's never set foot in the place since."

"Maybe she wants to be the Zelig of Broadgate."

"Well, it's a flaming cheek, whoever she thinks she is."

"Yes, Gran."

She goes upstairs to put her bag in the kitchen and comes

back with two cups of tea, humming "Onward, Christian Soldiers."

"I've just been thinking: you haven't been putting that electric blanket on too high, have you?"

"I'll go and see if there are any biscuits left in the tin, shall I?"

After a bit of a struggle, and quite a few digestives, we manage to staple the burnt orange velvet to the Peg-Board partition, and then I staple the leaves on top, and then prop the tree branch in the corner, with more leaves dangling from it, along with some of the smaller pom-poms. Then I get cramp in my leg and have to clamber back out while Gran goes outside to have a look.

"It still looks a bit bare."

"Yes, but we're only halfway through. I've still got the scarves to fold up and drape over the partition, and then there's conkers and dry leaves in that bag, and the rest of the pom-poms."

She gives me a blank look.

"See? Like this. I've threaded some of them onto nylon. I thought they could hang in little clusters."

She's still not convinced. Actually, I'm not that convinced, either.

"I've got to do something with them. Elsie spent hours doing them."

Gran sniffs.

Nearly an hour later I'm scattering dry leaves and arranging conkers in little heaps while Gran goes off to get doughnuts from the baker's. She thinks it all looks lovely, but I'm still not sure: there's still something missing, only I can't work out what. And all the dangling pom-poms are really annoying me.

I'm rearranging things when she gets back.

"Here we go. I got jam ones, I don't like their apple, they sometimes leave bits of peel on and it plays havoc with my teeth. Shall I put the kettle on?"

"Thanks, Gran. I'm nearly finished."

She goes upstairs while I cull a few pom-poms; I've decided less is definitely more when you're talking pom-poms.

"There, it's finished. What do you think?"

"It's lovely, dear. When will you put the pumpkins in?"

"You are brilliant, Gran, I'd forgotten about the pumpkins."

Two large pumpkins and three small ones later, it's looking more Shades of Autumn, and less Shades of Barking Mad, and we're standing outside on the pavement having a final check when Mrs. Davis comes out to tell us she thinks it's lovely, and glycerin's very good for drying leaves, which I bloody wish I'd known before I spent hours drying them on the bottom shelf of the oven.

We go back inside to eat our doughnuts.

"There's something I want to ask you, dear, only you must promise to tell me the truth."

Oh, God. I hope this isn't anything to do with electric blankets.

"Of course I will, Gran."

"Well, it's Reg. He's asked me to go on a little cruise with him, and I think I'd quite like to go, but I'm not sure."

"A cruise to France, do you mean?"

"No, a proper one. Mediterranean Medley, I think they call it, and we'd have separate cabins and everything. They do ballroom dancing, and there's a show every night, and I've always fancied a cruise. You fly to Madeira, and then they go round in circles, as far as I can make out. What do you think?" She's gone rather pink.

"It sounds lovely."

"You don't think it's silly, me going gallivanting off at my age?"

"I think your age is the perfect time for gallivanting, Gran. When would you be going?"

"Well, that's the other thing. It's over Christmas, and he needs to know because they're doing a special price at the travel agent's in Margate. I'd be back just after New Year, and it would stop your mother plaguing me to come over to Venice. But will you be all right, with me away?"

"Of course, Gran, we'll be fine."

She looks slightly hurt.

"If you're not gone for long, of course."

She drinks her tea.

"I've talked it over with Betty, and she says she can sit with the boys on Thursdays and whenever you need her, and she says she'll come shopping with me: they do whole outfits for cruising, apparently, in the shops in London."

I'm guessing she's not talking black leather trousers, but I'm not sure I can really see her in white culottes and a sailor's cap, either.

"I think you can wear what you like."

"They dress up in the evenings, Reg says, so I'll have to get some proper outfits for that. I wouldn't want to let him down or anything."

"You won't, Gran, you always look lovely. But we can go up to town, if you like. I'll take you up in the car."

"Would you? We could make a day of it, I'd really like that, but can we take Betty, too? Only I wouldn't want to hurt her feelings."

"Of course. I'm sure Connie will have the boys."

She smiles. "Honestly, who'd have thought it, me off on a cruise? I better go and tell Reg, then."

She goes off humming, looking very happy, and no wonder; I can't remember the last time she had a holiday, apart from coach trips with Betty. Mum's going to be furious; she hates it when anyone in the family does anything glamorous—apart from her, of course—and I think she was rather counting on me to get Gran over at Christmas, even though we've all told her she wasn't keen. Clever old Gran.

Elsie gives the window her seal of approval when she arrives and is busy showing Mrs. Geddings her collection of newspaper cuttings, even though I'm sure she's already seen them, while I tidy up and reorder some of the cotton we sold at the weekend, and then grab a quick sandwich from the baker's. There's a steady but mildly annoying trickle of old ladies who can't decide what color wool they want and keep getting their wheelie bags wedged in the doorway, and I'm in the middle of looking at photographs of Mrs. Bullen's new great-granddaughter, who's only six weeks old but is wearing a pink satin hair band and appears to have already had her ears pierced, when I realize it's ten to three.

I make it to school with only minutes to spare, which means I have to park miles away from the gates and then speed-walk into the playground. I'm standing panting as the kids start streaming out when Mrs. Chambers comes over with Jack and asks if I can spare her a minute for a little word. I'm quite tempted to say no, not at the moment thanks, but I'm not brave enough, so I exchange an anxious glance with Connie and walk toward the classroom, with Annabel Morgan giving me a very supercilious look, and before I know it I'm trying to balance on a very small chair, feeling like I've been kept in at playtime, while Mrs. Chambers searches through a drawer in a large plan chest, looking for the evidence, presumably. Bugger.

"I know it's here somewhere."

"Is there a problem with Jack?"

"No, not at all. I wish they were all like him."

Oh, God. It's Archie.

"How's Archie been getting on?"

"Fine, as far as I know, I haven't really seen him."

She carries on searching through the drawer.

"I had his class for painting yesterday, and he did a lovely picture of leaves, wonderful colors. And a dog. At least, I think it was a dog."

"That'll be Trevor."

"Sorry?"

I can't believe I actually said that out loud.

"He belongs to our neighbor, but he comes round to play quite a lot."

She looks at me like I might be one of life's Very Slow Readers.

"Here it is, I knew I had it somewhere, I must tidy this drawer, I saw it at the weekend, absolutely fascinating; it's an article about knitting."

Christ, what a stupid woman. If she'd only told me this was about knitting, I wouldn't have been sitting here in such a panic. Right, well, if this is about me doing a stall for the Spring Fair, I think she might be in for a bit of a surprise, because I'm not really up for spending hours wrapping tinsel round bloody jam jars. Start as you mean to go on, as Gran says.

"Is this about the Spring Fair, by any chance? Because I'm terribly busy at the moment."

I give her what I hope is a Firm Look, which she meets with a very convincing Firm Look of her own, and to be honest, hers is rather better than mine.

"No, not at all."

She gives me another Look, and while it's undoubtedly true that there's a special kind of pressure that comes from having to face thirty mixed infants every morning, especially if they've got paint and you're meant to be in charge of Art, I do wish teachers wouldn't always treat you like they're the busiest people on the planet and you just spend all day lounging about at home arranging flowers and occasionally doing a bit of light dusting. Because some of us are pretty busy ourselves actually, and we don't get thirteen weeks' paid holiday a year, with extra training days. In fact, we don't get any training days at all.

She hands me the article, and there's a big picture of kids in their school sweatshirts waving knitting needles, and my heart sinks. But Mrs. Chambers is looking Very Keen.

"Apparently teaching children to knit improves their numeracy and literacy skills, and there's an address here, where we can apply for supplies of wool and needles. But I need someone with the right expertise, to help me work out what we'd need, so of course I thought of you. I don't knit, you see—well, not at the moment—but I'm sure I could learn."

She gives me what I'm guessing she likes to think of as her Encouraging Smile; the sort of smile she'd give you if you were stranded at the wrong end of the wall bars in your PE pants. Bugger.

"Well, that does sound interesting, but—"

"I know, isn't it marvelous? We're going to be doing textiles throughout the school in the summer term, so I thought if every child could have the chance to knit something, just simple things, little scarves, pom-poms, that kind of thing, it would be wonderful."

Excellent. More bloody pom-poms.

"I thought we might try something more ambitious with the older ones, but I'd need your guidance on that, of course."

"They could make blankets, and then send them to charity when they'd finished."

"What a lovely idea. I knew you'd come up with good ideas like that."

Double bugger; I walked right into that one.

"We could put a note up asking for volunteers, so you wouldn't need to be in school for too much of your time, because of course I do realize you have your business to run. But if you could just help me with the initial planning. We'd need to come up with a program, so we're clear what we're trying to achieve, I do think that's important, don't you? Otherwise, it could so easily turn into lots of chatting and not many learning goals being met. We need to make some work sheets, so other members of staff can help deliver the target tasks for the older-year groups. It's so important to rescue traditional crafts and keep them alive for future generations, don't you agree?"

Christ, she's good.

"Oh, yes, definitely."

"And avoid the stereotypes."

"Sorry?"

"That only girls knit."

"Oh, yes, absolutely."

"Do your boys knit?"

"Jack's quite keen, but Archie's not convinced."

Actually, Archie refused point-blank last time I tried to get them both knitting, and then bent one of his needles out of shape by poking it down the back of the radiator in the kitchen.

"Well, I think it's wonderful, how it's having such a resurgence. It's an important art form, you know, going back to the Middle Ages. I've been doing some research, and it's fascinating; of course, it was mainly men then, making wool stockings and carpets, and they had guilds, so it was all taken very seriously. But it's always the same, I expect you've noticed; when men do something, it's an art, but when women do it, it gets relegated to being a craft. It's so annoying."

I'm liking her more and more. Damn.

"We could make a rug with one group. They could all knit strips and then we could weave them into a mat."

She beams at me.

"Excellent. How exciting! Shall I write off for supplies then?"

"Yes, and I'm sure we'll have some spare stuff in the shop."

There's no point in pretending anymore; I've been officially signed up.

"That's very generous of you. Once I've heard back from them, let's meet and start planning, shall we? I have a free lesson on Tuesdays, or after school if you prefer? I'll raise it at our planning meeting this week, but I know Mr. O'Brien will support us. He's very keen on whole-school projects."

"Tuesdays are fine for me."

Bloody hell. So now I've got to add Invent a Whole-School Knitting Project to my bloody list, along with Find Cruise Wear for Gran, and Sort Out Jack's Birthday Party. Christ. So many fabulous things to do, so little time.

Connie's waiting for me in the playground, looking rather worried. "What did she say?"

"She wants me to start a knitting project in school."

"For who?"

"The kids."

She laughs. "Porca Madonna!"

"Double porca Madonna, I think you'll find. Will you help me, when we get started?"

"Sure, as long as I don't have to be with Nelly."

"Christ, I hadn't thought of that. We'll have to fix it so we never get our own kids in our groups or it'll be chaos."

We walk back to the car talking about Jack's party. Connie's starting a new sideline for the pub, with Mark making cakes for special occasions, and we're going to be their first customer. Jack's birthday's just a few days before Halloween, so he's making him a giant pumpkin cake. I've done quite a few versions of Halloween parties. Last year we had a Vampire Adventure Playground party, which was particularly tricky because half of them were wearing plastic pointy teeth, which I had to hold while they went in the ball pool, and then they all got muddled up and Tadzio Holland-Blackman fell off the rope swing onto the soft mats and screamed so loudly three of the girls burst into tears, and Nick couldn't get home in time. But this year I think I've come up with the ideal combination, and we're having a proper birthday tea, with ten of his friends from school, as well as Nelly and Archie, and then a big bonfire party in the back garden. I've invited everyone from the Stitch and Bitch group, and Mr. Pallfrey's volunteered to do the bonfire. He's going to light a few fireworks, too, only that bit's meant to be a surprise; he's been filling buckets with sand and hiding things in old biscuit tins in the garage for days now, and he says Trevor loves fireworks, so someone will be facedown in the mud while Trevor drags them round the garden, and I'm really hoping it's not going to be me. The pile of wood for the bonfire is already enormous, and Mr. Pallfrey's still got more stuff to bring round, which is slightly worrying, but Tina's promised to bring her husband, who the boys now insist on calling Fireman Graham, and apparently he can put garden sheds out very speedily if he has to, which might be handy.

"Mark says he can bring soup, butternut squash, if you like?"

"That would be great. I thought I'd do baked potatoes and little sausages, and honey and mustard chicken, and salads, but soup would be great. I'm doing ice-cream cones and raspberry ripple ice cream, too, because they're his favorite. And then there's the cake, of course."

She smiles. "He's making a practice one tonight. So I can tell you tomorrow how it goes."

"Thanks, Connie."

"It's not a problem. I love it when he makes practicing cakes."

We do a quick supermarket sweep on the way home, and Archie smuggles cheese strings into the basket and then throws a complete fit at the till when I refuse to buy them, which causes some tutting from the woman behind us in the queue. He's still sulking when we get home but is restored to good humor by sausage sandwiches and salad and a strawberry yogurt, and then the boys sit watching telly while I put the last of the shopping away and try to summon up the energy to make a start on the teetering pile of ironing that falls out of the cupboard under the stairs every time I open the door. I've just put the ironing board up when my mobile beeps.

It's another text from Ellen. *Help. Now have 4569 stitches. And only meant to be a sleeve. E. x*

I text her back while I get the iron out. *Take back few rows and count. Will be fine. Remember to breathe. Gran off on cruise* with Reg and needs cruise clothes. Am now in charge of whole school knitting project. Help. Where are you? x

The phone beeps again. *At work, on at 6. Gran now getting more action than you!!*

I text her back: **** *off* and plug the iron in. I've just started on a pair of jeans when the phone rings.

"Aren't you meant to be in makeup?"

"Sorry?"

Bugger, I thought it was Ellen, but it's Maxine.

"We're back, and she wants you round now."

"Right now?"

"Yes."

"I can't. I've got the boys with me."

"Hang on . . . Yes, I'm talking to her now . . . Yes, but she's—"

Grace comes on the line. "Sorry about this, Jo, but can you come round, just for a minute? I need to show you, I've finished the little cardigan and it's so sweet, but I need you to do the sewing-up thing."

"I've got the boys here."

"Well, bring them, too. They can have a swim—would they like that? It's not too late, is it?"

"They'd love it, only—"

"Great. See you in ten minutes."

The line goes dead.

Damn, I better get round there, particularly since I've just signed the letter Maxine sent, with the truly staggering rate of four hundred pounds a day for being the official Knitting Adviser to Ms. Harrison, for a minimum of one day a month, which is brilliant, obviously, but it does mean I can't afford to say no.

I switch the iron off and start collecting up towels and swimming things while I drill the boys about Being Polite and not shouting, or running, or touching anything, and then I realize that I might have slightly overdone it, because they've both gone rather quiet.

"Put your shoes on, Archie, and then we'll go. It'll be fun, I promise. You can have a lovely swim; won't that be great?"

"And I don't need my armbands now, Mum, remember?"

"I know you don't, Archie, but just for today could you wear them until we see how deep the water is?"

He tuts.

"Please, Archie."

"Can we have chocolate on the way home?"

"Yes."

"A proper big bar each?"

In other words, no trying to palm them off with a packet of Maltesers to share.

"Yes. Come on, Jack, get your coat on, love."

I'm hyperventilating as I drive to the house, while Archie blows up his armbands on the backseat and then puts them on over his coat. I bet nobody else has ever arrived at Graceland with their armbands on over their anorak.

Grace is coming down the stairs when Maxine lets us in, and she's looking very pregnant in the kind of white silky caftan that nobody in their right mind would wear if they hadn't just been on a three-week trip to the Bahamas. But of course she looks divine; faintly tanned, but nothing too Eurotrash, with pink toenails and not a centimeter of anything wobbling at all.

"I thought we could all have a swim. Did you bring a swimsuit? I can lend you something if you like."

Maxine looks at me and we share a smile, because the chances of my fitting into any of Grace's swimsuits are nonexistent unless I can have some fairly major haunch-reducing surgery in the next three minutes. But it's very kind of her to offer.

"Thanks, but I've got mine with me." I'm not really looking forward to revealing my mottled bits to someone with world-famous legs, but never mind.

Grace smiles at the boys. "Would you like a drink or anything?"

Archie puts his hand up, which makes her laugh.

"Coke. Please. Thank you. Very much. Very very much."

Grace and Maxine both smile.

"We're only meant to have Coke at the weekends actually." Jack can't resist the opportunity to have an Older Brother Moment, even if it means he might lose out on a Coke. Everyone looks at me for a verdict.

"I think it'll be fine, Jack, just this once."

"So that's two Cokes, then. With straws?"

Archie claps his hands.

"Yes, please. Thank you very much."

I think I may have overdone it on the Be Very Polite thing.

Maxine goes into the kitchen while we walk down the corridor to the pool room, and the boys become temporarily speechless when they see the blue and green lights shining under the water; there's music playing, and the glass walls are shut, so it's lovely and warm. Grace leads us into the most stylish changing room I've ever seen, with heated mosaic tiles, and a huge walk-in shower with a wooden, grooved floor and a collection of lotions and shampoos, none of which are from Boots; it's all Jo Malone and Burt's Bees, and all the towels are warm. I wonder how long it would take for anyone to notice if I just moved in here for a few days' rest.

Grace dumps her caftan on a chair and goes out to the pool.

"It's lovely in here, isn't it, Mum?"

Jack's sitting on a white leather armchair in his Spider-Man pants, swinging his legs.

"Yes, love. Come and put these on. And give me your things and I'll hang them up."

Archie's armbands prove particularly tricky, since they seem to have welded themselves to the plastic coating on his anorak, and rude noises are produced whenever we try to pull them off, which go down extremely well.

"Do it again, Mum, do it again. Look, they've got a toilet to wash your bottom in, like in our hotel in Devon."

"It's a bidet, Archie."

"Yes, and Daddy said it was for your socks, but he was joking, wasn't he, Mum?"

"Yes, sweetheart."

"Daddy would like it here, wouldn't he?"

"Yes, Jack."

There's a silence, and I know I ought to say something, only I'm not sure what.

"We had a lovely time in Devon with Daddy, didn't we?"

They both nod.

"Do you remember when he fell over in the sea?"

He was trying to learn to surf, but soon gave it up when he realized just how many times surfers get smacked in the face by their own surfboards. But he spent hours playing in the waves with the boys, which they loved.

Jack's smiling. "Yes, and I was the champion. Dad said I was."

"Yes, you were. You were the champion six-year-old, and Archie was the champion four-year-old."

Archie finally gets his last armband off. "Yes, and I'm nearly ready for swimming now, Mum, so hurry up."

"Let's take your coat off first."

Grace breaks off from doing a series of very impressive laps and swims over to join us as we get in. The shallow end's just up to Archie's shoulders, so he's quite happy bobbing about, and the water's lovely and warm, so Jack isn't shivering like he usually does.

"This is fabulous, Grace."

She looks at Archie's armbands.

"I'll have to get some of those."

"They do little inflatable seats for babies, until they're big enough for armbands. Archie loved his."

She smiles, and Archie looks worried. "Yes, but I don't even need my armbands now, and I can go on my back, too. Look."

He hurls himself into a bit of backstroke and splashes us all.

"That's very good, Archie, but go on your front now, please."

Jack demonstrates how far he can swim with his face in the water and comes up spluttering. "It's called front crawling."

Grace applauds, and the boys start having mini-races while she does more laps. She doesn't seem to get even the tiniest bit out of breath, which is mystifying since I'm getting out of breath just watching her.

Archie manages a whole width without standing up, which is a new personal best, so he's very pleased with himself, and then he clings on to the strap of my swimsuit and demands a piggyback swim, like we used to do when he was little.

"You're too big now, darling. I'll go under."

Actually, I used to go under fairly frequently when he was little, too, since he was a pretty hefty toddler.

"I've got my armbands on, so it won't matter."

"Yes, but it would matter to me, because I'd be the one under the water."

He giggles.

"All right, bucking broncos, then, like Daddy used to do?"

Bugger. I was hoping he might have forgotten about the bronco thing, but he's said the D word, so I feel honor-bound to give it a go. He sits on my back with his arms round my shoulders, and I stagger along in a half crouch and then suddenly rise from the water and tip him backward. Jack wants a go, too, and what feels like an eternity later I've bucked them both off so many times I think I might have dislocated my right shoulder. Grace has been swimming round us, applauding occasionally.

"Can Grace do bucking broncos?"

"No, she can't, Archie, definitely not. And this is the last one, all right?"

"Okay. But when she has her baby out she can do it, can't she?"

Grace laughs. "I think I might get Bruno to do any bucking that's required."

Archie scans the pool. "Who's Bruno?"

"He helps me."

"With swimming?"

"Sometimes."

He nods.

"We have Mrs. Collins, and she blows her whistle if you're being silly and you have to get out and sit on the seat by the door. And when we go on the coach we sing songs, but only in our quiet voices because if you shout the driver might crash."

Maxine comes in with a tray of drinks. "There's a pot of decaf tea for you both, and Sam's done some fruit for the kids, to make up for the you-know-what. We've got some toys somewhere, for the pool. Hang on a minute and I'll find them."

She goes into the cupboard by the door and emerges with a huge net bag full of plastic hoops and balls. "Any good?"

"Brilliant."

She unzips the bag, and I start the boys off in a game of throw-the-ball-into-the-floating-hoop-without-trying-to-drown-your-brother while Grace gets changed, and then I nip into the changing room and get dressed, with the door open so I can still hear them, before I join Grace on a lounger; she's changed into a chocolate brown velvety tracksuit, which I instantly long for, if they do them in giant-bottom size as well as film-star petite.

"They're sweet, your boys."

"Thanks. They're even nicer when they're asleep. You'll notice that with yours. When they're asleep they're all completely adorable."

She smiles and passes me her floral knitting bag, which is something else I'm longing for, but I think I saw something like it in a magazine a while ago, and it was nearly six hundred pounds. So perhaps not.

She passes me a tiny cardigan in dark plum cotton.

"You're getting really good, you know. This is perfect."

She looks very pleased.

"I'll wash it and sew it up for you as soon as I can, and I've brought a new book for you to look through, with some great blankets, cot-size this time, rather than teeny."

I pass her the book and pour us both a cup of tea.

"I got it at the knitting show last week."

"The one you were telling me about, at Alexandra Palace, right?"

"Yes. I'd forgotten what a big place it is. There were hundreds of stalls, and crowds of people."

And it took me hours to get there, stuck on depressing roads in North London going in the wrong direction until I finally found the right road.

"Did you buy much?"

"A few books, and I'm sending off for prices on some lovely Scottish tweed and some Italian silk. There were some exhibitions by fashion students that were interesting; lots of knitted skirts with hoops, and dresses with three sleeves in gray silk, that kind of thing. And some Japanese women with sculptural things, like fishing nets, only in beautiful colors. Amazing."

"I like this one."

She's looking at a pretty cot blanket with baby animals in each square, mainly rabbits, ducks, and what I think are meant to be elephants.

"But not in these sickly colors."

"I'll bring some better colors for you to look at. I can drop them off with Maxine if you're busy, and she can let me know later. It might be nice in greens. I've got a lovely new apple green in, and a pale peppermint, which would work, or shades of browns and cream. Café au lait and caramel, that kind of thing."

"Great. Show me both."

I pour us some more tea. "How was Paris?"

"Fine, boring, the usual."

"I've never actually been. Is it beautiful?"

"You've never been to Paris?"

She looks at me like I've just said I've never been to a restaurant.

"Nick and I talked about going once, but then I had Jack and we didn't get round to it."

She looks at the boys, who are busy rearranging the hoops, with Archie wearing one round his neck.

"Archie, take that off, that could be dangerous, love."

He ignores me, but Jack takes it off and smiles at us.

Grace puts the pattern book down.

"Was he a good dad?"

"He was lovely with them when he was around, but he was away a lot, so we didn't always see him that much."

She gives me a thoughtful look. "You were a sort of semi–single parent, then?"

"Yes, I suppose so. Without the perks."

"Are there perks, then? Great, I love perks. Are there goody bags?"

"Not unless you count your Bounty pack, no."

"Your what?"

"They give you a free shopping bag full of stuff in hospital, samples and things."

"I'll be at the Portland, so they'll probably charge me fifty pounds for it."

"They're not that exciting, actually. I'd pass, if I were you."

She smiles. "What are the other perks, then?"

"Things like being able to stick to a proper bedtime routine and rules about sweets without him making you look like the Wicked Witch, overruling you whenever he feels like it. Not having to maintain the myth of how marvelous Daddy is, even when he's late home again and you're completely knackered, that kind of thing."

"So basically it's crap?"

"Yes."

"But having a dad around doesn't help that much, either?"

"No, not really. It's still mainly the mums who do all the boring stuff: you just go to any dentist during half term and you'll see. It's pretty much a one-woman mission for most people, I think."

"And no free gifts."

"Not really, no."

She laughs. "I think she got it wrong, you know, that Simone de Beauvoir. We're not the Second Sex at all, we're the bloody First. Everything would grind to a halt without women. I've been reading the research notes Max did for me, and that Jean-Paul Sartre sounds like a right wanker. She should have been much tougher with him, like that one who sat knitting by the guillotine. Madame de something."

"Madame Defarge?"

"Yes—get your knitting out and don't let the bastards grind you down. And she wore Chanel, you know."

"Who, Madame Defarge?"

"No, Simone de Beauvoir. So the clothes will be great, if I do it. If I ever get back to a normal size again. Have you read any of her books?"

"Maybe, at university. I can't really remember. I've got quite a few blanks about what I read years ago. I think it's a leftover from being pregnant. Sorry, I used to hate that, how people always tell you things like that when you're pregnant. It's like you become public property."

"I've been public property for quite a while, if you believe the papers."

"Yes, but people don't come up to you and touch your tummy, do they? They were always doing that to me, on the Tube, and I hated it."

She laughs. "Not unless they want to get up close and personal with Bruno, they don't."

"Anyway, there's some new research on how pregnancy actually improves your memory. I was reading about it at the weekend, I meant to bring it to show you. It increases something. They've done scans on how women's brains are different from men's, and it gets more pronounced after pregnancy. So we're not supposed to blame men if they can't multitask. Although they're very good at map reading, apparently."

"And quite good at multitasking when it's things they want to do, like shagging people behind your back."

"True."

"Did you ever meet her?"

"Who?"

"The woman your husband . . . Look, say if you don't want to talk about this, won't you?"

"It's fine. No, I never met her."

"Jimmy was always surrounded by women. They used to line up along the corridor in hotels, like a sort of buffet. Pick and mix, they used to call it."

"How horrible."

"I quite liked it at first. I could walk in and nobody would take any notice, because they were all completely focused on the Band. It was relaxing in a way, although it used to drive Max crazy."

"Yes, I can imagine that."

"But I knew he'd fuck it up, sooner or later. I was getting bored with him or I'd have sorted it out. You can always sort them out, if you really want to."

"It probably helps if you look like you do."

She laughs. "Maybe, but you know what I mean: you're only a victim if you want to be—my mum taught me that. It's hard sometimes, but that's the way it is; you just have to refuse to let it get to you. It's really bad karma if you let things diminish you."

Oh, God, I hope she's not going to start on about crystals or energy fields.

She smiles. "Nothing anyone does can really hurt you, unless you let it."

"Right. Nothing at all?"

"No."

I wonder if she'll still feel that way after she's had the baby. I'm guessing she might find a whole new chasm of vulnerability has opened up overnight, and there's no way she'll be able to karma her way out of it, however hard she tries. But I don't think I'll mention it, because apart from anything else, I don't like annoying people, whatever Archie might think.

"I still think it probably helps if you look as good as you do."

She smiles again. "Do you think you'd be divorced now, if, you know, if he'd still been around?"

"Yes, I think so."

"And he'd have wanted access?"

"I suppose so. God, I'd have hated that."

"Thank God Jimmy's not playing that game."

"Won't he be involved at all, then?"

As soon as I've said this, I realize I've crossed the invisible line.

"We'll see."

We watch the boys, who are still playing with the hoops, although they're slowing down now, and one of Archie's armbands is deflating, so he's gone rather lopsided.

"Are you hungry?"

"No, we ate before we came."

"Well, I'm starving." She picks up the phone and tells Sam she's hungry.

"Are you sure you don't want anything?"

I think this might be our cue to leave.

"No, really, I should be getting them home. But thank you, Grace, they've had a lovely time."

Archie's very tired and grumpy, like he always is after swimming, but at least this time we're not shivering in a chilly Formica cubicle while we get dressed, and he falls asleep in the car, much to Jack's amusement.

"I like it when he's asleep."

"Do you, love?"

"Yes. It's nice and quiet. Can we have stories when we get home?"

"Yes, if you get into bed quickly."

I manage to get Archie upstairs and into bed without any major dramas, and Jack's half asleep by the time I finish the first story. I'm back downstairs, sitting in front of the fire and trying not to fall asleep until I've finished writing my shopping list for the party, when Ellen rings.

"So has this Reg person got any young friends, then?"

"What, a former captain of the Bowls Club?"

"No, a nice handsome stranger who doesn't want to take you home to meet his mother."

"There's not much chance of that around here: I'd probably already know his mother, if he was a local, and they don't stay strangers for long. Before you know it, they're moaning about the way you cook bacon."

"You'll miss out on an awful lot of fun if you go on thinking like that."

"Maybe. But it makes my mornings much more relaxing."

She laughs. "You must miss the sex, though."

"Ellen!"

"Oh, please. You must."

"Well, I don't, not really. It just became part of the routine after a while; nice but nothing earth-shattering. There was one time, ages ago, when he came home in the middle of the night, and I was half asleep and I thought he was a burglar. But apart from that, no, not really."

"You thought you were shagging a burglar and you didn't wake up?"

"You know what I mean. It was unexpected, like when we first started seeing each other. But most of the time it was just sort of ordinary; comforting but ordinary, like the decaf version of the real thing."

"With blinding headaches if you have the real thing by mistake. Bloody hell, so I've got years of crap sex to look forward to."

"Not crap, just not amazing. You get used to someone, you're bound to. And anyway, I don't think I'm a terribly good example. I mean, he was sleeping with someone else, which can't be a very good sign. So maybe it was just me. I think he must have been quite lonely, you know. I know I was."

"What's brought all this on?"

"Something Grace was saying, about how you're only a victim if you want to be."

"Right. And she'd know, I suppose, looking like she does.

It's easy not being a victim if you've got all the power and all the money."

"I suppose so."

"I bloody know so, so you might as well just get out there and have some fun. Let's go shopping when you're up with your gran. That always works for me."

"Maybe."

"So that's a no, then?"

"I could do with some new boots."

"Hallelujah! Right, I'll be your stylist for the day. This is going to be so great."

By the time she's finished listing all the things I should be buying, I'm having a mini–panic attack.

"Don't forget we're meant to be shopping for Gran. And I want to get a present for Connie and Mark, for making Jack's cake."

"We can go to Liberty's—you're bound to find something there."

"I was thinking more M and S."

"Well, bloody stop it."

It's Saturday afternoon and it's Party Day, much to everyone's relief, because I don't think Jack could take much more party anticipation. He's already been in tears twice this morning, and Archie's not really helping since he's insisting on wearing his Spider-Man outfit.

"Yes, but it's not a dressing-up party, tell him, Mum."

"It doesn't matter, Jack."

"Well, I don't want him to come, then."

"Jack. Calm down."

He gives me a furious look and bounces off upstairs, while I carry on putting out Halloween paper plates; I've already hung up streamers and balloons, and solved my incendiary issues with the pumpkins by getting some small battery-operated candles from one of my catalogs. I've used them in the pumpkins inside the shop window, too, and they look great in the afternoon when it starts to get dark. We've moved all the furniture in the living room so there's more space, and anything breakable is upstairs, so I think we're all set: at least living in such a shabby house means it doesn't matter if anyone spills anything.

Mr. Pallfrey's outside, putting the final touches to the bonfire, with Trevor running round in circles with pieces of stick, and Gran's in the kitchen, making sausage rolls.

"I've done some cheese straws, too, they're in the oven."

"Thanks, Gran."

"Shall I go and give the boys a quick wash and brushup, then?"

"Great. I'll be up in a minute."

I'm feeling unusually coordinated today: I'm wearing my new boots, with my new dark green corduroy skirt and a green tweedy cardigan that I knitted last year. The shopping trip with Gran and Ellen was just as traumatic as I knew it was going to be, with Ellen doing her homage to Trinny & Susannah, although thankfully without insisting on seeing anyone in their pants. But I did end up with this skirt, and a brown velvet one, and two new vest tops, and Gran's now fully equipped for Dining Aboard, although she still wants to get a new suitcase, so it was definitely worth it. Betty got herself a new coat, and Ellen found a pair of beautiful suede platform shoes that she completely fell in love with, so she got them in three different colors, which gave us all a vicarious thrill. The highlight was definitely tea at the Ritz, which I'd booked as a last-minute surprise for Gran, who almost burst into tears she was so pleased; and even though it cost an absolute fortune, it was a real treat, and not just for the moment when the cakes arrived. Betty spent so long in the ladies' we thought we'd never get her out, and Ellen had to autograph two women's menus, and then they took pictures of us with their mobile phones, which Gran loved.

She's been busy with her comb when I go upstairs, and the boys have their hair slicked back with matching center parts.

"Are you sure you want to wear your Spider-Man outfit, Archie?"

"Yes, and Gran said I could, so you can't make me change it."

She laughs. "It was either that or have him in his vest and pants."

Jack giggles.

"All right, if you're really sure, but nobody else will be dressing up. You know that, don't you?"

"Well, I can be the winner, then. And I can help bring in the cake, can't I, Mum?"

"Yes, if you're sensible."

Jack doesn't look convinced.

"But don't let him hold it, Mum, or he might drop it on purpose."

Archie looks shocked. "No, I wouldn't. I'd never do that."

Gran gives him a kiss. "Of course you wouldn't, pet."

Actually, he would, but never mind.

The doorbell rings, and Jack freezes. "They're here, they're here."

It's Sophie Lewis, with her mum, and she's brought Molly Taylor with her, and they're both wearing party frocks and clutching presents.

Sophie's mum smiles. "They've got their coats, for the bonfire later. And I'll pick them up at seven, is that right?"

"Yes."

"Gosh, you are brave, having them all here."

She beats a hasty retreat as Jane Johnson arrives with a gaggle of small boys.

"Tom's dad will pick them up. Do you need a hand or anything?"

I've always thought Jane was particularly nice, and now she's just confirmed it. Offering to help at someone else's children's party is definitely gold star behavior, unless you're on very strong medication.

"I think it's all under control. For now."

She laughs. "Have a large gin. It'll help no end."

Bloody hell. The noise is incredible. We're playing Blind Vampire's Bluff, and we've already done Pinning the Tail on the Monster, and Pass the Pumpkin Parcel, and two rounds of Musical Chairs, and Archie and Nelly are now "helping" Gran in the kitchen, which is very brave of her, while Tina takes Travis upstairs because one of his front teeth has just come out, with copious amounts of blood, which he's loving. Connie's outside with Mr. Pallfrey, hanging up outdoor fairy lights; she's put the Cake in the kitchen, and it's totally fabulous. There are candles inside it, in a hollowed-out section at the top, and it's got windows, so we'll be able to see them flickering before I take the lid off for the birthday boy to blow them out. It's the cleverest thing I've ever seen, and Connie says the orange icing is delicious, and Nelly's already ordered one for her birthday, only in pink, so Mark's thinking strawberries. Or possibly a giant peach.

Tina comes back down with Travis, and we start playing Musical Statues, which goes down rather well until Nelly wobbles onto Marco and makes him move, and he refuses to be out because it wasn't his fault, and they both go into torrents of Italian, which is clearly their language of choice for Bickers. Everyone's terribly impressed, particularly Archie, who seems very taken with all the hand gestures and starts doing some arm waving of his own, and it takes another round of Pass the Parcel to restore the peace, so now I've got only one parcel left; and I've learned from bitter experience that you can never have enough Mystery Parcels when it comes to birthday parties, so it's all rather nerve-racking, and I'm sure we've got more children than we started with.

Gran announces the food's ready, so they swarm into the dining room and everything turns into a blur of pouring out glasses of apple juice and trying to stop Archie and Nelly having a sword fight with the cocktail sticks from their sausages. There's a lull of about three minutes when I drink a hasty cup of tea and Connie takes over the juice patrol, and then it's time to do the Cake.

"Shall I turn the lights off, dear?"

"Yes, Gran. Just give me a minute to light the candles."

I carry the Cake in on its silver cake board, staggering slightly because it weighs a ton, with Archie holding a tea towel and walking ahead of me so he feels like he's got a proper job, and we all sing "Happy Birthday" and everyone claps.

Jack goes very pink and wide-eyed as he stands up to blow the candles out.

"Make a wish, sweetheart."

"I already have."

He looks at me. I really hope he's not going to say something about Daddy, because if he does, I think I might burst into tears. Gran's standing behind him, looking pretty close to tears herself.

He smiles, and I give him a hug.

"Shall I tell you what my wish was?"

"You're meant to keep it a secret, but you can tell me if you really want to."

Please let it not be anything about Nick. Please.

"I wished for a dog of our very own, like Trevor. Only a puppy."

"Oh, right."

Gran smiles. "Shall we cut your cake up then, pet, and give everybody a piece?"

"Yes, please. And I can have a really big bit, can't I, because I'm the birthday boy?"

"Yes, lovey, you can."

I'm in the kitchen with Connie eating a large slice of cake, which is even more delicious than I thought it would be, when more people start arriving with presents; Elsie and Jeffrey and Martin, and Maggie, and Linda and her teenage daughter,

Lauren, who's wearing the shortest miniskirt I've ever seen, with sheepskin boots, and Angela Prentice, which is rather surprising because I didn't think she'd come, with a little present done up in train wrapping paper, and Betty and Mrs. Davis, who both disappear into the kitchen and keep threatening to start on the washing up while Gran makes them a cup of tea. Tina's husband, Fireman Graham, is outside helping Mr. Pallfrey light the bonfire, using approved Fire Brigade techniques, which seem to rely on lots of twigs and rolled-up sheets of newspaper rather than chucking half a can of petrol on it and then running away.

I open the French doors in the dining room so we can go in and out with plates of food, while Mark warms up a saucepan of butternut squash soup with cinnamon, with Nelly climbing up his leg while he doles out bowlfuls. Archie announces he loves orange food and will only be eating orange things from now on, and then it all goes a bit *Lord of the Flies*, particularly when we do the lucky dip, which seemed like a good alternative to party bags when I first thought of it, but in reality means I end up with sawdust all over the garden. The toffee apples go down very well, though, especially for jousting and dueling purposes; although they're not ideal if you take the cellophane wrappers off and then accidentally drop them back in the box of sawdust.

We stand watching Graham and Mr. Pallfrey guarding the bonfire and trying to stop the occasional shower of sparks from burning down the hedge. Cath and Olivia arrive, along with Cath's son, Toby, who's only fourteen but at least six foot two, with a very determined quiff in his hair, which seems to work for Lauren, who sidles up to him and starts chatting and giggling, which makes him go bright red. I volunteer Elsie for sparkler sentry duty while I collect up plates and try to stop Archie throwing baked potatoes into the bonfire because some idiot's told him they'll explode and he's desperate to have a go, and then Martin helps Mr. Pallfrey light the fireworks. They're fairly modest, thank God, but they get a very enthusiastic response, particularly from Trevor, who's having a fabulous time, stealing the occasional sausage and dragging Travis and a small boy called Philip round the garden, since they seem to have volunteered to try to keep hold of him. Elsie's making everyone with a sparkler stand arm lengths apart, with no poking anybody's hood, and only four at a time. She's got a bucket of water at the ready for anyone who Starts Being Silly, and they have to form a queue or she won't light their sparklers: I knew she'd be the perfect person to bring a bit of order to the chaos.

Martin comes over with a bucket of used fireworks: he's taken his bobble hat off, and his hair is sticking up in tufts. "I thought I'd better get rid of these, shall I put them in your bin?"

"Great. Thanks, Martin."

"There's a couple that didn't go off, but I've soaked them in water, so they should be fine. Just don't throw any lighted matches in the bin."

I'm having visions of my rubbish being airborne now.

"I'll try to remember that."

"I wanted a quick word, actually."

Excellent. This is the perfect time to be talking about Wood. "Oh yes?"

"I want to go in tomorrow to give them another coat of wax. Mum says I can use her keys, but I wanted to check that it was okay with you first."

"Of course, that's fine, and you must tell me what I owe you."

"You can pay me when I've finished. I've still got a few more bits to do."

"Well, if you're sure."

He smiles. "Did you have a nice supper with your friends? Fish pie, wasn't it?"

"Yes, although we all drank a bit too much and Ellen wanted to play strip poker, so you were probably better off with your hot pot."

He smiles again, but he sort of flinches, too. Damn, I didn't mean it to sound like that.

"I'm not sure your mum would approve of strip poker, would she?"

Christ, I'm just making it worse now.

"No, probably not, although what she does or doesn't approve of isn't exactly top of my list, you know."

"Of course not. I didn't mean—"

"No, I know you didn't, sorry. It just gets to me a bit, living at home. Still, the divorce will be through soon, and then I can get a place of my own."

"Will you stay around here?"

"Yes, I like it. It was nice to get away, move somewhere else, but now I'm back I realize how much I like it here. The way people talk to each other, you feel part of something, don't you?"

"Yes, you do."

"So if you hear of anywhere, especially anywhere with space for a workroom, I'd be really grateful."

"Sure. I'll keep a lookout."

"And I'll be in tomorrow, to do the shelves."

"Thanks, Martin. Archie, stop doing that. If you throw any more potatoes, you'll have to go back inside the house."

"I'm only playing."

"Archie."

"Okay, okay, keep your hair on. That's what Marco says, sometimes, to his mum."

"He does not."

Martin tries not to smile. "I'll just put these in the bin."

Tina's standing laughing as I collect up a few more plates.

"Just look at my Graham. He usually gets really twitchy round bonfires. We've got so many smoke alarms in our house, whenever I do him a steak the whole house goes off. It's terrible. But he doesn't seem bothered tonight; it's probably the dog, he's always saying we should get one."

"Well, have a word with Mr. Pallfrey, and I'm sure he'll let you borrow Trevor any time you want."

"No thanks. I got bitten by my aunty May's Jack Russell when I was little, and it put me right off. But look at my Travis, he's loving it. And I meant to say, Jo, thanks for asking him today. He was so pleased, getting his own invitation. He made me put it up on his bedroom wall, you know. Not that many people ask him to parties."

"He's been lovely."

"That's why I came with him. He gets a bit overexcited sometimes."

Archie runs past us, waving a toffee apple and a sausage, and joins the back of the sparkler queue.

"They all do, Tina."

She smiles.

Jack comes over, looking very happy.

"I love it in our new house, it's much better than stupid old London. Can I have a party like this one next year, Mum?"

"I expect so."

"Are there any more sparklers, because we're nearly running out."

"I think I've got a few more packets. I'll go and get them."

"Well, hurry up, because I want another go."

He gives me a hug. "This is my best day ever, Mum."

I walk round to the garage and open the boot of the car, where I've stashed the extra sparklers, feeling a weird mixture of relief and exhaustion; I always get a bit maudlin at some point on their birthdays, Nick used to call it my Flash-Forward Panic Button. One minute they're tiny and you're trying to work out how to get their clothes over their heads without pulling, and suddenly they're telling you about their Best Days Ever, like those depressing ads for mortgages where you see the young couple going into their first flat and then five seconds later they're playing with their grandchildren in a sunlit garden. It all goes so bloody quickly. Nick would have loved seeing them today, happy with all their new friends; he'd have really loved it.

I'm closing the boot of the car when I realize I'm crying, with no warning at all, and I can't seem to stop. I don't want anyone to hear me so I stand with my hand over my mouth, which only makes it worse. Oh, God. There's the sound of footsteps as someone walks past the garage door, and then stops. Damn. Please let it be Connie or Gran, and not one of the kids.

It's Angela Prentice.

"Are you all right, dear? I'm so sorry, I was just leaving, I didn't mean to intrude."

"I don't know what's the matter with me. It's just . . ." Oh, God, it's getting worse.

She puts her arms round me. "My dear, I'm so sorry. You've been so brave."

I try to wipe my face.

"Not really. It's just Nick would have loved this, so much."

I'm off again. Christ, I've got to get a grip, and preferably sooner rather than later. I try to smile, but I don't think either of us is convinced.

"I'm very proud of my daughter, too, I really am, and her partner, Sally. They've been so brave about finding a clinic."

Bingo. I appear to have stopped crying.

"And now the baby's nearly here. It's very important to tell people how proud you are of them, isn't it? I listen at the meetings every week, and you're all always showing your children how much you love them and how proud you are of them, I hear it all the time in the way you talk about them, all of you. I seem to have let Peter get in the way of that over the years. But it's never too late, dear, is it?"

"No, it's never too late."

"Because things happen, don't they, dear?"

"Yes."

"It's nobody's fault, they just happen."

"Yes."

She hugs me.

"Are you sure you're all right now? I can stay with you, or go and find your grandmother."

"I'm fine now, I think. But thanks, Angela."

She smiles. "No, thank you. You can't imagine what a difference it's made to me, coming along every week."

"I'm so glad."

"I'd better let you get back to your guests, but thank you, it's been a lovely party."

I walk her to the gate and then go back up the path, holding the packets of sparklers. I wonder if Penny's already heard the good news that her mum is undergoing something of a transformation. It'll be just what she needs when she has the baby. How lovely. I bet Angela's going to make a lovely gran.

The final sparklers get a rapturous reception, and then parents start arriving to collect their children, and things begin to calm down, thank God. Even Trevor's having a nice little lie-down.

Linda gives me a kiss as she's leaving. "Best party I've been to in ages."

"If that's true, you probably need to get out more."

She laughs. "No, it was. Fun, lovely food, and nobody having a fight. Perfect. Night, love."

It's nearly half past ten by the time everyone's finally gone, and Archie's fast asleep on the sofa. The last time I tried to carry him up the stairs I nearly collapsed halfway up, so I walk him up half asleep.

"Thunderbirds Are Go."

"Into bed, darling."

"I'm too tired to be in my bed tonight, Mum."

I know the feeling.

"Can I be in your bed?"

"All right. But just for tonight."

Jack follows us in and climbs into bed.

"Ooh, the sheets are all lovely and warm."

I check the electric blanket, which is on. And I didn't put it on. So Gran must have sneaked up and done it earlier.

"Mum?"

"Yes?"

"This has been my best day ever."

"That's good. Sleep time now, love."

"Has it been your best day?"

There's mud all over the floor downstairs, and I've got a feeling we'll be finding bits of sausage and toffee apple in all sorts of unusual places in the next few days, but yes, on balance, I think we can safely say it's been one of my better days.

"Yes. Go to sleep, love."

He smiles. "Soon it'll be Bonfire Night, and then it'll be Christmas, won't it?"

"Yes."

Christmas. God, I'd forgotten about Christmas.

Archie turns over and mutters, "Thunderbirds Are Go."

I know just how he feels.

7

TWINKLE, TWINKLE, LITTLE STAR

It's half past ten on a Monday morning, and my Christmas shopping list is getting longer by the minute. Gran's just called to recite the list of things she's packing on her cruise for the umpteenth time, if only she could find the perfect suitcase; we're off to Bluewater on Thursday, and if she can't find one I'll get one of those old-fashioned steamer trunks and lock her inside it until it's time for her to leave, because if we have one more conversation about whether it might be chilly in the evenings and how many cardigans she should take with her, I think I'm going to scream. And once we've addressed the Luggage Issue, I've still got to buy Christmas presents for practically everyone and their dog—literally, in the case of Mr. Pallfrey. I'm thinking a high-powered rifle and some tranquilizer darts might be good, but the boys want to get him a squeaky toy.

I've made a start on the packing for Venice, so there are piles of clothes all over the spare bed, and Mum keeps texting me lists of extra things she'd like me to bring over, which is Vin's fault because he should never have taught her how to text in the first place. But at least he realizes what an epic mistake he's made, because she's currently got him on a mission to find Gentleman's Relish, and some special kind of cracker that comes in a pale yellow box, only she can't remember the name, which given that he's still on a boat somewhere off the coast of Australia, might be something of a challenge.

I'm in the shop doing a quick stock check with Elsie, before I go to the supermarket to try to find Dad's favorite brand of marmalade, which Mum thinks is called Extra Chunky Orange, only she's not sure, when the door opens and Annabel Morgan walks in, with Gina Preston, who's secretary of the PTA and always wears her hair up in a bun. They look around and smile at each other, in a superior kind of way, which has Elsie bristling before they've even put their bags down.

"Such lovely colors, and your window display is so sweet."

I think Annabel's probably being sarcastic. I've got to admit I've gone rather overboard with the Christmas window, what with Elsie's knitted Christmas tree, and the Nativity scene and the knitted Advent calendar, surrounded by cotton wool and swathes of net and sparkly fabric, which all took ages to arrange, with the boys helping me by sprinkling large amounts of glitter everywhere, including inside my handbag. But the new fairy lights are lovely, and we've sold stacks of wool to people wanting to make their own Advent calendars, so I don't really care what snooty people like Annabel think.

She gets a notebook out of her bag and writes something down; Dreadful Lack of Taste, probably. I bet she's got everything beautifully color-coordinated at her house.

"Mrs. Chambers was telling us all about your little knitting project at the planning meeting last night, and I must say it sounds terribly ambitious."

She smiles, but it's not a very friendly smile.

"I was rather wondering, though, and I do hope you don't mind my asking, but do you have any formal training? We know you run your little group here, of course, but it's not quite the same thing, is it?"

She's giving me a very determined look, and Gina Preston takes a step backward.

"I think I'll just be helping out."

"Mrs. Chambers said you'd be forming a working group to establish a program for the whole school. As chair of the PTA, that does of course come under my remit. You'll be meeting in the new year, I take it? Do you have a date fixed?" She opens her diary.

Oh, God.

"Not yet."

"Well, do feel free to call on me, because I am rather experienced with this kind of thing, and proper presentation is so important when it concerns the education of our children, don't you agree?"

Gina's nodding so vigorously I think her bun might fall down.

Elsie stands a bit closer to me behind the counter.

"I'm sure Jo will manage. She used to be a top news producer on the television, you know, so I think she probably picked up a trick or two on paperwork and suchlike, don't you?"

Top news producer? I must have missed that bit. I remember the frantic news producer running up and down corridors clutching bits of tape, but I think the top bit must have happened while I was in the canteen with Ellen.

Annabel's clearly Not Happy. Very Not Happy, as Archie would say.

"Well, do let me know if you need any advice, because we must keep our standards as high as possible, and I'm always happy to help."

In other words, she's always happy to take the credit for other people's ideas.

"Now, there was one other little thing. I gather Grace Harrison shops here?"

Elsie seizes on her new Specialist Subject.

"Would you like to see the pieces from the newspaper? I've got them in my bag."

Annabel smiles. "No, thank you. My cleaning lady showed them to me."

Elsie stiffens.

"Does Miss Harrison come to your knitting group?"

"She doesn't really come into the shop."

Annabel exchanges a triumphant glance with Gina.

"No, I thought perhaps she didn't."

Elsie folds her arms. "No, Jo goes to her house, on a regular basis, for private consultations."

There's a small intake of breath from Annabel, and a distinct gleam in her eye as she turns to me.

"And I suppose the house is absolutely gorgeous? Is the furniture very modern?"

I think I'm meant to deliver top details, which she can trade on at her dinner parties, but luckily Elsie seems happy to continue in her new role as my official spokeswoman.

"I'm afraid we can't talk about it, because of confidentiality, you know. We do have to protect the privacy of our celebrity customers—I'm sure you understand. Now, can I help you with anything? Only we are quite busy this morning."

Blimey. Elsie's smiling, and there's a small silence, until Annabel says she's written to Grace to ask her to open our Spring Fair, but she's had a reply from some woman saying Grace can't be available on that day, so if I could just mention it that would be excellent, and I nod vaguely and there's an awkward silence until Gina rallies and says she's thinking of making a cardigan for her daughter, Fleur.

"Do you have any hundred percent cotton?"

I show her where the cottons are. Fleur's in the same class as Archie, and Horrible Harry, who's recently taken up Nipping, but only when he thinks the teacher isn't looking, although luckily he's still giving Archie and Nelly a wide berth, so I'm hoping there won't be any more pushing incidents.

Elsie's standing guard by the till, while Annabel halfheartedly looks at some of the mohair.

"This is a pretty color."

"Yes, that's the mohair we used for the shawls for Miss Harrison. You'll need four balls if you're making one."

Annabel pretends to ignore her but starts looking at all the different colors in earnest. A courier van screeches to a halt outside the shop, and a man in blue uniform bounds in, carrying a large padded envelope. I'm guessing it must be the shade cards that I ordered for new winter tweed, only they don't usually send things by courier. There's a flat white cardboard box inside the envelope, and Elsie watches as I open it, and then we both look at the set of beautiful black-and-white photographs of me sitting with Grace in the rowing boat, wrapped in my cardigan, with both of us laughing. There's a scribbled note on thick cream card: "Thanks for supper. Thought you might like these. Daniel."

"What lovely photographs." Annabel's leaning over the counter.

Elsie shuts the box.

"Yes, aren't they? So will that be four balls of the pink, then? It's quite a complicated pattern until you get the hang of it, so do feel free to pop in if you get stuck or anything. We'll be more than happy to help."

"Thank you but I'm quite an experienced knitter."

She hands Elsie her credit card.

"Well, we're here if you need us. Jo's often out with her private clients, of course, but I'm always here."

Christ, they look like they might start slapping each other in a minute. I think I'll go upstairs and look at the photos properly.

"I'll take these up, Elsie, and put the kettle on, shall I?"

"Right you are, dear."

I look at the photos while the kettle's boiling, and they're fabulous; what a nice thing for him to do. I dial the number on the card, and the phone's answered by someone sounding rather annoyed.

"What?"

"Daniel?"

"Yes. Who is this? I'm trying to get some fucking work done."

"It's Jo Mackenzie, I was just calling to say thank you for the photographs. They're absolutely beautiful, but I'll call back another time if you're busy."

"No, sorry, I thought you were from the agency. Hang on a minute."

There's a muffled sound in the background, and then he comes back on the line.

"Right, that's better. I got your address from Maxine. I thought you'd probably be in the shop. So you like them?"

"They're amazing, I normally look terrible in photographs, you've got no idea. Grace looks very relaxed. I suppose that's because she didn't know you were taking them?"

"Oh, she knew all right. She can spot a camera a mile off, and she'd have soon let me know if she wasn't up for it."

"Well, that was nice of her. I'm really glad she didn't tell me, though, or I'd have been doing my special Photograph Smiles. I do one where I look like I've just had a big shock, and another one where I look like I'm about to vomit."

"And do you alternate?"

"I try to."

"Good for you, it's important to vary your look. Yes, I won't be a minute. Christ, can I call you back, Jo? The models are getting humpy, and they've been a total nightmare all morning."

"Of course."

"Great. Talk to you later then."

What a nice man.

I take the tea downstairs and let Elsie have a proper look at the photos.

She's clearly itching to show them off.

"We could put them up in the shop, like in those restaurants, where they put up paper napkins signed by all their famous customers. Wouldn't that be lovely?"

"Maybe."

I've never really seen the point of the framed napkins thing; the signatures are always from people you've never heard of. Either way, it always ends up looking slightly tragic. But she's not giving up.

"We could put up photos of all our famous customers."

"What, like Mrs. Marwell?"

"Well, there's your friend Ellen, and we could put other ones up, too. Your gran's got a picture of you knitting, sitting on her settee, when you were little. She showed me when she was sorting through her albums, you've got your white school socks on, it's ever so sweet, and there's some of the shop, years ago."

"Actually, you might be right, Elsie. A collection of pictures of the shop would be rather good, and I could take some of the kids at school, too, once we get started on the knitting, and the Stitch and Bitch group. And we could do with something on the walls upstairs, they still look too bare."

She looks very pleased.

"That Mrs. Morgan's a terrible woman, isn't she? I don't know who she thinks she is, I really don't. Just because she's got one of those big houses up on the Estate, she thinks she's Lady Muck. She's always upsetting people, and she'd hate it if there was a picture of you and Grace Harrison up in the shop."

"True."

We both smile.

The supermarket doesn't yield anything remotely familiar in the chunky marmalade department, and the boys attempt a pasta boycott at supper, which is tricky since it's macaroni cheese, so I'm sitting knitting flower brooches and feeling rather shattered when Ellen calls. She's been out to another drinks party, and she's got lots of gossip to share.

I tell her about the photos. "Wasn't that kind of him? It really made my morning. Annabel Morgan was in, trying to put the frighteners on me again, although God knows why."

"Because you've shown up on her radar, that's why. She's just another playground bully, and you know how to deal with them, don't you?"

"Run away?"

"Outflank, outmaneuver, and then retreat to gloat."

"Yes, well, thank you, Lucrezia Borgia."

"Darling, where's the fun in letting her get away with it? She'll just get worse and worse if you don't stand up to her—people like her will knock you flat if you let them. The only way you'll get her off your case is if you frighten her off.

Now, talking of being knocked flat, what are you going to say to Fitzcarraldo when he rings back?"

"Nothing. Thanks, that kind of thing. It's no big deal, Ellen, he's only being friendly."

"Christ, what does he have to do? Take out a full-page ad in *Knitting Weekly*? What will you do if he asks you out for a drink?"

"What, next time he's in Broadgate, as opposed to New York, or Milan, or wherever he's off to next?"

"We definitely should have played strip poker, and then we'd know."

"Yes, well, I already know, thank you very much, and I'm very glad we didn't."

"We'll see. How are the texts from your mum going?"

"Hopeless. She's got me searching for marmalade now."

"Mine wants to know if I want a wok, from Aunty Paula."

"Doesn't she know you never cook?"

"Yes, but she thinks that's because I haven't got the right equipment. She got me some steamer thing last year that I've never even had out of the box. It's so annoying. You should try Fortnum and Mason for the marmalade, they're bound to have something."

"I was rather hoping to avoid buying the world's most expensive marmalade, but it might come to that."

"They're a fucking nightmare, mothers, aren't they?"

"Yes. If I ever get like that with the boys, I want you to promise you'll shoot me."

"I promise. But Archie would soon put you straight, don't worry, and anyway it's different for daughters; they seem to save all the real madness for us girls."

"I'm not so sure about that. Mine gets pretty twilight zone with Vin, too."

"Yes, but she's an exceptional case, your mother. She's always been barking mad. Now, let's talk about something much more important: my Christmas present. Have you got it yet?"

"No."

"You have, I know you have. Give me a hint."

Ellen loves getting presents; it's one of her favorite things. I've knitted her a shawl in sage green, which is one of her top colors at the moment, with tiny green beads around the edge.

"It will keep you warm on long winter nights."

"Johnny Depp in his pirate costume?"

"Yes."

"Excellent. Wrap him up and bike him straight over, would you? I could do with a treat, and Harry won't be home for ages."

Mr. Pallfrey's limp is getting worse, so we've taken Trevor for a few trial runs after school, before the official launch of Operation Dog Walk, and so far it's been going every bit as badly as I knew it would. He's fairly sedate at first, especially if the boys are holding his lead, but when we get to the beach, or the path leading up to the cliffs, he practically loops the loop, especially if he spots a seagull; and there's always a bloody seagull somewhere. We're on the beach today because the cliff path's muddy, and the tide's out, so it's all rather beautiful; very *French Lieutenant's Woman*, only with more fleece and less billowing silk.

Trevor's racing along when we see Lady Denby with Algie and Clarkson. Terrific; I bet she'll be giving me unsolicited canine tips before I get the chance to tell her he isn't my bloody dog.

"You mustn't let him pull you along like that. Oh, it's you, the knitting girl."

I'm quite pleased to be called a girl, but I'm rather dreading the lecture.

"Not yours, is he? Belongs to that man Plumley, doesn't he?"

"Mr. Pallfrey, yes."

"We see him quite often. Always running."

Jack smiles at her.

"We're helping him with Trevor, because he's got a sore leg."

She nods, then turns back to me, looking friendly but determined. Bugger.

"Well, I'll tell you how you can really help him, shall I? You can train his dog properly for him."

"I don't know all that much about dogs, to be honest."

"Any fool can see that."

We both look at Trevor, who's lounging on the sand and panting, looking like a rather scruffy foal.

"Right. Here's what you do. When he pulls on the lead, lean back and say, 'Heel.' Root yourself to the spot. It's absolutely vital you don't move at that point. Then, as soon as you get him back beside you, walk on slowly, and have a bit of spare sausage in your pocket to give him. It will encourage him. Always works."

Put a bit of sausage in my pocket, is she Mad? Archie would soon take care of anything spare in the sausage department.

"He walks very nicely for the boys."

"That's because he's playing with you. They're intelligent animals, dogs. Clarkson, stop that."

Clarkson is now lying down next to Trevor, looking totally dwarfed, and giving him a very flirty gaze. Suddenly he sits up.

"Blast. He's seen a rabbit up in the dunes."

There's a tangle of leads as Algie and Clarkson both make a break for it, and while she's sorting them out, Clarkson manages to give her the slip, closely followed by Trevor, who soon overtakes him.

"Oh dear."

I give Lady Denby what I hope is a supercilious look, but she produces a piercing whistle from the pocket of her Barbour and blows it twice. Miraculously, Clarkson slows down, then turns and comes back, looking like a sulky teenager who's just been told to turn his music down.

"Now remember, you'll be doing him a favor if you nip it in the bud."

"If he ever comes back, that is."

She smiles and sets off back toward the pier, while the boys run ahead to try to catch Trevor. They're having a lovely time running up and down yelling, and now it's starting to spit with rain. Christ.

My phone rings. If this is Mum with another Mystery Shopping Item, I think she'll be finding I'm Not in the Mood.

"Yes?"

"Is this a bad time?"

It's Daniel.

"No, sorry, it's just I'm out on the beach and Trevor's run off again. And Lady Denby says I've got to keep sausages in my pockets."

He laughs. "How attractive. Handy for picnics, though. Can you whistle?"

"No. Can you?"

"Yes, but I'm not sure he'll hear me from Berlin."

"True. God, I hate that bloody dog. The boys have gone after him, so that'll be all three of them covered in sand, and it's starting to rain. But apart from that it's all going brilliantly. How are you?"

"Wishing I'd got a dog, that's for sure. How's the shop going?"

"Quite busy, which is great, although we keep having to reorder stock at the last minute, because I haven't got a proper system worked out yet. But we're getting there."

"And how's Grace?"

"Great. Getting more pregnant-looking by the day, and more beautiful. It's so unfair; most people go all puffy, but she just looks more stunning. And I've been volunteered to do a knitting project at the kids' school."

"That sounds like fun."

"I'll put you down for Wednesday afternoons, then, shall I?"

He laughs again. "So all's well by the sea, then?"

"Yes, pretty much, and thanks so much for the photographs, Daniel. It was really kind of you."

"I wanted to thank you for that supper. You saved my life: I'm allergic to hotels like that one. How's your friend Ellen?"

"Great, but she keeps trying to find out what I've got her for Christmas."

"Are you getting her one of those Goats for Peace things I keep reading about in the papers?"

"No, mainly because she'd kill me. I got one for the boys, though, and they send you a little card with a picture on, it's terribly sweet. I got them a flock of chickens for an orphan in Africa, so at least they'll be getting one useful thing this year, in among all the plastic."

"What a great idea. I could get something like that for my lot. They could call it the Fitzgerald Flock."

"I meant to ask you, about the photographs, would the magazine people mind if I show them to people?"

"No, of course not. Just don't sell them to the papers, or they'll get very pissed off."

"Elsie's desperate to put one up in the shop."

"That's fine by me. So are you all set for Christmas?"

"No, I'm not, and if you've already got everything wrapped up on top of your wardrobe, please don't tell me; I haven't even started on most of mine yet."

"I usually do most of my gift panicking at the airport, so the chickens are going to be a real departure, especially for my mum. Are you still off to Venice for the duration?"

"Yes. Unless I can invent a mystery illness."

"I might be there myself at some point. We've got a rush job on and I need to meet the client, but I'm not sure about dates yet. If it works out, perhaps we could have a coffee or something. I'd like to see what your boys make of Florian's. Do they like hot chocolate?"

"Has the Pope got a balcony?"

"Any sign of the Wonder Dog yet?"

"No, but something dog-shaped has just run into the sea, miles up the beach, and I'm really hoping it's not him."

"Well, I'd better let you go and investigate then. Good luck."

"Thanks."

How nice; I knew he was just being friendly. And if he is in Venice at the same time as us, I might ask him to take some pictures of the boys for me. I could have my camera with me and ask him casually. It would be great to have some really decent photographs of them, although I should probably get a black-and-white film just in case, because I'm not sure professional photographers are that keen on free Bonusprint color films.

The boys have finally caught up with Trevor, who's covered in bits of gorse and looking very pleased with himself.

I grab his lead and wrap it round my hand. "Off we go, Trevor."

He lies down.

"Heel."

I tug at the lead, and he looks up at me and yawns. I pull a bit harder, and he narrows his eyes.

"Please, Trevor."

I pat my leg in what I hope is an encouraging manner, and he rolls onto his back. The boys start to laugh.

"Right. That's it. Let's start walking up the beach."

I drop the lead. "Naughty dog."

The boys roll their eyes but start walking, recognizing the telltale signs of Mother Close to Meltdown.

Trevor lopes along behind us, and Archie starts to giggle. "He's following us, Mum."

"Is he? Well, just ignore him. He's being very naughty."

They both sigh, and carry on walking.

"Why are you being such a grumpypotamus?"

Grumpypotamus is one of Archie's favorite new words, along with *catatonic*, which he overheard me saying to Ellen on the phone, and which he thinks is an alcoholic drink, and *masticate*, which he keeps saying at inopportune moments, like when we're standing in the queue at the baker's. But I know if I tell him I'm not keen on being compared to a bad-tempered hippopotamus, especially when I'm wearing my new jeans, which I had hoped were rather flattering, he'll be chanting it for months.

"He's still following us, Mum." Jack's getting anxious.

"I think he's trying to make friends."

I stop and pick up the lead, and glare at Trevor. "Walk, all right? Walk."

We start off quite well. He pulls a couple of times, and I yank and shout "Heel," and it seems to be working. How very brilliant. I have single-handedly trained a mad dog, in under ten minutes without the aid of sausages. Hurrah.

And then he spots another bloody seagull, busy showing off to its friends by perching on the railings and squawking. Trevor's ears go flat, and I lean back and brace myself as he leaps forward. He turns to look at me and pulls again, nearly yanking my bloody arm off, but I still hang on. And just when I think I've got the bastard thing under control, he does an enormous leap sideways and I fall over, right on top of him, which the boys think is brilliant. He struggles out from underneath me, looking very shaken: he probably thinks I'm going to try to ride him home.

"Right, let's go. And get up, Archie, or you'll get wet."

Trevor looks at me. I tug the lead. "Walk nicely, and I promise I won't sit on you again."

He walks, giving me the occasional worried look.

Excellent.

"I'm going to ask Father Christmas for a dog, just like Trevor, only a puppy. Of my very own."

"Archie, Father Christmas doesn't bring people dogs, I've told you before."

He ignores me and mutters "Grumpypotamus" under his breath.

Jack smiles. "A dog is for life, not just for Christmas, isn't it, Mum? People have that on their cars, sometimes, don't they?"

"Yes, Jack."

Archie smiles, too. "I bet he'll bring me one if I ask him."

I bet he bloody won't.

There are eight shopping days to Christmas, and Bluewater is just as appalling as I knew it would be. Reg drives us up there in his ancient Rover, which is very kind of him, obviously, but means I'm stuck in the back of the car for hours and hours, so I'm tempted to start counting lorries and whining for a drink. He never drives above forty and seems completely oblivious to the unusual hand gestures this prompts from other drivers, since he's busy chatting to Gran about the cruise, and offering round his packet of Murray Mints. He moves on to telling us all about his daughter's new carpet in her lounge, which isn't quite gray, but isn't blue, either, and by the time we've arrived I've practically slipped into a coma, and my legs have gone numb, which isn't the ideal way to start a shopping marathon. We have to tour round the car parks until we finally find a space on Squirrel Level 2, in the Green Zone. Or it might be Green Level 2 in the Squirrel Zone, but I'm so pleased to be out of the car I really don't care. Actually, I'm half hoping he won't find the bloody car again, and we can go home on the bus.

Gran spends ages finding the perfect suitcase, after making the poor man in John Lewis dismantle his entire display, much to his obvious annoyance, and then we all trot off to Lakeland, where Gran spends ages trying out all the lids on the plastic boxes and marveling at the extra-wide trays for soaking your oven shelves in. She tries to buy me one, which given I can't remember the last time I cleaned my oven, isn't exactly top of my Christmas list, but I divert her by showing her the yellow plastic boxes shaped like bananas.

"Isn't that a clever idea? I'll get one each for the boys for their school lunches, because there's nothing worse than a squashed banana."

Actually, I think the boys may feel differently, and turning up at school with a bright yellow plastic banana-shaped box in your lunch bag might be far worse, but never mind.

"I think I'll get one for Betty, too. She often brings a snack with her when we go on our coach trips, and she's quite partial to a banana."

"Good idea."

I leave them piling up the basket in Lakeland while I race round like I'm playing some very expensive version of that game where you put loads of objects on a tray and cover them with a tea towel, and then have to try to remember what was on the tray. I'm up and down escalators and along the hallways chanting "Sellotape" and "chocolate orange," and trying to remember what I need to get in Boots, until Gran finally emerges with lots of new plastic stacking objects, and Reg staggers backward and forward to the car stashing shopping bags while we search for something for Betty, who collects china rabbits and likes roses, and Elsie, who doesn't. I've bought Gran's suitcase as her main present from me, but I still need to get her something from the boys, and then she spots a teapot with a matching milk jug that she likes, so that's another thing off my list. We get one for Elsie, too, only with blue flowers on it, rather than pink, and then we spot a group of hideous china rabbits, including one clutching a posy of roses, so that's Betty taken care of. Naturally, Gran did all her Christmas shopping weeks ago, so she's quite happy to sit in a café with Reg having a toasted tea cake while I brace myself for round two.

I gather up bottles of bath stuff and candles in M and S for Connie and Lulu, along with smaller versions for the boys' teachers, and some spares for whichever bastard I haven't thought of who turns up with an unexpected gift, and some Christmas pants for Vin, because we always get each other really crap presents, before I head down to the food hall, where for some reason best known to middle management they've decided to put all the baskets outside the main doors, in the freezing cold, so you have to leave whatever shopping you've got in your arms in a pile on the floor, as lots of other people seem to be doing, or else take it outside with you and run the risk of being arrested for shoplifting. So that's all very helpful. I finally track down some chunky-looking marmalade in a vaguely familiar jar. I'm balancing two baskets on one arm, which leave big red marks, so I decide not to do any other food shopping as my personal protest about the new basket relocation policy. I bet that'll have Head Office rocking in their seats. But as Tesco keep telling us, every little helps, and maybe next time someone might join up the dots before customers are forced to abandon their shopping in little piles all over the bloody food hall. Christ, I think I might be developing shopping rage.

I still can't work out what to get for Nick's parents, Elizabeth and Gerald, who we've actually managed to see only twice since the funeral, which is making me feel rather guilty. The last time we saw them was when the headstone was ready, which Elizabeth insisted on organizing, although she did let me pay for it, and I'm still not sure about that gold lettering on black marble. It all looked a bit too pompous somehow, and she forgot to put the boys' names on, even though I asked her to, and I know he would have wanted their names, not just "Beloved Husband and Father." Oh, God, I think I'd better sit down somewhere for a minute and pull myself together.

I look at my list while I sit in Starbucks, practically inhaling a mince pie and a caramel macchiato and wondering exactly what it was I ever did to Elizabeth to make her treat me like someone who's just left muddy footprints all over her cream carpet, which I've never actually done, although Jack did have a rather spectacular near miss with a homemade jam tart the last time we were there, but I don't think she saw. I invited them over to lunch to see the new house and the shop when we first moved in, but they were too busy with golf things, and I've been putting off calling her for a while because she only wants to talk about Nick, and why I won't reconsider moving again and sending the boys to Nick's old prep school; although how she thinks I'd pay for that is anybody's guess. But we've fixed up a date for them all to come for lunch in January, although God alone knows what they'll make of the house. So that's something else to look forward to.

And then there's Nick's brother, James, and his wife, Fiona, who Elizabeth has always preferred; they live nearby and belong to the same golf club, and Fiona's in the same branch of the Women's Institute as her. They're always busy making things for the competitions; a matchbox full of as many items as possible, or a decorated thimble, that kind of thing, and the best ones get points each month and there's a silver cup at the end of the year and Elizabeth's won it, twice. I tried to show an interest at first, but I think I just annoyed her.

I'm pretty sure none of them will want a Goat for Peace for Christmas. Elizabeth collects expensive china figurines of the nonrabbit variety, and I'm quite tempted to get her a packet of Pledge dusters and some glue, ready for our next visit, but in the end I settle for a basket of herbs and things in jars from a posh Italian deli, which she'll hate, but I'm past caring, and a boxed set of gourmet oils for James and Fiona, ditto, and make-your-own-bead-bracelet kits for their girls, Elizabeth and Charlotte, which will mean beads all over Fiona's polished wood floors, as a sort of hidden bonus. I'll post them all tomorrow, along with the cards the boys made at the weekend, with extra glitter for added sparkle.

I've just got Mum and Dad left now. They are tricky to buy presents for because Mum always says she doesn't want anything because Christmas is such a con and she'd rather we didn't bother. But then she sulks if we don't get her anything, so I go for some of her favorite Body Shop stuff from the boys, and a book on Renaissance painters from me, and a big box of chocolate gingers for Dad, because they're his favorites and nobody else likes them so he won't have to share. I've got him some daft socks that play Merry Christmas from the boys, which he'll love, so I think I'm done. I'm carrying so many shopping bags they're cutting off the circulation in my fingers.

Gran and Reg are still in the café, but they've been making little forays out to get more stocking fillers for the boys, and a large box of biscuits for the Bowls Club.

"All done, dear?"

"Yes, I think so."

"Good. Let's have another pot of tea, shall we? You look done in."

"I'll go, Mary." Reg picks up the cups and goes back over to the counter.

"I nipped into M and S earlier and got us some custard tarts. We'll have to be careful, though, because I don't think they like you eating things that they haven't sold you. Mind you, the price they charge for tea, you'd think they'd be used to it by now. And I got you this."

She hands me a little plastic wallet with two tiny bottles of pink nail polish inside.

"How lovely. Thanks, Gran."

"There's a nail file and everything. I thought you could do them tonight, after the boys are asleep. You always loved me doing your nails when you were little."

I kiss her, and she smiles.

"I wonder how Betty's getting on. She was really looking forward to it, you know. She's got them a bag of sweets each—she was showing me yesterday. Just a few little things, mind. I told her you don't like them spoiling their tea. So you like the nail polish, do you? I can change it if you don't like the color."

"It's a lovely color."

"You're doing too much. You need to slow down a bit."

"I know, Gran, but there's so much to do."

"Well, remember, pet, Rome wasn't built in a day."

"Or Venice?"

She frowns. "I know I shouldn't say it, but your mother can be such a trial sometimes. I'm so glad I'm going on my cruise, I really am. Here, have a custard tart."

It's the end-of-term Assembly at school today, and I've got the Stitch and Bitch group tonight, so I'm sitting upstairs in the shop, putting the final touches to the flower brooches I've made as presents for everyone, before I wrap them up in tissue paper. I took Gran and Reg to Gatwick yesterday, and only just made it back to school in time to collect the boys, so I'm still feeling pretty knackered, and it's pelting down with rain, which I hope doesn't mean there are storms out at sea. They were both so excited, and Reg was already wearing his sailor's cap and his blazer, so I'm really hoping he hasn't had to swap it for a sou'wester.

Elsie's just brought me a mince pie from the baker's. She seems very chirpy at the moment, and she loved her teapot and milk jug. I'm still having the occasional bicker with her when she arranges new stock so it looks like someone color-blind has thrown things on the shelves, and she never writes down telephone messages, so I have to call everyone back and then get stuck for ages with salespeople from the bank asking me how my account is functioning, and did I know I could take out a loan on the shop and have the cash in my hand by teatime, with a free Parker pen, if I could just answer three questions, the first of which is "Are you a total idiot?" But apart from that we seem to have got past the constant tutting stage, and we're into something much more friendly, which is great. She still wants to put up the photos of me and Grace; she was busy showing them to Martin at the weekend, and he seemed very impressed, but I haven't seen him since because he's got some crisis job on at work and they're putting him up in a hotel.

I'm knitting the last flower for Tina, in pink cotton with a mohair center, and the smell of the woodsmoke and the feel of the wool is making me feel much calmer. I think I'll put another log on the fire and finish this, and then I'll check what else needs doing.

Fuck. Double fuck. It's half past one and I've just woken up.

Elsie said she didn't like to wake me because I looked so peace-ful, which was sweet of her, obviously, but means I'm in serious danger of being late for the bloody Assembly. I race down the stairs and then race back up again to get my bag, and by the time I get to school I'm feeling as if I've been entered into one of those half marathons as a surprise, like one of those peo-ple who wear amusing outfits and take nine hours to complete the course. I'm wearing my new boots and my green corduroy skirt with my tweed jacket because I wanted to look a bit smarter than usual, but now I wish I'd gone for something I could bloody run in.

The hall's already packed, but Connie's saved me a seat next to her and Mark, so I sit down, rather red-faced, and An-nabel Morgan turns round and gives me an especially unim-pressed kind of look. Cow.

Everyone's chatting and smiling, apart from her group at the front, who are all stony-faced because this year Mr. O'Brien has decided against the traditional Nativity play, which the PTA usually help organize. According to Jane Johnson, who knows the school secretary, he's said it takes up too much time, and doesn't really benefit the kids, especially those who don't get to be Mary and Joseph, so instead each class will have a moment onstage to share what they've been doing this term. And while this seems extremely sensible to most of us, with the added bonus that nobody has to stay up until midnight making a sodding sheep costume, Annabel's completely furious about it. She'd probably already had her sheep costume professionally made.

Mr. O'Brien comes in, and everyone quietens down.

"Good afternoon, ladies and gentlemen, and thank you for joining us for our end-of-term Assembly."

He asks us to remember not to stand up to take photographs, because it puts the children off, and Connie nudges me, because we've heard about last year's summer concert, when Mr. Dale fell over and fractured his elbow while trying to walk backward as he was videoing his daughter's solo. Fireman Graham had to administer first aid out in the corridor until the ambulance came, and Mrs. Nelson had to play a loud medley of her favorite show tunes to cover up the sound of Mr. Dale swearing.

The Reception class climb up the steps onto the stage, holding pictures of Christmas trees covered in tinsel, and what I think are paintings of reindeer, only it's quite hard to tell because some of them are more figurative than others. They're looking nervous and very small, apart from one girl who steps forward and begins belting out "Rudolph, the Red-Nosed Reindeer" before the piano has even started, which gives the rest of her classmates a sudden jolt of recognition, but they rally, and despite singing at a variety of tempos, and to slightly different tunes, they manage to meet up by the end, and we all clap.

Then Archie's class troop in and my stomach does that thing it always does when you see one of your offspring standing on a stage in front of a live audience. They're holding papier-mâché models of stars, which are all roughly the same size and decorated in shiny silver paper, apart from Harry Morgan's, which is much more professional-looking and twice the size of all the others; if he could find a plug, it would probably start revolving and playing a tune. I bet Annabel was in the classroom "helping" on the day they made them, unless she broke in at midnight to remodel it for him.

They line up on the stage, and Nelly drops her star, which rolls off the edge of the stage and drops onto the floor. There's a silence, and Connie and Mark both lean forward; Connie's holding Mark's hand really tightly, but just when I think it's all going to end in tears, Archie does a rather spectacular jump off the stage, lands in a little heap, picks himself up, and hands Nelly her star, then runs round to the side of the stage and climbs back up the stairs again. He takes his place next to Nelly in the lineup, and she turns to him with such gratitude on her face you can almost hear the entire audience smiling. Connie reaches for my hand. So now all three of us are holding hands and sniffing.

Mrs. Berry announces that they're going to sing "Twinkle, Twinkle, Little Star" for us. It was written by Jane Taylor in 1806, which is a very long time ago, but first the class would like to tell us some interesting facts about stars, and then assorted small people tell us that stars are born in big clouds of gas, and there are over seven thousand stars that you can see in the sky without a telescope, and they were named after animals and gods. And then Seth Johnson, who's very clever, steps forward. I can see Jane stiffen, willing him to get his line right.

"Stars twinkle because air is never still, so when light goes through the air on its way to us on Earth, it looks like it's twinkling."

He seems to understand what he's talking about, which is

more than I can say for most of the audience, me included; it's all very impressive for someone who's only six. Then the piano starts up and they're off. The first group manage their verse, more or less together, and it's all going well when Archie and Nelly step forward in their group, ready for their verse. This is the bit I've been really worried about, because it's fifty-fifty whether Archie will be singing the official version or going for Jack's alternative, "Winkle, Winkle, Little Bra." This reduces them both to complete hysterics every single time they try to sing it, which they've been doing pretty much every day for weeks now. Archie stands up straight and puts his shoulders as far back as he can, which means he's going to be Singing as Loud as He Can. Oh dear.

Then the traveler in the dark
Thanks you for your tiny spark.
He could not see which way to go
If you did not twinkle so.

Thank God.

They rejoin the line, and Archie waves his star at me. Then it's time for one more round of the chorus, in which I think I hear a faint trace of "Winkle, winkle," but I'm not sure, and everyone claps as the children line up and jostle their way back down the stairs. Archie turns for one final wave, and then he gives me the thumbs-up sign, which he always used to do with Nick, which nearly finishes me off completely. We've all been enjoying the occasional dab and sniff in the customary aren't-they-so-sweet kind of way, but I'm now getting perilously close to My Life is a Total Travesty sobbing, so I look for a spare tissue and find an extra-strong mint at the bottom of my bag, which is a bit of a result even if it is covered in glitter. Christ, this is going to be a long afternoon.

I've just about pulled myself together, after a spirited rendition of "The Holly and the Ivy," with real holly, when Mrs. Chambers leads her class in. Jack's looking pale and nervous, but Marco seems relaxed and grins as he waves to his mum and dad. Connie's holding Mark's hand again. Mrs. Chambers has outdone herself on the Artistic Effort front, and they're all holding big sheets of paper with paintings and collages of stockings and little mice, and rooftops and a red silk Father Christmas, with lots of tinsel and gold stars.

Two girls step forward and announce that their poem was written by a man called Clement Moore in 1823, and it's very famous. They pause and then we're off:

> 'Twas the night before Christmas, when all through
>   the house
> Not a creature was stirring, not even a mouse . . .

Everyone with a picture of a mouse holds it up and jiggles it. They're doing four lines each, and there's the occasional moment of hesitation, but they're managing pretty well, and

then Jack and Marco step forward, and Jack goes even
paler.

> *So up to the house-top the coursers they flew,*
> *With the sleigh full of toys and St. Nicholas, too.*
> *And then in a twinkling I heard on the roof*
> *The prancing and pawing of each little hoof.*

Christ, what a relief. He's been so worried he'll forget his words, I
practically have to sit on my hands to stop myself clapping as the
next two start their verse and more paintings are waved. And
then suddenly they're at the end, and they all take a bow and we
clap and Mark does a loud whistle, which Jack and Marco love.

We're treated to a very lively "Jingle Bells" next, and then
"While Shepherds Watched Their Flocks by Night," which
seems to go on forever, before the top class sing "We Wish You
a Merry Christmas." They all look very grown-up, particularly
some of the boys, who are obviously far too cool to bother with
singing in assemblies, so they stand at the back and practice
their slouching. Mr. O'Brien thanks us all for coming, and reminds everyone to take their reading books home, and then we
all shuffle our way out and try to collect PE bags and congratu-
late our budding stars.

We've just about made it to Nelly and Archie's classroom
when Annabel Morgan looms into view, full of Christmas spirit.

I smile at her.

"Wasn't it lovely?"

"I prefer a proper Nativity play myself, but it was fine, if you
like that sort of thing."

Connie looks annoyed. "I thought it was very lovely."

"Yes, but being reminded about the true meaning of Christmas is so important, as I'm sure you agree. And a proper Nativity is the best way to do that, in my experience."

"Not if you have to be a donkey. I had to be, how do you say, the donkey's . . ."

Mark laughs. "Bottom."

"Yes, the donkey's bottom. And it didn't teach me a thing about Christmas."

We're attracting a bit of an audience now, and Annabel is starting to look Annoyed. Again.

I try another smile. "Maybe they can do a Nativity play next year, but I thought this was lovely, and they all felt equally important, which has got to be the point, surely? And we didn't have to make any costumes, and that definitely gets top marks from me."

"I'm so glad you liked it, Mrs. Mackenzie, isn't it?"

Bugger. It's Mr. O'Brien. "Yes."

"Mrs. Chambers tells me you've offered to help us with our textiles project next term, which is very kind of you. I try to make it a rule that we don't have anything taught in the school that I don't have a go at myself, so you'd better put me down for the first session, but I think I should warn you that teaching me to knit might be your toughest challenge yet."

"It's very easy. I'm sure you'll pick it up in no time."

"I doubt it—I'm hopeless at that kind of thing—but we can but try. Now, I wanted a word with your son. There he is. Archie, come here for a minute, would you, young man? I want to tell you how pleased I was to see you being so kind and helpful in our assembly. Let's shake hands, shall we?"

He holds out his hand, and Archie shakes it, looking very pleased with himself.

"Very well done, Archie. Here, have a toffee."

He hands him a toffee wrapped in shiny paper from his jacket pocket.

"But please save it for later, there's a good boy. Now then, I must find Mrs. Finch, I think she's been looking for me." He heads off up the corridor, stopping to chat to children as he goes.

Annabel's sulking as we go into the classroom to collect paintings and book bags. Hobnobbing with the Head and a toffee for Archie: I'm not sure I could have been more annoying unless I'd got a special T-shirt printed with "I Hate Mrs. Morgan" on the front. Shame, as Ellen would say.

"I remembered it, Mum."

I'm helping Archie put his coat on. "You did, darling, and you were brilliant."

I risk a quick hug, even though we are technically still in public and this is a clear breach of the rules. There's a muffled "Get off! Get off!" and he emerges, slightly red-faced.

"Can we go and find Jack now? I want to tell him Mr. O'Brien shaked my hand, and gave me a sweet, because he only does that if you've been very good."

"Okay."

"I was the best, wasn't I, Mum?"

"Yes, love, you were the best in your whole class. And Jack was the best in his."

He looks at me and smiles.

"Yes. But only I got a sweet."

It's just past midnight and I can't get to sleep; I think I've eaten too much, but Connie arrived with two trays of pastries from Mark for our Stitch and Bitch Christmas party, and they were so delicious we'd eaten half of them before anyone else had arrived. And then Cath brought a quiche and Tina and Linda had made sausage rolls, including some cheese-and-chive ones for Olivia, who's decided to be a vegetarian, mainly to annoy Cath, we think, but we're trying not to take sides, and Maggie and Angela both brought cakes, too, so I feel like I've been eating for hours and hours.

Angela was proudly showing off her photographs of Penny and Sally holding baby Stanley, who's got lots of wispy hair. There were a few photographs of Stanley's dad, too, who looked very nice, and Tina said she thought Stanley was a very lucky baby to have three parents who obviously love him so much, which was just about the perfect thing to say really, and Angela looked very pleased. And then we had a competition to see who was having the most hideous Christmas lunch, and Cath won, with seventeen grown-ups and five children. Connie's going to lend her some chairs because she hasn't got enough, which I think is probably the least of her problems. I can't imagine cooking for that many people without requiring professional assistance, but she seemed quite relaxed about it, unlike Maggie, who told us that she might be out of a job in the New Year, because they all got called into a special meeting at the library today, and apparently the council are looking at merging branches, and a property developer has already put in an offer for the building. We're all going to try to help, and Cath's starting a petition, which cheered Maggie up a bit.

It'll be terrible if the library closes, because lots of people won't be able to travel to wherever the new branch is, and some of the older ones pop in nearly every day for a chat, according to Maggie, to meet their friends and look at the papers. The children's section is really sweet, with lots of paintings on the wall and beanbags, and I'm going to make an extra effort to take the boys in more regularly, because it's obviously a case of Use It or Lose It. The only potentially tricky moment was when Angela said she hoped Peter wasn't involved, which he's bound to be, what with him being on the parish council and being the local estate agent. But we all pretended we hadn't heard her, and Cath started talking about making posters to put up in all the shop windows.

It's ten past one, and I still can't get to sleep, so I'm downstairs making tea and wrapping up the knitting-needle case I've made for Grace for Christmas; I'm seeing her tomorrow, and I hope she's going to like it, because trying to work out what to get for someone with impeccable taste and vast amounts of money isn't easy. I haven't seen her for a while because she's been busy with meetings about the new films, and it looks like she's definitely doing the French one next year, and possibly a remake of *Bedknobs and Broomsticks,* with lots of special effects and more sex. I don't remember there being any sex at all in the Angela Lansbury version; but I do remember loving the rabbit and the bits when they were all bobbing along under the sea.

Christ, I wish we were staying here for the holidays and we could sit by the fire and watch *Bedknobs and Broomsticks* and eat too much chocolate instead of being satellites revolving round Planet Mum. Dad will disappear as much as he can; he's like the bloody Invisible Man sometimes, only with carpentry tools. And I really hope he hasn't Made Something with Wood for the boys, like the year he made me a Noah's Ark. It must have taken him ages, and he was so proud of it, but secretly I hated it because all the animals were different sizes, so the rabbits were nearly twice the size of the sheep, and what I really wanted was one like my friend Alison's, with plastic animals with faces and a Mr. and Mrs. Noah who had clothes you could take off. While Dad was making us toys we didn't appreciate, Mum was always trying to ignite some artistic flair in us; she'd give us boxes of expensive modeling clay or fabulous paint sets, and then look bewildered and irritated when we weren't that interested. She liked taking us round museums on Sundays, too, when she'd tell us all about the Surrealists in such a loud voice that people used to look at us, until Vin started refusing to get in the car.

I always end up feeling that I'm being Disappointing when I'm with Mum. I used to feel it with Nick, too, sometimes; like

I wasn't quite up to scratch. But it's different now. The past year has made me feel that I'm not just someone who spends all her time at home, redecorating everything in sight while her brain slowly melts, not that I ever was that person, but I used to feel like her sometimes. What with a new house and a new business, and new friends, I feel I've started to achieve something. So if Mum thinks she's going to play her usual game of I'm a Very Special and Artistic Person and You're Not, then I think she might be in for a bit of a surprise.

8

STRESS IN VENICE AND THE CHOCOLATE ORANGE

It's four o'clock on Christmas Eve and we're at thirty thousand feet somewhere over France. Archie's sitting by the window, looking small and wide-eyed with the thrill of it all, and Jack's busy being the debonair, jet-setting older brother, listening to Harry Potter on CD, which we borrowed from Maggie at the library, and occasionally sneaking excited glances through the window when he thinks Archie isn't looking. I'm completely knackered, but after a large gin and tonic and a packet of crackers, I feel a tiny bit less like running down the aisle screaming, "Let me off! Let me off!"

The food arrives, and it's just as revolting as usual, and scaldingly hot, but the boys enjoy buttering their rolls with their little plastic knives. Stewart, our flight attendant, comes round with the teas and coffees. Archie gives him one of his best smiles and waves a piece of roll at him.

"I'm masticating."

Stewart hesitates for a second, teapot in midair, but since he's obviously a seasoned professional, he rallies and carries on pouring my tea, with a rather fixed smile on his face.

"Archie, there really isn't any need to tell people when you're chewing your food, I've told you before. People don't really want to know."

Stewart relaxes slightly and rests his teapot on my tray. "Don't worry, you'd be amazed what people get up to when their trays are down, madam. Honestly, nothing would surprise me in this job. Would he like another roll?"

"That would be great."

"I'll be back in a sec. I can't wait to tell the purser, he's going to love it."

Archie looks puzzled.

"Who's the purser? Does he do the money?"

"Yes, poppet, that's exactly what he does. And precious little else, if he can help it. Back in a minute."

After Stewart's collected our trays, and the purser has been down for a quick look at the Masticator in 25A, it's time for trips to the toilet, which are a big hit with Archie, who particularly enjoys pressing the flush mid-wee to see if he can get sucked down the toilet and out into the clouds, just in case Father Christmas is having an early practice run on his sleigh.

"Don't do it again, Archie."

"Yes, but if you did get outside, it would be lovely."

"No, it wouldn't, it would be very cold."

"I could put my hood up."

I'm pretty sure finding yourself on the wrong side of the

emergency exit at thirty thousand feet would mean that getting the hood of your sweatshirt to stay up might be the least of your worries, but I don't want to frighten him, and anyway he's pressing buttons on the sink now, and if I'm not careful I'll end up with a soaking-wet trouser leg.

By the time we're back in our seats and playing endless rounds of Animal, Vegetable, or Mineral, but without the Minerals because Archie just makes them up, my trousers are starting to dry. And then the captain announces we're beginning our descent and preparing for landing. Jack checks that his seat really is in the upright position, to the sound of tutting from the man behind us; although he's in no position to tut as far as I'm concerned because his daughter has been standing on her seat for most of the flight, doing a kind of in-flight cabaret performance of I'm a Very Gifted Child in an annoyingly nasal voice. I'm sure we're all meant to be applauding and wishing we had such a marvelous child, but I don't think I'm alone in wishing she'd just shut up and sit down. She kicks the back of my seat for a while, then stands up and leans over to ask me if I know how to say "Hello, my name is Sophie" in Italian, because she does.

I try to pretend I haven't heard her, but she tells me anyway, and then sits down and resumes her kicking. I wonder how many air-rage incidents are sparked off by middle-class children; quite a few is my guess, especially on flights to Venice.

Jack gets nervous while we're landing, and grips my hand very tightly, while Archie gives us a running commentary on what he can see on the ground, including things he must be making up unless Italy's gone back to the Jurassic period during our flight.

We finally make it through passports and into the baggage hall, which in typical Italian fashion is very beautifully designed but doesn't appear to be working. There are hordes of people crowded round stationary luggage carousels, and an atmosphere of mild hysteria, but it's such a relief to be off the plane and away from the sound of Sophie telling everyone about her favorite food that I really don't care.

The boys are getting chilly, so I find their woolly hats at the bottom of my bag and reassure myself that I've still got the passports, for the hundred and eleventh time. Jack finds a luggage trolley by running and sitting on the first one he sees, and since we're in Italy nobody hurls him to the floor, and he's very pleased with himself as he wheels it back toward me. Archie's sulking because Marco Polo Airport doesn't give out free packets of Polos, but he cheers up when Jack starts wheeling him backward and forward on the trolley, at a very sedate pace because I think they both realize I'm not in the mood for any Nonsense.

I'm just starting to relax when I hear the unmistakable tones of Sophie and her parents, who come and stand right beside us. Excellent.

"Daddy, I want a trolley to sit on like that boy."

"There aren't any trolleys left, darling."

There's a definite hint of gritted teeth in his tone now. Shame.

"But I want one."

He turns to me and smiles, as if to signal that I should be turfing my children off our trolley and donating it for Sophie's sole use. Like that's going to be happening any time soon.

"I want one now."

All the English passengers in the vicinity who've got trolleys hold on to them more tightly.

Jack turns round. "You can have a go on this one if you like, but just a go."

Everyone smiles at him, apart from Archie and me, who are both completely horrified.

"No. I want one of my very own."

Sophie's mother finally cracks. "Sophie, don't be silly. Say thank you to the nice boy."

"No."

"I know you're tired, darling, but it was very kind of him to offer."

This slight hint of public criticism is too much for Mr. Sophie.

"For God's sake, leave her alone—it's not as if it's his personal trolley."

I stare at him, and he reddens. And Mrs. Sophie raises her eyebrows. Christ, the poor woman; it just goes to show there's always someone worse off than you. I must try to remember that during the next few days.

Sophie continues whining, and hits her father with her Barbie bag, which is gratifying, and we're finally reunited with our suitcase and our big black nylon bag, which looks much flatter than the last time we saw it. I'm so glad I didn't bother to take the Fragile stickers off. We're trundling toward the automatic doors with Archie balanced on top of the suitcase, giving Sophie the evil eye whenever he catches a glimpse of her, when a torrent of Italian greets us as the doors open, and we are surrounded by crowds of people standing waving and kissing. And then we spot Vin and Dad, and I feel like bursting into tears, but I always feel like crying at airports, so I'm hoping this is only temporary.

Dad pretends not to recognize the boys because they've got so big, and we hug as Vin pushes the trolley toward the exit.

"Good flight?"

"Oh yes, fabulous. Packed full of horrible kids and snooty parents, and that was just the row behind us."

He laughs. "Well, I can top that big time, we had a three-month-old on ours, all the way from bloody Australia, and she never stopped screaming. Me and Lulu had to walk her up and down for ages to get her to stop, and every time we tried to sit down she started up again."

"That was nice of you."

"It was the only way to shut the little sod up, I remembered it from the midnight shuffle when Jack was little."

"You only did that once."

"I know, but it's stayed with me."

We both look at Jack, and I say a silent prayer of thanks that he no longer requires walking up and down to get him off to sleep.

"How's Mum?"

Vin rolls his eyes.

"And Lulu?"

"Great, and dying to see you. Come on, we're over here. We have to get the bus to the boat."

Bugger. I'd sort of forgotten about the boat thing.

"Dad's borrowed one from his friend Gianni, so we won't need to catch the ferry."

"Lovely."

Oh dear. The last time I saw Dad in charge of a boat we were in Greenwich Park and he bashed it into the side so hard Jack nearly fell out; and a lagoon is a lot bigger than a boating pond. Bugger. I wonder if there's anywhere I can buy a couple of life jackets.

It's foggy and cold outside, and getting the luggage onto the bus takes a fair bit of heaving, and lots of sarcastic comments from Vin, but when we get to the port, Dad's friend Gianni is standing smiling and waving at us, next to his beautiful and highly varnished water taxi, and before we know it we're racing across the lagoon in a very glamorous fashion, feeling like visiting VIPs. The boys are madly impressed, as well they should be, since this has got to be the most expensive way to arrive in Venice. Dad's telling them about all the different kinds of fish you can catch off the little islands.

"Are you doing lots of fishing, Dad?"

"A fair bit."

Vin shakes his head. "Don't get him started. He goes out with all his mates for hours, it's his new excuse for disappearing."

Dad smiles.

"And then they all come home drunk."

"Well, you have to take a nip of something to keep the cold out."

The lights of Venice start twinkling at us through the mist, which is rather magical. There's still enough light to see, but all the edges are blurry, and there's something slightly unreal about the way the city suddenly rises from the water like Atlantis, only with much better shops. The boys keep standing up to look out of the windows as we chug up and down canals, which are all a bit eerie and silent apart from sudden bursts of light and noise as we pass little squares. I remember how knocked out I was the first time I came here with Nick. We were supposed to be attending a television festival, but we were stuck in a hotel miles from the center, so we pretty much gave up trying to get to the festival events and just wandered about getting lost and having a blissful time.

The boat stops beside some stone steps, in front of a rather grand-looking building with a large gray wooden door, and Dad and Vin start getting the luggage off. We thank Gianni, who kisses me four times and calls the boys *bambini*, and then the door opens and Mum comes out, wearing clogs for some reason, and a long purple skirt with a dark green poncho. She's looking very bohemian, with her hair in a velvet turban, and kisses me in a very Italian lots-of-cheek-kissing kind of way, and then turns to the boys.

"Now, darlings, you must remember to call me Mariella. None of that dreadful Granny nonsense, because I couldn't bear it."

They both nod.

"And Josephine, darling, what on earth have you been doing to yourself? You look dreadful. It must be working in that shop. I told you it was a bad idea, didn't I? You need to be using your brain, not working on a till all day."

She laughs, as if she's being very witty, and turns to Jack.

"So what do you think of Venezia?"

"It's lovely."

She smiles. "And Archie? Do you think it's beautiful, too?"

"Yes, but where are the ice-cream shops? Mum said there were shops full of ice cream."

Trust Archie to let the side down.

"The really important thing is all the beautiful museums we can visit, full of beautiful pictures. You'd like to see them, too, wouldn't you?"

"Not really."

I give him a firm look.

"We'd love to see all the pictures, wouldn't we, Archie?"

"Oh yes, but we'd like to see the ice cream more, that's all."

Vin laughs. "I know just what you mean."

Mum sighs.

Lulu helps us get the luggage indoors and whispers that Vin has been bickering with Mum all day and she's really glad we're here. We go up the stairs, and suddenly we're surrounded by marble and gilt in a very grand but undoubtedly dilapidated palazzo. There are bits of plaster missing from one of the walls, and a faint smell of damp, but the marble floors are beautiful, and there are huge sets of double doors leading off the corridor. Mum leads the way up two more flights of stairs and into a large bedroom.

"I've put you in here. You get marvelous views from this window over the rooftops."

She opens the shutters. The room's enormous, with a massive wooden bed and two rather rickety-looking camp beds, and a huge dark wooden wardrobe with carvings on the doors of little cherubs and bunches of grapes.

"Isn't it beautiful?"

"It's lovely, Mum, thank you."

It's also freezing, but never mind; it'll make it feel more like home.

Dad's looking worried. "The only thing is, I wouldn't go out onto the balcony because those railings could give way any minute."

Excellent. I wonder which one of us will be first to fall headlong into the canal.

"There used to be keys, but we've lost track of them."

"*You've* lost track of them, you mean, Derek, I've never seen them. I have told you." Mum sounds irritated.

"I'll tie the doors shut with a scarf or something; it'll be fine. It's an amazing place, Mum."

She nods. "Yes, we're very lucky. Giancarlo lets us use all the rooms when he hasn't got tenants in, and the rest of the time we have our lovely flat downstairs, of course, so it's perfect. It's such a shame he's not here at the moment. He's such a lovely man, so cultured. He's a count, you know, and his family have lived here for generations."

In fact, I already know from Vin that he's a Milanese banker, and not terribly cultured at all, with a very blond wife who likes to wear lots of gold jewelry. They rent the house out to tourists in the summer and only keep it because of something to do with tax.

Dad plugs the ancient fan heater in, and it wafts warm air around our feet.

"The boiler's a bit temperamental, so the radiators don't

always work up here, but this will take the chill off. Are you hungry, love? I could do you some soup, if you like."

"Don't fuss, Derek. She's perfectly capable of making herself some soup if she wants to."

"Well, I just thought, after the journey, you know . . ."

"We'll be going out to eat later, anyway. I'm sure she can wait."

"Actually, Mum, I think the boys might be hungry, so some supper would be great."

"You're in Italy now, Josephine. Nobody eats supper at this time; you don't want to look like a tourist, do you, darling?"

Actually, I don't care what we look like as long as the boys aren't hungry, but I know she'll only get annoyed if I argue.

Dad's looking anxious again. "I could do them some toast or something, just to keep them going?"

"That would be lovely."

Vin winks at me, which I think Mum notices.

"Let's all go downstairs. I want to show you the formal rooms: they're really lovely, and there's a wonderful quadratura in the dining room."

What I'd really like to see in the dining room is some hot food, but never mind; I should probably try to avoid catapulting myself back into teenage sulking within ten minutes of getting here.

"Your mum got some of your special tea for you. Earl Grey, is that right?"

I hate Earl Grey with a passion. It's like drinking stale

perfume, and we've had countless conversations about it. But still, it's the thought that counts.

"Lovely."

It's Christmas morning and I'm sitting in the palatial dining room with the quadra thing ceiling, while the boys shoot Lego cannonballs at each other and I try to calm down; Mum made me one of her special triple espressos for breakfast, and my hands are still shaking, but it was either that or more bloody Earl Grey, and at least it woke me up. We've opened our presents, and Vin and Lulu have gone back to bed, much to Mum's annoyance. Dad's busy doing something to one of the doors in the hall involving a screwdriver and a plane, although why he has to do it now is anybody's guess, while Mum's banging saucepans around downstairs in the kitchen, because she hates cooking. We all offered to help, but she said she wants to do it by herself; only I think she meant with us as the admiring audience rather than just letting her get on with it.

It's only half past ten and I'm already feeling like I've been up for hours; but supper last night was a real treat, even if it did mean we got home late. We went to a tiny restaurant in the nearby square, run by Gianni's son Luca and his wife, Gabriella, and it was packed with all their friends and family. We were so hungry we practically inhaled our pasta before the traditional Christmas Eve main course arrived. Roasted eel wasn't exactly what I was expecting, and judging from the look on Jack's face, not what he was expecting, either, but Gabriella was sweet with him. She gave him a tiny forkful to try, and when he risked it and pronounced it delicious, he got a round of applause from everyone for being *bravissimo,* so Archie ate all his quite happily, too, which was another minor miracle. Maybe I could add a nice bit of roasted eel to the menu for the relentless round of weekday suppers when we get home; it would certainly make a change from fish fingers.

On the way back to the house, we passed three men dressed as Father Christmas standing up in a gondola singing and waving at everyone, which the boys thought was thrilling and made hanging up their stockings even more exciting than usual. In fact, things got so exciting that Archie collapsed his camp bed and had to be retrieved in a highly agitated state, but they both finally conked out at around one, and then were awake again what seemed like minutes later, bouncing on my bed and yelling "He's been! He's been!" and waving their stockings at me. The miniature cardboard kaleidoscopes went down well, and the clockwork monkeys that do somersaults, but I'm never letting Gran get them mini-trumpets and maracas again. Ever. Although they did mean everyone else was awake by the time we went downstairs for breakfast.

Archie's already eaten his chocolate orange: I've always thought a satsuma at the bottom of your stocking is a bit of a swiz, so the chocolate orange has become something of a family tradition. Jack's rationing himself to a couple of segments a day, like he always does, partly because he likes to make it last, but mainly because he knows it upsets Archie. I almost forgot them last year, and Nick had to rush out and get them on Christmas Eve, which he wasn't very pleased about. It seems so much longer than just a year ago, and being in Venice makes it seem even more distant, but I'm still bracing myself for a Daddy-would-have-liked-this moment.

I should probably be taking them upstairs to get dressed, but I can't quite face the bathroom; there's some kind of medieval boiler above the bath that you have to adjust with a spanner to get hot water. Dad explained it all to me yesterday, and if you turn the lever too far to the right it blows up, and if too far to the left it just goes out, and then blows up. So I'm thinking I might boil a kettle and we can all have a nice little wash instead.

Mum's standing in the kitchen looking at a pile of potatoes.

"I'm taking the boys up to get dressed, Mum. Can I boil a kettle for some water?"

"Yes, but can you hurry up, please? I think I've got it all under control, but if you could peel these for me I could be peeling the carrots, and the *cavolfiore*."

"The what?"

"The cauliflower."

I wish she'd stop speaking Italian; it's getting quite annoying actually.

"And you could do the *fagiolini*—just top and tail them, and while you're doing that I'll start on the table. I thought I'd do my special *crostini* to start with?"

"Lovely."

"And I've made *zuppa inglese* for pudding. I thought the boys would like that and I got a marvelous recipe from Gabriella."

"That's trifle, right? They'll love that."

She hands me the vegetable peeler.

"It's rather more sophisticated than trifle, darling. Could you do the carrots, too, while I pop up for a quick bath? And keep an eye on the capon, would you?"

"Sure."

Porca Madonna. So that's me down for cooking Christmas lunch again then; what a surprise.

The boys sit at the kitchen table and build their pirate ships, which were their main present from me, while I start on the potatoes. Vin and Lulu have got them some extra pirate kit, including a crocodile and a Playmobil dragon with chains round his legs, and Vin rather brilliantly organized their presents from Mum and Dad, too, so they've got islands with sharks to add to the collection. They're desperate to get the ships built so battle can commence.

Jack smiles at me. "I think I'll have another piece of my chocolate orange in a minute."

Archie sighs.

"I'll just do the veg for Granny and then we can go and get dressed. We could go for a walk later, if you like."

"She said we had to call her Mariella, Mum."

"I know, Jack. I keep forgetting. Sorry."

Archie looks puzzled. "We don't have to call Gran Mariella, too, do we, when we get home?"

"No, darling."

"Good. Because I like calling her Gran. Will the ice-cream shops be open when we go out?"

"I'm not sure, but we're having a very big lunch, so you probably won't have room."

He looks at me like I've suddenly gone daft.

"Can I go and wake Uncle Vin up now, so he can help us with our castles?"

"That's a good idea."

You never know; maybe he'd like to peel some potatoes while he's at it.

Lunch turns into a joint production between me and Vin, while Mum takes ages to get the table just how she wants it, which seems to involve trailing lots of ivy everywhere and stenciling stars on the tablecloth, only she can't find her special little brush, which she accuses Dad of stealing. After we've got past that mini-crisis, Dad moves on to fixing a wobbly handle on a cabinet in the living room and manages to superglue his thumb to it in the process, so Lulu has to spend ages dabbing away with special solvent and trying not to laugh, while Mum wafts off somewhere in search of candles.

Vin opens a bottle of champagne, which improves things slightly, and we're all in festive mood by the time we're actually sitting at the table, especially since Vin's brought a box of crackers with him. Mum's not that keen on them since they clash with her color scheme for the table, but everyone apart from her sits wearing their paper hats and swapping tragic jokes, while Dad hacks away at the capon with a carving knife he found at the back of the drawer. On balance, I wish Vin hadn't got crackers with whistles in them, but we'll certainly be able to attract attention in an emergency, which might be useful when we're out walking along beside the canals.

Mum gives me a rather narky look.

"Where's the blue jug with the bread sauce?"

"What bread sauce?"

"Honestly, do I have to do everything? There was a packet on the table, the one your father likes, I got Vincent to bring it over for me. What did you think it was for?"

"I didn't see a packet."

Vin pours himself some more champagne.

"That's because I didn't bring any, Mum. Sorry, I forgot."

"Honestly, Vincent, it's your father's favorite."

"Actually, dear, I'm not really that keen on bread sauce."

"Well, you might have said. I wish you wouldn't keep changing your mind about things, Derek, it's very annoying when you're trying to cater for large numbers. I think I'll have a little siesta after lunch, I'm completely exhausted. Why don't you all go out for a lovely walk, and get some fresh air?"

"Won't everything be shut?" Vin's not looking very keen.

"The hotels will be open, so you can have a coffee. Go over to San Marco. Derek, take them past the Accademia, it looks like a lovely day for a walk."

I'd already decided a walk was probably a good idea, but now I've heard about the siesta plan, I think it's pretty vital. The boys aren't terribly good at lying quietly in darkened rooms in the middle of the day, and if we stay here much longer, there's a strong chance I'll be poking her with her special stenciling brush.

Lulu pours herself some water. "I'd love a walk."

Archie's waving his fork in the air, and his paper hat has

slipped down over his eyes. "Can we have ice cream when we go for our walk?"

"Yes, love, I'm sure we can."

It's the day after Boxing Day and the shops are open again, thank Christ, because I'm in serious need of a little retail therapy, even if it's only buying a few postcards and more ice cream. Mum wants to take us out on another leg of her My Favorite Paintings tour, which isn't the sort of treat that will have the boys jumping up and down by the front door. And she's got another bloody drinks party tonight, which I could do without: six people turned up in the evening on Christmas Day, and fifteen of the sods trooped round yesterday, including a man called Julian, who thought I was a waitress and handed me his coat with a very snooty look on his face, then asked me to get him a mineral water in the kind of voice you use when you're speaking to someone who's mentally defective. Mum was in her element holding forth in the living room while we all scuttled around with trays of drinks, and Lulu put the finishing touches to her mini–tomato tartlets, which she'd spent most of the afternoon making. The boys coped fairly well with being shown off to guests and having their cheeks pinched repeatedly before being dismissed to lurk in the kitchen, but then Archie threw a major fit at bathtime, and I was already on edge because of the bloody boiler, so we ended up having a screaming match. So a nice relaxing day out without any History of Art lectures might be a Top Plan.

Vin wants to go to the fish market, and Dad tells us the

flood alerts have been on the radio so we'd better wear our wellies, which worries Jack.

"Does the water go right in the shops, Grandad?"

"Yes, sometimes it does, but they have metal barriers they put over the doorways. You have to climb over them to get in, but don't worry, today won't be too bad. It'll be tomorrow that you'll really see it."

Archie's thrilled. "If the water comes in big, will we have to swim?"

Dad laughs. "It's not usually that deep, but it might come over the top of your wellies."

Lulu puts an arm round Jack. "They put tables out as walkways, don't they?"

Dad nods, and Archie grins. This gets better and better: water in the shops and walking on tables. How perfect.

"Quick, let's go before the water goes."

We set off for the Rialto in a little procession, with Vin leading the way, since he's insisted on holding the map, while Lulu and I dawdle along behind, looking in shop windows. It's a lovely sunny morning, and all the different colors of the buildings are beautiful: the pinks and oranges and all the pitted marble and the faded wooden doors. It's so lovely you just want to sit somewhere and watch, and each time you think you've seen your favorite square, with the perfect mix of old buildings and churches and busy shops and cafés, you turn the corner and something even more lovely catches your eye.

We pass a wool shop with a window full of sweaters with pictures knitted on the fronts, so we go in and nod admiringly at the woman sitting knitting, and look at the huge range of different colors. I'm not that keen on complicated picture knitting, it always seems a bit Val Doonican to me, but I'm definitely jealous of the colors, particularly the greens and yellows. I buy a sweater with van Gogh's *Sunflowers* on the front to take to school for the knitting project, and we carry on walking until Lulu finds a lovely secondhand clothes shop full of flimsy blouses and lace. She buys a pretty white cotton camisole, and I'm tempted by a cream shirt with lots of tiny pleats on the front, but the boys are starting to get bored and it's very expensive, so I manage to resist.

The fish market's amazing. The boys are particularly impressed with the huge swordfish lying on a slab of ice and looking like it'll be swimming off at any moment. They want to buy one for supper, but I'm not sure Mum would be too pleased if we came home dragging a swordfish along behind us. The old men behind the stalls seem to spend most of their time talking to each other, while the younger ones do all the flirting and haggling, and the whole place is so lively and friendly you'd never get tired of it if you lived here; and you'd definitely eat more fish, especially with all the kissing and waving, which would improve our local supermarket no end. We walk past vegetable stalls piled high with beautiful arrangements of fruit, and an old woman in black gives Archie a clementine and kisses the top of his head.

"Inglese?"

"Sì."

She beams and kisses Archie again, much to his horror, as I stop to buy a bagful. They're cold and sweet, and smell wonderful.

Vin spots a butcher's shop in the corner of the square and heads over to look in the window. If yesterday is anything to go by, Mum won't have a meal planned for after the drinks thing and the boys will be starving, so it's probably a good idea to get something for supper. There's a picture of a black horse above the door, which Vin announces is Black Beauty.

The boys look horrified.

Lulu shoves him. "Of course it isn't."

There's a dog sitting on the marble step of the shop doorway, wagging its tail and looking very keen, and the man behind the counter smiles, rolls some mince into a ball, and throws it to the dog, who catches it in his mouth. The boys clap, and the man laughs and does it again.

Archie's very impressed.

"Trevor could do that, if we teached him."

I can't quite see our local butcher going in for chucking bits of mince to assorted dogs, but this is obviously a regular routine, because the dog makes no attempt to go into the shop but sits waiting patiently as a woman with a little girl goes in. The woman smiles and nods at the butcher, who throws the dog another meatball. The boys clap again.

"Please can we buy something, Mum, and get him another bit of meat?"

"All right, come in and help me choose something."

We get some nice-looking chops, which I'm sure are far too small to belong to anything that used to be able to neigh, and the dog gets another treat and wags its tail so hard it nearly falls over, so everyone's happy, and then we sit in the café in the square so the boys can carry on watching the dog. Lulu's ordering toasted sandwiches when my mobile starts to ring; I'm still very impressed with myself for having a phone that's so international, but I still half expect it to be someone speaking Italian.

It's Mum, sounding stressed.

"Are you still at the fish market?"

"Yes."

"Get some prawns, would you, but not the big ones."

"Sure."

"Do you know how to make vol-au-vents?"

"Not really."

She's sounding even more stressed now.

"Are you sure?"

"Pretty sure, yes. I'm not very good with pastry, especially not the puffy stuff. It never puffs for me. I could do you flat ones if you like."

She sighs.

"Do try to be helpful, Josephine, please. I've just heard there's a rather important American woman coming tonight, and she's part of the Guggenheim set and their parties are always wonderful, so don't be late back. I'd like you all to look your best this evening. Do the boys have something smart to wear, by any chance?"

"Not really, no. I'll put them in clean shirts, though. Will that do?"

"I suppose so."

"Is there anything else you want me to get?"

"I don't think so."

"Shall I still get the prawns?"

"No, I'll do my spinach and ricotta things with pine nuts; everyone always loves them."

"Great."

Vin grins as I put the phone back into my bag.

"Don't tell me. That was Mum, right?"

"Yes, and it's formal evening dress tonight, so I hope you remembered to bring your dinner jacket."

"What?"

Lulu smiles. "She really gets you both going, doesn't she?"

"And she wants you to make fifty mini-quiches, Lulu, when we get back, and if they're not up to professional catering standards, you'll be in big trouble."

"You're joking, right?"

"Not entirely."

She laughs. "Christ."

My phone rings again. "Yes, Mum?"

"Sorry?"

It's Daniel. He rang yesterday to say he was due in Venice today, and we're meant to be having tea with him in Florian's this afternoon, but I bet this is him ringing to cancel.

"I got here earlier than I thought, and I'm at the Gritti if you fancy some lunch. Where are you?"

"We're at the fish market, and the boys are in their wellies in case the flooding kicks off this afternoon, so I'm not sure about lunch at the Gritti."

"What flooding?"

"Dad said they reckon it'll be a really high tide, especially tomorrow."

"Great, that'll be me soaked again. Christ, every time I come here in winter I end up wading through fucking water."

"Didn't you bring your wellies?"

"My what?"

"I'm sure you could buy some. What size are you? I'll have a look for you if you like."

"That's very kind of you, but they sell plastic things you can put over your shoes when it gets bad. I haven't worn wellies since I was a kid."

"Fair enough. Just don't come crying to me when you've got wet socks."

He laughs. "So if you're not up for lunch, shall we meet earlier for tea?"

"That would be lovely. It'll take us a while to get over there, though, especially since Vin's got the map."

"Around three?"

"Perfect."

"How's the chocolate orange thing going?"

When I talked to him yesterday, the boys were mid-bicker about a missing segment.

"Still pretty tense, but they've negotiated a cease-fire, for now."

He laughs again. "I'll see you all later, then."

We carry on wandering, heading vaguely in the direction of the Grand Canal, and the boys become fixated on all the bakery shops with their beautiful displays of marzipan animals and nougat, so we stop for another coffee in a little café with marble-topped tables and they try some nougat, which goes straight to the top of their list of Top Sweets and renders them silent while they chew, so it's pretty high up on my list, too.

Vin orders himself another panini. "So who's this bloke we're having tea with, then?"

"Daniel Fitzgerald."

Lulu puts her cup down. "Like the famous photographer?"

"Yes. He's meeting someone about a job taking pictures of Venice, I think; I'm not really sure."

"You mean he actually *is* the famous photographer?"

"Yes."

"God, I wish I'd known. When you said we were meeting a friend for tea, I thought you meant someone normal."

"He is normal, well, fairly."

"Yes, but at least I could have worn my clean jeans. Did he take those great pictures you were showing us?"

"Yes. He came down to do the magazine shoot with Grace, and Ellen invited him to supper, so he ended up playing football with Trevor and the boys, didn't he?"

They both nod, but their mouths are jammed full of nougat, so they can't speak. I must remember to buy lots to take home.

Vin finishes his panini.

"Well, I'm glad to hear he plays football, because for a minute there I thought we were going to be stuck all afternoon with someone else poncing on about light, and we get quite enough of that with Mum, thank you very much."

Lulu smiles.

"It's not funny. Either she's giving you one of her History of Art lectures or she's treating you like a flaming waiter for one of her parties, and they're all such"—he hesitates and looks at the boys—"such interesting people."

We cross the Rialto bridge and head toward San Marco, and the shops start getting smarter and more expensive-looking. And then we see another wool shop, full of amazing hand-dyed silks and some fabulous cashmere, and despite protests from Vin, we go in for a quick look round. They've got lots of beautiful hand-knitted cardigans and wraps, and skeins of wool hanging from wooden poles and more stock in glass-fronted cupboards. It's all incredibly elegant, and I buy some of the silk in a really deep olive that I can't resist, and take a price list and a leaflet about the cashmere to look at when I get home; maybe if it's not too expensive, I can ask Connie to call them for me and put in an order.

The water's starting to lap round the edge of the canal steps as we cross the little bridges and make our way to St. Mark's Square, and workmen are putting out linking trestle tables as walkways, ready for tomorrow's high tide, which the boys think is very exciting. Vin promises to bring Archie back tomorrow so he can walk on the tables, and I promise to stay indoors with Jack.

Daniel's sitting in a window seat when we get to Florian's. He hands Jack and Archie a paper bag each, with a chocolate orange in.

"I thought these might come in handy."

Archie jumps up and down with the thrill of it all.

"Oh, thank you, thank you, because I've run out of mine."

"So I heard."

Jack's looking very pleased, too. "Yes, and now I'll have nearly one and three quarters."

Lulu gives him a hug as Archie starts unwrapping his.

"Just have a little bit, though, Archie, yes?"

"Yes. This time I'm going to make it last. Or I might not. I haven't decided yet."

We drink glasses of thick hot chocolate and try some of the delicious cakes, while Lulu tells us about her friend who kept all her Easter eggs on a shelf in her bedroom, untouched in their boxes, just to annoy her sister, and Archie rolls his eyes. Daniel's telling Lulu he's in Venice for a meeting about a special project for the Biennale, while I try surreptitiously to wipe hot chocolate off Archie's face.

"Can we have more cakes?"

Lulu laughs. "You can't possibly have room for any more, Archie, and anyway, Uncle Vin's going to take you up the tower in a minute."

"Oh yes, I'd forgotten about that. Can we go now?"

"In a minute." Vin sighs. "Anyone care to join us?"

Lulu shakes her head, and I tell Daniel that Vin and the boys are going up the Campanile as I start getting their coats on.

"Actually, I was hoping you might take some photographs of them for me, with my camera, because I haven't got any really nice ones of them since they were little. I know it's a terrible cheek, but would you mind? It's got a film in it."

He looks at my camera. "Not with that, I can't."

"Oh, right. Sorry."

I suppose it was a bit of a cheek to ask him really.

He lifts up a battered old camera from beside him on the seat.

"I'll give it a go, but I'm not very good with kids, so don't expect anything brilliant. What are you after?"

"Sorry?"

"What sort of pictures do you want?"

"Ones with both of them in, without the tops of their heads cut off, and not scowling or pushing each other."

He smiles. "I think I can probably manage that. The light's pretty good now." He looks at Archie. "Does he have to wear that hat?"

"Why?"

"Because it makes him look like he's got a pointy head."

Jack shrieks with laughter, and Archie takes his hat off and throws it on the floor.

"Thanks, Daniel. Archie, put it back on, and I'll fix it so it doesn't go pointy. Come on, or you'll get cold. Any more style tips you'd like to share with us, Daniel?"

"No, they're fine."

"Good, because I can make your hat go pointy, too, if you like."

"I haven't got a hat."

"We can soon fix that."

After an initially tricky moment when everybody goes rather stiff and self-conscious, Daniel gets us all running round the square, shouting orders to us in such a bossy voice we're all leaning up against pillars and balancing on one leg before we know it, and two rolls of film later he's finally happy.

"They're only snaps though."

"Of course."

"I'll get Tony to send them over."

"Oh no, I don't want to put you to any trouble. I can easily get them done in Boots."

"Boots? Are you mad? I'm not having my stuff done in Boots. I do have some standards, you know."

"Well, if you're sure. But you must let me pay."

He smiles. "I do all my work with them. It'll just get lost on a client's bill, don't worry about it. So where are we off to now?"

"Shopping, I think, while Vin does the tower thing."

"Great. Gucci? Prada? Bags or clothes? I'm great at shopping. In small doses."

"Tea bags. Mum's only got Earl Grey."

"Just tea bags?"

"Yes."

"You're the only woman I know who'd come to Venice and only go shopping for tea bags."

"And a hat for you, of course. I thought maybe one of those velvet carnival ones, with the bells. I've seen them on all the stalls."

We head off down a side street and find a shop selling lots of different kinds of glass beads, which I can't resist; they'll be great for beading on shawls and scarves. I buy a few packets of the smaller ones and a box full of the larger ones in lovely deep colors, and Lulu spots an old glass cake stand on one of the shelves, in pale pink glass, and a smaller one in pale green, which are both so pretty I'm really tempted, until I see the price.

"They'd be great for your new Teatime window display."

I'm thinking of teapots and tea cozies and little knitted fairy cakes for the new window display in the shop, and I was talking to Lulu about it yesterday, while we made the tomato tartlets.

"I know, but they're really expensive."

Daniel sighs. "Honestly, you two are hopeless. This is Italy; haggle."

"I hate haggling, it always makes me feel like I'm being mean."

"Oh, for God's sake, go and wait for me outside."

We can't resist peering through the window, and there's a fair amount of arm waving before Daniel comes out with a bag with two tissue-wrapped parcels inside.

"Done."

"Oh, thank you, that's brilliant. How much do I owe you?"

"I don't really want to talk about it."

Lulu looks puzzled. "But you got lots off, right?"

"No. Actually the price went up at first."

We both start to laugh.

"But that was because the green one was part of a set or something. I got the pink one for half price, I think. Now, can we talk about something else, please?"

I finally persuade him to let me pay for them, but only after a fair bit of bickering, and we walk back to the square to find the boys have loved the Campanile, but Vin's exhausted.

It's starting to get cold.

"I think we should probably be heading for home."

Vin nods. "Good plan. I'm crackered."

Lulu puts her arm round him and kisses him, which makes Archie giggle.

"Damn, I forgot to get tea bags."

Daniel smiles. "I've got some tea back at the hotel, if you want it. Why don't you all come back with me? Or we could put the boys in a water taxi with your brother and you two can come and get it, and we can have a drink?"

Vin looks enthusiastic. "Sounds like a good plan to me. Except I'll do the tea bags and the girls can do the water taxi. I could do with a beer right now."

Lulu shakes her head. "Oh no you don't. I'm not having you coming back singing rude songs in the middle of one of your mother's parties. No, Jo can get the tea and we'll take the boys back."

"Spoilsport."

"Don't whine, Vin. I've told you before: it's not very attractive."

Daniel laughs. "Right, well, that's sorted then. Yes?"

Everyone looks at me.

"Okay, but tell Mum I'm on my way, will you?"

"Sure. Come on, boys, we're going home in a boat."

They cheer.

We put them all into a water taxi, and I make the boys promise to stay sitting inside in the warm, and then we walk to the hotel, which is very splendid and hushed, and smells of woodsmoke and polish, in a non-Pledge kind of a way. Daniel walks straight past the reception desk and toward the lifts as a beautiful young woman comes out from behind the desk with an envelope.

"This arrived for you, Mr. Fitzgerald."

"Oh, right. Thanks."

She smiles at him, but he doesn't seem to notice.

"Is there anything else you need?"

"Yes. Tea bags, lots of them, but no Earl Grey."

"I'll send some up directly."

"Great."

The room turns out to be a suite, with a living room looking over the Grand Canal.

"Bloody hell, this is amazing."

"I guess you'd like some tea now, right?"

"That would be lovely."

"Do you want cakes or anything? I think they do quite good ones here."

"No, thanks, just tea, please."

We sit talking and drinking tea while we watch the boats going up and down the canal, and the occasional gondola full of tourists, as it starts to grow dark. The tea's lovely, and he's very easy to talk to.

"So why are you in Venice in this fabulous room all by yourself?"

"I told you, I've got a meeting tomorrow."

"I know, but you must know someone who'd like to spend a couple of days of splendor in Venice with you."

He smiles. "I do. But she's married."

"Oh, sorry. I didn't mean to pry."

"It's okay."

"Is it?"

"No, not really, but it's nice to be able to talk about it. She's quite high-profile, so it's tricky."

"Oh. Right."

"Or rather it used to be tricky. She just gave me my cards, just before Christmas, actually."

He starts to look rather sad, and tired.

"Oh dear. Tell me about her."

"What?"

"Tell me about her, if you'd like to. How you met, everything. Just don't tell me her name."

He looks pleased. "I'd like that. Tea and sympathy, right?"

"It helps sometimes, talking."

"God, I'm sorry. I forgot."

"What?"

"About your husband. Look, let's have a proper drink, shall we? Do you fancy a whiskey?"

"Yes, please."

He walks over to a large wooden drinks cabinet and pours two tumblers.

"Ice?"

"Please."

He hands me a glass and sits back down.

"So, do I start at the beginning, then?"

"Yes."

"Well, she's Swedish, and we met on a job."

"Right."

He stares at his feet. "I remember thinking she was the most beautiful woman I'd ever seen."

Three large glasses of whiskey later I'm feeling very mellow, although I'm not sure I can stand up anymore, and Daniel's telling me about his first girlfriend, who was called Flora.

"She sounds sweet."

"She was. I should have stayed at home and married her. I'd probably have kids by now, and a proper life instead of this fucking traveling circus I seem to have got myself into. God, I'm really hungry. Are you? Shall I get some food sent up?"

"Yes, that would be—Christ, what time is it?"

"It's nearly eight."

"Fuck, I'm meant to be at Mum's, serving canapés with a cheery smile on my face, not sitting getting pissed with you."

"Sod her."

I laugh.

"I mean it. This is your holiday, right?"

"Yes, but."

"So sod her."

"Actually, you're right, I don't really need to be there. In fact, it'll be hobble." Christ, I can't say *horrible* now: I think I must be drunker than I thought. Maybe some food would be a good idea.

"I just need to call Vin and check on the boys."

"I'll get some menus sent up."

Vin's delighted. In fact, he thinks it's brilliant. "She's been going absolutely tonto."

"Oh, God."

"Stop it; it's fine. You stay and have supper. It'll give me and Lou a brilliant excuse. We'll say we've got to take the boys out for a pizza, and that way we all get to escape."

"She'll be furious."

"It's a good job she isn't coming with us, then, isn't it? Look, it's not like she really needs us here, we're only background interest. Anyway, I can't stand here gabbing to you.

I've got to go and break the news to Mum. God, this is going to be so great."

"See you later, then."

"Sure."

"Are you sure the boys are okay?"

"They're fine, and we've nearly finished building their pirate ships."

The menus arrive, and we order steak and chips and salads, which come with a bottle of wine and a waiter, who sets everything up on a table by the window and then leaves.

"This looks wonderful."

"Good. Go on, it's your turn now. Tell me all about your sordid past."

"There's not much to tell, really."

"Make something up, then. Or tell me your top tips. I love getting top tips from girls."

He pours us both some wine.

"I can't think of anything. Apart from how it's not the end of the world."

"What isn't?"

"When things change. It feels like it is. But it's not. I thought losing Nick was going to ruin everything, completely. And it did, of course, in some ways. But in some ways it's better. Is that a terrible thing to say?"

"No."

"It is. He deserves better than that—everyone does. But it's true."

"Do you miss him?"

"All the time. Mainly for the boys, but not just for them. I'd like to tell him things, show him how we're doing. I want him to see how they're growing up. He'd be so proud of them, I know he would. But it's not as hard as I thought it was going to be. You carry on, even if you don't think you can, somehow you do."

He leans forward and kisses me. Bloody hell.

"Why did you do that?"

"Because I wanted to."

"Oh."

"I might do it again. If you don't mind?"

"Well, let me eat my chips first, would you?"

He laughs.

"Sure. We could have a secret signal or something, if you like."

"A what?"

"A secret signal, so we both know when a kiss might be on the horizon."

"Like when they say 'Brace, brace, brace,' when your plane's crashing?"

He laughs again. "Something like that, only maybe slightly more upbeat?"

"Okay. Like what?"

"I don't know."

We carry on eating, and I can't help smiling.

"It's not much of a secret signal, is it?"

"Not really."

"I think I've thought of one."

He puts his fork down. "Go on, then."

I lean across the table and kiss him.

"That works for me."

It's nearly midnight now, and I'm feeling all glamorous and wanton, and I've always wanted to feel wanton. It's absolutely brilliant.

"I really should go."

"But baby, it's cold outside."

I hit him with a pillow.

"Look, I'm sure your mum will cope, if they wake up or anything."

"Not unless they need an urgent bit of stenciling she won't."

"Please. Just stay a little bit longer."

Christ, it's nearly one now. "I've really got to go. Where's my bag gone?"

He grins. "I've got no idea."

"Thanks. That's very helpful."

"You'll have to learn to keep track of your gear when you go out gallivanting, angel."

"I don't go out gallivanting."

"You could have fooled me. Shall I ring down for a taxi?"

"Won't they be asleep?"

"Then they can wake up, can't they? That's kind of how twenty-four-hour room service works. It doesn't mean just when they're not asleep, you know."

"It does in the hotels I stay in."

He picks up the phone as I go into the bathroom. My hair's gone all tangled, and I've got a weird mark on my neck. Excellent.

"The taxi's on its way."

"Great."

"So when are you flying home?"

"At the weekend."

"I'm off back to New York later today."

"Oh. Right."

"And then we've got a job in Germany, I think. Tony knows all the details, at least I hope he does, or we're going to look pretty stupid at the airport. So I'll call you, shall I?"

"Sure."

"You don't sound very enthusiastic. Is this you telling me you don't want to see me again?" He's smiling.

"No, of course not. I'm just trying to be realistic, that's all."

"Well, don't be."

"You'll be busy flying round the world with your supermodels, and I'll be at home with the boys, not flying anywhere. So maybe we shouldn't try to turn this into something it isn't."

"You're a total sweetheart, did you know that?"

"Most people are, when you get to know them."

"Not the ones I meet."

The phone rings.

"The taxi's here. And by the way, it's on the hotel account, so don't go paying him. Shall I come down with you?"

"No, stay up here in the warm."

I kiss him on the cheek and leave.

Christ. I've somehow turned into the kind of woman who has passionate interludes in Venice and gets water taxis in the middle of the night. How bloody brilliant. I'm so pleased with myself I could almost skip. Although perhaps not out here on the jetty, because I don't want to launch myself into the Grand Canal.

I'm just getting into the water taxi when Daniel appears, wearing a hotel bathrobe and clutching a plastic bag.

"You forgot your tea bags."

The doorman and taximan both give us rather interested looks.

"Oh. Thanks."

He grins. "Christ, it's fucking freezing out here."

He hands me the bag and kisses my cheek. "Night, angel."

"Night, Daniel."

The taxi glides away from the jetty, and he waves at me and then turns and goes back inside. I sit and watch the buildings float past. Bloody hell. I wonder how long I'll have to wait before I can call Ellen. A few hours, at least. Bloody hell.

Mum's sitting in the kitchen in her dressing gown when I get in.

Bugger.

"I see you've finally decided to grace us with your presence."

"Sorry, Mum. Didn't Vin explain?"

"Yes. He said you were having supper with Daniel Fitzgerald. The photographer."

"Yes."

"When you knew I had people coming for drinks."

"Yes, but they weren't coming to see me, were they?"

"No, but I'm sure they would have liked to meet him. He is rather famous, you know."

"Oh, I see, that's what you're so annoyed about. Missing out on a celebrity guest."

She glares at me.

"Look, Mum, it's late. Can we do this tomorrow?"

"No, we can't. You've always been the same, totally selfish. By rights the shop should have come to me, you know. I could have used the money to get us a little flat over here, but oh no, she gives it to her favorite, as usual."

"I don't think a wool shop in Broadgate would buy you much in Venice, Mum, and anyway, isn't it up to Gran who she gives her money to?"

"And what about Vincent? He seems to have rather lost out, too, doesn't he? It's absolutely typical of you. You always have to be the center of attention, especially where she's concerned."

"Mum, Nick died, I didn't do anything to be the center of attention. It just happened. And Vin's fine about it, you know he is, and I've told him I'll sell up if he ever needs the money."

"Oh yes, he always takes your side."

"Please let's not argue, Mum."

"You could have stayed in London and gone back to work. Running a little wool shop isn't exactly what I had in mind for you. When I think of the years I put into you two, and look at you, one off playing on boats and the other one playing shops. Honestly, it's so disappointing. It's important to make a difference, Josephine, do something special with your life."

"I am."

"In a wool shop?"

"Yes, and it's making me really happy, for the first time in ages. The boys are happy, and it doesn't get more important than that, not for me, so please don't start. I'm going up to bed now."

"I see. So you're not in the mood for a bit of honesty, then? What a surprise."

Oh, bollocks to this.

"All right, let's give it a go, let's be really honest for once, shall we? You can tell me what a crap daughter I am, and I'll tell you what a crap mother you are. Yes? Because once I get started, there'll be plenty to talk about. Mariella."

She looks rather shocked.

"Not keen? No, I thought you might not be. I'll see you in the morning. And one crack, one sarcastic comment, and I'll be off, because I'm not having you upset the boys. And I mean it, Mum. I really do. Good night."

Blimey. I'm shaking as I walk up the stairs. Passionate interludes and standing up to Mum, all in one night. How completely brilliant is that? God knows what I'll be getting up to tomorrow, but I think I'd better get some sleep.

It's seven in the morning and the boys are still asleep, so I'm calling Ellen while I've got the chance.

"God, you total trollop. How fabulous."

"I know."

"When will you see him again?"

"God knows. Probably never. But I don't care. It's weird, but it feels like a one-off. It's like I'm still married and this is just a mad moment. I don't know, it'll probably end in tears, but it was worth it."

"Everything ends in tears, darling. It's the beginnings that count. And the middle bits."

"I felt so grown-up, Ellen, I can't tell you."

"I'm so pleased for you."

"It was lovely, just being with someone else."

"By 'being,' I assume you mean shagging, right?"

"Trust you to lower the tone. Yes, and it was great. And I wasn't embarrassed or anything."

She laughs. "Why would you be embarrassed?"

"Oh, you know, my thighs, supermodel thighs, spot the difference, that kind of thing."

"And we don't have to have the condom conversation, do we?"

"No, we do not, thank you very much."

"Good. Boys like him usually travel equipped."

"Ellen, please!"

"I don't think you're in any position to go all coy on me, darling, not with what you've been up to."

"I keep getting flashbacks. It's very disconcerting."

"Don't worry, they'll wear off after a bit. Now, it's vital you don't call him, you know that, don't you?"

"Ellen, I don't think this is going to turn into anything serious. I mean, think about it. What on earth do I want with a photographer who's surrounded by the most beautiful women in the world, flying off at a moment's notice? It'd be like Nick, only ten times worse, and I wouldn't just be worrying about UN workers."

"Right. So this is about Nick, then, is it?"

"No."

"It bloody is. You meet a drop-dead gorgeous man who most women would give their right arm for, and you're too scared to go for it because your husband cheated on you."

"I went for it, Ellen, trust me."

"I know, darling, but why not see him again?"

"I might. I'm not saying I won't, but I'm not holding my breath, either. He's thirty-two, Ellen, and he's free and single, and I'm not. I'm thirty-eight with two kids and a life, and anyway, he's in love with someone else, we talked about it."

"Really? Who?"

"Someone, nobody, it doesn't matter. The important thing is I'm fine about it, I really am, and this way I won't be waiting for him to call and wondering what he's doing and getting all involved, because I really don't want that. We can be friends, proper friends maybe. Not because I'm some tragic wounded person still in mourning, although funnily enough I feel like I've got past a point on that front, somehow. It's like I'm moving forward, and not just making the best of what's left. But more importantly I've realized how happy I am, for the first time in ages. And I don't want to change that."

"Bloody hell. Good for you, darling."

"Of course it might all change."

"Of course."

"But for now I'm feeling pretty pleased with myself, I can tell you."

"I bet. What's the plan for today, then?"

"Nothing much. I've seen a nice shirt in a secondhand shop near the house which I might get, and the boys want to try out more ice-cream shops. But nothing too strenuous, because I'm totally knackered."

She laughs. "One-night stands I can take, but vintage shopping is too much. I think you're having a breakdown, and you need international rescue. I'll be on the first plane."

"Or I could see you next weekend, if you fancy Sunday lunch?"

"All right, but promise me you'll take it easy. It's a lot to get used to, and you might have overload issues going on."

"I promise. If I find myself by the till in Gucci by mistake, I'll call you, okay?"

"Great. Or you could just buy a present for your best friend. Pretty much anything in Gucci would be fine."

"I've already got your present."

"Tell me."

"No."

"*Tell me.*"

"It's a gondola that lights up and plays a tune."

"Fabulous. 'Just One Cornetto,' right?"

"How did you guess?"

9

IN THE BLEAK MIDWINTER

I'm kneeling in the window of the shop, humming "I'm a Little Teapot" and trying to de-glitter before I put the tea cozies in; I've already put the teapots in and the cups and saucers, and the hot-water-bottle covers and the scarves are on the shelves at the side, but this bloody glitter is really slowing me down. I've borrowed one of Gran's tablecloths, a floral cotton one I remember from birthday teas when I was little, and I've left a string of white fairy lights up, because I think January's exactly the kind of month when you need fairy lights. It's bloody freezing today, and we had sleet for most of yesterday, mixed in with thick fog, so maybe the lights will lure people into the shop for a quick warm by the fire and a small purchase. It's been pretty quiet since Christmas, so we need all the help we can get.

Gran and Betty are upstairs knitting fairy cakes, while

Gran runs through her cruise highlights with Betty for the umpteenth time. She's got four packets of photographs and enough anecdotes to last her all year, and they're already talking about going on another one in the summer, and she's trying to persuade Betty to come with them. Reg came home with a light tan and a new sailor's cap because the other one blew off somewhere outside Funchal, and he won a trophy for playing quoits, whatever they are. He's going to ask his friend William to join them next time so they can make up a four for bridge, not that Betty actually plays bridge, but Gran's got a book from the library, so they're going to learn together.

The phone starts ringing, but by the time I've managed to clamber back out of the window Gran's already answered it, and is telling Ellen all about her cabin.

"They keep everything spotless, you know, you really should try it, and they go all over, Greenland if you like whales, or hot places, everywhere really and they're so big you hardly know you're moving. They do all sorts of classes, you know: bridge or flower arranging or painting. A woman at our table did a lovely one of a sunset. Oh, here she is now, dear."

She hands the phone to me and mimes "Do you want a cup of tea?" I nod and she goes back upstairs humming "I'm a Little Teapot." It must be catching.

"Bloody hell, I think she's just booked me in for a week cruising round Wales."

"She's a born-again cruiser now, she wants everyone to have a go."

"In the non-swinging sense of the word, I hope?"

"Ellen, please. This is my grandmother we're talking about."

"What's sauce for the gander, darling."

"What gander?"

"The light's green: drive, you moron, for fuck's sake."

"Are you in the car by any chance?"

"Yes, so speak up, darling, I can hardly hear you. This hands-free thing is complete crap. Has he called yet?"

"No, and the photographs haven't arrived yet, either, but it's fine. Actually, I think I'd almost prefer it if he didn't ring, in a way."

"Oh yes? And what way is that? The tragic I-have-no-life way?"

"No, the I-have-a-lovely-life-and-I-don't-want-to-fuck-it-up way."

"You might be right. I think he could be a tiny bit too high-maintenance for you, arty types always are. You want a nice background boy, off making shedloads of money, who's a bit shy, but brilliant when he gets going."

"Oh yes, and do you know anyone like that?"

"Not really, and if I do spot one I'm ditching Harry and keeping him for myself. But if he's got a friend, I'll let you know."

"What's Harry done now?"

"Gone off to Dublin for a two-day jaunt with his mate Liam. He rang last night, and he was so pissed I thought he was a heavy breather at first. Fucking taxis, same to you, wanker."

There's the sound of a car horn being pressed repeatedly.

"You know, what I really need is an air horn like lorries have, the ones that are so loud they make your seat vibrate. Do you know where I can get one?"

"No, but I'm pretty sure they're illegal in cars."

"I won't use it on police cars, darling, although I'd like to see their faces if I did, bastards. Forty-two miles an hour in a thirty, like there's nothing more important going on in London at ten o'clock at night. Talk about wasting police time. I should have made a citizen's arrest."

"I don't think citizens' arrests are for traffic policemen when they stop you for speeding."

"Well, they bloody should be. God, I wish I'd thought of it at the time. The papers would have loved it, and I'd have probably got a one-hour special out of it."

"True. And Jeremy Clarkson could be your new best friend."

"There is that. Still, every silver lining has its cloud."

"Talking of which, Mum rang me last night."

"How was she?"

"Still sulking. She's talking about coming over for a visit in the summer, because she says she misses the boys, not that she's ever missed them before, and Vin's still not speaking to her. So that'll be ten years with half the family not talking."

"Oh dear."

Vin and Mum had a huge row on the last day, and he stormed off to the airport straight after breakfast, because Mum had started having little digs at Lulu.

"She'll never change, you know. Mothers don't. They just get worse and worse. What am I meant to be, fucking psychic? Indicate, you wanker."

"I'm sure your mum didn't mean it."

"She bloody did. She spent the whole time going on about how much she'd like a grandchild before she was too old to lift the fucker up, and then when I told her she was really freaking me out, she pretended she didn't know what I was talking about. There's a bus lane, you wanker. Bloody go in it and stop blocking my lane."

"Ellen, wouldn't it be better to get a cab to work?"

"No, it bloody wouldn't. If I want to sit in a car with some man droning on for hours, I can go out for a drive with Normal Neil. At least I won't be paying the bastard."

Neil is Ellen's latest co-anchor, who crawls round management all the time and gets lot of fan mail from middle-aged housewives who think he's lovely, although perhaps not quite as lovely as his boyfriend does. His wife seems oblivious, or maybe she just doesn't care, which is Ellen's theory.

"So how's it going with Mr. Smarm, then?"

"We're putting espressos in his decaf now, so his hands keep going shaky. It's really freaking him out, it's brilliant. What time do you want us on Saturday?"

"Any time that suits."

"Great, because I'm really knackered, so I want to have a lie-in and then go for a swim."

"You want to go shopping, you mean?"

"Yes."

"That's fine. Will Harry be back from Dublin?"

"Yes, although God knows what state he'll be in."

"Does he know I've got the in-laws for lunch on Sunday?"

"No, I thought that could be a nice little surprise for him. Oh, and if I bring his sweater down with me, could you fix it? One arm's definitely longer than the other, it'll make him look deformed."

"Sure."

"Great. Lift the fucking pole up. Yes, I'm talking to you. Thank you. God knows where they get these security people from, they're all morons. Talk later, darling."

Blimey, I'm almost feeling sorry for poor old Neil.

Betty comes downstairs with another fairy cake and a cup of tea.

"Here's another one finished, love. The tea cozies look nice, don't they? That blue one's like the one my mum used to have. We always had a proper tea on Sundays, you know, with cake, and we'd sit and listen to the radio in the front room. I can remember it like it was yesterday."

Gran's made a blue-striped tea cozy, and Elsie's just finished one with ruffles in pink and cream, and I've made a couple of more minimalist ones in cotton. They hardly took any time to knit, but they look rather fetching, especially the one with pom-poms.

"I'm nearly ready to start putting them in the window."

She puts the cake next to the others on the counter, on one of the glass cake stands from Venice.

"These plates are pretty, and these cakes would make nice little pincushions, you know, not that there's much call for pincushions nowadays."

"The Victorians used to make them as presents for new mothers, but they didn't put the pins in until the baby had arrived safely. Isn't that sweet? I've been reading about it as part of my research for the school knitting thing."

She smiles. "Your gran says you're off to see Grace Harrison later. Is that right?"

"Yes."

"I thought I might knit something for her, for the baby, but I wasn't sure what to make. I don't expect she'd think much to a pincushion, though, would she?"

"Probably not, but what about one of your shawls? Although she's got quite a few things already."

Betty makes lovely baby shawls, and she knows all the patterns off by heart, just like Gran does.

"I'd like to make her something, it can't be easy for her, being on her own like that, with everyone wanting to know what she's doing, it doesn't matter how rich she is. I'll get some wool before I go; I like having a bit of knitting on the go, it keeps me busy in the evenings."

"Well, don't forget you get staff discount now, so it'll be a third off. And I can always sell them in the shop, if you want to make more. I'll give you the wool, and I'd pay you for your time."

"Elsie won't like it, you know."

"Let's not tell her, then."

She smiles. "You're a good girl. Now, drink your tea while it's still hot, love."

It's raining as I'm driving to see Grace, and one of the wipers isn't working properly, so there are smears all over the windscreen, and then I get stuck behind a gritting lorry, which sprays grit all over the front of the car. I park as far away from the black Jeep as I can, and Maxine comes out, looking anxious.

"She's in a terrible temper."

"Oh dear, why?"

"I'm not really sure."

"Shall I see if I can cheer her up a bit, then?"

She smiles. "Please. We'd all be eternally grateful. But be careful: she hates being Handled."

"I wouldn't dare."

I've never really seen Grace in a temper, although it's obvious to anyone within fifty yards of her that she's used to getting her own way: she's always been completely charming to me, which probably means she's never been that relaxed, which makes me feel rather sad.

She's lying on one of the green sofas looking very pregnant and very annoyed.

"Oh, it's you. Great. Could we have some drinks, Maxine? If it's not too much trouble, of course. I wouldn't want to get in the way of your telephone calls."

Maxine looks at her feet.

"Water for me, and not that plastic crap, and I'd like a bagel. Toasted."

"I'm not sure if we've got bagels, but I can—"

"Well, go out and get some, then. You're my assistant, right? So assist me. Or send Sam. I don't really care."

"Of course. I'll get right on it."

Maxine closes the door, and Grace turns to look at me. She's very pale.

"What's the matter?"

She gives me a surprised look. And rather a terrifying one, too, if I'm completely honest.

"You seem a bit upset."

"That's because I fucking am."

"Can I help?"

"No."

"Can anyone help?"

"No."

"It's not anything to do with the baby, is it?"

There's a small hesitation.

"No."

She turns her head away from me, like Archie does when he's sulking.

Bless.

"Does your back hurt? When I was having Jack, I had terrible backache. You get so uncomfortable by the end, nothing really fixes it for long, does it?"

"No."

"I remember feeling very panicky, too. I don't think you ever feel completely ready for something like this, do you?"

"No."

Her shoulders are heaving now, so I think she might be crying. Or maybe she's just laughing at my pathetic attempts to be reassuring.

"I was just as bad with Archie, too, and then he ended up being an emergency cesarean because he was getting distressed—although not half as distressed as I was, I can tell you. And I remember thinking, when they handed him to me, that they'd give me a quick look and then hand him over to someone more sensible to take home, someone more like a proper mum."

She turns round and sniffs. "I didn't realize you had a cesarean."

"Yes. And I bloody wish I'd had one with Jack, too."

"Really? Don't you think natural childbirth is better, then?"

"No, I don't. I think all that too-posh-to-push stuff is rubbish. I don't think it's better at all, it's just cheaper. When I was in with Archie, there were three doctors having babies on my ward, and they'd all had elective cesareans, so that's got to tell you something."

She smiles. "So you don't think it's a cop-out?"

"No. Natural births aren't always flute music and getting your breathing right, you know. And having your baby delivered by forceps isn't exactly ideal, especially for the baby, or having the poor little thing dragged out with one of those horrible plastic suction cap things so it gets a pointy head. And what's so natural about crawling about in agony on all fours for hours, anyway, that's what I'd like to know. It can't be very nice for the baby, can it, all that yelling; I've always thought it was pretty daft spending nine months playing the poor little sod Mozart, and then for its introduction to the world all it gets is yelling and screaming and hearing its mum telling everyone to fuck off."

"Did you tell everyone to fuck off then?"

"Oh yes, and I punched Nick so hard he nearly fell over. It was brilliant, and it really made the midwife laugh, and she'd been a bit of a cow up to then. He was meant to be massaging my back, but he just kept sort of prodding and it was annoying me."

She smiles.

"Seriously, Grace, if men gave birth, do you really think they'd do it with a bit of gas and air and a bloody beanbag?"

"But what about breast feeding? Someone was telling me it's harder to get going with that after a C-section."

"I didn't have any problems. I mean, it's really weird at first—you can't quite believe it works—but everyone gets that. Who was telling you it's harder?"

"One of the midwives at the hospital."

"That's because most of them hate C-sections, because they don't get to be in charge. It's like asking a member of the Countryside Alliance for an impartial view on hunting: they just start frothing at the mouth. And you'll be different. You won't be having an emergency cesarean after hours in labor so you're so exhausted you can hardly see straight, let alone have a go at breast feeding. You'll be fine."

"But what if I can't cope—when it's out, I mean? What if I'm just totally fucking useless?"

"Of course you'll be useless; everyone is at first."

"That's very bloody encouraging, thanks. You were almost helping there for a minute, but now you've totally blown it." She's smiling.

"Grace, nobody feels ready for this, and if they say they do, they're either thick or lying. But do you know what's clever? The baby doesn't know you're making it up as you go along. They just know you're their mum. They look at you, and you become sort of invincible."

"Well, I don't feel invincible, I can bloody tell you. I've been in tears half the fucking morning. And if you say it's hormones, I'll throw something at you."

"You've got yourself into a right old frazzle, haven't you?"

"A what?"

"A frazzle. It's a technical term for someone who's eight months pregnant."

She smiles. "I'm not even nesting, and all my books go on about nesting."

"I didn't, either. Lots of people don't; I think it's called anti-nesting."

"What did you do, then, when the baby was born?"

"Sent Nick out emergency shopping, with my friend Ellen, and she sorted it all out for me."

"Does she have kids?"

"No, but she's very good at shopping. It's her specialist subject."

Maxine comes in with a tray and puts it down on the table. "Sam's gone to get bagels. He won't be long."

"Thanks, Max. And I'm sorry, about earlier."

Maxine looks surprised. "That's fine." She winks at me as she passes me my tea.

"I bloody saw that."

"I'll bring the bagels straight in, shall I?"

"Yes. Thanks, Max."

Maxine curtsies and goes out.

Grace smiles. "So, tell me, how was Venice?"

"Great. I got some lovely new wool for the shop. I'll show you, if you like."

"I've nearly finished my blanket. Do you want to see?"

"I'd love to, and I've found a pattern for a sweet little baby sleeping bag, which I thought you might like to try next. It would be handy for car journeys."

"Do they like sleeping in cars?"

"At the risk of frazzling you even more, sometimes it's the only place they'll sleep, as long as you keep driving."

"Looks like Bruno's going to be busy, then."

"Mum, Mum, quick, get up, it's snowing. Look."

Archie is jumping on my bed, at half past seven in the bloody morning.

"You're supposed to play quietly in your bedroom until the big hand is on the eight, Archie."

"Yes, but it's *snowing.*"

I get up and look out of the window, and he's right, it is. But it's not really settling, thank God.

"Can we go out and make a snowman?"

"I don't think there's enough snow for that yet, love."

"Will there be more later?"

I bloody hope not, because I've got my Stitch and Bitch group tonight and I'm supposed to be meeting Mrs. Chambers at school this morning to talk about the knitting project.

"We'll see."

The boys insist on walking to school for maximum exposure to what is now much closer to sleet than snow. Archie tries to collect handfuls to make snowballs and gets very annoyed when it melts, while Jack trudges along behind me, moaning that we haven't got a sledge, and then we see Mr. Pallfrey's daughter, Christine, taking Trevor out for his morning walk, which means we have to stop to say hello, and Trevor puts muddy paw prints all over the front of Archie's coat while I ask Christine how Mr. Pallfrey's doing; he went into hospital on Tuesday, and he had his operation yesterday.

"I think he's in a fair bit of pain, but he was sitting up last night, and they're getting him walking today. I gave him your card and the picture, and he was ever so pleased."

Archie drew him a picture of Trevor, in case he was missing him.

"So when will he be home?"

"At the weekend, or maybe Monday—it depends on how he's doing."

Please let it be Monday. I really don't want to have to take over full-time dog-walking duties on the weekend when Elizabeth and Gerald are here for lunch.

"Give him our love, won't you? And let me know if you think he'd like a visit."

She smiles. "Between you and me, I don't think he's that keen on people seeing him in his pajamas. He's having enough trouble coping with me going in."

"Well, let me know when he's coming home and we'll bring a cake round. Come on, Archie, put that down. What do you want a dirty, wet stick for?"

"For Trevor."

"Give it to him quickly, then, or we'll be late."

"I'm not sure I like this one. I might need another one."

"Archie."

"Oh, all right. Grumpy big potamus."

The playground is even more chaotic than usual, with everyone under twelve trying to get as much contact as possible with whatever is available in the snow department, and everyone over twelve desperately trying to stop them. Mr. O'Brien's blowing his whistle and Mrs. Berry's ringing the bell, but there's still a great deal of Milling About before they start to line up and go in.

Connie's looking very cold and fed up.

"Are you okay?"

"Yes, I'm just tired. Christmas was so busy, and it seems like this cold and fogging will be forever."

"Why don't you have a break at half term? Go home and see your parents?"

Her face lights up for a second at the mention of home, but then she sighs.

"We can't afford to close for a week, not now. Maybe in the summer. Mark has a friend, he might come and do the restaurant for us, but he's in Germany now."

"Well, let's go shopping somewhere nice and have lunch, maybe one day next week?"

She smiles. "Perfect."

The school secretary takes me into the staff room while I wait for Mrs. Chambers. It's full of piles of leaflets and folders, and half-drunk cups of tea, with a whiteboard on the wall, and a selection of felt-tip pens on the ledge underneath it. There are various notes on it in different kinds of handwriting, some of which are definitely C+. Apparently, the word for today is *rhyming*, and Mrs. Nelson and Mrs. Connell are down for wet playtime duty, poor things. I'm trying to work out why someone has written "Punctuality!" on the board, and hoping it isn't aimed at parents, when the door opens and Mr. O'Brien comes in. I feel like I've been caught snooping, but he doesn't seem to mind.

"I see you've noticed our planning board. We meet most mornings, and I find it helps us focus, although I'm not sure all my colleagues would agree with me. Actually, I think some of them would quite like me to be banned from the staff room entirely."

I think he's probably talking about Mrs. King, who's been at the school for decades and likes to do things the way she's always done them.

"Mrs. Chambers will be along in a minute, she's finishing her register, and then I'm doing poetry with them; it's my favorite part of the day, when I'm in class, especially with the younger ones. They're so spontaneous. You'll see when you do your groups, it's the smallest ones who sometimes have the biggest ideas, especially with things like poetry; it really gets them going, particularly anything rude."

"I can imagine that."

"Here she is. We were just talking about how much our children like rude poetry."

Mrs. Chambers smiles. "I'd avoid anything to do with snow, if I were you. They're all rather overexcited."

Mr. O'Brien nods. "James Pelling was just telling me how to

survive in an avalanche, quite fascinating; apparently, you have to swim up to the surface and try not to swallow. And it's okay if you do a wee. Although personally speaking, I'm not sure I'd have that much choice in the matter."

Mrs. Chambers and I both laugh.

"Still, it's good to know, isn't it? It might come in handy later, just thought I'd pass it on: swim to the surface. Now, where's my book gone? There's a lovely one about a cat that always goes down well." He goes off down the corridor muttering "Slinky Malinki" to himself.

Mrs. Chambers closes the door. "Would you like a coffee? It's such a treat for me to be in here during lesson time, I think I'll have a biscuit, too."

Half an hour later Mrs. Chambers is heading back to her classroom and I'm walking across the playground with a long list of things to do, including working out a pattern for knitting rugs, and experimenting with knitting with string and raffia and bits of plastic bin bags, and finding some more historical nuggets for the older ones so they can do a timeline. Mrs. Chambers has found a picture of some rather tragic-looking knitted leggings from ancient Egypt, and I've got one of a knitted lace dress from the Great Exhibition which had nearly one and a half million stitches, but we need a lot more. The sleet's starting up again, so I put my hood up and walk as fast as I can, which turns out to be not very fast at all, particularly since the wind keeps blowing my hood off.

Elsie's upstairs lighting the fire when I get to the shop.

"You look half frozen. Come and sit down, and I'll put the kettle on. This weather's shocking, isn't it? I thought I'd better light this now, because it's so chilly up here and you've got your group tonight, haven't you? Oh, and there's a parcel for you."

"Thanks, Elsie."

There's a large padded envelope on the table, which looks like it might be the photographs from Venice. Hurrah.

They're brilliant, especially the one of the boys leaning against a pillar and giggling, with a shadow falling across the stone. There's a lovely one of them running toward me in the square, with the sun sparkling on the water behind us, and there's a plastic wallet full of negatives, and a scribbled note from Daniel saying work's gone crazy but talk later.

"Aren't they nice? Your gran will love them. Shame you didn't have them in color, really. I'll go back down, then, but I meant to say, I sold another tea cozy, to Mrs. Lewis."

"Great. I'll be down in a minute."

"They're proving ever so popular, you know. Shall I start on another one? I've still got some of that dark green left."

"Lovely."

I'd like to call him and say thank you, but I'm not sure about the protocol; maybe I'll just call Ellen and check.

"Morning, darling. Is it snowing down there? I was going to call you. You'll never guess what."

"What?"

"Harry's broken his leg. Well, he's fractured it. Silly sod."

"Christ, how?"

"Falling down some steps in Dublin, outside the hotel. He's just called me from the hospital, sounding totally pissed off. They're putting it in plaster, and he says it hurts like hell. He's flying home later on, but they're on easyJet so they'll probably make him buy an extra ticket for his crutches."

"Poor thing. You don't sound very sympathetic."

"That's because I'm not. It's his own fault for going off on a bender."

"Well, give him my love, won't you? And go easy on him. He'll probably be in a lot of pain."

"I know, and I will, I promise, but I don't think we'll be able to make it down at the weekend now. I could put him on the roof rack, I suppose. If I had one."

"Of course you can't come down here, don't be daft. Poor thing. Will they get him a wheelchair at the airport?"

"Yes, I'm sorting it out, although he wants an ambulance; he's being a total baby about it."

"He's probably in shock."

"Yes, and he's going to get another one if he thinks I'm playing night nurse; I'm not really a Florence Nightingale kind of a girl."

"Call me later, when you've got him home."

"Okay, darling, and sorry about the weekend."

Bugger. I was counting on Ellen being around for Sunday; she's so good at diverting people's attention. I think I'll call Daniel later, when I've worked out what time it is in New York. Poor Harry. We'll have to make him a card, and maybe I can knit him a footrest or something. I wonder if he'd like a tea cozy.

Maggie's the first to arrive for the Stitch and Bitch group, and she's very impressed with the new window display. "I love tea cozies, there's something so comforting about them. Are they easy to make?"

"Very, and they don't take much wool, either."

"Perfect project for a winter's evening, then?"

"Yes."

"Great. Well, I'm up for it, if you can sort me out a pattern."

We're downstairs choosing colors when Linda and Tina arrive, and decide they'd like to make one, too.

"And those knitted cakes are a good idea if you're on a diet. We should have some at our Weight Watchers."

By the time we're all sitting upstairs round the table, everyone's decided to join in with Project Tea Cozy, much to Connie's amusement.

"A little hat for a teapot, it's so English."

Tina smiles. "Don't you have teapots in Italy?"

"Not really. Some of the hotels do, but not really at home."

"Well, there you are. You could be the first person to bring tea cozies to Italy—you'd probably make a fortune. This cake is lovely. You've got to tell your Mark to stop making such lovely cakes, you know, I'm meant to be on a diet. How many calories do you think there are in one of these?"

Linda sighs. "About three million."

Tina hesitates, before reaching for another one. "Oh, well, in for a penny, in for a pound."

I'm showing Cath how to knit a row of bobbles. "Where's Olivia tonight?"

"At home, sulking."

Linda puts her cake down. "What have you done now?"

"Told her she can't go to an all-night party on a school night. She's not allowed to go to all-night parties on any night actually, but especially not on a school night."

"You cruel thing."

"I know. She's furious."

"She'll get over it. They're always furious about something at that age."

"She told me I was a helicopter parent the other day; she read it in one of her magazines. Apparently I'm always fussing, and I'm on permanent hover, ready to swoop down and muck things up for her. And everyone else will be going, so I'm totally out of touch."

Linda laughs. "Everyone with a mum who doesn't give a bugger, more like. You can't win, can you? Either you let them do what they want, and they end up on drugs and get chucked out of school and they hate you, or you stand up to them and then you're a helicopter and they hate you."

Maggie helps herself to another piece of cake.

"I went in a helicopter once, at an air show, and it was bloody awful. I had to be sick in a paper bag."

"I might try that with Olivia if she carries on sulking. At least it might shut her up for a while. Sometimes she talks to me like I'm something she's found on the bottom of her shoe."

Maggie smiles. "I blame the nineteen sixties. Before that you were either in a sailor suit or in a twinset and pearls like your mother, busy embroidering a tray cloth. But now they have to be teenagers. It's like they're honor-bound to be revolting, or there's something wrong with them."

"I do know how hard it is for them, I really do. I look at Livvy sometimes and I admire her so much—she's much braver than I was at her age. But I can't help worrying."

Linda smiles. "Of course you can't, that's your job. Everyone needs someone to worry about them and make sure they've had a proper breakfast. That's what mums are for."

We sit knitting for a while, listening to the wind outside and catching up on the latest gossip about Mrs. Taylor at the chemist's, who's apparently having an affair with the man from the wholesaler who delivers the vitamins and health supplements.

"I'm sure I saw her getting out of his van the other day."

"Maybe he was just delivering something?"

Linda doesn't look convinced. "In the car park behind the beach? I don't think so. And she looked ever so furtive; you can always tell when people go all furtive. Have a look next time you're in there. Honestly, she's got vitamins practically stacked to the ceiling she's put that many orders in. Mr. Taylor doesn't seem to have noticed, though, silly sod: too busy mooning after that new woman they've got in to do the prescriptions. Mind you, he'll catch on sooner or later, and then there'll be hell to pay." She pours herself some more coffee. "I keep meaning to ask you, how's our local film star doing? The baby must be due soon, isn't it?"

"Yes, I think so, and she was fine, last time I saw her. Getting a bit nervous, though."

"I don't blame her, I was reading something in one of the magazines in the salon about all the things you're meant to do with babies now. God, I'm glad they weren't going in for all that when I had mine. Baby maths, violin lessons, all sorts, before they can even walk."

Angela nods; now she's a proud grandmother, she's become a bit of an expert on babies. "Penny's got a book on sign language, it's all very clever. You can teach them signs they can do with their hands, so they can tell you when they want a drink."

Linda laughs. "Mine have been doing that for ages; my Lauren's got one particular one she's been using for years."

Angela giggles. "I know. I did think it might not be a terribly good idea, but I don't want to interfere."

"Good for you, Ange. You couldn't nip round and tell my mum about that, could you? Because she's always going on at me about my two. Mind you, my Lauren did tell her to piss off and get a life this Christmas."

Maggie laughs, and we start talking about the library. Cath's got nearly a hundred signatures on the petition, which is brilliant, but Maggie's still worried.

"They're having a meeting at the library with the parish council and someone from the planning department, so they can view the site, which doesn't sound very encouraging, does it? It's like they've already made their minds up."

Angela goes slightly red. "When I mentioned it to Peter, he went into a huff and said it's far too early for anyone to be talking about it, which if I know Peter means it's all practically signed and sealed. So I think we might need more than a petition if we're going to stop them. I'm very sorry, dear."

Cath puts her knitting down.

"There's plenty of other things we can do. We could hold a protest outside the library when they arrive for their meeting. They'd hate that, and maybe we could get the local paper to do a story on it, or even the radio. What do you think, Jo? You know about the press: would they be interested?"

"It would be better if we could come up with something new, rather than just standing outside. Something visual."

Angela coughs nervously. "Could we all bring our knitting? Sorry, that's probably a terrible idea."

"No, it's rather good. We could call it a knit-in, and that would make it more interesting for them."

Angela looks very pleased. "We could sit in a circle knitting, and tie ourselves to things."

"Brilliant. We could all be in the entrance hall when they arrive and they'd have to step over us to get in. We could call it Knit for Victory, like in the war, only without the air-raid shelters."

Maggie's getting enthusiastic. "Do you really think the press would be interested, Jo?"

"Definitely, if we get enough people, which I'm sure we will if I ask Gran and Elsie to spread the word. If it's a slow news day, we might even get one or two of the nationals, and maybe the local telly might do a piece; it's just the kind of thing they like."

Everyone's getting into the idea now.

"Peter would hate it."

Maggie smiles at her. "Yes, but don't tell him, will you? Let's keep it secret for now, so we can surprise them."

I'm so tired by the time I get home I can't face ringing Daniel, so I send him a chirpy text thanking him for the photographs. He texts straight back: *Glad they arrived, will call you later, up to neck in summer fashion shoot at moment. PS Shorts are back! Dx.* I text, *Not round here they're not.* Which is all very gratifying: light and friendly and not awkward at all, and I'm rather relieved; Venice was wonderful, but now we're back to normal life, what I'd like most is for us to be friends, maybe with the occasional interlude, but nothing serious, nothing I have to worry about. Great. So now all I've got to do is mastermind the knit-in, and work out what to knit with string and raffia, and I'll be fine. Excellent.

It's Sunday morning and I've been up cleaning the house since six. It's all still a long way off Elizabeth's pristine standards, but I'm way past caring.

The phone rings, and I'm really hoping it's them calling to cancel, but it's Grace to say she's finished her flower blanket and wants me to go round to collect it.

"I can't right now. I'm really sorry. I've got my ex-mother-in-law coming for lunch, former mother-in-law, I never know what to call her. Anyway, her and the brother-in-law and his wife and their two girls."

"Oh, right. Well, that'll be nice."

"It would be if they didn't all hate me."

She laughs. "I'm sure you're exaggerating."

"I am not. Elizabeth hates me because she never thought I was good enough for her precious son, and James just thinks I'm trouble. He got drunk one Christmas and told me, so I know it's true. And Fiona hates me because she thinks I'm a slut."

"Did she get drunk and tell you that, too?"

"No, I just know. She's got a cleaning rota on the notice board in her kitchen, with special jobs for every day of the week so she can keep on top of things. She offered to print me off a copy last time I was there."

"What a bitch."

"Exactly. And the house is still messy, and Archie's in a foul mood because he woke up too early, so it's going to be a nightmare. Sorry, you probably don't want to hear any of this. I can come round tomorrow, if you like."

"Sure. I think we're out in the afternoon, but the morning will be fine. But listen, if you let them get to you, they will. You just need to focus and behave like everything is fine and the house is perfect and you're so happy you can hardly bear it."

"I think you probably need professional training to pull off that kind of thing."

She laughs. "Will you take them to see the shop?"

"Yes, I thought we'd do a little detour on our way to the pub for lunch. I couldn't face cooking for them—which is another thing Fiona won't approve of."

"Make sure you talk it up, tell them how brilliant it is, how people are queuing up to get in most days, and you feel like you've found your true calling."

"I'll give it a try."

"Don't sound so negative. If you don't believe it, they won't. I'll see you tomorrow, and can you bring some more of that new silky stuff in that olive color?"

"Sure."

I'm moving a vase of flowers on the table by the window when I see a huge silver Jeep pulling up outside; James has obviously got a new car. We go out to admire it, and the boys are very impressed.

"Can it go really fast?"

James looks pleased with himself. "Yes, Archie, very fast. But don't tell your aunty Fiona."

Fiona turns to me and simpers. "I don't like him breaking the speed limit, but with a car this powerful, he does find it so hard to resist."

I try to look suitably impressed, but it's bloody freezing, and what I'd really like is for them to stop milling about so we can go back indoors, but I don't think James is finished yet. He's showing the boys the boot now, for some reason best known to himself, and Jack's trying to look interested, bless him. Maybe I should follow his good example and attempt to be extra-friendly to Fiona, because apart from anything else, being married to such a total prat can't be easy.

"It's so lovely to see you all, and haven't the girls grown? They're so big now, aren't they?"

They're both standing next to their mother looking uncertain, wearing matching navy coats with velvet collars.

Fiona hisses something at me.

"Sorry?"

"Lottie's very sensitive about her weight, so we're trying not to talk about it."

"Oh, right. Sorry."

She gives me an annoyed look, and now she's mentioned it I notice Lottie's coat is rather more of a snug fit than Beth's.

Bugger.

"Let's go in, shall we?"

We walk up the path.

Elizabeth looks pointedly at the straggly rosebush by the door. "Haven't you found a gardener yet, dear?"

"No. I keep meaning to sort the garden out, but I haven't got round to it yet. I thought I might do it myself, actually."

She smiles. "I'd get one if I were you, dear. Our Mr. Jenner is a marvel; I don't know what I'd do without him. Of course, I can't let him buy plants—he's got no taste at all—but he keeps the lawns in very good condition, and nothing is too much trouble."

I'm trying to smile back, but it's quite hard, particularly since I know Mr. Jenner hates her guts, and they have massive rows every year about how she plants things too early and then blames him when the frost gets them.

"Good Lord, what's that?"

We turn to see Trevor bounding toward us up the path, followed by Christine. Bugger.

"Sorry, he gave me the slip again. I didn't realize you had visitors. I'm so sorry." She's looking rather out of breath.

Trevor runs up the path and leaps up at Archie, and both the girls start to scream.

Oh, Christ.

"Trevor, get *down*."

He gives me a puzzled look and starts to run round in circles, wagging his tail. I grab his collar.

Archie's outraged. "Don't shout at him, Mum. He's only saying hello."

Jack grins, and pats him, and the girls cower behind their mother, who's looking horrified.

"He's very friendly, don't worry."

I hold the front door open a bit wider, and they all belt into the hall and huddle together like there's a large killer beast on the loose.

"It's only Trevor, he belongs to our neighbor, he often comes round to play with the boys, he's fine, honestly."

Elizabeth in particular is now looking at me like I'm a total nutter, as Christine gets hold of Trevor's lead.

"I'm so sorry."

"It's fine, don't worry about it. In you come, boys."

"Can't we play football with Trevor?"

"Not today."

James makes a rather sarcastic-sounding noise. "Does he play football, then?"

"Yes. Why? Do you fancy a quick game?"

He looks appalled. "I don't think so."

"You don't know what you're missing. He's very good in goal."

Gerald laughs. "Is he? I had a dog like that when I was a boy."

Elizabeth gives him a furious look.

"Well, I did. Pointer bitch, very good at rugby."

Oh dear, now he's said "bitch" in front of Beth and Lottie, so Fiona's Not Happy, either.

She turns to me, looking rather thin-lipped. "Shall we put our coats over here?"

"Yes, sorry. Let me hang them up for you."

She hands me her coat. "Thank you. Are we in here?"

She looks toward the door of the living room and I'm very tempted to say no, you're back outside in your stupid car, but I smile nicely and show them in. God, this is going to be a long day.

"What a sweet little room. Isn't that the same sofa you had in London? How clever of you, to keep the same furniture. You can buy new sets of covers, you know, if you want a little change. What interesting wallpaper. Super view of the garden. Oh, I forgot our presents. Do go and get them, darling."

James goes to the car, and I notice him looking nervously down the path before he steps out of the door. He comes back in with three presents wrapped in rather odd-looking brown paper with green splodges on it, and bits of twig tied on with green ribbon.

"What lovely paper."

"I made it myself. I made all our wrapping paper this year—it's simple to do and it makes things so much more per-sonal, don't you think?"

Christ.

"Lovely."

I open my present, which is a cookery book called *Easy Entertaining,* although not quite as easy as taking everyone to the pub, by the look of things. There's a whole chapter on Seasonal Table Arrangements. Dear God. If only.

"How lovely. Thank you so much."

Serves me right for fobbing them off with gourmet olive oils, I suppose.

The boys both get French dictionaries, which they manage to look suitably grateful for, after an initial tricky moment when Archie looks like he might be about to Say Something.

"It's so important to learn other languages, don't you think? The girls do French every week now, don't you, darlings?"

They both nod unenthusiastically, especially Lottie.

Elizabeth sniffs. "Nicholas was very good at French."

Oh, God, here we go.

"I'll just make some coffee, shall I?"

Fiona follows me into the kitchen and tells me all about her new oven, which has a rotisserie spit, and then James spends so long telling us about his latest triumphs on the golf course that I'm almost ready to spit, too. Elizabeth's gone silent, which doesn't bode well, and Gerald appears to have fallen asleep, although he often does this; he tends to put himself into standby mode until the food arrives.

"I thought you might like to see the shop, on the way to lunch."

Elizabeth frowns. "Aren't we eating here, then?"

"I thought the pub would be more fun."

Gerald reactivates himself and sits up, looking alert. "Pub? Jolly good idea."

I try to point out all the interesting architectural features of Broadgate as we walk to the shop, which isn't easy because we haven't really got any unless you're into 1950s British Seaside (Faded), and the tour of the shop seems to leave them all underwhelmed, too, so I'm starting to feel mildly suicidal when a large black Jeep pulls up outside.

"Look, Daddy, that one's much bigger than ours."

James scowls and Lottie giggles; actually, I'm rather warming to Lottie. The door opens and Bruno gets out, and then Grace emerges, waving, as if she was at a premiere, and sweeps into the shop and throws her arms round me.

"Darling, I simply couldn't resist when I saw you were here. I just had to pop in and give you this. I'm off up to town, but I thought I could pick up some more of that gorgeous wool you were showing me."

Bloody hell. I don't know what she's playing at, but it's certainly having quite an effect.

"Of course. I'll get it for you."

She hands me a bag full of the squares for her flower blanket and turns to Fiona, whose mouth is slightly open.

"Do excuse us." She turns and winks at me. "Aren't you going to introduce us, darling?"

Christ.

"Oh, yes, sorry. This is Elizabeth and Gerald, and Fiona and James."

Fiona looks totally gobsmacked, and even Elizabeth's looking impressed.

"Lovely to meet you all. Aren't you thrilled with the huge

success Jo's making of her gorgeous shop? Isn't it completely wonderful? I could spend hours in here—so many treasures. She's such a genius, isn't she?"

I hand her the bag of wool, and she turns to the boys. "I hope you're both going to come and swim in the pool again soon. It was such fun last time, wasn't it?"

They both nod.

"Lovely to see you again, darling. I must be off." She kisses me again.

God, even I'm feeling rather dazzled now.

"I'll call you later."

Fiona has recovered herself and clearly wants to make an impression.

"We're all such fans of your work."

Grace gives her a dismissive look. "Are you? How sweet."

"And you're, well, you're even more beautiful in the flesh than in your films."

Grace smiles. "Thank you, Leona. I must remember to tell that to my makeup and lighting team. They'll be thrilled."

"Actually, it's Fiona."

"Sorry?"

"My name: it's Fiona, not Leona. You said Leona, and I thought perhaps you hadn't heard me."

There's a small silence. Grace gives her an imperious look, then turns, kisses me again, winks, and goes out.

"Darling. Speak later."

Bruno gives me the thumbs-up sign as he opens the car door, and they drive off.

Christ. How completely brilliant.

I turn to Leona, as I think I'll be calling her from now on, at least inside my head, and smile.

"I didn't realize you knew Grace Harrison. I mean, we saw the thing in the papers about the shawls, but I didn't realize you actually knew her."

She's looking a bit shaken, and Elizabeth and James are, too. In fact, only Gerald seems oblivious. "Who was that, then?"

James groans. "Honestly, Father, do try to keep up. That was Grace Harrison, an important actress. Do you go to her house often, Jo?"

"Fairly often. Shall we go to the pub now? I think our table will be ready."

We walk up the hill, and I start to feel like I'm no longer the uncouth person who's not quite up to the standards of the rest of the family. It's just brilliant. And then my phone beeps with a text from Maxine: *Grace hopes recent guest performance was helpful. See you tomorrow. Max.* How lovely of her. I can't believe Grace did that for me, and I'm very touched. I text back *Million thanks*, which is the best I can do while I'm walking.

Fiona smiles at me. "Nothing important I hope?"

"No. Just a message from Grace's assistant."

"Oh. Right."

Who knew all I needed was the intervention of a megastar to get my in-laws back on track.

Lunch goes very well, apart from Elizabeth and Fiona trying to get me to agree to ask Grace to come to one of their Golf Club things. Even James says the food is fabulous in the pub, and he's usually very snooty about restaurants and likes a great deal more servility and bowing and scraping from waiters. The only slightly tense-making thing is that Connie's promised to hit Elizabeth with a spatula if I give her the signal, except I'm not entirely sure what counts as a signal, so I'm slightly worried I'll push my hair back behind my ears and inadvertently launch Operation Fish Slice, but thankfully we manage to avoid any unpleasant incidents. Lottie gives me a very sweet smile when she gets ice cream for pudding like her sister, instead of the fruit salad her mother's been hinting at, and after another cup of coffee back at the house, they're off, thank God. Elizabeth promises to ring me later in the week with possible dates for the Golf Club dinner, despite my explaining that I think this is a bit of a long shot; why she thinks Grace would do guest appearances at Golf Club dinners is beyond me, and I can only imagine Maxine's face if I asked her, so I think I'll just ignore it and tell them she's busy.

We stand waving them off as they drive down the street.

"Lottie said 'bloody' when we were eating our lunch."

"Don't tell tales, Archie."

"But she did."

"Well, never mind."

"I don't mind. I like Lottie."

Actually, I think I do, too. She must have the recessive family gene—and she's going to need it with those two for parents, bless her.

"Can we take Trevor out for a walk now, Mum? You promised we could."

Bugger.

"Yes, all right. But not for too long, Jack. It'll be getting dark soon."

Christine's very pleased to see us, and full of apologies about earlier, and we head straight for the beach as the perfect choice for a late-afternoon walk in a freezing gale. Jesus Christ. I'm standing watching the boys throwing sticks for Trevor and losing the will to live when my phone rings and it's Daniel. Damn. Why can't he ever ring when I'm sitting down somewhere in the warm, ready for a bit of sparkling banter, instead of half frozen and sniffing.

"Look, I'm sorry I haven't managed to call you. It's just been mad."

"Don't worry about it, and thanks so much for the photographs: they're lovely."

"You're welcome. So how are you? Nice to be home?"

"Yes, apart from the weather. It's bloody freezing here."

"Don't talk to me about freezing, I've spent the last few days digging Tony out of snowdrifts in Sweden."

"Oh dear."

"I'd have been better off with a bloody husky for an assistant. He's been totally fucking useless."

There's the sound of scuffling in the background.

"Tony says hello."

"Say hello back to him for me."

"She says, 'Fuck off, you total loser.'"

"Where are you?"

"At the airport."

"Off anywhere nice?"

"Barbados."

"Oh, please. Enough."

"Sorry."

"It'll make a nice change from Sweden, that's for sure."

"Yes, although that's kind of what I'm calling about. Hang on, I'll move somewhere quieter."

I hear flight announcements for a few seconds, and then he comes back on the line.

"That's better. Yes, Sweden. It wasn't just work. Liv was over, staying with her parents actually, and we met up. And, well, to cut a long story short, she's left him. And moved in with me."

This doesn't sound good.

"Who's Liv?"

"Sorry, I never told you her name, did I? She's called Liv Bergstrom. You've probably seen her in things?"

Fucking hell. She's almost as famous as Grace.

"Yes, I have. She was in that film with the bank robbery, wasn't she?"

"Yes. That's how we first met, on a publicity shoot for *Vanity Fair*. But she's very real, too, if you know what I mean. I think it's the Scandinavian thing: they seem to be much more grounded over there, apart from all that pickled herring bollocks, of course. So I just wanted to let you know. Bad timing or what? I'm really sorry."

"It's fine, Daniel, honestly. And I'm really pleased for you."

"Are you, really? That's so great. I was hoping you might be, and I'm sure you'd get on. She knits, you know, she loves it. She's been doing it for years. Maybe next time we're over we could all meet up?"

"I'd love that."

"Great. She's got a film starting in a few weeks, but I think we might be around in the summer."

"Lovely."

"Great. I'll call you then. And say hello to the boys for me, and Trevor. Bye, angel."

Damn and bugger it. It's not like I feel as if my heart has been broken or anything, but still. Damn. Time to go home, I think. I've got a large chocolate cake, which I bought in case they all stayed for tea. But now I think crumpets in front of the fire and a large slice of chocolate cake are just what I need. I'll call Ellen later. And I can finish off the baby shoes I'm knitting for Grace. And try to forget that little jolt when he called me "angel." Damn.

10

THE GREAT ESCAPE

It's my first proper day in the shop for nearly a week, thanks to a combination of Archie having a cold, and then Jack, culminating inevitably in me catching it. After a nightmare week of boxes of tissues and hot drinks merged with high temperatures and hacking coughs, I've realized that, while in my head I like to think of myself as a proper mother who has cool hands ready to soothe fevered brows, and endless reserves of cheerful patience, it turns out that actually I'm not very patient at all, and rather prone to shouting things like "Just stop whining, for God's sake," and tutting when people leave their tissues all over the living room floor. I managed to lose my voice completely by the end, so I was reduced to banging saucepan lids together to get them to be quiet. Which on reflection probably wasn't quite as good an idea as it seemed at the time, because Archie's taken to doing it every time he wants a bit of attention.

It's Valentine's Day soon, and I'm in the shop tying knitted pink hearts onto gingham ribbon to hang up in the window, although God knows why I'm bothering, since I've always hated Valentine's Day, and this year looks like being a particular corker.

I think I'll give Ellen a call for a bit of moral support.

"I'm feeling completely crap."

"Getting-over-a-cold crap, or just in general?"

"Just general, and bloody Valentine's Day isn't helping."

"Tell me about it. I was thinking of taking Harry off to Paris this year for a mini-break, but I'm not sure I fancy it with him still on his crutches. Although you'd be amazed what he can get up to with his leg propped on a cushion."

"Please. That's exactly the kind of thing I don't want to be hearing about."

"Are we talking about Daniel now, by any chance?"

"No."

"Good, because I think you're well out of that one, darling."

"Do you? Well, that's good, because I don't think I've got much of a choice about it."

"You want to steer well clear of men who are carrying torches for their former lovers. They always end up whining on about them for hours; there's no future in it."

"I didn't want a future with him, but a few more interludes would have been nice."

"It's just bad luck, darling. Don't let it put you off."

"Please tell me you're not going to say there are plenty more fish in the sea."

"Well, there are. You could try a nice bit of skate next, or chub. Actually, what are chub?"

"I've got no idea. But knowing my luck, I'll get one of those ones that puff up to twice its size and then give you an electric shock."

She laughs. "Well, there's always old Dovetail to fall back on."

"Stop calling him that, Ellen, he's been really kind."

"Yes, and I bet he'd be even kinder if you gave him half a chance. Still, you know best. I know, let us two go to Paris and leave Harry with the boys."

"On crutches? He wouldn't stand a chance. And anyway, I haven't got the money. I could do you a weekend down here, though, and we can rent movies and eat too much chocolate and watch the boys tying Harry to a tree. How does that sound?"

"Perfect."

"It's nearly a year now, you know. This time last year Nick was still in Jerusalem."

"I know, sweetheart."

"It seems much longer than a year, doesn't it?"

"Yes, it does. How are the plans for your knit-in shaping up, by the way? Have you decided on your media strategy yet?"

"Get the boys to watch less cartoons?"

"If you get the Diva along, I could probably swing it to come down and do a piece."

"I'm still not sure she's up for it. She sounded quite keen when I told her about it, and Max thinks she might do it, it depends on how she feels on the day. She's very pregnant now."

"Well, I'll mention it at the meeting and see what I can do.

It's human interest, isn't it, and that always works, especially if a megastar might be in the mix. When is it again?"

"Friday morning."

"It might be a laugh. I could interview you if she doesn't turn up, and then we can go to the pub."

"Can't you interview someone else? Linda would be great; she never stops talking. Or Gran—she'd love it, although it might turn into a piece on the wonders of cruising."

"I'll call you after the meeting, but start practicing, just in case."

Oh, God.

I've just finished sewing the last heart onto the ribbon when Mark comes in, carrying a large Tupperware box.

"I've got a new recipe I want to try out on you. Can we have a coffee?"

"Is it cake?"

"Yes."

"You're on."

We go upstairs and sit by the fire. The cake turns out to be a dark chocolate one with glossy icing, and something else, only I'm not sure what.

"This is lovely."

"You don't think the prunes are too much, then?"

"What prunes?"

"Great. That's all I need to know."

He drinks his coffee and looks rather nervous.

"Is something the matter?"

"Not really. It's just, well, I'm a bit worried about Connie."

"Why?"

"Well, she's being quiet, and she's never quiet. So I wondered if she'd said anything to you. I mean, I know you talk and everything, and I wondered if she'd mentioned anything."

"You mean you thought you'd bring a cake round and I'd tell you all our secrets."

"Yes."

"Not a chance."

He smiles. "Fair enough. But there aren't any secrets I should be worrying about, are there?"

"No, sorry, of course not. I was only teasing. I think she just needs a break, that's all. Honestly."

"The trouble is, there's never a good time with the pub."

"I know. That's what used to happen with me and Nick, there was always something that needed doing, and you just gradually drift apart."

He seems rather horrified. "You don't think that's what's happening to me and Con, do you?"

"No, sorry. I've just been thinking about it a bit, recently. No, I think you're both fine. Only it's hard when you're so busy."

He looks at his feet. "I was thinking I could book a ticket for her to go over to see her mum for a few days. I think she'd like that, maybe with the kids, at half term. I thought I'd tell her on the morning of the flight, so it would be a surprise. What do you think?"

"I think that's the kind of surprise that works best if you haven't got to pack for two kids for a week."

He nods. "True, and I don't think I could afford to go, too, not if it meant closing, so maybe it's not such a good idea."

"Why don't you get her mum and dad over here, then? You could ask them over for half term or Easter."

"That's a brilliant idea. She'd love that, she really would. And it could still be a surprise, if I went and picked them up at the airport without telling her, couldn't it?"

"I'd tell her now if I were you. That way she'll be able to look forward to it."

"Yes, but if I tell her now she'll want to redecorate the spare bedroom."

"But that's all part of the fun, isn't it?"

"I suppose so, unless you can come up with something that doesn't involve me holding a paintbrush?"

"Sorry."

He smiles. "I can't wait to see her face when I tell her."

"Well, remember, any time you need a food taster, you know where to come."

"Shall I put the rest of this in the kitchen?"

"No, please. If you leave it here, I'll have eaten the whole thing by lunchtime."

"Fair enough."

"I'll see you on Friday, then, at the knit-in?"

He sighs. "Do I have to?"

"Reg and Mr. Pallfrey are coming."

"Yes, but will they be knitting? Connie says I've got to be knitting and she's going to show me how to do it, but I really don't fancy it, to be honest. It's a bit too girlie for me."

"Reg will be knitting—he learned in the army—but Mr. Pallfrey's just going to hold a ball of wool, I think."

"I can do holding things. I'm really good at holding things. And anyway, she's not very patient, so I'm not sure how her teaching me will work out. I'll probably end up looking like a total tosser."

"Russell Crowe knits."

"Exactly. And before you ask, no, I'm not wearing a bloody toga."

"What a brilliant idea. We could do the whole thing in fancy dress. I'll put you down as a gladiator and tell everyone to dress up."

"Christ. Me and my big mouth."

It's Friday morning, and we're all standing outside the library with our knitting, ready to storm the barricades. Although actually, we're rather short on the barricade front, but we have got a rather nervous-looking policeman who Gran knows because he does the Neighborhood Watch meetings where you're supposed to call him Mike and tell him about any suspicious incidents. He takes notes, apparently, and there's a special number you can use if you think you've spotted a bogus caller. He's just told us we're not allowed to cause an obstruction in the lobby, so we're standing outside on the pavement in a sort of semicircle, feeling rather self-conscious, until Angela rather surprisingly takes charge.

"Do you think we ought to sit down? We could go and get some more chairs, I've got two folding picnic ones in my car, and then it would look like more of a demonstration, wouldn't it? Like those people who lie down in the middle of roads."

Linda's not convinced. "I'm not lying down in the road with my back, Ange, thanks all the same, and anyway it'll be filthy and I've just had this coat dry-cleaned. And you know what some of those bus drivers are like: they'd drive right over you."

"Yes, but we don't have to actually be in the road, we can stay on the pavement. I think it would look more serious than if we're all standing about chatting."

Elsie nods. "Yes, and we've still got nearly an hour to go before the meeting, and that's quite a long time to be standing up, especially with my legs."

Twenty minutes later we've got a collection of camping stools and picnic chairs and a deck chair, and we're all sitting knitting and having a fabulous time. Gran and Reg are passing round beakers of tea from the giant thermos flasks they've borrowed from the Bowls Club, and Mark and Connie have brought a selection of mini-muffins, which PC Mike is looking at rather longingly, but when we offer him one he says he'd better not because he'll probably be tucking into a banana muffin just as his sergeant drives past, and it's not really approved police procedure at public demonstrations. But he puts one in his pocket for later, which as Gran says will be a nice treat for him when he gets back to the station.

Reg hands me a plastic cup full of tea. "No sugar, that's right, isn't it, love?"

"Yes, thanks, Reg."

"We should have a song. We always had songs in the war, and it keeps your spirits up if you're all singing."

Gran smiles at him. "Go on, then, start us off, Reg."

We're singing "I Do Like to Be Beside the Seaside," and Maggie and Miss Kingsley, the head librarian, are standing watching us from the window, looking delighted, when Lady Denby arrives on a very rickety old bicycle, which she leans up against the railings.

PC Mike steps forward. "I'm afraid you can't leave that there, madam."

"Don't be ridiculous. I always put it here when I come to the library."

He gets his notebook out of his pocket. "Can I have your name, madam?"

"No, you cannot. Absolute cheek."

PC Mike is looking a bit shaken now and starts writing something down in his notebook as Angela comes to his rescue.

"Could we just move it over here, Lady Denby? It'll be out of the way, and we wouldn't want to risk it falling on anyone, would we? Oh good, I see you've brought your knitting."

Elsie stands up and offers Lady Denby her seat, and Angela wheels the bike to the railings by the pedestrian crossing.

Reg holds up his thermos. "Would you like some tea, Lady Denby? It's only beakers, I'm afraid."

"I would, thank you."

Gran hands her a yellow plastic beaker.

"What shall we sing next then, Reg? What about 'Daisy,

Daisy, Give Me Your Answer, Do'? Does everyone know that one?"

"Shouldn't we be chanting as well? You know, like they do on the telly."

Tina looks at Linda. "What do you mean, chanting?"

"You know, where they say, 'What do we want?' and 'When do we want it?' 'Now.' That one."

Everyone thinks this is an excellent idea, and we're having a practice run when the man from the local paper arrives. I think they must have sent their most junior reporter, because he isn't the same one who did the piece on the shop, and he looks only about fifteen. He's brought his camera with him, though, and nearly gets run over standing in the road trying to fit us all in. Cath helps him get all our names written down and gives him a muffin, which cheers him up, and then everything suddenly steps up a gear. Ellen arrives with an outside-broadcast van, which half blocks the high street, and Maxine rings to say Grace is on her way, and they've told a few people about it, so we'd better brace ourselves for snappers, and then we're surrounded by young men in jeans and woolly hats snapping away and shouting things like "Over here, darling" at Gran and Betty, who are thrilled and doing their best smiles.

Lady Denby starts giving an interview to the man from the local paper, dictating to him and making him read back what she's said about how important local libraries are for the community, and how she likes a good Agatha Christie herself, or historical fiction, and she's just read a marvelous one about India, only she can't remember the name, but it had a dog in it, and then a familiar black Jeep arrives and Grace gets out and the boys in the woolly hats go into a complete frenzy.

I'm standing with Ellen, watching Elsie and Betty surreptitiously trying to move their chairs a bit closer to the action.

"This is fabulous. So what's the plan now, darling?"

"Plan?"

"You want her sitting in the middle of you all, otherwise they'll just run with ones of her, and the library won't get a mention. And then you'll have to get them to back off for a bit while I do my interview. Yes?"

"Oh, yes, right."

I spot Maxine standing by the car, and together we manage to get Grace sitting on Tina's deck chair with her knitting, which is the perfect shade of lavender cotton to match her dress, and PC Mike starts talking on his radio as the photographers go into overdrive again. Getting Grace back up out of the deck chair turns out to be a bit more of a challenge than I'd anticipated, and with hindsight perhaps it wasn't the perfect choice of seat for a heavily pregnant megastar, but she copes very well and Tina's thrilled to have been of assistance. We make our way over to Ellen, but before we get to her Lady Denby nips in for a quick word.

Maxine nudges me. "Christ, it's that mad woman who came round the house. You'll have to rescue her, I got stuck with her for hours last time. Go on, quick, before she gets going."

"I'm terribly sorry, Lady Denby, but we need Grace over here for a moment."

"Right you are. Isn't it all absolutely marvelous? This'll put a spanner in their pipes."

We walk toward Ellen, and Maxine steps forward, back in professional mode. "Grace, this is Ellen Malone, who's doing the interview we talked about."

"Oh yes, sure."

Ellen does one of her Big Smiles. "It's lovely to meet you, and thank you so much for agreeing to talk to us."

Maxine stays standing in front of Grace. "No problem. Two minutes, and no questions, right?"

"Of course. I thought maybe over here?"

Grace stands in front of everyone and does her piece to camera, looking very beautiful and completely calm, while everyone sits knitting and trying to look determined. I'm standing to one side with Maxine and feeling rather nervous; this would not be a good time for Ellen to ask one of her tricky questions.

"So, Grace, why are you here today?"

Grace smiles and looks directly into the camera, which is usually a mistake, but of course with her it'll be great.

"Because they're threatening to close our local library, and I've always been passionate about libraries. My mum used to take me every week, and it opened up a whole new world for me. And I want to help make sure that other children have the same chance."

She pauses for a second or two and puts her hand on her tummy. "Making sure our children have access to as many books as possible, for free: it doesn't get much better than that, does it, Ellen?"

"So you'll be bringing your baby here, when it's old enough?"

Grace smiles. "I'd love to. I'm really looking forward to reading some of my favorite books again, ones my mum used to read to me when I was little, and I'm hoping we can come here and read with the other children. But we won't be able to if they've closed the library, which I'm sure you'll agree would be a complete tragedy. We need lots more libraries, not less."

Maxine steps forward, and Ellen nods.

"Let me just check we got that."

The cameraman gives her a thumbs-up.

"Thanks so much, Grace, that was great. And any time you fancy an interview, you know who to call, right?"

"Sure."

"And good luck with the baby."

"Thanks."

"When's it due?"

Grace laughs. "Yesterday, tomorrow, next month, who knows? Lovely to have met you, Ellen." She turns to Maxine and me. "Jo, walk with us to the car, would you? Oh, look, here come the enemy."

Two men in very smart suits are walking toward the library steps, carrying expensive briefcases and looking extremely annoyed.

Cath starts up the "What do we want? To save our library" chant as they go inside, rather quickly. In fact, they almost sprint up the steps.

"Thanks so much, Grace. You were brilliant."

"Happy to help."

Maxine smiles. "We've got a statement ready if we get any calls, so just put them onto me if they ask you anything about Grace, yes?"

"Of course."

"And thanks, Jo, this was great. Ed's really pleased. It's exactly the kind of thing we want to be doing—local issues and all that. I'll call you later, and let you know what calls we get, shall I?"

"Thanks, and I'm sorry about the deck chair."

Grace smiles, and there's another flurry from the snappers as she gets back into the car, and a round of applause from everyone sitting knitting and chanting, which goes down very well because she opens the window and waves as the car drives off, and she doesn't usually do that.

Ellen's looking very pleased. "That was great."

"She was brilliant, wasn't she? I was a bit worried it seemed so short, though."

"No, it was fine. She knows exactly what she's doing, and it was great that she said my name. Very classy. Her skin's bloody amazing, isn't it?"

"I know."

"Oh, here we go, they've brought in reinforcements. It's amazing how megastars always bring out the top brass."

She turns to look at a police car arriving with its blue lights flashing.

"God, I hope they haven't come to arrest us."

"What for? Knitting in a public place?"

"No, but they don't look very happy, do they?"

A rather senior-looking policeman arrives and goes over to talk to PC Mike, while the driver gets out and starts rather unnecessarily directing the traffic.

"Go over and do one of your special charm offensives, would you, please, Ellen?"

"Oh, Christ, do I have to? I thought we could go to the pub."

"I can't go to the pub in the middle of the knit-in. And anyway, it's shut; Connie and Mark are both here. Just go over and sort him out, please, before he arrests Lady Denby or something."

The snappers take a few more photographs of us all sitting knitting as the councillors and the people from the Planning Department start to arrive, and Ellen signs autographs for PC Mike and the new grumpy one, and shows him inside the camera van, and he starts looking a great deal happier and stands by the doors of the library, evidently quite pleased with himself while the snappers take lots of pictures of Ellen, and then the men in the smart suits come out and walk very quickly back up the high street.

Linda laughs. "Looks like the meeting didn't last quite as long as they planned. Should we stay here until the rest of them come out?"

"Let's give it a bit longer, shall we? They're bound to come back out soon."

I'm standing with Connie and Ellen when the man from the local paper comes over, looking a bit panicky. "I don't think I got any good photographs of Grace Harrison. I mean, I tried, but they kept pushing me out of the way; they're very aggressive, some of those photographers. She won't be coming back by any chance, will she?"

"Sorry."

"I got one of you and Miss Malone, though, and I got a good one of her getting back into the car. Do you think that will be enough?"

Ellen smiles. "I'm sure it will."

"I couldn't have your autograph, could I? Only I know my boss would like it, and it might help when he sees my photographs. He tends to throw things when he gets angry."

"Of course. I'll give you a quote, if you like. Would that help?"

"That would be brilliant."

The Planning Department people come out first, in a little huddle, and practically run up the road, and then the local councillors, including Angela's husband, Peter, who looks livid.

"What on earth are you doing here, Angela? I thought I made myself perfectly clear."

We all pretend we're not listening.

"I'm making my own mind up for a change, Peter."

"I beg your pardon?"

"I'm just doing what I think is right."

"It's only a proposal, I've told you. It might not happen."

"Well, it had better not."

He starts to splutter.

"I mean it, Peter."

He stomps off toward the car park.

Tina laughs. "You certainly told him where to get off, Ange."

Angela's gone pink. "I think it's about time, don't you? I've let him have his own way for far too long."

Linda stands up. "We're all off to the pub for a sandwich. Why don't you join us?"

"Do you know, I think I might."

Linda smiles. "Good for you. Right, then, everyone back to the pub, and mine's a double. Come on, Connie, we'll race you."

Bloody hell. Nearly all the papers have run pictures of Grace sitting in a deck chair knitting, with a line or two about the library, and Ellen's piece ran at six and ten, and everyone's been in and out of the shop looking at themselves in the paper and having a marvelous time. Maggie says the council are already backtracking and saying they never meant they were going to close the library, they were just exploring options, and they've all been told not to talk to the press if anyone calls, so it looks like we might have won, although we won't know for sure until the next Planning Committee meeting in May. Cath has delivered the petition, and we're all feeling very pleased with ourselves. In fact, the only person in the whole of Broadgate who doesn't seem delighted is Annabel Morgan, who was definitely giving me the evil eye in the playground again this morning, but I was too busy talking to Connie about the wallpaper for her spare room to take much notice. She wants me to go shopping with her next week, and I've promised to help her put it up because she's never done wallpaper before, but she's much happier now she knows her mum's coming over.

Elsie and Gran are in bliss with all the excitement, and

Elsie's bought a special album for all the press cuttings, so they've been holding court in the shop all day, and by the time I'm picking up the boys from school, I'm so exhausted that all I really want is a nice little lie-down. I don't think I'm over my cold properly yet, and yesterday's excitements seem to have made me even more knackered than usual. But apparently I promised we'd take Trevor for a walk after school, which I'd completely forgotten about.

"You promised, Mum."

"All right, but finish your juice and then go up and get changed. I don't want your school trousers getting all sandy."

They look at each other and shake their heads just like Vin and I used to do with Mum, which is rather annoying. They've been doing it quite a lot lately, in between their usual routine of light bickering punctuated with occasional bouts of actual bodily harm.

"And you'll have to wear your wellies, Archie."

"I'm not wearing wellies. Only babies wear wellies, and girls. Molly Tanner wears hers all the time, and they're pink. And I hate her."

Jack starts to giggle. "That's only because she wants to be your girlfriend."

Archie glares at him. "She does not. And anyway, I don't want a girlfriend. If you've got a girlfriend you have to do kissing." He starts to make being-sick noises.

Jack looks superior. "I might have a girlfriend when I get bigger. But I don't want one who gets hormones."

Hormones? Who's been telling him about hormones? Damn, I'm not really up to a hormones conversation right now.

"Marco told me his dad says it sometimes when his mum gets in a temper, and then they do kissing in the kitchen. Did you and Dad do kissing in the kitchen, Mum? I can't remember."

Oh, God. "Yes. Sometimes."

Not often enough probably. But sometimes.

"Well, I might do that, when I'm grown up, I haven't decided yet, but I might. And we can all live in a big house, can't we?" He looks at me rather seriously.

"Yes, or you could live in your own house and we'd see each other all the time, like with Gran."

He's horrified. "No, we can all live together, and you can do the cooking."

"Okay."

"Because people die, don't they, Mum?"

"Yes, darling."

"But you won't, you'll just be old like Gran, won't you?"

"That's the plan, sweetheart."

Archie seems worried.

"Can I live in the house, too?"

Jack looks at him very carefully, as if he's weighing up the pros and cons of the application.

"Yes, you can. And we can have dogs. And televisions in our bedrooms."

Archie's delighted. Harry Morgan has a television in his bedroom, and they've both been on a mission to join him in this audiovisual paradise ever since they heard about it.

"Hang on a minute. I'm not sure about televisions in bedrooms. Wouldn't it be really noisy?"

They both shake their heads. "Yes, but we'd be grown-ups then, Mum."

"I know, Jack, but the funny thing about being a grown-up is that, however grown up you are, you'll still be my baby."

He nods, but Archie's less convinced. "But we won't have to wear wellies, will we?"

"No, Archie, probably not."

"And sometimes we could have tickle fights, like we used to at our old house. We did, didn't we? And Daddy always won."

They both smile, and look at me, expectantly, which I think is probably my cue to go into tickle monster mode. Bugger.

I start waggling my fingers.

"Oh dear. Quick. I think the tickle monster might be back, and the last person up the stairs is going to get seriously tickled."

They both shriek and run for the stairs.

Double bugger.

It's ten past eight in the morning and I'm trying to make packed-lunch sandwiches while simultaneously extolling the virtues of Weetabix as the breakfast cereal of choice for superheroes, when Maxine calls.

"We're at the hospital."

"Oh, God, so it's today, then?"

"Looks like it. Grace wondered if you'd like to come up, around three?"

"Yes, of course I would. I'd love to."

"I'll meet you by the main doors. And just ignore the press."

"Okay. Is there anything you need?"

"Me?"

"Yes. I can bring you some food if you like, or bottles of juice or something. Those machines are always so horrible."

"No, I'm fine, but thanks."

The news breaks while I'm driving to the hospital, and they're saying she had a baby girl early this morning. Ellen calls me.

"I'm on my way there now. Maxine rang."

"God, you're definitely on her friends and family list."

"I know. I never thought she'd ask me to the hospital."

"I would, if it was me."

"I should bloody hope so."

"No, I mean if I was her I would. You've had two of your own, so you know what it's like, and more importantly, you're discreet. Practically everyone else trying to get through those doors only wants to be there so they can tell everyone about it. They don't really give a fuck about her."

"Well, I do. God, I hope she's all right."

I'm suddenly feeling rather tearful. Actually, I've been feeling pretty close to tears ever since Maxine called me.

"She'll be fine. So call me and tell me everything, off the record, of course."

"Of course. That'll be me doing the discreet thing, will it?"

She laughs. "All right. Give her my best, will you, and say many congratulations. I've sent her some flowers, but I doubt she'll even see them."

"That was nice of you."

"Darling, trust me, everyone and their dog will have sent her flowers."

"Oh, God, I haven't. Should I stop and get some, do you think? I've knitted a crib set, a blanket and a little duck, and a shawl for her, in cotton, and some little shoes. I knitted a pink pair and a blue pair, I couldn't resist, they're so sweet."

"Sounds perfect."

"So I don't need flowers then?"

"No, but you do need to call me. And if you can get a snap or two of the baby, we can both go to the Bahamas for a month."

By the time I get to the hospital, there are hordes of press outside. Maxine's waiting for me by the doors and takes me straight up in the lift.

"How is she?"

"Great. Brilliant, actually. But it's all been a bit manic."

We walk along a corridor to a side room full of flowers, where Ed's talking on his mobile phone.

"Dump your stuff and I'll take you in. We've had all sorts of nutters turning up with teddy bears and posing for the press: actresses, studio people, producers, people we've never heard of—you name it, they're all turning up."

"God, how awful."

"Don't worry, we've got Bruno on the door, and nobody gets past Bruno."

Ed waves to me as Maxine leads me back along the corridor toward Bruno.

"She's in here."

I hesitate, and she nods. "Go on, she's waiting for you."

I open the door, and there she is, lying in bed and smiling and holding a tiny baby wrapped up in a pink sheet.

"Hello, Jo. I'd like you to meet Lily May Harrison."

She looks so proud as she lifts the baby up so I can see her face.

"Oh, Grace, she's beautiful."

"She is, isn't she?"

"She's absolutely perfect."

We both smile.

"And how are you? You look wonderful."

"I feel wonderful, and you were right, it was great. Amazing, actually. One minute they were asking me to tell them if I could feel anything, and the next minute they were handing her to me. And she didn't cry, you know, she just opened her eyes and looked at me. It was the best moment of my life."

I can feel myself smiling as she looks down at the baby.

"I can't take my eyes off her. She's so perfect. Would you like to hold her?"

"I'd love to."

"Just don't move more than six inches from the bed. I can't have her more than six inches away."

"Of course."

She hands me the baby, who hardly weighs anything at all: I'd forgotten how tiny they are, especially when they're not yours. She opens one eye and then closes it again.

"She keeps doing that. She's got really blue eyes, and look at her fingers, can you believe it?"

"They're beautiful."

She opens the presents and immediately puts the shawl round her shoulders. "This is perfect."

The pink shoes are a big success, too.

"How did you know that she'd be a girl?"

"I just knew."

"Oh."

I show her the blue ones in my bag.

"They announced it on the radio while I was driving up."

"Did you hear that, sweetheart? You're a media star and you're not even a day old yet."

"She's obviously a very clever baby."

"She's already had two feeds, well, two and a half, really, but then she fell asleep."

"Has she? Well, that was very clever of her, and pretty clever of her mum as well."

"She's a very advanced baby."

"I'm sure she is. And Lily's such a lovely name."

"My mum was called Lily, and my nan was May."

We sit in silence and look at the baby.

"I can't wait to take her home."

"How long will you be in?"

"As long as I want; a couple more days, I think. I get this out tomorrow." She holds up her arm, which has a drip taped to the back of her hand. "And then it depends on how I'm feeling."

"Well, don't rush it. It's weird, going home. Take your time."

"Max has sorted me out a nurse for the first few weeks, and a nanny for her, so we should be fine. At least, I hope we will."

"Of course you will. You'll be great."

Maxine comes in.

"Ed wants to check if it's okay to give them a statement."

"Fine."

"Shall we give them the name?"

"Yes, that's fine."

"Only Ed thinks we should wait, and give them her name when you leave?"

"Okay, that's probably better."

"Do you need anything?"

"No, thanks."

All the time she's been speaking, Maxine's been looking at the baby.

Grace smiles. "Would you like to hold her now?" She turns to me. "I asked her earlier, but she was too nervous. But she's dying to hold her, I know she is. Jo will show you, Max, you'll be fine."

"Oh no, really."

"Max, shut up and hold her for a minute. You'll like it, I promise."

Maxine looks very nervous as I put the baby in her arms. "Oh, God."

The baby stirs and then settles.

"Oh, God. She's . . . I don't know. God, she just opened her eyes."

"She must like you, which is handy since it'll be you help-ing me walk her up and down in the middle of the night if the nanny's on a break. Now give her back to Jo and go and sort Ed out."

"Okay."

She doesn't move; I think she's gone into a trance. "I didn't know they were so little."

"They get bigger, Max. Jo, you'd better help her."

Grace is starting to look tired.

"Sure, and then I should leave you to sleep. Shall I put her back in her crib?"

"Please."

I lie her down, and she's fast asleep as I put the blanket over her and tuck it under the mattress like I used to do with the boys when they were tiny.

"Thanks for coming, Jo. I wanted you to see her."

"I wouldn't have missed it for anything. And promise you'll let me know if you need anything, anything at all."

She smiles. "Some pink wool would be nice, when I get home. I think I'd like to make her a blanket with her name on it. Pale pink, though, and soft."

"Of course. Blush and pale rose?"

"Perfect."

I give Maxine a hug as I'm leaving, and she hugs me back, and we're both slightly tearful, which makes us laugh, and then I make it back to the car just in time: there's a parking warden lurking round the corner, and the meter's only got ten minutes left. As I'm driving back through the City, the sun comes out, which makes the Tower of London look even more like a stage set than it usually does. I'm thinking about the boys when they were babies, and remembering how nervous Nick was when he first held Jack, when I start to feel a bit wobbly. I'm starving, so I pull into a McDonald's and get some chips and a coffee, and suddenly I've got tears rolling down my face. I've almost pulled my-self together when I see the blue shoes in my bag, and that sets me right off again. Bloody hell, this is getting ridiculous. But she was so tiny, and Grace was so happy; and so it begins again. The circle of life and all that bollocks; it's like a miracle, every time.

We're in the shop on Saturday morning, with the boys cam-paigning to go to the beach, even though it's freezing outside. Gran's at the hairdresser's, and I'm trying to sort out some wool for Grace, who's due home tomorrow. I've ordered in some pink silk for her, and some baby cotton, and I'm trying to arrange it all in a basket, but it's not looking quite how I want it to, and then Jack spills juice on his sweatshirt and starts fussing about it and blaming Archie.

"Stop whining, Jack."

"It's not fair. He did it on purpose."

"It's only a tiny bit of juice. And, Archie, stay there, sit on that chair and stop being so annoying or we won't go to the beach. You promised you'd be careful with your juice, and you're not a baby. I should be able to trust you to sit quietly for five minutes."

He glares at me.

"Don't start, Archie. I'm not in the mood."

I take Jack upstairs to dry his sweatshirt, and when we come down Archie's not on his chair. There's a kind of glitter-ing space where he should be sitting. And total silence. Christ.

"Elsie, where's Archie?"

"Didn't he go upstairs with you?"

"No."

We look at each other.

"Are you sure?"

I run back up the stairs.

"Archie?"

Oh, God.

I go back downstairs, willing him to be sitting on the chair; if I close my eyes, I can see him sitting there. But he's not. I move the pattern books, like he might be hiding underneath a small plastic folder.

Oh, my God.

Elsie's got her arm round Jack's shoulders. "I'll nip along to the salon and see if he's gone to find your gran."

"That's a good idea."

"You stay here. He'll probably have gone to the shop for sweets or something, don't you worry."

I stand by the counter, holding Jack's hand.

"Is he lost, Mum?"

"No."

Oh, God. Please. He can't be lost. He'll be at the salon.

Elsie comes back with Gran in a plastic cape, and Tina, and Angela Prentice with curlers in her hair, and Martin, who was in the newsagent's when she went in to see if Archie had been in for sweets.

She's out of breath.

"There's no sign of him. Let's split up; he won't have gone far. You go home, love, he might be waiting there for you, and I'll stay here in case he comes back. Martin, you go to the beach, and everyone else can do the high street and the park. And Mary, you should probably go and check your house in case he's up there."

Thank God Elsie's so bossy; at least one of us is being organized.

Gran's looking shaky. "Shouldn't we call the police?"

Tina puts her arm round her. "Let's see if we can find him first, Mary. We'll meet at Jo's house in twenty minutes, and then we can call them, but I bet we'll have found him by then. You'll see."

We all go off in different directions, and Jack and I race back to the house, half running and half walking, while I frantically scan up and down the street as we go, but there's no sign of him. I'm having visions of him falling over a cliff, or lying crumpled in a little heap in the road, or being bundled into a car by a shadowy figure. Oh, God, I can't do this, I'm going to lose it in a minute and start screaming, and I'm not going to stop until I've got him back. Jack's gone very pale and is trotting along beside me, looking like he might start to cry at any minute.

"Where is he, Mum?"

"I don't know, darling, but we'll find him."

Right, I've got to keep calm for Jack. "Don't worry, sweetheart."

He squeezes my hand.

Mr. Pallfrey's trimming the hedge in his front garden as we

turn in to the street, and Trevor bounds toward us, barking and wagging his tail.

"Have you seen Archie?"

"No. Why? Has he gone missing?"

I nod. I don't think I can speak, not without risking hysterics.

"I'll go and check the beach. I'll take Trevor—he'll soon find him, don't you worry, pet. Have you checked at home? He might be in your back garden. I wouldn't have necessarily seen him, I've been in the back."

We run up the path to the house, but he's not there. I sort of knew he wouldn't be, somehow.

"He's not here, Mum. I thought he'd be here."

Jack's looking even paler now.

"Will you stay here with Jack, Mr. Pallfrey, in case he comes back? I can't just sit here waiting."

"Of course I will, love."

"Where are you going, Mum?"

"I'm going to find Archie, love. Stay here with Mr. Pallfrey. Promise?"

"I promise."

I walk back down the garden path toward the gate, and the tears start. Please let him be safe. Please.

And then I see him. Walking down the road, holding Martin's hand.

For a second I think I might have dreamed it, but they carry on walking, and then he runs toward me, and I'm kissing him and hugging him too tight, and kissing Martin as well, who goes rather rigid.

Archie's squirming to get away, but I'm not letting go of his hand, probably for quite a while.

"I went to the beach to see if Trevor was there, and I crossed the road by the green man. That was good, wasn't it?"

Christ, he crossed the main road all by himself. Suddenly I feel completely furious with him.

"No, it wasn't. You frightened me, Archie, and Jack. Really frightened us."

"Why was Jack frightened?"

"Because he loves you, and we didn't know where you were." Oh, God, I think I'm really going to cry now.

"Shall I say it now?" He looks at Martin, who nods.

"I promise to never ever do it again, ever, and I'm very sorry. What was the last bit?"

Martin whispers, "I hope you'll forgive me."

Archie nods. "Yes. And I hope you will give me. Can I have something to eat now? I'm starving hungry. Have we got crisps?"

"In a minute. And you're not having crisps. People who go off and frighten people don't get crisps."

He sighs.

"I don't know how to thank you, Martin, really I don't."

He looks rather panicked; he's probably worrying I'm going to kiss him again. "Well, maybe we could go for a drink sometime?"

Christ, I really didn't expect him to say that.

"If you're not too busy. You're probably too busy."

I look at him, standing there, wearing the bobble hat his mum made for him, because he doesn't want to hurt her feelings.

"I'd like that."

He looks surprised. "Really?"

"Yes, I would. And you must let me know what I owe you for the shelves, because I still haven't paid you, and I feel awful about it."

"I enjoyed it. It gave me something to do in the evenings and got me out of Mum's way—there's only so much *Emmerdale* a man can take. And I only bought a few bits of glass, it was no big deal."

"Well, let's make it dinner, then. I'll buy you dinner somewhere expensive to say thank you."

He smiles; he's got a lovely smile. I wonder why I've never noticed it before.

Lady Denby comes puffing up the street with Algie and Clarkson.

"Oh, good, he's back. I was halfway home when it occurred to me that he was rather small to be out on the beach on his own. Gave you the slip, did he? Mine were always doing that to Nanny. Still, glad he's back safe and sound. Now then, young man, don't ever do that again. Understood?"

Archie nods.

"Not until you're much older."

He nods again, looking contrite, and then he giggles as Clarkson starts licking his feet.

"I suppose you could always get him tagged with one of those electrical things they're always going on about in the papers."

"I'll look into it, Lady Denby. And thank you."

"You're welcome, my dear. Go and have a large brandy. You look as if you could do with one. Very good for shock."

She passes Connie and Gran, who are half running down the street, Gran with her black nylon cape billowing out behind her.

"Oh, thank the Lord. Come and give your gran a cuddle, pet."

We end up with quite a gathering in the street, with everyone needing to pat Archie on the head to reassure themselves that he's back safe and sound, which he tolerates with unusually good grace before escaping with Jack into the back garden to play football with Trevor. Tina takes Gran back to the salon to sort her hair out; God knows what'll have happened to her perm, but I'm guessing it'll be a lot more curly than usual, and most of Angela's curlers have fallen out, so Tina says they might as well start all over again.

Martin's still smiling. "I'll go back to the shop and let Mum know."

"Thanks, Martin. And tell her thanks from me, for being so sensible. I'd probably still be standing there panicking."

"I'll see you later, then, and we can fix up that dinner?"

"Yes."

He's whistling as he walks back up the street.

Connie puts her arm round my shoulders as we go into the house. "When Angela came into the pub, she was nearly crying. You must have been so worried. Sit down, and I'll make you some tea."

"Thanks, Connie."

"Were you very frightened?"

"Terrified."

"And did you cry?"

"A bit, not much. I was too terrified."

"Perhaps you will cry now, yes?"

"No, I'm fine."

She hugs me, and I burst into tears.

"I thought he was lost. For a minute or two, I really did. I thought I'd lost him. And I kissed Martin by mistake when he brought him back."

She laughs.

"It's not funny. We're going out to dinner, and the poor man probably thinks I'm a total trollop."

"Trollop? What is trollop?"

"The kind of woman who kisses men when they're not expecting it."

"I think you should be a trollop. It sounds nice."

"I haven't got the right kind of clothes. Or the right kind of lipstick."

She laughs. "When we go shopping for wallpapers, we can get you some."

"Okay."

"He crossed the road down by the seafront, you know. All by himself."

Connie says something rude-sounding in Italian.

"I don't think he'll do it again. Well, he'd better bloody not, but still. I really thought I'd lost him, Con. And it was my fault. I never should have left him sitting downstairs like that."

"I ran away once, when I was little. I went shopping, but Aunt Rosaria found me in the market and took me home."

"What did your mum do?"

"Screamed for hours. And then made me my favorite supper."

We both smile.

"It doesn't get any easier, being a mum, does it?"

Connie shakes her head. "And it gets worse, I think."

"I know. We've still got sex and drugs and rock and roll to get through."

She smiles. "I think Nelly will be terrible."

"Christ, I was just starting to feel a bit calmer, and now I can see Archie with a quiff and an unsuitable girlfriend, telling me to fuck off and get a life."

"Maybe she will be nice."

"Who?"

"The girlfriend."

"Jack's might be, but Archie's going to go for the kind of girls you don't take home to meet your mother, I'm sure of it."

"Mark says he thinks Nelly will be wheels on hell."

"Hell on wheels."

"Yes."

"God, you think getting them through the phase where they can choke on bits of carrot is tough enough, but it's a doddle compared to the rest of it."

"Yes, but at least it's not boring. If everything went in straight lines, it would be terrible, yes?"

"I quite like straight lines."

She laughs. "Are you all right now? I should go back to the pub—Mark will be busy."

"Sorry, Connie, I never thought. Of course, go. I'm fine. And thank you."

I hug her as she leaves, and then go into the kitchen and stand watching the boys playing football. I'll make some sandwiches for lunch in a minute, and get them a drink; we can have a picnic. They love picnics, and I don't do them often enough. I'm feeling much calmer now: I think having so many people out there looking for him has reminded me how much safer it feels down here. I think we really belong now. That doesn't stop terrifying things happening, of course; nothing can stop that, I suppose, although I'm going to have a bloody good try. I think I'll start on the picnic; and we can eat out in the garden and I'll put the wigwam up for them if Trevor has gone home by then, because he's not very keen on wigwams. Even if it is cold, at least it's not raining, and we can wear our coats.

I'm opening a tin of tuna for Archie's favorite tuna and lettuce sandwiches, but no tomato, when Jack comes in.

"Can we have a drink?"

"Yes, love. I'm just making lunch."

"Oh, good, are we having a picnic?"

"Yes."

He grins. "We're playing football, but it's halftime."

"Right."

"I'm quite glad Martin found Archie, aren't you?"

"Yes, love."

"Because I don't want to play football with just Trevor."

"No."

"It was very naughty of him to go to the beach on his own, wasn't it, Mum?"

"Yes. Very."

"You have to be much older before you can go for walks on your own, don't you?"

"Yes."

"How old?"

"Twenty-six."

He nods.

"Were you scared, Mum?"

"Yes, darling."

"So was I, a bit. But now it's all right, isn't it?"

"Yes, love."

He picks up the beakers of juice and starts walking very carefully toward the door.

It's moments like this when I wish Nick were here. He was so much bolder than I am; he'd be making a joke of it by now, teasing Archie and making me relax. He could be the brave, exciting one who encouraged them to take risks, and I could be the one in the background with a drink and sandwich. He was always planning impromptu picnics, and then halfway through a sandwich he'd get bored with it and throw it over his shoulder, which the boys thought was brilliant. And now I have to be the one who makes the sandwiches and then throws them in the sand.

But at least this year has shown me I can cope with almost anything as long as the boys are all right, although God knows what kind of stunts they're going to pull as they get older. Although you never know, they might be the kind of teenagers who hold doors open for old ladies and take up interesting, quiet hobbies, like stamp collecting or excessive numbers of pen pals. The house will be magically transformed into a temple to shabby chic, instead of just being shabby, and the shop will start making proper money, and everything in the garden will be lovely, including the tragic old rosebush by the front door, which will burst into bloom. It might not be much of a plan, and it might not be how I thought it was going to be, but I think we'll be all right. And if it's not, then I'll just have to make it up as we go along, like I always do.

Turn the page for a sneak peek at Gil McNeil's sequel

to *The Beach Street Knitting Society and Yarn Club*,

Needles and Pearls

1

TWO WEDDINGS
AND A YEAR AFTER
THE FUNERAL

FEBRUARY

It's half past seven on Sunday morning and I'm sitting in
the kitchen knitting a pale pink rabbit and trying to work
out what to wear today. All those programs where women
with tired hair and baggy trousers emerge a small fortune later
with a new bob and a fully coordinated wardrobe never seem to
give you tips about what you're meant to wear when you visit
your husband's grave on the first anniversary of the funeral.
Especially when you've got to combine it with lunch with
Elizabeth, the artist formerly known as your mother-in-law,
who'll definitely be expecting something smart, possibly in the
little-black-suit department, or maybe navy, at a pinch. And
since I haven't got a black suit, or a navy one, come to that, I
think I might be in trouble.

Perhaps if I'd actually got some sleep last night things
wouldn't feel quite so overwhelming, but the sound of the wind

and the waves kept me awake, which is one of the disadvantages of living by the seaside; it's lovely in summer, all beach huts and day-trippers coming into the shop when it starts to drizzle, but I'm starting to realize that winter can be rather hard going. It's all freezing mists and gales, and when there's a storm down here, you really know about it. Maybe if the house wasn't ten minutes from the beach I might not have quite so many dreams where I'm shipwrecked and trying to keep two small boys afloat.

I finally managed to drop off around two, and was promptly woken by Archie shuffling in to let me know he'd had his space-monster dream again. Which is something else that's not quite as good as it sounds on the packet: how five-year-olds manage to combine being far too grown-up to wear vests now they're at Big School with still needing night-lights and special blankets as soon as you've got the little buggers into their pajamas. Not that Archie really goes in for special blankets—unlike Jack, who's seven but is still firmly attached to the fish blanket I knitted him in honor of his new seaside bedroom—but he's still perfectly happy to wake his mother up in the middle of the bloody night to talk about monsters and the possibility of a light snack.

I'm writing another version of my never-ending Things I Must Do Today list, while the rain pours down the kitchen window in solid sheets. We might not be able to match Whitstable for stripy sweaters and artistically arranged fishing nets, but we can certainly match them for pouring rain. We do have an art gallery in the High Street now, that goes in for smart window displays involving a large wooden bowl and a spotlight, so we're starting to get there; and what's more, we've got houses that normal people can afford, and a rickety pier and newly painted beach huts that don't get sold in auctions for more money than most people paid for their first house. Gran's been renting hers for years, which reminds me, that's something else to add to my list: I need to take another towel down next time we go to the beach; we took Trevor the annoying Wonder Dog for a walk yesterday, and Archie ended up in the sea again.

I'm making a pot of tea when Archie comes downstairs, with his hair sticking up in little tufts, wearing his pajamas, and the belt from his dressing gown, but no actual dressing gown.

"It's no good just wearing the belt, you know, love. You'll get cold."

"No I won't. I like it like this, it's my rope, for if I need to climb things. And I'm not having Shreddies for my breakfast. I want a sausage, just sausage. I don't have to have Shreddies because it's the weekend. At the weekend you can say what you want and you just have it."

How nice; I think I'll order eggs Benedict and a glass of champagne. Or maybe a nice bit of smoked haddock.

I'm rather enjoying my Fantasy Breakfast moment while Archie looks in the fridge and starts tutting. "We haven't got no sausage."

"I know."

"Why not?"

"Because you said you hated sausages when we had them for supper last week."

He tuts again. "I was only joking."

Jack wanders in, looking grumpy. "I don't want sausages. I want jumbled-up eggs."

Apparently I am now running some kind of junior bed-and-breakfast operation. Perhaps I should buy a small pad and a pencil.

"Well, since we haven't got any sausages, what about lovely scrambled eggs, Archie, before we get ready to drive to Granny's?"

"Yuck. And anyway last time you made them you put stupid cheese in and they tasted absolutely horrible."

"Well, it's Shreddies or scrambled eggs. That's it. So make your mind up."

He sighs, while Jack stands in the doorway looking like he's still half asleep.

"Did Daddy like cheese in his scrambled eggs?"

Bugger. There's been a lot less of the Did My Lovely Daddy Like This? lately, but I suppose it was bound to resurface today.

"Yes, love, he did."

"Well, I want mine with cheese then."

Archie hesitates. "Well, I don't. He liked them without cheese in too, didn't he, Mum?"

"Yes, love."

"And there's no sausages?"

"No."

"Are you sure?"

Does he think I'm hiding a packet inside my dressing gown or something?

"Absolutely sure, Archie."

"Well, I'll have jumbled eggs, with toast. But not the eggs on the toast—toast on another plate."

Christ.

Ellen calls while I'm washing up the breakfast things.

"You'll never guess what. Ask me who's calling."

"I know who's calling, Ellen. It's you, Britain's Favorite Broadcaster."

"Yes, but ask me anyway. Just say, 'Who is this?'"

"Who is this?"

"The future Mrs. Harry Williams. He asked me last night, when we were having dinner. On bended knee and everything— he'd even got the ring. Tiffany. Serious diamonds. The works. It was absolutely perfect."

"Oh, Ellen, that's brilliant."

"I know, although why he couldn't have done it on Valentine's Day is beyond me. He said he wanted to wait until his leg was out of plaster, in case he got stuck kneeling down, but I think he just couldn't cope with the hearts and flowers thing."

"That sounds fair enough."

"I've always had a crap time on Valentine's Day, so it would have made up for all those years when I didn't even get a card."

"You always get cards, Ellen. For as long as I've known you you've always got loads."

"Only from nutters who watch me on the news, not from proper boys."

"Well, now you've got a proper boy, and the ring to prove it."

"I know. Christ. I still can't really believe it."

"Tell me everything. What did he say? What did you say? Everything."

"I tried to play it cool, so I said I'd get back to him once I'd reviewed my options, but then the waiter brought the champagne over and I just caved. Who knew he'd turn out to be the future Mr. Malone? Isn't life grand?"

"I suppose we'd better stop calling him Dirty Harry now. It's not very bridal."

"Oh, I don't know: Ellen Malone, do you take Dirty Harry as your lawful . . . I quite like it."

"What's the ring like?"

"Fucking huge."

"Clever boy."

"So will you be my bridesmaid then?"

"Don't thirty-eight-year-olds with two kids have to be matrons?"

"Bollocks to that—it's too *Carry On Night Nurse*. I want you to be my bridesmaid; I'm thinking pink lace crinolines. With matching gloves."

"Oh, God."

"Or possibly Vera Wang."

"That sounds more like it."

"And the boys in kilts."

"Harry, in a kilt?"

"No, you idiot, my godsons."

"My Jack and Archie, in kilts?"

"Yes. What do you think?"

"I think it depends on how big the bribe's going to be."

"Huge."

"No problem then, although we'd better not let them have daggers in their socks or it could get tricky. Have you told your mum and dad yet?"

"I'm building up to it. Actually, it's going to be one of your main bridesmaid duties, stopping Mum trying to turn this into a family wedding. I hate most of them anyway, and they hate me. I just want people I really, truly like."

"So no need for a big church then, since there'll only be about six of us."

"Exactly. Here, talk to Harry."

"Morning, Jo."

"Congratulations, Harry."

"Thanks, darling, and you'll do the bridesmaid thing, because I'm counting on you to calm her down."

"How exactly do you think I'm going to pull that one off?"

"Drugs? One of my uncles knows a bloke who can probably slip us some horse tranquilizers; that should slow her down a bit. You'll have to do something or I'll be forced to make a run for it."

"Don't you dare. Anyway, she'd find you."

There's a scuffling noise, and Ellen comes back on the line.

"Harry's just fallen over."

"Has he? How mysterious."

"I don't think his leg's completely up to speed yet."

"No, and it won't be if you keep pushing the poor man over. He's only just had the plaster off."

"He tripped. Look, I'd better go, darling, he's making toast and he always burns it."

"Put a new toaster down on your wedding list then. A Harry-proof one."

"Christ, I'd forgotten about the wedding list. God, the amount of money I've spent over the years on bloody lists. Brilliant: it's finally payback time."

"John Lewis do a good one, I think."

"Please. I'm thinking Cath Kidston, the White Company. Actually, I wonder if Prada do a list—I bet they do—and I'm thinking registry office, like you did with Nick, so my mum doesn't get the chance to cover the local church in horrible satin ribbon."

"That might work, you know, like that man who wraps up whole mountains."

"Yes, but Christo doesn't dot mini-baskets of freesias everywhere, or make everyone wear carnation buttonholes. God, I wish I could see you. Why don't you come up here for the day and Harry can limp round a museum with the boys while we start planning?"

"I'd love to, but I've got lunch with Elizabeth and Gerald."

"Oh, Christ, I'd forgotten. Sorry, darling."

"Do I have to wear black, do you think?"

"Of course not, sweetheart. Wear what you like."

"She wanted us to go to the morning service at the church, but I said we couldn't get there in time, so they'll all be in their best Sunday outfits. James and Fiona and the girls will be there too. God, I bet they all have hats."

"You could always wear your bobble hat."

"So they look like they're off to Ascot and I look like a tramp?"

"Just wear what you feel comfortable in."

"You don't think turning up in my pajamas will look a bit odd?"

"Not if you top it off with a woolly hat; very bohemian and deconstructed: Björk, with a hint of grieving widow. What about your black trousers, the ones you wear with your boots?"

"I've already tried them, but I can only get the zip done up if I lie on the floor. I think they must have shrunk."

"Shrunk?"

"I think I may have been overdoing it slightly on the biscuits when I'm in the shop. And it's bound to rain. Do you remember how much it rained at the funeral? I thought the vicar was going to fall in at one point, or Archie, and Christ knows how much therapy you'd need after falling headfirst into your dad's grave. Quite a lot, is my guess."

"The bastards would probably make you sign a direct-debit form before they let you in the door."

"Do you think I should take flowers? The boys have written letters and drawn some pictures."

"Sweet."

"They spent hours on them. Jack's done one of the new house, to show him where we're living now, and Archie's done one of Trevor, and a boat. But I haven't got anything to take."

"Darling, you should have reminded me. Look, I can drive down. What time are you leaving?"

"No, it's fine, I'm just fussing. Flowers will be fine. I'll get some at Sainsbury's on the way, and you have a lovely day celebrating with Harry. I'll call you when I'm back."

"Sure?"

"Definitely."

"But?"

"Nothing. It's just I feel such a fraud. I should be the grieving widow, but I'm still so furious with him. I thought I'd be into the acceptance thing by now, or maybe even forgiveness, but I'm not. I mean I forgive him about the affair. It's weird, but I'm really past that. Maybe my mini-moment in Venice with Daniel helped me with that one, sort of put everything into perspective, and stopped me feeling like a total reject."

"I'm sure it did, darling."

"But I still can't forgive him for planning to leave the boys. I'm nowhere near closure on that one. Nowhere near."

"Of course you're not. Why would you be? Christ, he finally gets promoted and you think you're off to a new life as the Wife of the Foreign Correspondent, but it turns out he's having an affair and wants a divorce, and the night he tells you he manages to kill himself in a car crash. Why would you have closure on something like that? It'll take years."

"Thanks, that's very encouraging."

"Darling, you're doing great, fantastic, actually. Instead of going under you've got on with it, with all the debts and the second bloody mortgage he didn't even bother to tell you about. You've sold up and moved to the back of bloody beyond so you can work in your gran's wool shop, and before you say it, yes, I know it's your shop now, and you've made a brilliant job of it and you're new best friends with the Diva and everything. Official knitting coach to Amazing Grace, but still. I'd be fucking furious with him. In fact it's a good job he crashed that car because I'd have killed him myself if I'd got my hands on him. Bastard."

That's one of the best things about Ellen: she's so brilliantly partisan. She never sees both sides of the argument, or tells you to calm down and think about it from someone else's point of view. And she was so great last year, with the funeral and everything. Christ knows how I'd have got through it without her.

"I know, Ellen, but it was partly my fault, you know."

"Oh, please, not the guilt-trip thing again. How could it possibly have been your fault?"

"I should have known, about the money. I should have worked it out. And if I'd been less wrapped up in the boys, maybe I would have noticed how bored he was getting. When I think about it, I could see he was unraveling, but I tried to ignore it. He got so furious when I tried to talk to him about it, so I left it."

"And I suppose it was your fault he was shagging the teen-age UN worker, was it?"

"She was twenty-six, Ellen."

"Twenty-six, sixteen, makes no difference, just better clothes. Now pull yourself together, darling. He fucked up, big time. And it wasn't your fault, but you're left picking up the pieces. It's bollocks whichever way you look at it."

"I suppose so. Although I love living here now."

"I know you do, Pollyanna. You've always been good at seeing the bright side . . . what's that lemon thing again?"

"If life deals you lemons, you just make lemonade."

"Christ."

We both start to giggle.

"What a load of rubbish—it sounds just like something your Diva would say, like her line about how people can only turn you over if you let them; it's all in your karma."

"Yes, but I think there's some truth in that, you know."

"Oh, definitely. It's very good karma if you're incredibly rich and freakishly thin and your last three movies were hits. Not quite so easy if you're working in Burger King and the onion rings have just got flame-grilled into oblivion."

"True."

"How is our Amazing Grace, by the way? Is motherhood suiting her?"

"Very much, last time I saw her. And she's looking even more fabulous than before she had the baby, sort of glowing. I know it sounds like rubbish, but she really is. And the baby's gorgeous. I'm doing a new-baby window display for the shop; I've been knitting baby things for days now. It's been a bit weird—it reminds me of knitting when I was pregnant with Archie, which hasn't exactly helped."

"You'll be fine today, you'll see. Now are you sure you don't want me to come down?"

"Sure. You're right. It'll be fine, and at least there's been some good news today."

"What?"

"My best friend's getting married, and I'll be in peach Vera Wang with gloves and a bobble hat."

"Call me when you get home, promise?"

"Yes."

"And if Elizabeth gets too annoying, just hit her. Pretend you've gone into widow hysterics and deck the old bag. You'll feel so much better, trust me."

"I must just try that."

"Hurrah. God, I really wish I was coming down now."

READING GROUP GUIDE

Attention: Some plot spoilers in this guide.

1. Do you have a hobby or creative outlet, such as knitting? Why do you pursue it—to express yourself, to relieve stress, or for some other reason? If you were given the chance to make your hobby a full-time job, or otherwise make a living from it, would you?

2. Ellen Malone, Jo's best friend, is a source of constant support and levity to Jo. Do you have an Ellen in your life? In what ways do you depend upon your closest friend, and does he or she depend upon you?

3. Talk about the range of emotions Jo experiences as she processes not only Nick's death but his revelation hours before the car crash that he was having an extramarital affair and wanted a divorce. How does she deal with these feelings? What would you have done in her position?

4. When Martin and Daniel were first introduced, what did you think of each man? Did you imagine that Jo would have feelings for either of them? And did you guess which one she'd eventually "fancy"?

5. One of the book's subplots deals with international film star Grace Harrison, who purchases an estate in Broadgate Bay and befriends Jo. What do you think of Grace? What does her friendship mean to Jo? Does Grace help Jo?

6. Discuss the different members of Jo's knitting circle. Do you think each woman joins just for the knitting experience, or are they looking for some other kind of camaraderie or fulfillment? What do you think each woman gets out of the group, particularly Jo?

7. At the novel's end, the members of the knitting circle organize a "knit-in" to protest the closing of the village library. Besides being an act of social protest, what do you think the knit-in means to its participants? Does it mark the end, or beginning, of something for Jo and the other women?

8. If Nick hadn't died, how would the book have been different? What do you think would have happened to Jo? Do you think she would have left Nick and taken over Gran's shop?

9. What do you think the overriding message of *The Beach Street Knitting Society and Yarn Club* is? Did you learn anything having read it?

© Jerry Bauer

Gil McNeil is the author of *Needles and Pearls*. She lives in Kent, England, with her son, and comes from a long line of champion knitters.